PENGUIN BOOKS

THE LATE MR. SHAKESPEARE

Robert Nye was born in London in 1939. His novels include *Merlin*, *The Memoirs of Lord Byron*, *Mrs. Shakespeare*, and the award-winning *Falstaff*. A poet, journalist, and critic, he lives near Cork, in Ireland.

The Late
Mr Shakespeare

ROBERT NYE

PENGUIN BOOKS

PENGUIN BOOKS

Published by the Penguin Group
Penguin Putnam Inc., 375 Hudson Street,
New York, New York 10014, U.S.A.
Penguin Books Ltd, 27 Wrights Lane,
London W8 5TZ, England
Penguin Books Australia Ltd, Ringwood,
Victoria, Australia
Penguin Books Canada Ltd, 10 Alcorn Avenue,
Toronto, Ontario, Canada M4V 3B2
Penguin Books (N.Z.) Ltd, 182–190 Wairau Road,
Auckland 10, New Zealand

Penguin Books Ltd, Registered Offices:
Harmondsworth, Middlesex, England

First published in Great Britain by Chatto & Windus 1998
First published in the United States of America by Arcade Publishing, Inc. 1999
Published in Penguin Books 2000

1   3   5   7   9   10   8   6   4   2

THE LIBRARY OF CONGRESS HAS CATALOGED THE ARCADE EDITION AS FOLLOWS:
Nye, Robert.
The late Mr. Shakespeare: a novel/ by Robert Nye.—1st U.S. ed.
p.   cm.
ISBN 1-55970-469-1 (hc.)
ISBN 0 14 02.8952 6 (pbk.)
1. Shakespeare, William. 1564–1616—Fiction.   2. Great Britain—History—Elizabeth,
1558–1603—Fiction.   3. Great Britain—History—James I. 1603–1625—Fiction.   I. Title.
PR6064.Y4L35   1999
823'.914—dc21   98-50763

Printed in the United States of America
Set in Bulmer

To
Giles Gordon

and in memory of

Glenn Gould
Georges Perec

Contents

Our pleasant Willy, ah! is dead of late

Edmund Spenser
The Tears of the Muses

The Late Mr Shakespeare

A never writer to
an ever reader:
News.

Chapter One

*In which Pickleherring takes his pen
to tell of his first meeting
with Mr Shakespeare*

For instance, William Shakespeare. Tell you all about him. All there is that's fit to know about Shakespeare. Mr William Shakespeare. All there is that's not fit, too, for that matter. Who he was and why. Where he was and when. What he was and wherefore. And then, besides, to answer several difficult questions that might be bothering you. Such as, who was the Dark Lady of the sonnets? Such as, why did he leave his wife only his second-best bed? Such as, is it true he died a Papist, and lived a sodomite? Such as, how come he placed that curse on his own grave? All this, and more, you will find answered here. But better begin at the beginning, while we can.

Who am I? Reader, I will tell you suddenly. My name is Robert Reynolds *alias* Pickleherring and my game is that of a comedian and believe me I was well-acquainted with our famous Mr Shakespeare when I was young. I acted in his plays. I knew his ways. I played Puck to his Oberon. To his Prosper, I was Ariel. I washed my hands sleep-walking too, as the Scottish queen. Why, once, at Blackfriars, the man was sick in my cap. I loved the lovely villain, ladies and gentlemen.

By the time I have finished I think you will have to admit it. There is no man or woman alive in the world who knows more than old Pickleherring about the late Mr Shakespeare.

I call to mind as if it was just yesterday, for instance, the first time I ever clapped eyes on the dear fellow. He was wearing a copataine hat. You won't know those hats now, if you're under fifty. They were good hats. They wore good hats and they wrote good verse in those days. Your

copataine hat was a high-crowned job in the shape of a sugar-loaf. Some say the word should be COPOTINK and that it comes from the Dutch. I call a copataine hat a copataine hat. So did Mr Shakespeare, let me tell you. I never heard him say that his hat came from Holland. And in his tragical history of *Antony and Cleopatra* he has the word COPATAINE. Which part, friends, he wrote first for your servant: Cleopatra. I never wore a copataine hat myself, but then I was only a boy at the time we are speaking of.

I was living in those far-off but never to be forgotten days in a cottage made of clay and wattles just outside the north gate of the city of Cambridge. That cottage stood by a fen. Fatherless, motherless, I was being looked after by a pair of sisters, whiskered virgins, Meg and Merry Muchmore, two spinsters with long noses for the smelling out of knavery.

It was the pleasure of each of these ladies in turn to spank me naked while the other watched. I think they liked to see my little pintle harden. Meg's lap smelt of liquorice but there was no pleasing Merry. I had a well-whipped childhood, I can tell you.

All their long lives these two weird sisters had dedicated themselves to piety and good works, and I, the bastard son of a priest's bastard, conceived in a confessional, born in a graveyard, was one of the best of them. I mean, what better work than Pickleherring?

I was a posthumous child. Of my father, I heard from my mother only that his mouth was so big and cavernous that he could thrust his clenched fist into it. How often he performed this trick for her amusement I know not. I know only that he could do it, and that also he had some interest in the occult. That is an interest which I do not share.

Reader, don't get me wrong. I believe in ghosts and visions. I pray only to be spared from seeing them.

My mother died when I was seven years old. She smelt of milk and comfrey fritters. She used to tell me tales by the chimneyside. It was from her sweet lips that I first heard of Tattercoats and of Tom-Tit-Tot and of Jack and his beanstalk. She sang to me, too, my mother – all the old English songs.

I remember her singing me to sleep with a ballad called *O Polly Dear*. But she died of a fever and then there was no more music. My bed was under thatching and the way to it was up a rope ladder.

I had never before been spoken to by a man in a copataine hat. Mr Shakespeare was tall and thin, and he wore that hat with an air of great authority. He had also a quilted silken doublet, goose-turd green; grey velvet hose; and a scarlet cloak. Never believe those who tell you he was not a dandy.

This first meeting of ours took place in the yard of a tavern called the Cock. A small rain fell like brightness from the air. Ah, what a dream it seems now, seventy years away.

One thing I can tell you that you'll perhaps not learn elsewhere. Mr William Shakespeare never minded a bit of rain. He sat under the springing mulberry tree that grew in the middle of the Cock's back yard. He had a damask napkin over his knee and a little knife of silver in his hand. He was opening oysters.

As for me, I had climbed up on the red-brick wall to keep him in my sight. My friends mocked me. One of them said the man was from Wales, and an alchemist. They said he could make gold, and fly in the air. They said he was in Cambridge for blood for his lamp. I pretended not to care. I did not want his art, but I had no father.

'Pickleherring's mad again!' piped my playmates.

Then they all ran away and left me on my own to face the necromancer.

Mr Shakespeare must have seen me watching him. But I don't believe that his eyes ever left the oysters.

His voice was soft and gentle when he spoke. But it was the sort of softness that you stop and listen to, like the sound of the theorbo.

'Boy,' he said, suddenly.

I nearly fell down off the wall. Instead I said, 'Yes, sir?'

I was shaking in my boots.

'Say this, boy,' he said. '*I am afraid, and yet I'll venture it.*'

What kind of spell was this?

I looked at Mr Shakespeare.

He looked up from his oysters and looked at me.

Something in his look made me take him straight. So I forgot all about spells and I said the words he said. I said them simply. I do not think I can say that I said them well. But I said them more or less as he said them, which is to say that I spoke the speech trippingly on the tongue, not mouthing it, not sawing the air with my hand.

It was, as I learned later, the way he liked it. He never could abide the ranting sort. Truth to tell, I had never then acted in my life, so I knew no worse. Also, I *was* afraid, which helped me to say that I was as though I meant it.

My performance seemed to please Mr Shakespeare.

He took off his hat to me.

'Good,' he said. And then, 'Good, boy,' he said. And then again, after a little while, 'Good boy,' Mr Shakespeare said finally.

He swallowed an oyster.

'Say this,' he said. 'Say that.'

I mean, I can't remember now all Mr Shakespeare bade me say then. He sat there downing oysters while I recited. Sometimes he said 'Good' and sometimes he said 'Good, boy' and once he said 'Good boy' again and more than once he said nothing but just wiped his mouth with his napkin.

I do recall that he asked me at last to sing.

So I sat down on the wall and I sang for Mr Shakespeare.

I had a good voice in those days.

I sang for him the ballad of *O Polly Dear*.

The sweet rain fell and the drops ran down my face and I sat there in the rain, legs dangling, singing *O Polly Dear* that my mother used to sing to me.

Mr Shakespeare listened with his eyes as well as his ears.

When I finished he nodded and he clapped his hands three times together.

It was the first applause I ever had.

Then at Mr Shakespeare's instruction I jumped down off the wall.

Chapter Two

*In which Pickleherring makes strides
in a pair of lugged boots*

The first part I ever played for Mr Shakespeare on the London stage was that of young Prince Arthur in his play of *The Life and Death of King John*. That's why he asked me to say *I am afraid, and yet I'll venture it*. It is what that poor boy says before he kills himself by jumping from the battlements of the castle where he is confined.

When I jumped down off the red-brick wall and into the back yard of the Cock Tavern, Cambridge, Mr Shakespeare stopped eating his oysters and he asked me my name and where I lived and who my father was. So I told him of the cot beneath the thatch and my fatherless fate.

As I spoke to him of fathers, I saw tears run down his cheeks. I thought it was rain.

'O my poor Hamlet,' Mr Shakespeare said.

Like a fool, I repeated the four words.

Mr Shakespeare flushed. His face was all at once a crimson rose. He blinked at me in anger through his tears. I think he thought that I was mocking him. Then he must have realised that I'd mistaken what he said for another speech to try. He pinched his nose between the thumb and the first finger of his left hand, shaking his head a moment as he did so. When he looked at me again his eyes were clear.

'Do you have perfect pitch?' Mr Shakespeare asked me.

I told him that I had. (It was a lie.)

Then Mr Shakespeare took my hand, unsmiling, and he promised me that if I chose to come with him to London and join his company he could make me a player like himself.

My heart thumped in my breast. I felt as if I had suddenly grown taller by an inch.

Well now, my dears, it happens that this part of Prince Arthur might contain the key as to why Mr Shakespeare first noticed me and thought to give me employment as a player.

I think perhaps that I put him in mind of his son.

I was wearing, do you see, a pair of lugged boots. Those boots were all the rage that year of our first meeting. They were boots of soft leather, hanging loose about the leg, turned down and fringed. I think they called them lugged because the fringes looked like ears.

Be that as it may. I learned later that young Hamlet Shakespeare begged for a pair of these boots to wear as he lay dying. He was eleven years old. It was Mrs Shakespeare herself who told me that she got them for Hamlet to wear as he tossed on his death-bed. He never so much as walked in them anywhere.

So it might be that my lugged boots were what caught Mr Shakespeare's eye.

But then (you ask me), what has this to do with that other boy Arthur in *King John*?

Permit me to tell you.

Little Hamlet died not long before I first met Mr Shakespeare. I think that Mr Shakespeare was still writing *King John* in his head that day in Cambridge, and that in any case he was thinking of his own son when he has Queen Constance in Act III Scene 4 lament the fate of her son Arthur in these lines that follow:

> *Grief fills the room up of my absent child,*
> *Lies in his bed, walks up and down with me,*
> *Puts on his pretty looks, repeats his words,*
> *Remembers me of all his gracious parts,*
> *Stuffs out his vacant garments with his form:*
> *Then have I reason to be fond of grief.*

Of course, I could be wrong. My linking of the writing of this speech with what Mr Shakespeare may possibly have felt about the loss of his own (and only) son might deny the man's imagination or at the least insult it. Or it could be that I mistake or misconstrue the way the mind of a poet works upon the things that happen in the poet's life.

I confess that I never dared to question Mr Shakespeare directly in the matter. But I remember a night at the Mermaid when having recited those

tender lines which he gave to Queen Constance, I expounded my theory and quizzed his fellow playwrights as to what they thought.

Mr Beaumont said I was right, and wiped away a tear.

Mr Fletcher said I was wrong, and that my supposition accused Mr Shakespeare of a want of heart, or a want of imagination, or of both wants together, and only went to prove my mediocrity.

Mr Ben Jonson said nothing, but belched and hurled a flagon at my head.

It was an empty flagon, naturally.

Ladies and gentlemen, Beroaldus (who was a wise doctor) will have drunkards, afternoon-men, and such as more than ordinarily delight in drink, to be mad. I am of his opinion from my own experience. They are more than mad, much worse than mad.

Speaking of which, before we quitted Cambridge finally Mr Shakespeare saw fit to try to teach me the joys of tobacco. He was not one of those who suppose that plant divine in its origin or its powers. But he liked his white clay pipe. He gave me sweetmeats also, and called me his doxy. It was not for such things that I loved his company.

As to why Mr Shakespeare liked mine, if he did, who now can rightly say?

I suggest only that the least that can be supposed – leaving lugged boots and young Hamlet out of it – is that the great man was pleased when he found that rainy afternoon that I said his lines plainly and true even when perched upon a red-brick wall. And perhaps it pleased him further when he discovered that I had some rudimental feeling for the shape of English verse. The Sisters Muchmore had taught me rhythm on the arse with their striped tawse.

For whatever reason, or none, Mr WS took me along with him like a prize bull-calf when he went back to London to rejoin his company of actors.

They were called the Lord Chamberlain's Servants* and they played at that time at the playhouse called the Curtain, in Shoreditch. Our master was Mr James Burbage, a stubborn old man with an anchor on his thigh, who died of a surfeit of lampreys the Easter after I made my first entrance.

I wore my lugged boots and I made great strides.

---

* The threefold nature of the name of the company of actors to which WS belonged has not always been well understood. Here, then, let me spell it out that the Lord Chamberlain's Servants had formerly been known (before my time) as Lord Strange's Men, and that after the accession and patronage of King James I we were proud to be known as the King's Players.

Chapter Three

Pickleherring's Acknowledgements

I was thirteen years old in that long-ago summer when I first met Mr Shakespeare and made my entrance on the London stage. I am 81 now, or maybe 82, or 83. I can't remember, and it does not matter. Besides, I may not be so old at all. I may be a 13-year-old boy wearing an 83-year-old mask. That's how I feel sometimes. You think about it. How old would you be if you didn't know your age?

Here I am, at all events, a little wearish monkey in a red cotton night-cap.

The last time I looked in a looking-glass what did I see?

I saw a wretched elf with hollow eyes and cracked rawbone cheeks. I saw a pantaloon with a blubber-lipped mouth. I saw a sickly visage, and a shrivelled neck like a chicken's.

Sometimes I wear a false beard, but not today. One does not put on a false beard to write the Life of William Shakespeare. I have pointy ears, though, and I wear long pointed slippers that curl up at the toes. My belly bulges from the stomach down. Once I could pull it in like everybody else, but not any more. I can only see my sex by bending over. It must be a good twelvemonth since I bothered.

If I still had a mirror what would I see in it? A white worm, that's what.

But enough about even imaginary mirrors. My grandfather the bishop used to say that looking in the mirror made you go mad. I submit, gentlemen, that I have a subject which is not myself, and mighty. I aver, ladies, that you will not have long to bear my less than charming company.

Let me put it this way: I am one who has in his possession a vast argosy of tales about Mr Shakespeare. A thousand stories, ladies. A thousand and one, good sirs. And if it pleases you, gentles, Pickleherring will tell them all.

I shall tell you stories to beguile you.

I shall tell you tales to keep me alive while I do so.

Not all these tales and stories will be my own. I mean that a book like this might be said to be long in the making, and to have enjoyed the intercourse of many several begetters. My mind is what Mr Shakespeare said of his Dark Lady. It has been a bay where all men ride, and it has been the wide world's common place. Yet in the end I am no whore, but our Shakespeare's true and loyal servant. I served him first on the stages at the Curtain and the Globe. I put myself now upon the stage for him again. This book is my theatre. The play's not done.

Before I begin my story proper, I wish to express my thanks to all those who have helped me (even unwittingly) in the gathering of the matter for it. You see, although the writing of this book has come late in my life, I think I was preparing for it all along. It is the outcome of a lifetime of labour, and testament to a lifetime's love as well. From *King John* on, I worshipped Mr Shakespeare. I thought him more a god than a mortal man. And so it was that I lapped up all there ever was to learn about him. Like Autolycus in his *Winter's Tale* I was littered under Mercury and have been likewise a snapper-up of unconsidered trifles. (In that play, though, I played the part of Hermione.)

Chief among my memorists and informers have been my fellow actors in the theatre, now most of them dead (and God rest their souls every one). Therefore it is a pleasure to me now to recall and name first in pride of place the leading members of our company as it stood at the death of Mr James Burbage, all of whom gave me something of our Shakespeare that was their own: Mr Richard Burbage (old James B's younger son, and a Protean actor – the first Hamlet, the first Othello, the first Lear); Mr Thomas Pope; Mr John Heminges (the original Falstaff); Mr Augustine Phillips; and Mr George Bryan. I might mention even that flame-haired ticklebrain Mr William Kempe, though Mr Shakespeare never much liked him on account of his habit of working in jokes of his own when on stage and being generally too conceited in his jigs.

Then, also, and no less, in the years that followed, these men, the principal actors, besides myself, in all of Mr Shakespeare's later plays: Mr Henry Condell (one of WS's closest colleagues, remembered in his will); Mr William Sly; Mr Richard Cowley; Mr John Lowin (the original Henry VIII, now landlord of the Three Pigeons Inn at Brentford); Mr Samuel Cross; Mr Alexander Cooke; Mr Samuel Gilburne; Mr Robert Armin (a far better clown than Kempe); Mr William Ostler; Mr Nathan Field; Mr John Underwood; Mr Nicholas Tooley; Mr William Ecclestone; Mr Joseph

Taylor (who took over Hamlet when Dick Burbage died, and if anything surpassed him in the part); Mr Robert Benfield (played kings and old men); Mr Christopher Beeston; Mr Robert Goffe; Mr Richard Robinson; Mr John Shank (who was a gentle dancer); and Mr John Rice.

These were my fellow students of our Shakespeare. They went to school with me in the universality of his wit. Each of them told me something about the man, or confirmed perhaps a tale I had heard from another. All of them taught me a part of what I had then to learn as a whole for myself. Just remembering them now, and reeling off their names, renews for me the pleasure of their company and our fellowship. They were my companions in comedy and tragedy alike, on stage and off. They were my fellow players. They were also my friends.

I acknowledge too the assistance (and sometimes the obstruction) I have been given over the years by the late Mr Shakespeare's rival playwrights, chief amongst them these notables: Mr Francis Beaumont; Mr George Chapman; Mr Henry Chettle (whom Mr Shakespeare prized for one sweet song); Mr Samuel Daniel; Mr Thomas Dekker (fond of cats); Mr Michael Drayton; Mr John Fletcher; Mr John Ford; Mr Thomas Heywood (whose boast was that he had had a hand or at least a main finger in 220 plays); Mr Ben Jonson (who said that Mr S lacked art, but was author of the chief eulogy in the Folio of 1623); Mr John Marston (red hair and little legs – and became a priest); Mr Philip Massinger (Papist); Mr Thomas Middleton; Mr Anthony Munday (became a playwright after being hissed off the stage as an actor); Mr Samuel Rowley; Mr George Ruggle; Mr Thomas Tomkis; Mr Cyril Tourneur (whose nature was as lovely as his name); Mr John Webster (kept a skull always by him); Mr George Wilkins (wrote the first two acts of *Pericles*, and much of *Timon of Athens*); Mr Arthur Wilson (a great dueller until he risked his life to save a laundry maid from drowning, took up mathematics, and died a Puritan).

For personal information regarding Mr Shakespeare I am also much indebted to the Poet Laureate, Sir William Davenant. Sir William is certainly Mr Shakespeare's godson. I do not believe (as Sir William himself has sometimes claimed late at night) that he is also Mr Shakespeare's natural son. His *Ode in Remembrance of Master Shakespeare* may assuredly be commended as a remarkable production for a boy of twelve. I am sorry that he lost his nose to the pox.

I suppose that I am grateful to the late Dr Simon Forman for his horoscope of Mr Shakespeare imparted to me privately. I glanced at this before I threw it away.

Nextly, I wish to mention all those in Mr Shakespeare's native county of

Warwickshire who submitted to my importunate interview of them after his death, telling me tales of his boyhood and early manhood, and then his later years spent in retirement in Stratford-upon-Avon, the town of his birth. Principal among these is his widow, Mrs Anne Shakespeare, born Hathaway, a woman whose serene silence on the subject of her husband should have taught me at least to hold my tongue when I am not sure that I know what to say. Mrs Shakespeare, despite her reticence, might be counted my main source of understanding of the home-life of the poet. She was a woman like no other I have ever known. Expressionless, for me she expressed wisdom. On one occasion which I remember with especial feeling she drove me from the Shakespeare residence at New Place, Stratford, with a stout birch broom in her hands. Admittedly at the time I was dressed in her second-best petticoats.

I have then as well to thank another redoubtable woman, Mr Shakespeare's sister Joan, latterly Mrs William Hart of Stratford, who regaled me in her final years with many sweet remembrances of her brother. The poet's daughters Susanna (Mrs John Hall) and Judith (Mrs Thomas Quiney) were also most generous to me with their memories, especially the former, whom I always found to be a woman (as her tombstone now declares) witty above her sex. Mr Shakespeare's son-in-law, Dr John Hall, of Hall's Croft, Stratford, and then New Place, was a mine of information on matters medical and religious, as well as concerning Mr Shakespeare's gout, and the day that he died. On a small personal note, I owe also to Dr Hall the cure of my scurvy by means of his Scorbutick Beer.

Others who assisted my enquiries in pursuit of *anecdota* in Warwickshire include Mr Shakespeare's granddaughter Elizabeth, now Lady Bernard, and her husband John, of Abington Manor, near Northampton, to whom I am also grateful for hospitality. Concerning Mr Shakespeare's domestic life while he was working in the theatre I am indebted to details furnished long ago by his landlord Mr Christopher Mountjoy, in whose house on the corner of Monkswell and Silver Street near St Olave's Church in Cripplegate ward the poet sometime had his London residence.

It is a great privilege and pride to acknowledge at all points in what follows the influence upon my own writing of the work of my friend and patron the late Sir Thomas Urquhart, of Cromarty, translator of the immortal Rabelais and author in his own right of *Logopandecteision*, a scheme for a universal language. It has been said that Urquhart's Rabelais is not exactly Rabelais. But I say that it is exactly Urquhart. Besides, it reproduces the *spirit* of the original with remarkable felicity and force. I love it as I loved the man himself. Never let us forget that he died laughing.

As to my wife Jane, I acknowledge that without her I would not be as or where I am today.

Finally, I may say that all I perform in these pages that follow is what I was taught to do in the theatre. Namely, to hold a mirror up to nature. Take it or leave it, my motive in writing this book cannot be better expressed than it was by my old comrades from the tiring-house Mr Heminges and Mr Condell when introducing the volume of Mr Shakespeare's works which they gathered together and published after his death. That Folio sits to my right hand now on the table where I write, just beside the tattered pile of my own actor's copies of Mr Shakespeare's plays. Here is what they say in their preface, Mr Heminges and Mr Condell – that they work *without ambition either of self-profit or fame,* but *only to keep the memory of so worthy a friend and fellow alive as was our Shakespeare.*

So now do I. No more. No less.

But a word as to the manner of my writing. Apart from the exemplar of the admirable Urquhart already noted, this wretched style of mine has something (I think) in common with the playing of Mr Armin, our company's clown, author of *Fool upon Fool, or Six Sorts of Sots* besides. He created Feste in *Twelfth Night,* as well as playing the part of Dogberry. An excellent round man, and a pupil of the great Tarlton.

Armin could not only act the fool like a wise man. He would ask the audience to shout out a subject, and thereupon produce a poem out of his head, composing extemporarily. He was what the Italians call an *improvisatore.* Mr Shakespeare made good use of this talent in his comedy called *As You Like It,* where Armin took the part of Touchstone. When Rosalind (your author) appears with Orlando's verses, Touchstone (Armin) retorted with a few more of his own, composed on the spot, made to the moment, a different set each night of the 20-night run. It was doggerel, of course, but it made you laugh.

That's just what I do, ladies.

I play the fool, gentlemen, yes. And like a good clown in cap and bells I make it all up as I go along. I write a sort of motley, though this motley I make up has been formed and informed by the many wise men and women acknowledged in this chapter.

But enough of Pickleherring.

It is high time I started to give you my Life of Mr Shakespeare.

Chapter Four

*About John Shakespeare and the
miller's daughter*

William Shakespeare was born in the town of Stratford-upon-Avon on St George's Day, Sunday the 23rd of April, 1564. His father was a butcher. His father's name was John. *JOHN SHAKESPEARE* said the sign over the door of his shop on the northern side of Henley Street, Stratford, *JOHN SHAKESPEARE: BUTCHER & WHITTAWER*. It was a busy crowded *omnium gatherum* of a shop, the sort of place where people like to stand and pass the time of day. Dealing in skins and leather as well as meat, Mr John Shakespeare was master of his trade, and a popular man.

Our hero's mother was born Mary Arden. She was a farmer's daughter, and she grew up under the apple-boughs in the sweet village of Wincot, which lies three miles to the north-west of Stratford in leafy Warwickshire. But this Mary was almost not Mr Shakespeare's mother. How so? It came about like this.

Near by John Shakespeare's butcher shop, on a small tributary of the River Avon, there stands a mill. It is ruined now, that mill, another casualty of the late Civil Wars. The place closed down for a lack not of corn but of men who knew how to grind it, in the old ways, to the ancient specifications, with water and stones, furrows and thumbs. In Shakespeare's day there was always a miller there.

The miller's taste was in his thumb. The art, on the other hand, is in the stone. It looks crude, it looks easy, two girt stones grinding together, what could be simpler? But in the cut and clarity of the furrow, the way the miller marks his stone, or the miller's man, his amanuensis, there you have it, the whole lost art.

When he opens the gate the stream runs straight. If he opened it full it

would bring the mill down. So he opens it half, and the water flows through, the green water, and round and round the wheel goes, and the chalky walls shake and you can smell the flour fly, the oatmeal in the air, in the low gloom, though it's a long while now since they bore sacks up the thin stair, spread corn to warm on the worn stones, lit the fire under, and let the wind spin the chimney as it would. When you look up it still moves slightly, that chimney, then the whole twisted roof moves, and you're lost. Have you noticed millers always have bad breath?

Now when young Mr John Shakespeare was first making his way in the butchery business, the miller in that mill had a beautiful daughter. She had long silky hair and her lips pressed together like two red rose petals. Her name was Juliet, wouldn't you know. John and Juliet did not marry because their fathers spoilt it. How did they spoil it? By plotting matrimony.

'Listen, John,' said his father to him, 'I want you to marry the miller's daughter.'

'Juliet, listen,' her father said to her, 'I want you to make a good catch for yourself – that John Shakespeare, the butcher boy, for instance.'

'Speak nicely to her,' said Shakespeare's father's father.

'Be agreeable to the man,' commanded the miller.

Next day the would-be lovers met.

'Mr Shagsper,' said Juliet, 'my father told me to marry you.'

'Is that so?' said John Shakespeare. 'Well, in that case I think we should sleep together first to find out if we're suited.'

The miller's daughter did not demur or delay. That night they lay together in her bed above the mill wheel. The air was salty with flour. His eyes pricked. She gnawed her lower lip in the blue darkness.

'Mr Shagsper,' she whispered at last.

'Yes, my love?' John whispered back.

'Did you come round the mill pond by the dovecots?' Juliet asks him.

'Yes, my darling,' John says, panting.

'And did you notice a great big heap of dung under the wall?' asks Juliet.

'I did,' John Shakespeare answers, somewhat surprised by the question.

'Well,' says Juliet, 'that's mine.'

'Yours?' John Shakespeare said.

'I did it,' Juliet told him, 'every bit.'

The miller's daughter was a lovely lovely creature, but she did have the one shortcoming which makes me glad she was not our hero's mother – she lacked conversation.

Chapter Five

*How to spell Shakespeare and
what a whittawer is*

So Mr John Shakespeare married Mary Arden——
But before we get into that I'd better say something about the way
Juliet the miller's daughter said the family name.

Shakespeare is a not uncommon surname in Warwickshire and the
counties round about, along with little variations on its martial music:
Shakelaunce and Brislelaunce, Lycelance and Breakspear. One of the tribe
last-named, Nicholas Breakspear, even became Pope, the only Englishman
to have sunk so low, calling himself Hadrian IV when he sat down in the
papal chair.

What the miller's daughter said – *Shagsper* - is just one possible spelling
and pronunciation of the name. Both in Stratford and in London people
say it variously, and I have come across it in many different forms. Here are
a few of them:

Shakaspeare	Shakespey	Shakstaff
Shakispeare	Shaxpur	Shakeshaft
Shakyspeare	Sakesper	Sacaspeer
Shakespire	Shaxberd	Sakeespeer
Shakespeier	Shexper	Shakeschafte
Sakespeier	Schacosper	Shakespere
Saxpey	Scakespeire	Shaxber
Saksper	Saxper	Shakespaye
Sakspere	Saxberd	Schakkyspare
Shagspere	Schaftspere	Shakespur
Shaxbere	Chacsper	Shakespure

15

Shagspare	Saxshaffte	Shaxpay
Shaxpear	Chacspeire	Chacsberde
Saxpar	Sacksper	Sexper
Shakesbear	Shakesides	Shagstuft
Shuckspere	Shagsshaft	Sexspear

The saying and the spelling being so mutable, you might conclude that all this speaks of a quality of mystery in the man himself. I'd not deny this. But I spell it SHAKESPEARE. Why? Because that's how Mr Shakespeare spelt it himself in the printed signatures to the dedications of his two narrative poems *Venus and Adonis* and *The Rape of Lucrece*, when his mind must have certainly been on the job. It is in fact the form in nearly all the printings of his plays in my possession. And it is also the way his name is spelt in the text of all the legal documents relating to his property that I have seen, and in the royal licence granted to him in 1603 in his capacity as a player.

So while I must admit that you could find his father's name spelt 16 different ways in the Council books at Stratford (the commonest being Shaxpeare), it is my firm conclusion that all these variaments express the way that *other people* said the family surname. As such, each variance bespeaks how these others perceived a member of the family. (*Shagsper*, for instance, tells what the miller's daughter had in mind.)

But, in sum . . .

SHAKESPEARE is how our poet wrote it (for the most part).

SHAKESPEARE is also how he said it.

SHAKESPEARE is finally how I always knew and called him.

Quod erat demonstrandum, gentlemen.

Ladies, you may take it that SHAKESPEARE is how to spell Shakespeare.

By the way, a whittawer is a white-tawyer, which is to say one who taws skins into whiteleather. (I love these old country words.) This tawing was the second side of the senior Mr Shakespeare's trade in Henley Street, though in his later life it became his main line, so that some have spoken of him as a glover. The truth is that he was always a man with different coloured hands. For instance, he dealt in wool from the sheep he slaughtered, as well as their meat.

I confess to a certain disease at having told you that the sign above his shop said BUTCHER & WHITTAWER. This seems to me unlikely, even though the building was quite commodious – in fact it was *two* premises knocked into one, as can still be seen. However, I have been assured of that BUTCHER & WHITTAWER wording by several ancient citizens of Stratford, including Mr William Walker, the present Bailiff, who is Mr Shakespeare's godson,

and who was remembered in the poet's will with the gift of 20 shillings in gold.

The disposition of having meat and leather for sale in the same shop is scarcely salubrious. But then things were ordered differently a hundred years ago, and not always for the better. Perhaps all that needs to be remarked, for our present purpose, is that Mr John Shakespeare made such a success of his various trades in the first two acts of his life that he rose to be Bailiff himself in 1568, and then in 1571 Chief Alderman. It was while he was Bailiff, and his son William still a boy, that the players first came with their plays to Stratford, at the town's expense. His fortunes declined in acts three and four, but more of that later.

Wincot, let me also tell you, is the way that Mrs Anne Shakespeare used delightfully to say the name of the village her mother-in-law came from. I have retained that particular spelling in affectionate memory of the many happy hours I spent in her company while she divulged to me little or nothing concerning her late husband. The proper spelling of the place is Wilmcote. However you spell Mary's place of origin, as an Arden she might have been descended from the Ardens of Park Hall, a family mentioned in the Domesday Book. Mary Arden was certainly something of a minor heiress, her father having left her lands at Wincot, as well as money, so we may suppose that it was not just the miller's daughter's conversational shortcomings which put off Mr John Shakespeare from her marrying.

Speaking of the Domesday Book, and suchlike records, I have turned up a pretty pair of Shakespeares who managed to make their marks before our man. The first is one William Saksper, of Clopton, in Kiftesgate Hundred, Gloucestershire (about seven miles from Stratford), who in 1248 was hanged for robbery. At the other extreme, consider that Isabella Shakspere who was prioress of Wraxall Abbey at the start of the last century. There is no evidence whatsoever that either of these was related to our poet. Yet I must say I relish the fact of them.

The late Mr Shakespeare remarked more than once in my hearing that he held within himself a devil and an angel, and that his life was their warring together, and his work the resolution of that war. So it pleases me to picture a young abbess picking apples in his family tree, her skirts kilted high to show a plump leg perhaps, while a robber dangles executed from one of the branches. Of such confusions is the best poetry made.

Before we resume our story, permit me lastly to explain to you how I can write conversations which I did not overhear. (I anticipate your criticisms, madam.)

The truth is Mr Shakespeare lessoned me. Do you think I learned nothing from all that playing in his plays? And had you supposed he listened to King Lear?

Chapter Six

About the begetting of William Shakespeare

So Mr John Shakespeare married Miss Mary Arden. But just as Mary was nearly not William Shakespeare's mother, so John was nearly not his father, or thought he wasn't. How so? Listen and you'll find out.

It happened, you see, that John was a very jealous husband. He was so jealous that he couldn't bear another man to be so much as looking at the ground where Mary's shadow had passed. She had already borne her husband two daughters, though neither lived long after christening. John was still jealous. And he desired a son.

One night in the year before our poet's birth there was a great storm that raged across all England. It was unseasonably cold. Sleet blew in the wind. People lit fires and huddled in their houses. Standing at the window of the room over the shop in Henley Street, Mary calls to John to come and look out and see something else that's strange in this unnatural night. A fine coach has turned over on the road below, its axle broken, its horses run off, harness trailing.

Then there's loud knocking at their big front door.

John Shakespeare goes downstairs and opens it.

It's a tall dark-haired man in a black cloak that's asking for shelter. John says he can give him food and a bed for the night.

The man is obviously of gentle blood. Some say it was Edward de Vere, the young Earl of Oxford. (I doubt this myself – the Earl was too young at the time.) Whoever, the man has great presence, and fills the room up with his charm. He wears his hair long, with ribbons tied in it. His sword swaps between his legs like a monkey's tail.

As this man sits there warming his long thin hands by the fire and looking at the lady of the house, it comes into John Shakespeare's head that

anyone glancing in at the mullioned window just now would think what a splendid married pair they make, Mary and the stranger, and himself no more than an interloper thrown up by the storm where he doesn't belong.

You have to understand that the Ardens had for a long time been somebodies. The Shakespeares were not nobodies, but they were still over-eager to make that known. As for the stranger, Lord Oxford or not he was certainly a Somebody with a capital S.

Now, as John Shakespeare rubs his temples with this line of thinking, the stranger leans back his head and yawns. He has an uncommonly pretty red mouth and a most artful style of yawning. The next moment, almost as if to answer him, Mary yawns too.

'It's a sign,' thinks John Shakespeare to himself. 'It's a secret sign between them that they want to go to bed. She must have known this rogue before I married her, when she was Mary Arden.'

He sits furiously in the chimney corner. He is still and passionate, nursing his grief.

Now if Mr John Shakespeare had met a former lover of his wife's on the road or in the tavern, he could have cut him dead or knocked him down. But this elegant fellow with the raven locks and pink mouth has come to him cunningly, in search of sanctuary from the storm, and is now a guest within his house. You can't cut guests, and neither can you throttle them.

They eat their venison pie, the three of them, with gravy, by the hissing fire, with little speech, and none of it from John. He sits sullen. He looks sunken in his skin.

When the stranger has disappeared upstairs with his candle (and out of this book), John Shakespeare goes to the old sea-chest and takes from it a hank of hempen rope. His wife he gathers by the wrist. 'Come,' he commands. And he leads her out into the dark.

Mary is frightened. Going out through the door she has thrown on her cloak, but it's small enough protection against the storm.

'What is it?' she cries. 'What is it you're wanting with me?'

'Love,' shouts mad John Shakespeare. 'I want love, and I want the simple truth.'

'But you have them both,' cries Mary. 'My dear, you have always had them.'

'And I mean to keep them,' promises her husband. 'I mean to keep you true, madam, which means not opening your legs for that old flame of yours who's up in the house.'

His wife holds up her hand in the wind and the rain. 'I swear to you,' she

cries, 'by my own hope of heaven, I am innocent of this sin which you say is mine. I never saw that man before in my life!'

'Strumpet!' roars Mr John Shakespeare. 'If that's true, then weren't you the quick one to be making the signs of lust – smiling between your fingers, yawning when he yawned, and all the wicked rest of it.'

He's in a fury now, our Mr Shakespeare's father, the bold butcher and whittawer. His fingers burn as he fashions a noose in the end of the rough hempen rope. His wife cannot believe what her eyes are seeing. He drops that noose about her neck, and pulls.

John leads Mary through the dark towards the Forest of Arden.

The wind is dropping but it still blows hard enough. They are bent in their struggle to reach the ragged trees.

As they go, John and Mary Shakespeare, a noise of wild wings goes with them. It's a flock of small birds, fluttering against the ends of the storm, whirling above their heads where they bend into the wind.

And the moon rides out. There's a pool of moonlight now for them to move through, like people underwater, as they reach the first tree of the forest. John Shakespeare throws his rope over the lowest bough.

Up goes the rope, and it crosses the branch, but it does not lodge there.

The birds are there first, you see, hopping and dancing, and the rope slides when it hits their beating wings, and it snakes away, and it falls back to his hand.

John Shakespeare curses. Then he tries again.

Up goes the rope, the birds' wings beat once more, down falls the rope without purchase.

They're beating off his rope with their small wings.

'We will go,' proclaims William Shakespeare's father, 'to the next tree in the forest. It's an oak, if my memory serves me right, which will be the more suitable.'

With a tug at the rope, he leads his wife on by the neck.

Mary weeps as she walks there behind him.

But when they reach the great oak, the two Shakespeares, the same thing happens that has gone before. The birds are there. The rope is repulsed by the beating of their wings.

John Shakespeare drags his wife from tree to tree.

But it's the same scene at every tree he tries. The birds are there before him. They fly through the night, in the howling storm, and their wings repulse the rope each time he throws it.

His face black with anger, Mr John Shakespeare shouts: 'Madam, I know one tree where your friends the birds can't save you!'

What he means is the gallows. That hanging tree stands at the dark heart of the forest, where all the ways meet to make a crossroads.

Mary Shakespeare's weeping without ceasing now. Mary Shakespeare knows he means the gallows.

Her husband drags her on through the black wood.

When they reach the gallows John Shakespeare coils the end of the rope and then hurls it. It goes up. It seeks purchase on the crosstree. But even as the rope is snaking and looping through the air, the air is suddenly full of wings and the moon spills on them. And the moon spills on the gallows too, and on the man hanging there, and John Shakespeare sees the flock of little birds fly down once more in a bright cloud, and settle on the crosstree, so that his rope won't rest there. And this time there are more birds than ever, scores of them, hundreds, centuries of birds, the air's all birds, and birds all over the dead man too, sitting on his skull and on his twisted shoulders, swallows mostly, but fieldfares and martens as well, and blackbirds and thrushes, rooks and red-legged crows, throstles and bunting larks and ouzel cocks, pigeons and turtle doves, crows, sparrows, choughs, finches, blue wings and black wings in the swing of the moon, birds falling off and hanging in the air, birds fighting for places, birds perched on every spar and splinter of the gallows, birds, birds, birds, their small bright wings a-flicker in the night, so that it might as well be water the rope is trying to hold, it might as well be the Avon or the sea.

John Shakespeare was a fool, but he's not an idiot. He knows a miracle when he's witnessed one.

He lets loose the rope from round about Mary's neck. He falls down on his knees. He kneels before her and the gallows in the moonlight.

'Forgive me,' said John Shakespeare. 'Forgive me, wife. It is I who have sinned against you.'

Nine months later, to that very night, the poet William Shakespeare came into the world.

Chapter Seven

All the facts about Mr Shakespeare

It has been said that all the facts about Mr Shakespeare's life could be written on a single page. Here they are then:

KNOWN FACTS ABOUT WS

26th April, 1564:	Christened.	'C. Gulielmus filius Johannes Shakspere.'*
27th November, 1582:	Granted licence to marry.	'Item eodem die similis emanavit licencia inter Willelmum Shaxpere et Annam Whateley de Temple Grafton.'
26th May, 1583:	Christening of his daughter Susanna.	'C. Susanna daughter to William Shakespeare.'
2nd February, 1585:	Christening of his twin son and daughter, Hamlet & Judith.	'C. Hamnet & Judeth sonne and daughter to William Shakspere.'
11th August, 1596:	Burial of Hamlet Shakespeare.	'B. Hamnet filius William Shakspere.'
8th September, 1601:	Burial of his father, John.	'B. Mr Johannes Shakspeare.'
5th June, 1607:	Marriage of his daughter Susanna.	'M. John Hall gentleman & Susanna Shaxspere.'
9th September, 1608:	Burial of his mother, Mary.	'B. Mayry Shaxspere, wydowe.'
10th February, 1616:	Marriage of his daughter Judith.	'M. Tho Queeny tow Judith Shakspere.'
25th March, 1616:	Signed his will.	
23rd April, 1616:	Died.	
25th April, 1616:	Buried.	'B. Will. Shakspere, gent.'

* All bits in italic are words I have copied out from the parochial records at Holy Trinity Church, Stratford, or (in the case of the marriage licence) from the Bishop of Worcester's Register.

These twelve facts are all that there is to be known for sure about William Shakespeare from the public records.

But a man's life does not just consist of facts.

Least of all, the life of our Shakespeare.

Chapter Eight

*Which is mostly about choughs
but has no choughs in it*

When in the last chapter but one I named some of the birds that helped save Mr Shakespeare's mother from the hanging tree I must admit that I took a few of their names from his plays and his poems. Why not? How else could it be when you think about it? My mind is printed with his words and phrases. (Sometimes I think he dreamed me.) I was his page, sir. Now the page writes the book.

Remember, madam, I am an ancient actor. I strutted in my time on the ivory stages.

To be an actor, what is that to be? It is to be a man who turns himself into all shapes like a chameleon. But the whole damned craft is strange, and rooted in mystery. Why does one man's yawning make another man yawn? How, when standing in the jakes, should one man's pissing provoke a second? These are questions impossible to answer except in terms of some common nerve of human sympathy. But what if that sympathy be betrayed by art? What if your first man is not tired or pissy? He is your actor. He pretends a yawn he does not have in his jaws. He peacocks a piss when there's nothing in his bladder. In all this he's as false as those witches and old women that can bewitch our children. The forcible imagination of the one party moves and alters the spirits of the other. And behind the phantom of the player stands the god of the playwright. I was myself created by Mr Shakespeare. My real name is Nicholas Nemo. I am no fowler or ornithologist, no catcher of birds or discourser upon their several kinds and conditions.

And yet not all is art. It is plain fact and verifiable that I have seen with my own eyes in the country around Stratford-upon-Avon certain among

those birds I mentioned. For instance, finches. But others I know only from my trusty Folio – the chough, for instance, which I believe is not an inland bird at all, but more probably to be discovered at the sea-coast of Cornwall, where it builds its nest in the cliffs.

Reader, my procedure is to give you the warp and the weft of Mr Shakespeare's world. His mind held choughs, and his verse found places in it for those birds to fly, therefore it seems to me right that they should be here in the tale of his begetting in the night of the great storm.

Instances are on record of choughs being taught to speak, but Mr Shakespeare appears to have entertained no great opinion of their talking powers. He speaks in *All's Well that Ends Well* of 'chough's language, gabble enough, and good enough', and then in *The Tempest* the usurping Duke of Milan, talking of 'lords that can prate', says

> I myself could make
> A chough of as deep chat.

Falstaff, in the scene with the Prince and Poins, when they are met to rob the travellers at Gadshill, speaks of the victims as 'fat chuffs' – no doubt from their strutting about with much noise.

By the by, Mr Shakespeare sometimes says choughs when I think he means jackdaws. For instance, in the second scene of the third act of *A Midsummer Night's Dream*, where in my part of Puck he had me speak of

> Russet-pated choughs, many in sort,
> Rising and cawing at the gun's report.

Russet here is the French *gris*, a fine grey, and the head of the jackdaw about the neck and ear-coverts is precisely that colour. The head of the chough, like the rest of its body, I believe to be perfectly black.

But if you ask me our poet certainly means the cliff-haunting chough, your chough *graculus* or *Pyrochorax*, when he has Edgar at Dover in *King Lear* pronounce

> Come on, sir; here's the place: stand still. How fearful
> And dizzy 'tis to cast one's eyes so low!
> The crows and choughs that wing the midway air
> Show scarce so gross as beetles; half way down
> Hangs one that gathers sampire, dreadful trade!

Sampire did you know is the herb of St Peter (San Pierre)? It was used in the old days for pickles. But I digress.

For instance, carp is a muddy fish.

For instance, old Mr Burbage had an anchor on his thigh.

For instance, I anchor my mind fast upon Mr Shakespeare.

(One must needs scratch where it itches.)

So if I tell you now of some of the things in the country-side about Stratford, my dears, you may take it as read that I speak of what I have seen with my own eyes.

No choughs in this chapter.

The country about Stratford is pretty, well-watered, and uninteresting. A few miles away rise the Cotswold hills. These have a bold beauty, very pleasant after the flatness of the plain. The wolds towards Stratford grow many oaks and beeches. Farther east, they are wilder and barer. Little brooks spring up among the hills. The nooks and the valleys are planted with orchards. There are grey farm-houses and little grey villages. There are sheep.

Michael Drayton called Warwickshire the heart of England. (And I heard Mr Shakespeare once call Michael Drayton seven sorts of an ass.) Other wise men remark that none of our counties is richer in truly English features, and that none has more verdant or more pleasing meadows than you can discover in the neighbourhood of Stratford. Certainly the Avon is an agreeable river. There are always the swans.

This famous Shakespeare country, then, is what? Let me spell it out in his own words, as I did with the birds. It is all lady-smocks and cuckoo-buds, and it is oaten straws and cowslips' ears. Marigolds. Mary-buds. Undulating farm-lands broken with coppices, I say.

Soho! Soho! So how did Mary Arden's garden grow?

How do you think? The same as any other for miles around.

She planted it when the frost broke in March. She set out thyme and hyssop, garlic, parsley for stuffing rabbits, saffron to colour her pale pies.

Rank fumiter grows in the hedgerows round about her village of Wincot, its flowers sometimes yellow, sometimes waxy red – as red that is to say as sealing-wax.

Idle weeds choked the corn in the bad days: hardokes, hemlock, nettles, cuckoo-flowers. (And quite what those hardokes were I have no idea. In the Quarto of *Lear* the word is printed hor-docks. But he always made me say it out as hardokes. Yes, madam, Pickleherring played Cordelia.)

Well, I think that's quite enough pastoral for one night. The truth is I've got little to say about the country. The country doesn't exist, so far as I'm

concerned. It is Nothing turned inside-out and painted green in spring and golden in the autumn. It is all illusion. All the same, I like it. I also like the town. Pickleherring is not hard to please, you see.

As for Mr Shakespeare, I once heard him give his opinion of Stratford-upon-Avon in four words. Three of them were Stratford-upon-Avon. The other was a verb he never used in his plays.*

But today I feel scurrile – idle, dull, and dry. Reader, you cannot think worse of me than I do of myself.

What am I? I am an antic actor now turned writer to be thought a polymath and get a paper-kingdom. This book is my common theatre. The subject of my discourse: William Shakespeare.

I remember a night not long after I first came to London in Mr Shakespeare's company. We were eating carp quick cooked in butter. I spilt some of their shitty grease on the front of my shirt. Instantly, seeing my embarrassment, Mr Shakespeare thrust the forefinger of his right hand into the hot dish and smeared the front of his shirt to look like mine. I never dreamed of such courtesy before. I have not seen it very often since.

Mr Shakespeare's face was always full of the vivacity of his mind. His habitual look was that of an aloof but sunny spirit. He was a man alive to his fingertips.

I was a witness to some of Mr Shakespeare's life. I was not much of an actor in any of it. Nor am I exactly his bard, though of course he is mine. He has been my guiding spirit all my days.

He was my master, and my genius. I am a dwarf. He was a giant. Yet a dwarf sitting or standing on the shoulders of a giant may see farther than the giant himself. So, telling you Shakespeare's story, I tell you at least one story which Shakespeare could not tell.

O my tautologies. O my toys and fopperies.

All that's too bold, though. (Not like the pancake country round about Stratford.)

This chapter has been a rhapsody of rags gathered together from several dung-hills. The next one should be better. In it I'll have the birth of our hero for my theme.

---

* Though he does have Sir Hugh Evans allude to it punningly in *The Merry Wives of Windsor*, where he asks 'What is the focative case, William?' Mr Shakespeare informed me that this character he based on his Welsh master at the Stratford Grammar School.

Chapter Nine

About the birth of Mr WS

The Misses Muchmore always used to claim that April was the cruellest month. I don't know why. Meg would speak of memory, and Merry of desire. 'Pinch him!' Meg squeaked. 'And burn him!' squealed Merry. Then they would strip and spank me in their parlour.

It was in April, cruel or not, that Mr WS was born and christened. Here's how it happened.

The first nightingale sings each year in the Forest of Arden on the 23rd of April. It was in the late evening of that day in the year of Our Lord 1564, after a day when all day April had been unpicking the blossoms on the whitethorn, a day when expert April had been unlocking the earliest blossoms on the whitethorn, a day when April with shy smiles had been unclenching the first fists of whitethorn blossom, that William Shakespeare, our hero, son of John, was born at Stratford-upon-Avon, in the shire of Warwick.

It was a Sunday and St George's Day.

At the coming forth of the babe the town clock stopped. The small hand pointed to heaven, the big hand to hell. It was half an hour before midnight when the bard was born.

The midwife, whose name was Gertrude, and who hailed from the neighbouring village of Snitterfield, cut the birth-cord with a sword she kept close for the purpose.

Then she kissed the caul that covered the baby's head.

'Here's one who will be fortunate,' she noted.

Then she kissed the black spot, no bigger than a sixpence, on the infant's left shoulder.

'And he's of the devil's party too,' she said.

This Gertrude was a small woman, plain and eager, an intense little mouse living in hope that a big tom-cat would one day jump on her. Blissfully shy, tremulously silent except when telling stories, suffering from piles and a need to be loved, she quivered through what passed for life in Warwickshire wearing a gown with a pattern of faint-green moss on it, her hair drawn up and coiled at the back of her head in a shape which suggested a bun, mittens on her paws, the eyes behind her spectacles on sharp look-out for symptoms of insincerity, moral facetiousness, or otherwise offensive brilliance in those she met.

She was serious and fussy, this Gertrude, liking sunsets and waterfalls, the kind of person afflicted with aphorisms in the presence of either – and that is all your author intends to say about her for now.

That's a good word that BUN though. Have you noticed it's the simple words, the words we take for granted, that are strangest when you stare at them? Nobody really knows where bun comes from. Bugnets is French for little round loaves – lumps made of fine meal, oil or butter, and raisins. The Frogs eat them during Lent, but then France is a dog-hole. Still, there's an old French word *bugne*, meaning swelling, and this might have led to a puffed loaf (a bugnet), and thence to our good plain English BUN.

But as I say it's doubtful. One thing I do know for certain: In Scotland buns are sweeter. They put more sugar and spice in them there, the Scotch being sourer to start with.

It was Mr Shakespeare awakened me to language. But I think you won't find a bun in his plays nor in his poems. I like a buttered specimen myself to my breakfast.

Mary Shakespeare's labours had lasted seven days and seven nights. Her women were about her at the birth, but her husband busied himself outside in the shed where he sometimes cobbled slippers from his surplus whitleather. He was always on the make was Mr John Shakespeare. Now as he watched he saw the house catch fire and burn in flames that spired sky-high. He ran to the Avon with a bucket for water. But Gertrude came to the door of the house and cried: 'Be still, the child is born.' The house was not burned, neither had a single flame harmed the inmates. John Shakespeare was dumbfounded, until he took thought and remembered his Bible, how Moses saw the burning bush – the flames that burned yet consumed nothing. (*Exodus* iii. 2–4.)

Gertrude placed salt in the child's cradle and sewed a speck of iron into the seams of his blouse. The child was sained then. Tallow candles were lighted and whirled about the bed in which mother and infant lay. This whirling was done three times, in the name of the Father, and of the Son,

and of the Holy Ghost, and in the direction in which the sun moved round the house.

A word about cauls. The old wives used to think they stopped you drowning. They used to sell them to sailors if they could. Haly how, sely how, a lucky cap, a holy hood, which midwives like Gertrude called a howdy or a howdy-wife.

According to some, and not all of them fools, the keeper of a caul would know the health of the person who was born in it. If firm and crisp the caul, then he (or she) alive and well. If wet or loose or slack, then dead or ill. The colour of the caul was important also. Black caul, bad luck. Red caul, all that is good. Diadumenus was born with a caul. He became emperor.

The poet William Shakespeare came veiled into this world, then, for his head, his face, and the foreparts of his body, all were covered with such a thin kell, or skin.

John Shakespeare, seeing this, and being as I have told you a man much given over to jealous fantasies, convinced himself that the local vicar, the Reverend John Bretchgirdle, must be the real father of Mary Shakespeare's son. It was so like the clergyman's cowl, that caul on baby William.

So on the Monday morning up jumps John Shakespeare bright and early hammering on the vicar's door and threatening to kill him with his little cleaver.

'Warlock!' he shouts. 'Fat villain! Whoreson upright rabbit! I'll caul you! I'll puncture your testicles!'

'God's mercy!' protests the priest. 'But I am an innocent man, Mr Shagspierre. Sit down upon this hassock, sir. I will pray for you while you wait.'

John Bretchgirdle, oh yes, the Reverend John Bretchgirdle, for the best grin through a horse collar, John Bretchgirdle always won first prize at the Stratford Fair. His eyes were the colour you see otherwise only in a mountain lake, an intelligent clear colour. His complexion was perfect gallows. He was given to winking, not blinking, strong on charity, hard on heresy. His hair was very dark brown, so dark as to appear almost black. In his youth this same Bretchgirdle had been anxious to distinguish himself by committing new sins. He had sat brooding at Christ Church, Oxford, trying to work out exactly what the sin against the Holy Ghost might be, so that he could commit it, never be forgiven, and become immortal in the memory of men as a saint-in-reverse. (Unless the sin against the Holy Ghost is writing blank verse and concealing it in prose, then your author doubts if even he has committed it.)

On the occasion of his first visit to the house in Henley Street this venial

vicar did not address a single word to Mary Shakespeare, and when at John's request he dined there two days later the only notice he took of the lady of the house was to command her to sit at the same table.

Bretchgirdle's condescension in allowing her to share the dinner she had cooked for him did not go unremarked by Mary, although his habit of rejecting his meal from his stomach and chewing it over again, as a cow the cud, some twenty minutes after its original ingestion, caused her no little wonder.

It was Bretchgirdle's pleasure to continue this second chewing for no more than an hour, after which he would always counsel against both Puritans and the tyranny of the Pope.

It fell to the Rev. John Bretchgirdle to christen William Shakespeare. This act he performed in his parish church at Stratford, with John Shakespeare watching his every move with a beady eye.

After the christening feast had come to an end, and the godfathers and godmothers of the child had eaten and drunken lustily (as was the country custom in those days), all set forth on their way homeward. But the night was wet, and they were weary, and they minded not all their steps to be careful of them. And so it came to pass that one of the godmothers carrying the child (it was the wife of WS's uncle Harry) caught her foot upon a stone and fell into the ditch with little William in her arms. She and the baby came out all covered with mud. But as weeds cannot so easily come to harm, the child was not hurt, though he looked like a soot-black imp.

When they got home, Mary washed her child clean in good hot water.

Thus was William Shakespeare in one day three times christened. First, according to the prayer book. Then in the mud of the ditch. And at last in sweet warm water.

So it is always with poets, I have heard. Even in their infancy, strange and wonderful things foreshow their future greatness.

Chapter Ten

*What if Bretchgirdle was
Shakespeare's father?*

But what if the Reverend John Bretchgirdle really was our poet's father? Could that be possible? Let us consider the facts.

Bretchgirdle became vicar at Holy Trinity Church, Stratford, in January 1561, three years and three months before the poet's birth. He was a portly man, and a comfortable one, and a man of parts, made B.A. at Oxford in 1545 and M.A. some two years after. Before he came to Stratford this shrewd prelate was curate at Witton in Cheshire, serving also as master of the school there. Bretchgirdle never taught in the Grammar School at Stratford, but one of his brightest pupils at Witton, John Brownsword, loved him so well that he followed him like a little dog to Stratford to schoolmaster there. More of that in a minute.

Visitations by Bretchgirdle to the house in Henley Street followed regularly upon each other after the occasion already chronicled when he ate his dinner twice, and condemned both Pope and Puritans. Truth to tell, hospitality was offered him more in duty than through any liking, and neither John nor Mary Shakespeare warmed to their vicar until one Sunday post-Communion afternoon when the butcher and whittawer, in the act of handing a cup of sherris sack to his guest, regretted that his latest apprentice had run away.

'Then I will help you,' the Reverend Bretchgirdle said, with every assumption of impulsiveness. 'I know nothing of butchery, but cobbling comes naturally to me,' he added, 'and at the least I can do as well as one of your adolescent labourers.'

John Shakespeare thought that the fat ecclesiastic might be joking. So he did not reply. But later when he witnessed his guest trotting out to the shed

33

and attaching insoles to the bottom of a pair of wooden lasts and fastening the whitleather down with lasting tacks, he had no choice in the matter – speech proved beyond him.

John stood watching goggle-eyed as Rev. Bretchgirdle pierced round the insoles with a bent awl, and it was only when he realised that this was not play-acting and that the priest was hard at it, that he ran to him, and begged him to desist.

'It's not right that your reverence should so demean himself,' he protested, forgetting in his admiration the correct churchly mode of address.

'There's nothing demeaning about it, Mr Chackosper,' purred Bretchgirdle, placing the uppers on the lasts and drawing their edges tightly round the edges of the insoles. 'Cobbling is the only secular work in which a parish priest may profitably interest himself,' he lied. He fastened the uppers in position with lasting tacks. 'Without prejudice to his immortal soul,' he added.

Lasting is a crucial operation, as John Shakespeare knew too well, for unless the upper is drawn neat and tight upon the last, without a crease, without a frown or wrinkle, the shape of the shoe will be spoiled.

The Reverend Bretchgirdle did not falter. He inseamed as if he had been born with an awl in his fist. Then he pared off the rough edges and levelled the bottoms with a piece of tarred felt.

'It was the hobby of many of the patriarchs,' he explained. 'And of Cranmer himself, in his spare moments.'

That night their rector shared the supper of the Shakespeares yet again, and for many a night thereafter, so that soon it was common knowledge in Stratford-upon-Avon that the ecclesiastical eccentric was in some sort of partnership with John Shakespeare, the butcher and whittawer who cobbled as well when he could. It was not so commonly known, however, that the priest had also taken the education of the Shakespeares in hand – slipping frogs, toads, and mice into the marital bed, teaching John and Mary to play with slow-worms and grass-snakes, measures to ensure that they developed an attitude of honest indifference to those things which might otherwise engender wasteful impulses of fastidiousness or fear.

But did the Reverend Bretchgirdle share in John Shakespeare's bed? Had that great whited sepulchre known Mary?

There is a Latin poem by John Brownsword which is a key document here. Brownsword was reckoned a good Latinist. He was schoolmaster in Stratford from 1565 to 1567, having taught in Macclesfield School before that. When Bretchgirdle died (some say of exhaustion) a few years after

christening William Shakespeare, Brownsword returned to Macclesfield, and taught there for many years until his own death in 1589. He wrote three poems addressed to Bretchgirdle, which are of no interest whatsoever, to our purpose, save that we might register their tone of sycophantic amatory tenderness. A fourth, which is probably also addressed to Bretchgirdle, or which is at the least about matters which concerned him, may be only a fragment. A cryptic and broken-backed acrostic, it runs as follows:

> MARE, *ignis, et mulier sunt tria mala!*
> ARDUA *molimur: sed nulla, nisi ardua, virtus.*
> arENAs *mandas semina.*[*]

I have put capitals to the concealed acrostic name so that you may see the more readily that it is MARE (or Mary) ARDEN. In the margin of the page Brownsword has written in his crabbed schoolmaster's hand, *Dux femina facti* ... (Which is to say, 'There's a woman at the bottom of it.') And beside this, scribbled in a macaronic mixture of English and Latin, *'No!' (dixit) 'no!' 'No!'*

What is the significance of this? Let Pickleherring elucidate the mystery. In themselves the lines might be nothing but the complaint of a splenetic spirit thwarted in its love for an inappropriate object, but taken in conjunction with a tale still current in both Stratford and Macclesfield they are at least peculiar, and peculiarly haunting. That tale goes thus:

John Shakespeare having one day to journey to London on business, he says to his wife, 'Listen, while I am gone you're to say No to that Rev. Bretchgirdle.'

'Say no?' says Mary. 'What do you mean say no?'

'I mean say No to him,' John Shakespeare says.

'Nothing but no?' says Mary.

'No, no, no, no, no, all the time No,' John Shakespeare says. 'Say No in thunder, woman. Always answer No, whatever he says to you, however he comes pleading and wheedling, that lecherous old goat. And never add another word to No. Do you understand?'

Mary Shakespeare said she understood.

Her husband went on his way. He trusted his simple stratagem would prevent any harm befalling his wife.

---

[*] Englished: The sea, fire, and women are three evils! We essay a difficult task: but there's no merit save in difficult tasks. You are sowing the sand, i.e. you waste your seed.

The Reverend Bretchgirdle's in through the back door of the butcher shop in about five minutes.

'Good morning, Mrs Shagshaft,' says the scoundrel, bowing low, and then wringing his plump white hands and studying the palms of them as one might refer to an index of human vanity. 'You'll be missing your husband already, I expect?'

'No,' says Mary Shakespeare.

'Oho,' thinks vile Bretchgirdle, 'what can this signify?'

That Mrs S is not missing her husband sounds mighty promising to the lusty vicar.

Then before long he discovers that the young wife answers No to all the things he says to her.

Bretchgirdle sees his chance. He's as clever as a bag of weasels. And persistence is his strong suit. 'Well,' says he, 'if I put my hand on your knee, Mrs Sexspire, you won't mind then?'

'No,' says Mary Shakespeare.

'And if I lift up your gown, Mrs Shakespay,' says the happy priest, his round cheeks dimpling, 'you won't be complaining and telling your husband when he gets back?'

'No,' says Mary Shakespeare.

So the Reverend wretched Bretchgirdle puts his hand on Mrs Mary Shakespeare's white-stockinged knee, and he lifts up her grass-green gown of linen taffety, and he takes down her mockado drawers. His mind is smelling like a rich man's funeral. His bulging eyes roll.

'Pray tell me, Mrs Sackstuft,' he says politely, 'would you object if your rector was to futter you?'

'No,' says Mary Shakespeare.

So the false friar futters her, and when he has finished he says, 'There, Mrs Sexbear, you'll be satisfied now.'

'No,' says Mary Shakespeare.

'Hallelujah!' cries the Reverend Bretchgirdle.

He futters the docile lady all over again, concentrating the while in order to delay the moment of ejaculation upon certain collects of Cranmer's.

'Will that do, Mrs Shagspeer?' the priest enquires solicitously when he comes to his amen.

'No,' says Mary Shakespeare.

Bretchgirdle falls out of bed. He wolfs a dozen oysters and a loaf of cockelty bread. Then he's back at it again.

This time he just pumps away and keeps himself going with fantasies that he is loose in a harem of virgin Turkish girls. Some of the girls are

choirboys. Some of the choirboys are angels. He has to inspect, resolve, and satisfy them all. Then they must satisfy him – first the girls, and then the choirboys, and then the angels. Then angels, choirboys, and girls all come together and Bretchgirdle's the Pope and they all have to do what he says. He doesn't say much but they do it all anyway. Meanwhile the lady beneath him claws at his back and watches a fly over his shoulder that squats upon the ceiling rubbing its hands together.

'Mrs S,' pants the priest, 'isn't that,' (he collapses), '*enough?*'

'No,' says Mary Shakespeare.

Confused, exhausted, and contrite, a sadder and a wiser man in all ways, his balls drained, his heart pounding, his imagination in tatters, his eyes starting out of his head, his knees knocking together and his breath coming in great shuddering gasps, the unworthy Reverend Bretchgirdle withdraws, defeated, and creeps speechless away to his church by the swan-ridden river.

Nine months, nine days, and nine hours later, William Shakespeare made his entrance into this world.

Chapter Eleven

About this book

Y ou understand, madam, that I do not mean to say that the late Mr Shakespeare *was* the bastard son of a priest. (Though in all honesty there are worse things to be, and I am myself the bastard son of a bishop's bastard.)

I only tell you stories about Shakespeare. I only tell you tales which I have heard. You are not required to believe any particular one of them. Nor is it necessary to salvation that you should. But from the over-all impress of the various stories may you perhaps come to know our poet thoroughly. One story might cancel out another. But the whole book will be more than the sum of its parts.

For what it is worth, sir, I think Shakespeare was the son of a butcher (and whittawer). Or perhaps a glover's son.

But, having said that, what have we said in any case? What, in other words, do we mean when we say Shakespeare?

Who is Shakespeare? What is he? (that all our swains commend him). Yes, good reader, *what* is Shakespeare? That is the question my book is trying to answer. *What is Shakespeare?* Where is he to be found? How can we tell the man from the work, and both from the stories about him? Why did the sly fellow leave so little information about himself, so few facts in the way of footprints made in Time? Why did he cover his tracks so cleverly, leaving not a rack behind? What is the proper name for the subject of our study: Shakespeare or 'Shakespeare'?

Sometimes I think that no one has ever been so many men as this man. Like the Egyptian Proteus, he exhausts all the guises of reality.

That Proteus was a minor sea-god, herdsman of the flocks of the salt sea, its seals and its dolphins and so forth. He was a daimon, servant to

Poseidon. He had this power to assume all manner of shapes, but if held till he resumed the true one, he would answer questions. And so in this book I try to hold the late Mr Shakespeare.

Not that WS was a god, you understand; nor even a demiurge or daimon. He was just a man like any other man. Only he was just a man like every other man, and more so. This means that we must think of Shakespeare as always more than we can say about Shakespeare. And, as he remarked to me once, in an unguarded moment, a moment when weariness and excitement made the mask slip and his tongue lose reticence, we must think of Shakespeare as always *less* than we can say about Shakespeare too.

What he said to me that day at the bear-garden was in fact that sometimes he did not feel as though he had written his own works. He said that sometimes he felt as if his works had been written by someone else of the same name. I do not think this betokens undue modesty. He was talking in part about inspiration, of course – that feeling all true poets must have, that their best work comes from somewhere else, from something other than their minds, and that they are merely the conduit for it. The poet takes; he does not ask who gives. 'Not I,' he cries, 'not I, but the wind that blows through me.'

But I believe my master Shakespeare meant more. That afternoon at the Paris Garden he was making reference to a certain quality or condition of being anonymous which is to be met in much of his writing. He becomes the men and women he writes about. Yet none of them is him. And then the character of his language has the same property. It attains a self-sufficing anonymity, so that no name is needed at the bottom of the page to qualify or identify what it says. It is not William Shakespeare who speaks in these plays and these poems. It is the English language speaking itself.

I say that the true life of William Shakespeare is in his plays and his poems. Yet the man himself, to my fingers, we touch nowhere in the work.

Mr Shakespeare is the hero with a thousand faces, and none.

Even the spelling of his name makes him elusive as a sliver of quicksilver. Shakespère was my father.

William Shakespeare, William Shakespeare – the day will come when everyone will know the name, I tell you. I knew him well, sir, and I know him not at all. Madam, there was this man, called William Shakespeare, a certain man who was a fine man too, greater than Tubal Cain or Roger Bacon, an upright downright honest man, subtler than Avicenna, wiser than Paracelsus, knowing at least as much as Cornelius Agrippa himself of the doctrine of sympathy and antipathy in the mineral kingdom, and of the

mystery which is fire (whose faithful secretary he was) – I mean, the mystery which is the fire of language – a man who lived in the old days, not so long ago, and who will live again, if you'll hear me out, for as long as this book lasts, at least.

William Shakespeare was the son of a butcher. During his christening feast, when many guests were seated round his father's table to eat a fatted calf, little William, being then but a few days old, was seized by a griffin and carried away. Over land and over sea the griffin flew, until it came to its stinking nest on top of a cliff in the western isles of Scotland, where it deposited the fledgeling lad. One of the griffin's brood, wishing to reserve such a delicate poetic morsel for its own delectation, caught up our hero in its talons and flapped away to a neighbouring tree. But the branch on which this junior monster perched was too weak to support a double load. It broke. The startled griffin dropped its Shakespeare in a thicket. Undismayed by thorns, young William crawled from the griffin's reach, taking refuge in a cave. A delicious surprise awaited him there, for he found within the cave three girls who had escaped from the griffins in the same way——

Your author doesn't think that is going to do. Try again, Pickleherring. Writing makes history possible. Least among lies is the lie told in jest (*mendacium iocosum*). These fictions are jocose, and not officious. These fictions are fantastic, and not pernicious. These fictions are a comedy, and not malicious. These fictions presently form a story of beginnings. There will be middles enough and endings too, to come. Your author tells of the late Mr William Shakespeare. Your author gives an account of his origins and originals, to feed a need for stories, and to supply a Life.

Here are no legends, sagas, myths, or mysteries. Your author tells you stories about Shakespeare, and he is only too willing to explain whenever he can. For instance, Brownsword. Brownsword's love for Bretchgirdle was more Latin than English, and even more Greek than Latin in his heart. We know no less from his verses. But Bretchgirdle's lust for Mary Shakespeare is quite another matter. Bretchgirdle's lust for Mary Shakespeare is mere gossip. A distinction must be drawn. Yet gossip plays its part too in the life of a man.

This book takes account of such gossip, as it takes account of the stage. The late Mr Shakespeare had his exits and his entrances, and he was one man who in his time played many parts. Nor does Pickleherring mean this merely as Jaques meant it in terms of age. Mr Shakespeare was both poet and player. I speak not just of his profession, but of his identity. He was author and actor. In a word, Mr Shakespeare was an AUCTOR.

That's a good word, that AUCTOR. It comes as near defining what WS *did* as any other single word I know. It's the ancient way to spell the word author. But it is more than that. An auctor is an author and an actor. And I don't just mean that in Mr Shakespeare's case he was a playwright who was also a player in his own plays. (Although he was.) I mean that any man is both the author and the actor of his own life. He is its auctor. Both in the world of the stage and on the world's stage.

It is not just because I am a comedian that I keep coming back to stage business and play-talk.

I act, therefore I am.

We are all players.

What if what we like to call the self is just a series of masks and poses?

An actor's question, and the actor's dilemma, no doubt. But let the audience beware and go home wondering. I mean you, sir. And you, madam. Are you more than your mask? Is there a person to know behind the persona?

Now then, regarding Mr Shakespeare, what we might call the identity question is of course the wildest thing. Which is why some think that someone else wrote his work. (We shall come to this in due process. Also, the portraits.) But if his identity is the wildest question, then a mild thing is the matter of his birth-date, which so far I have taken quite for granted.

The truth is that we can't take it for granted.

The truth is that truth is what we can never take for granted.

What do I mean?

Madam, I mean we all know that Shakespeare was born on the 23rd of April, 1564 – and that he might well not have been.

In other words, that birthday belongs to beauty, not to truth. April 23rd is of course St George's Day. April 23rd is also without doubt or dispute the day on which Shakespeare died in 1616. So we round out our man's little life with a timely coincidence, a chime or rhyme of dates, linked St George's Days. But to say that WS was born on that feast is conjecture. The life of Shakespeare starts with a conjecture. We want him to be born then, so he was.

This is the story of the life of William Shakespeare. It is a story neither cosmogonic, theogonic, anthropogonic, nor eschatological. (Scatological it may be, here and there, but then I did not invent John Shakespeare's dunghill outside his house in Henley Street.)* It is a story inspired neither

---

* Twelve years before our hero was spawned, on the 29th of April, 1552, John Shakespeare paid a fine of one shilling for keeping this *sterquinarium* by his door.

by hope nor fear, but a desire to come at the truth by telling lies. Mr Shakespeare was my master in this desire.

This book must not be thought of as a fable or an old wives' tale. Nor is it so much a cock and bull story as you might care to think. Being jocose, it could even be said to be not incompatible with a taste or a hunger for truth. It offers you no information about the world as a whole. On the question of the meaning and end of life it has nothing to say. This is the story of William Shakespeare. It is a pack of lies, and my heart's blood.

Chapter Twelve

Of WS: his first word,
& the otters

What was the boy William's first word spoken? This is plainly a matter of some pith and marrow.

His sister Joan insisted it was *'Roses!'* – which word she said he learned to say when sat upon his pot in the rose-arbour in his mother's garden. But Joan was five years younger than her brother, so she most certainly never heard this for herself. It may have been family tradition. It could have been Joan's idea of a joke – I mean, the contrast between the roses and the pot. She was an odd woman, married to a hatter called Hart, her madness always having the oddest frame of sense, as the Duke in *Measure for Measure* remarks of Isabella (not one of my best parts, though perhaps I should not say so).

Besides and all, poor greasy Joan was old when she told me this, and her wits sometimes wandered. Her own son was named William, and she might have meant him. *'Roses!'* in my opinion is altogether too poetical a thing to be true as a poet's first comment upon the world. I have known many poets in my time, and none of the good ones was poetical.

'Cheese!' seems much more likely. It was Mr Shakespeare's brother Edmund told me this. The first word the Bard ever uttered, he said, was a good round *'Cheese!'* on account of their father's fond habit of feeding his chicks little morsels of the stuff as they sat up at table. This might well have been so. The fact that Edmund was sixteen years younger than William makes me even more prone to believe it. Notice he did not claim his own first word was *'Cheese!'* Poor Edmund was a modest soul, and gentle. He told me their mother always said that her William's first word was *'Cheese!'* and I can credit it. *'Cheese!'* has at least a petty ring of truth, or probability.

Both Mr John Shakespeare, by report, and WS himself, in my own experience, were always very fond of a nice piece of cheese.

Chaddar (which some miscall Cheddar) was by way of being his favourite. And why not? Your Chaddar is a large, fine, rich and pleasant cheese – and so it should be, for I have heard that in that village near the Mendip Hills in Somerset where it is made, all the milk of the cows is brought every day into one common room, where proper persons are appointed to receive it, and they set down every person's quantity in a book kept for the purpose, which is put all together, and one common cheese made with it.

But Cheshire cheese was also to Mr Shakespeare's taste. He was partial in particular to it toasted. In *The Merry Wives of Windsor* he has Falstaff say, ''Tis time I were choked with a piece of toasted cheese', and I heard him say no less more than once himself. But the poet noted also that eating toasted Cheshire makes your breath stink.

Parmesan pleased him less. He reckoned it was for men who lived like mice and run squeaking up and down. And as for Banbury, pah! Nothing good ever came out of Banbury, said Mr Shakespeare. 'Not even the buns?' I asked him. 'Not even the buns,' he said. 'Not even the fine lady upon the white horse?' I asked him. 'Least of all, her,' he said. 'She would have been a Puritan,' he added. I think I know exactly what he meant. It's an odious town, that Banbury, and all the people there come loaded to their boots with religious zeal. Your Banbury-man is a bigot, sir. Your Banbury cheese is nothing but a paring. Bardolph compares Slender to Banbury cheese. It's no use at all, not even with pippins.

Of cheese in general I once heard Mr Shakespeare declare that a cheese, to be perfect, should not be like

(1) *Gehazi*, i.e. dead white, like a leper;

(2) not like *Lot's wife*, all salt;

(3) not like *Argus*, full of eyes;

(4) not like *Tom Piper*, hoven and puffed, like the cheeks you get from playing of the bagpipes;

(5) not like *Crispin*, leathery;

(6) not like *Lazarus*, poor, or raised up from the dead;

(7) not like *Esau*, hairy;

(8) not like *Mary Magdalene*, full of whey, or maudlin;

(9) not like the *Gentiles*, full of maggots or gentils;

and

(10) not like a *bishop*, made of burnt milk.

I must admit that I never comprehended number 10 in his list of cheese

negatives until one day during the late Civil Wars when my dear wife Jane burnt the porridge and when (mildly) I complained she shouted, 'So the bishop put his foot in it, that's all!' It turned out to be a country saying where she came from, remarked of milk or porridge that is burnt, or of meat that's over-roasted. I daresay it derives from the bishops in the bad old days being able to burn whosoever they lusted.

Well, that's sufficient I think about cheese, although truth to tell Mr WS could never get enough of it himself. I would like it to be true, what Edmund told me.

He was a sweet ineffectual fellow, Edmund, with long hair the colour and consistency of tow. The youngest of the family, he followed William to London to join our company, playing minor female parts and second messengers. It is not true that I was jealous of him. He fathered a bastard son, Edward, who died of a trembling fit before he could speak and we buried him at St Giles, Cripplegate, in the year Mr S wrote bits of his *Timon of Athens*. I think it was 1607, that bad year. Edmund himself died at the end of it. He was buried on New Year's Eve. In St Saviour's, Southwark. I remember the snow falling on his coffin as we carried it into the church, and the forenoon knell of the great bell over our heads. That cost Mr Shakespeare £1. If he had buried his brother outside, with the smaller bell, it would have cost no more than three shillings. Edmund's funeral was held in the morning so that all his fellow actors could attend.

After the funeral, we played at cards for kisses. Mr Shakespeare won. He had me dress in my costume as Rosalind before she went to the woods. He cut himself on a card. (He was very thin-skinned.) I recall him looking at his fingertip and saying, 'His silver skin laced with his golden blood'. This made no sense to me. He sniffed at his fingers also, and said that he smelt a strange invisible perfume. But then perfumes are always invisible, I should say.

Of course, I made no such comment at the time. My dress was blue as they say the Greek sea is. It was made of silk-shag and it rustled when I crossed my legs. I wore silk stockings too, and garters pulled tight like roselets. By the time our game was finished, and all forfeits paid, Mr Shakespeare's Rosalind had nothing on but a pair of hair-coloured satin stays and a scanty quilted petticoat.

Rosalind was always one of my favourite parts. I have reason to know that Mr Shakespeare favoured it as well.

But about that Pickleherring will be silent, for the present. My lips are sealed. They might open another night.

I only just now remembered that game of cards – thinking of Edmund's

burial after telling you how he told me his brother's first word was *'Cheese!'* Sometimes the mind works strangely, but I count this the best way to remember. The trouble with thinking about something often is that it becomes more and more your memory of the thing rather than the thing itself remembered. So it's just as well I'd forgotten this till this minute.

Edmund Shakespeare had a long and ironical face.

He died of brandy, which in those days we called brandy-wine. Brandy is Latin for goose. Here, madam, is a pun between *anser*, a goose, and *answer*, to reply. What is the Latin for goose? Answer (*anser*) brandy!

Reader, my guest, I am myself a water-drinker. I drink no wine at all, which so much improves our modern wits. I am a rude writer too, loose and plain, I confess it. I call a fig a fig and a spade a spade. What my mind thinks my pen writes. I respect matter, not words. With Mr Shakespeare it was otherwise.

Let us consider then the time when the child Shakespeare rose up in the night, while his mother and his father slept.

He went from his cot out into the darkness. In the morning he came back. He was wet through, though it had not been raining. There were green weeds in his hair and about his shoulders. He looked, they thought, like the Old Man of the Sea.

The next night his mother could not sleep for worry about the boy. She saw her son go out again. She followed him to see what it was that he did.

Little WS went down through the moonlit meadows to the river. He walked along its banks till he came to the weir. On the shallow side of the weir he entered the water. He walked into the Avon until it came up to his neck.

There the child stood. There he stayed. He did not move. He did not cry out. No sound escaped him. The dark hours passed. The river flowed all around him with moonlight upon it. Mary watched. Her heart was sore for her son but her feet would not carry her to his rescue nor her tongue cry out. She was as one spellbound, witness to a mystery.

William Shakespeare did not come forth from his vigil in the River Avon until daybreak. Then he walked up the green bank, and he knelt down upon it, and he prayed. And, behind him, two otters came following, bounding from the shallows, slippery through the gloom, and they stretched themselves in his shadow in the thin morning sunlight, and they warmed his feet with their breath and they dried them on their fur.

Chapter Thirteen

Was John Shakespeare John Falstaff?

Mr John Shakespeare suffered badly from indigestion.

'Are you aware,' said the Reverend Bretchgirdle, 'that the bile in your belly could burn a hole in the carpet?'

'Go on,' said John.

'I tell you true,' promised the lumpish ecclesiastic. 'In the third and fourth centuries, Lampridius and Jerome established this,' he added, 'not to say Isidore. Your bile is one of your four humours: *sangius, melancolia, phlegma,* and *cholera. Cholera*'s what you've got. It's what makes you so irascible, Mr S.'

'Sometimes I belch hubbubs,' admitted John.

'Hubbubs?' the priest invigilated. 'What colour hubbubs?'

'Hubbubs the colour of pixies,' said John Shakespeare. 'Green ones and black ones. I can't stand my own smell when I do.'

'Do you eat a lot of butter?' asked Bretchgirdle. Then, without waiting for any answer, he went on, 'Just last year, so I heard, Dr Timothy Bright poured half a pint of green bile onto a Turkey carpet at St Bartholomew's Hospital in Smithfield. Do you know what happened?'

'A hole,' John suggested.

'A hole as big as a saucer,' Bretchgirdle says.

'But my bile's mostly black,' John Shakespeare counters hopefully. 'It's only my hubbubs come green. Will I have to be purged?'

'Not at all,' his priest tells him. 'Mr Shakstaff, yours is the black choler, Trevisa's *cholera nigra.* All we must do is to shave off the foreign ferment from your crude ventricle.'

While the poor bewildered whittawer is failing to digest this, and before

he can open his foam-flecked mouth to reply, Bretchgirdle hands over a folded sheet of paper.

'Read this,' he says.

It was a holograph manuscript in cursive script, the signature sprawling and sea-stained.

John Shakespeare read as follows:

I have been a martyr to <u>cholera</u> for five years, went to divers surgeons and physicians, gained no benefit. I essayed everything, but was unable to take solid food. My wife advised BRETCHGIRDLE'S DIGESTIF CORDIAL. *After using it, I improved, and was able to enjoy buttered pippin-pies and to consume a mutton chop at will. Now I carry a flask of* BRETCHGIRDLE'S DIGESTIF CORDIAL *in my pocket when I go on any voyage, and drink a sip of it after each and every meal. It has been to me a godsend.*

(signed) Sir Francis Drake, Admiral;
MP for Bosinney, Cornwall.

John Shakespeare never bothered to learn to write, and he's a very slow reader. When he's read the commendation through he whistles, and then taps at his front tooth with it. 'That's remarkable,' he says at last. 'Can I ask you one thing though – do you take this drink yourself?'

'Each bottle blessed by Edmund Grindal, the Archbishop of Canterbury,' his vicar says neutrally. 'It tastes just like honeysuckle,' he explains, 'but believe me it's manna by the time it comes to meet all that thick acrid fluid secreted in your kidneys. Choler, farewell. Indigestion ceases *instanter*. You can eat anything, Mr Shakestaff.'

'Anything?' John Shakespeare asks slyly.

'Take two sips after each confession but before making your communion,' advises the Pelagian.

Reader, you will have noticed in this colloquy that Bretchgirdle twice addressed our hero's father as *Shakstaff* and *Shakestaff*. This is not idle fancy on Pickleherring's part. In fact I have inspected a document in which the late Mr William Shakespeare's father is listed as Richard Shakstaff. That makes it quite thinkable that John Shakespeare could be known as John Shakestaff. But where is all this *staff*-stuff leading us, you wonder?

Sir, I would like to suggest that the character of Sir John Falstaff is based directly on Mr Shakespeare's father John! Madam, consider it without tilting your nose, if you please. I do not mean only to say that they had indigestion in common. Nor big round bellies.

Members of the poet's family proved understandably reticent when I broached this subject. I cannot blame them. Who would want to admit to the fat cowardly knight in his family tree – that liar, that misleader of youth, that great drunkard? Joan Hart (Shakespeare's sister) looked away when I mentioned it. Susanna Hall had her Puritan husband show me the door. Only Judith Quiney, the poet's younger daughter, did not bat an eyelid at my theorem. Dear Judith, but I don't know what she thought. She seemed never very interested in her father's work. It was long after her own tosspot of a husband had upped and left her that I got around to asking if it had ever crossed her mind that Falstaff and her grandfather were the same. As I say, she didn't bat an eyelid. She just stared at me. One of her tricks was to wear a medal low on her chest. Whenever I asked to see it, instead of drawing it out she leaned forwards for me to look. Although I often asked to see that medal, I never did find out what it represented.

But think of what I'm saying. John Shakespeare was a drunkard. He was fat. He was witty. He spent most of his time in the ale-house. He told lies. He rose Alderman-high* in Stratford before he fell ruffian-low. The boy William's first memories of him would have been of a great man in a red gown with white ermine collar and trimmings. And John's fall from grace must have come in William's youth. I am sure John Shakespeare cast a long shadow over his son's life. Yes, and a fat shadow too, I'm convinced of that.

But don't take my word for it. Look at the names on this black list. It's a list that I turned up in Stratford – of men not attending Trinity Church in the year of 1592:

Mr John Wheeler
John Wheeler, his son
Mr John Shakespeare
Mr Nicholas Barnhurst
Thomas James, alias Giles
William Baynton
Richard Harrington
William Fluellen
George Bardolfe

It is said that these nine come not to church for fear of process for debt.

I have underlined the three names that prove there must be something to my case. Here we see John Shakespeare linked in disrepute with two of

* Falstaff in *Henry IV, Part One* goes out of his way to say that when younger he 'could have crept into any *Alderman's* thumb-ring'. This is followed by a passage in which he says to Hal: 'Thou art my son.'

Falstaff's cronies: Bardolph and Fluellen. Of the real-life Fluellen I know nothing, save that his widow died in the Stratford almhouse. But George Bardolfe was much like the rogue in the plays – in *Henry IV*, *Henry V*, and *The Merry Wives of Windsor*. He started as a mercer and a grocer, and ended up as a drunk. Writs of arrest were issued against him for debt. He was imprisoned for it in the year he appeared on the list. They say he had friends in high places, and that the under-sheriff of Warwickshire, Basil Trymnell, let this Bardolfe out to drink in a tavern in Warwick but when warned that he might escape kept him 'in a much straighter manner' and secured him by 'a lock with a long iron chain and a great clog'.

The character and nature of John Shakespeare and his associates seems to me as near a match as you will find for the character and nature of John Falstaff and his associates. Who says the people in the plays are not real people? I think they had flesh and blood in our poet's mind.

Besides which, Thomas Plume, the Archdeacon of Rochester, told me that Sir John Mennis once saw Mr John Shakespeare in his shop in Henley Street. This would have been at the end of the last century. He was a merry-cheeked old man, he said. He said also that the father said that Will was 'a good honest fellow', but he 'durst have cracked a jest with him at any time'. Who else can this remind you of but Falstaff and Prince Hal? *Do thou stand for my Father*, as the poet has the prince say true to Falstaff.

I should not be surprised one day to learn that John Shakespeare died crying out 'God, God, God', as Mistress Quickly says John Falstaff did. Some say he died a Papist, like his son. But more of that later.

That hubbub's an Irish war-cry: *Ub! Ub! Ubub!*

As for Doctor Timothy Bright, he was a very fine physician in his day, and the odious Bretchgirdle's invoking him should in no wise be permitted to detract from his excellent fame. In addition to his treatise on preserving health, called *Hygieina*, he wrote a good one on restoring the same commodity, *Therapeutica*. He also invented a shorthand system that was used by Robert Cecil and his spies. His *Treatise of Melancholy*, published in 1586, distinguishes between the mental and the physical roots of that affliction. The late Mr Shakespeare was fond of this little book. I often saw him reading in it, and he may even have derived from thence the phrase 'discourse of reason' which comes in Hamlet's first soliloquy.

I doubt myself that Dr Bright ever poured bile on any carpet. Nor would Grindal have blessed a bottle. He leaned towards Geneva in such matters.

I met John Shakespeare myself, but just the once. I'll be telling you all about that when we come to it.

Chapter Fourteen

*How Shakespeare's mother
played with him*

Some say that the first word spoken by William Shakespeare was neither *'Cheese!'* nor *'Roses!'* but that as soon as he came forth from his mother's womb he cried out with a great voice and what he cried was this: *'Drink! Drink! I want drink! Bring me ale to drink!'*

No doubt you do not believe the truth of this first saying of Shakespeare's after his nativity. No more do I. But tell me, if it had been the will of God that the babe should cry out not as other babes do but in this wise, would you still say that little Willy could not have done so? I tell you, it is not impossible with God that a child should speak in the first moment of his life, and that he might call out for a pot of ale, if he wanted one.

Be that as it may, the midwife Gertrude told me on her oath that at the sound of his father's flagons clinking the baby William would of a sudden fall into an ecstasy, as if he had then tasted of the joys of paradise. So that every morning his mother would strike with a spoon upon a glass or a bottle, and at the sound her son would become happy, lolling and rocking himself in his cradle, nodding with his head, a perfect little tosspot.

And if he happened to be vexed, or if he did fret, or weep, or cry, they had only to bring him some ale in a bottle with a teat, and he would be instantly pacified, and as still and as quiet as they could wish.

WS was by all accounts a fine handsome boy, and of a burly physiognomy. In fact he cried little, and laughed when he could. He beshat himself very smartly every hour. To speak truly of him, as Dr Rabelais says of the infant Gargantua, he was wonderfully phlegmatic in his posteriors.

So what did Shakespeare do in the days of his beginning?

He did, sir, what you did, and what I did, and what even you did,

madam. That is to say, he passed the time like any other child since the birth of the world. He passed his time in drinking and in eating and in sleeping. And he passed his time in eating and in sleeping and in drinking. And he passed his time in sleeping and in drinking and in eating. And he passed his time in eating and in drinking and in sleeping. And he passed his time in sleeping and in eating and in drinking. And he passed his time in drinking and in sleeping and in eating.

And, sometimes, as I say, he shat himself.

And as soon as he learned to walk he learned to run. He may even have learned to run before he could walk. Before or after, in no time at all the boy Shakespeare was chasing after butterflies. And in no time at all he had trod his shoes down at the heel.

What were his very first games?

He blew bubbles at the sun through a yarrow straw. He shooed his mother's geese, sir, and he pissed in his breeches and his bed.

What were his very first fancies?

He hid himself in the river for fear of rain. He hoped to catch larks, madam, if ever the blue skies should fall.

What else did he do?

He shat in his shirt. He wiped his nose on his sleeve. He let his snivel run down into his porridge, and then gobbled up the brew. He slobbered and he dabbled in the ditch. He waddled and he paddled in the mire. He sang sweet songs and he combed his hair with a bowl of chicken gruel.

What else did he think?

Why, he thought that the moon was made of green cheese, and that if he ate cabbage he would shit beets, and that if he beat the bushes he might catch the throstle-cocks.

So what was his first ambition?

To run away.

Is it true that Shakespeare was a lecher, even as a child?

It is true, so they say, that little WS was always groping his nurses and his governesses, upside down, arsiversy, topsiturvy, handling them very rudely under their petticoats in all the jumbling and the tumbling he could get into.

How could this be?

He had already begun to exercise his tool, sir, and if you will forgive me, madam, to put his codpiece in practice.

But how did he know what to do, and him so young?

On account, I am told, of his mother.

His mother?

His mother.

Mary Shakespeare who had been Mary Arden?

The same.

Are you telling us that she taught him the facts of life?

You may believe it, or not, just as you please. I only tell you stories I heard in Stratford.

Who told you this one?

The midwife Gertrude, speaking on her oath.

A midwife told you that Shakespeare's mother told him the facts of life when he was still a child?

No, sir. The midwife Gertrude told me that Shakespeare's mother *taught* him the facts of life when he was still a child.

How so? How so?

I'll tell you how so, both of you. Mary Shakespeare would take her son's little member very pleasantly in her hands, and she would pass her time with it there between her fingers, and she would cherish it and dandle it and play with it, and do all sorts of tricks with it, rubbing it softly in her silks as well as briskly in her palms, until the thing fairly throbbed at her slightest touch, until it beat like a captured nestling in her grasp, until it stood up stiff as any little thorn for her. Mary Arden was a farmer's daughter. She had milked many a cow in her days on the farm. Not that she milked her son William, you understand. He was too young to be milked when she started to play games with him. She called his prick her pleasure, her pride, and her pillicock. She called his little balls her sugar-plums. She whispered all this in his ear as he lay beside her in his father's bed, and his father away at the ale-house. She took him out by the hand to the green mossy banks in the Forest of Arden also, and mother and son lay together in the long grass, and she did it there too. She said sweet William was her pretty rogue, and that he was equipped like any knight, and that he would go far since the world was his already.

Did Mary apply her red lips to it?

Don't be disgusting, sir. We are speaking of his mother!

But you say that she played with it?

Madam, let's change the subject———

Chapter Fifteen

What this book
is doing

Was there *really* a sign over John Shakespeare's shop saying BUTCHER &
WHITTAWER?

Of course not. Well, it's highly unlikely, to say the least.

But it's made you think, hasn't it? I made you remember it.

That's what Pickleherring is about. That's what this book is doing.

I make you remember certain things I tell you about the late great Mr
William Shakespeare and those round about him. I want you to think for
yourself about all of them.

For instance, take that matter of Shakespeare's mother and what she
may have done to him. Perhaps she did awaken her son's first passions.
Perhaps she did not, perhaps she did no such thing. What is certain is that
Shakespeare was precocious in what he has Hamlet call 'country matters',
and someone must have taken him in hand. He was only 18 years old when
he came to marry. His bride was eight years his senior. And their first child,
Susanna, was born less than six months after the date of the marriage.

I have heard it said that WS married an older woman. But the truth is
that Anne Hathaway married a younger man. The average age of marriage
for women in parishes in the Forest of Arden in the period from 1575 to
1599 was 26·3 years old. The average age for men was 29·7. So while Anne
was exactly punctual to the nuptial pattern, Will was eleven years early.
Think it out for yourself. Then read *Venus and Adonis* over again.

It's wonderful what you can prove with the facts in parish registers.

Besides which, BUTCHER & WHITTAWER is only *philosophically* true.

Though I believe myself that John Shakespeare was more likely a glover.

Or a dealer in skins, and in wool perhaps. And in timber and in barley and in leather.

And, later, without question, more than a bit of a usurer. (I'll be coming to that.)

Chapter Sixteen

Shakespeare breeches

When our little William Shakespeare came of sufficient age, his father John bestirred himself and determined that the boy should have a pair of breeches.

Shakespeare breeches were no ordinary breeks. They were, in fact, a kind of galligaskins, very wide and flopping in the leg, like shipmen's hose but tight into the arse, fashioned of thick stiff whiteleather to withstand the winter's fury, without points to truss them up but with the vest growing as it were spontaneously out of them, a sort of natural over-all, like branches and leaves that have sprung from the rotundity of some great oak tree.

Furthermore, to ensure goodness, these breeches had to be made in a church, upon consecrated ground.

Now this could not be done by day in Stratford, for the Reverend Bretchgirdle did not approve of tailoring on God's premises. So John Shakespeare called on Martin Jimp the tailor in his shop in Sanctity Street, and promised him that if he would consent to make the breeches by night in Holy Trinity Church he would pay him treble wages.

Jimp agreed. He was a very able tailor, as swift and deft a needle-jerker as any in Warwick.

Some three years previous, so it is said, Mr John Shakespeare had won a considerable wager as a result of this Jimp's alacrity. What happened was that the glover (and/or butcher) bet an acquaintance of his, the same George Bardolfe already mentioned, that by 8 o'clock on a particular evening he would sit down to dine in a well-woven, well-dyed, well-made suit of apparel, the wool of which had formed the fleece on sheep's backs in the Shottery meadows at 5 o'clock on that same day's morning. It is no wonder that among the class of persons accustomed to betting such a wager

should eagerly be accepted, seeing that the achievement of the challenged result appeared all but impossible. Martin Jimp was entrusted with the work.

At five in the morning of one fine June day he caused two South Down sheep to be shorn. The wool was washed, carded, stubbed, roved, spun, and woven. The cloth was scoured, fulled, tented, raised, sheared, dyed, and dressed. The tailor was at hand, and made up the finished cloth into garments. And at a quarter past six in the evening Mr John Shakespeare sat down to dinner at the head of his guests, in a complete damson-coloured suit that had been thus made – winning the wager, with an hour and three quarters to spare. Of course every possible preparation was made beforehand; but still the achievement was sufficiently remarkable, and was long talked of with astonishment in Stratford-upon-Avon.

Jimp liked a challenge. So in the matter of the Shakespeare breeches it was not so much the glamour of the triple money that attracted him, but the knowledge that the Stratford church was haunted, and the imputation – which he resented that a tailor might not be brave enough to spend a night there. For Martin Jimp was well acquainted with what is said of tailors: that it takes nine of them to make a man, that a tailor's sword is only a needle, that a tailor's wound is a stab in the back, and so on.

Jimp was a spruce little fellow with a mop of white hair. He walked with a stoop and wore a black patch made of velvet over one eye, but he was not without honour.

So night comes, and Martin Jimp comes to Holy Trinity Church. He approaches it from the north, passing down the avenue of lime trees that smell sweet from a sudden shower of rain, entering the building by picking the lock in the door in the porch with his clever tailor's needle, and crossing himself with the same sharp blade in hand as he slips in.

It's cold and dark inside. The air is dewy from recent burials in the crypt. The stonework seethes with damps that creep in with the fog from the nearby Avon. You can hear mice rustling among the smooth pews. Those pews gleam in sudden shafts of moonlight falling through high pointy windows as the moon rides fast. There's a smell like rotting quinces from the charnel-house.

I should tell you that Trinity Church is cruciform in plan, consisting of a nave with aisles, a chancel (where the wearer of the breeches now lies buried), transepts, and a central tower with a spire made of wood. The charnel-house stands just beyond the chancel. It's a place of horror. The sexton digs up bones and throws them there, to make room for new graves in the church and the churchyard as more people die. I think this place

loomed large in the boy Shakespeare's nightmares. In *Romeo and Juliet* he writes:

> *Or shut me nightly in a charnel-house,*
> *O'ercover'd quite with dead men's rattling bones,*
> *With reeky shanks, and yellow chapless skulls.*

And then there's all that Yorick stuff in *Hamlet*. I think that the closeness of the charnel to the chancel in the Stratford church is one reason for the curse Shakespeare put on his grave. But I run on too fast, sir. All things in order, Pickleherring. No hasty puddings, thank you.

Jimp sits down cross-legged on the tomb of a knight and his lady just beside the choir stalls. The tomb is comfortable enough, the effigy of the lady having been removed by Bretchgirdle, with a result that there is plenty of room for a tailor on that side of the bed.

Jimp lights his candle with a spark from his tinder-box. He puts on his thimble. He threads the stout thread in his silver needle. Then he sets to work, making the breeches.

Jimp worked hard and well. The seams grew. The stitches flew. Loop, double chain, tambour, lock – he's throwing in the lot for luck, and to celebrate the extreme dexterity of his fingers, his mastery of his trade, for this Jimp's no bodger, he's the finest gentleman-tailor in Stratford-upon-Avon, which is why Shakespeare's father has employed him for such important business.

Look, madam. Watch spry Jimp at work. It is always a pleasure to see a man at one with what he is doing.

The candleflame flickers high. It illumines not just our busy little tailor crouched to his task but the choir stalls beside him. His shadow's at work on them, stitching and stitching. Those choir stalls are tall and handsomely carved. They are covered with grotesques on their misericords.

Now, all at once, Jimp sees his bright candleflame shiver.

It sputters.

He watches it.

It shakes.

He watches it.

Then the shivering and the shaking seem to stop. The flame burns bold again. His shadow on the stalls is big as ever.

Perhaps, thinks Jimp, it was just a breath of wind under the door. A draught in this draughty church. At worst, some foul exhalation from a crack in the ancient pavement. But he feels an icy chill creep to his heart.

He can hear a sound like the scratching of rats' claws. He can hear a sound like the slithering of rats' tails.

But it is not rats.

And it was not a breath of the wind.

And it is not a draught or exhalation.

The candle shakes again, and again, and again. Big drops of wax flake off from it, and drip like blood. Then the flame flares and spills and suddenly goes out. And the stone floor starts cracking open at the entrance to the charnel-house.

Gazing wide-eyed with his one good eye through the chancel in a sudden bolt of lightning, Martin Jimp the tailor sees a head thrust up through the floor. It is a scaly and an ugly head, like a fist upraised, the hair long and black and matted on the skull, the eyes dreadful and staring. The mouth of the head yawns open, deep and red. Its voice when it speaks is like dead leaves rustling together on the ground, doing what children call the devil's dance.

The voice says to Martin: 'Do you see this great head of mine?'

'I see that, but I'll sew this,' says Jimp the tailor.

His heart is thumping as if to get out from the coffin of his chest. He rocks from side to side as he squats on his haunches. But he stitches and stitches away at the Shakespeare breeches.

Then, as the thunder rolls over the church, there's a cracking and a ripping sound, louder than any thunder, and the head of the thing by the entrance to the charnel-house comes up higher through the floor. The glass in the altar windows rattles and seems to splinter as poor Jimp watches. And the neck of the thing from the charnel-house comes into view, and terrible it is to see, with its throat cut, and the veins hanging out like blood-red worms, and a plague sore weeping on its Adam's apple.

The voice speaks again through the red red mouth to Martin: 'Do you see this great neck of mine?'

'I see that, but I'll sew this,' says Jimp the tailor.

He trembles and he reels to and fro as he works with his needle. His gorge rises in his throat, making him spit. But he stitches and stitches away at the Shakespeare breeches.

The storm bursts over the church. Head and neck of the thing from the charnel-house rise higher yet through the broken-open floor. Now our brave little tailor can see the chest and shoulders of a vast enshrouded dead thing thrusting up through the fissure. It is like nothing so much as a tombstone with flesh growing on it.

Again the voice speaks to Martin: 'Do you see this great chest of mine?'

And again Jimp answers: 'I see that, but I'll sew this,' and though mad with fright he keeps on stitching, stitching at the breeches.

Thunder and lightning come together now as the dead thing keeps on rising through the pavement of Holy Trinity Church. Rain lashes the wooden spire as the thing writhes and shakes a long pair of arms with the bones poking through at the fingers in poor Jimp's face.

Then it cries: 'Do you see these great arms of mine?'

'I see those, but I'll sew this,' answers Jimp the tailor, wailing, moaning, stammering, yet ever mindful of his grammar.

And he stitches and stitches the harder at the Shakespeare breeches, for he knows that there's not much left in the way of time now. Disgust swells his bosom, but still he won't stop from his task.

Trinity Church seems shaking from crypt to spire in the grip of the storm, and Jimp is nipping off threads with his foxy little teeth and taking up the long stitches when the thing uses its horrible arms to pull up one of its legs through the floor of the chancel.

'Do you see this great leg of mine?' the thing cries, and its voice doesn't whisper any more, it sounds louder than the thunder.

'I do, sir, oh I do indeed,' Jimp answers. 'I see that, but I'll sew this, all the same!'

His fingers burn to be done. His thumbs prick to be finished. He bites his tongue. The sweat runs down his cheeks. There is blood on his fingertips. His lips are gnawed through and through where he has chewed at them. His good eye rolls in its socket. But he will not give up. His needle flashes in the lightning that strikes through the church. Jimp pants. He gasps for breath. But he pulls all the stitches fast tight in the Shakespeare breeches.

It is said that the last stitch came right under Martin Jimp's needle just as the thing from the charnel-house pulled up its other leg out of the rotting stinking darkness from under the floor of the church.

Jimp snapped the thread.

'Ho hum!' he cried. 'Time to go!'

He jumped down from the tomb where he had been working. Turning his back on the thing, he ran down the aisle as fast as his legs would carry him, and out through the porch and out of Holy Trinity Church, with the completed Shakespeare breeches under his arm.

Once out of the church and Martin Jimp was safe. The thing could not follow him. Such things are held fast, so they say, by consecrated ground.

Never had night air smelt so sweet to his nostrils. The storm had passed as suddenly as it begun. The agony of the brave little tailor's soul found

vent in one long loud shriek of triumph as he held up the Shakespeare breeks and showed them to the moon.

Jimp did not go home straight away. He washed his hands in the Avon and then went back. He could hear the thing still ramping and stamping up and down the nave of Trinity Church. Climbing up on a rain barrel, he peeped in through a crack in a stained-glass window and he saw it sitting in the font and eating corpse flesh, both hands full and its red mouth dribbling blood.

As Jimp watched, the thing looked up and saw him. It started to howl. Then it held out a handful of corpse meat, and it started laughing. The look on its face, Jimp said, was the look of a delicate glutton. The thing beckoned him, Jimp said, with an air of great politeness, as if it would invite him back to come and share its feast.

That sight was the last straw for Jimp the tailor.

He ran away. He ran as fast as he could.

He ran and he ran till he came to John Shakespeare's shop in Henley Street. There they found him crouched in the doorway as dawn broke over Stratford.

It was this adventure that left the little tailor's hair as white as snow.

But the Shakespeare breeches were delivered and William Shakespeare wore them.

Chapter Seventeen

Pickleherring's room
(in which he is writing this book)

I would like to describe for you this room in which I write.
It is a small room in the shape of a triangle. My door is at the point of it.
All three walls are lined with my bookcases. There's a small window like an
eye in the middle of the wall that's opposite my door. I have my table there, to
get the light. My bed's to the right of the table. Sometimes I move the table
and push the bed under the window and work in bed. Sometimes at night I
push the bed into the door and sleep with my feet against it. The exercise is
good for me, and an old man can't be too careful these naughty days.

I'm on the third floor. Downstairs is a whorehouse. In the basement, a
pie-maker's. So you see I'm well catered for.

Madam, don't fret yourself. Pickleherring jests. It's 20 years since I
bothered with a woman. And I keep a spare diet, sir. It's 30 years since I
bothered with a pie.

All my work is done here.

All my life is in this room.

In addition to my books I have 100 small black boxes stacked along my
bookshelves. Each box is tied with red ribbon and sealed with red sealing-
wax. These 100 boxes contain all my notes and queries concerning Mr
Shakespeare. I take a box down and I work. My boxes hold little objects
also – things cogent to the subject of the papers in them. While writing that
last chapter, for instance, I had Martin Jimp's bright needle on my table.
Touching it was inspiring. It gave me ideas. I have to do stuff like this since
I am not really a writer. Such things are my props. I'm just one of your
harlotry players after all.

I am seated at my table writing this.

To my left, on the top of a little drawer-desk, stands a green lacquered tray bearing a cup and saucer, a jug of water, and a silver egg-cup with its egg as yet unboiled but waiting for me. Beside the egg-cup there's my (once) white napkin lying. That's rolled in a whorled napkin ring in the shape of two snakes coupling.

Those boxes contain all the matter I've accumulated for my chapters. For instance, names and dates and figures copied out from parish registers. For instance, stories that I heard in Stratford. For instance, play-bills.

Under the bed I've a porcelain pot which I piss in.

It's been bitter cold this winter. That I welcome. The snow lies on the roofs I see from my window. The blessed snow does not discriminate. It blesses both the taverns and the stews. No doubt it even blesses the Bishop of Winchester. This Liberty of the Clink lies under him. But I can't see St Mary Overy's from here.

There's a view, could I lean out, of five fine prisons – the Marshalsea, the King's Bench, the White Lion, the Counter, the Clink itself. Once upon a time you could have seen our Globe from this same window. But that was torn down by Cromwell, who was no play-goer. Before that, of course, it caught fire in 1613. We were doing *King Henry the Eighth*. I was playing Anne Bullen. (Not much of a part, but by then I was well past my prime.) It was old Heminges' fault. The text calls for hautboys. So he goes and gets trumpets. Then to go with those trumpets he has this great ordinance set off. The effect was dramatic. But wadding from out of the barrel set fire to the thatch. It took only two hours to dissolve Shakespeare's Globe after all. The mercy is no one killed, though that Sly the critic had his breeches set on fire, which would perhaps have broiled him, if he'd not by the benefit of a provident wit put it out with bottle ale.

Here I sit every day to my great work. I wear two coats to keep the winter out. It's not warm in this room, though you'd think the heats below would filter up. On *very* cold days I wrap over my coats that vasty black star-spangled cloak that was once part of my costume as Cressida. The whole working suit is bound round my body by a leather girdle.

In the trunk by my feet I keep my costumes, though some hang up on pegs between my books. There is Cordelia's wig. Here Portia's law gown. I sometimes still sleep in the nightgown of Lady Macbeth for a treat on a warm summer's night. But I wear my jerkin over it, not to speak of my leggings. I have to. My blood would stop, otherwise.

My boots are covered with patches. No surprise in that. They've been my companions now for 33 years.

I feel the cold keenly. I put my feet in a box of straw under my table

when I'm sitting working. If you keep your feet warm then the rest of you doesn't seize up. I wear mittens on my paws. Two pair when I'm writing.

I won't list all my books, since that would be tedious. Sufficient to say it's a good job the girls downstairs can't read. If one of them learned to, and took it into her unpretty little head to creep up here, then she might come to the conclusion that there's some kind of Aladdin's Cavern above her in the attic of the whorehouse.

I'll mention only that I possess all the necessary books. Which is to say: Holinshed's *Chronicles*, John Stow's *Annals*, North's translation of Plutarch, some anonymity's Plautus, Belleforest's *Histoires Tragiques*, Cinthio's *Hecatommithi*, an execrable French version of Ser Giovanni Fiorentino's *Il Pecorone*, Arthur Broke's translation from the Italian of Bandello's *Novelle*, and Golding's great Englishing of the *Metamorphoses* of Ovid.

Who gave me these books?

Mr Shakespeare did.

Yes, madam, he loved me, but that's not the only reason. I've told you he covered his tracks. These were his source books, you see.

For example, the plot and much of the matter for *Romeo and Juliet* comes straight out of Broke's rendering of that old Bandello story. Nor do I believe that I dishonour Mr Shakespeare in pointing this out. While he makes little change in the plot, he impregnates it with his own poetic fervour. His Mercutio and his Nurse relieve in their different ways what was mere solemn melodrama in the original. He compresses what takes nine months in Broke to a single week of hot days and hot nights, and he reduces Juliet's age from fifteen to thirteen. As for the language which he gives the two young lovers – it is on fire, where Broke is not even kindling. Imagine the balcony scene with turd like this:

> *What if your deadly foes, my kinsmen, saw you here?*
> *Like lions will, your tender parts asunder would they tear.*
> *In truth and in disdain, I, weary of my life,*
> *With cruel hand my mourning heart would pierce with bloody knife.*

That's from Broke's *Romeus and Juliet*. Pyramus and Thisbe, eat your hearts out. If alchemy is what they say it is – the art of transmuting base matter into gold – then Mr William Shakespeare was an alchemist.

By the way, friends, while everyone knows that this is one of Mr Shakespeare's earliest plays, I believe that I can date the thing precisely. Forgetting Verona, wholly caught up in creating the part of the Nurse, he

has her declare *'Tis since the earthquake now eleven years*[*] – and there hasn't been an earthquake in England since 1580. Which must mean Mr Shakespeare was writing it in 1591, in the 27th year of his age. Well, I like to think so, anyway. He revised the piece considerably after its first playing, augmenting the part of Juliet just for me. You'll see that for yourselves if you care to compare the First and Second Quartos. (I bore the fair copy for the latter, in '99, on behalf of Cuthbert Burbie to his printer Creede at the Katherine Wheel in Thames Street.)

My pride is of course my First Folio of Mr Shakespeare's plays. This was given to me by the printer William Jaggard for a fortieth-birthday present. It sits to my right hand on my table whenever I write. I refer to it each time I quote for you, having only an actor's memory; I mean, I can recall *verbatim* my own parts, but not the others.

I have all my prompt-books too, from the days when I served with the Company. These I keep under the bed, to the left of my piss-pot.

I am not poor. I am not rich. *Nihil est, nihil deest*: I have little, I want nothing. All my treasure is in Minerva's tower.

All the same, somewhere in this room – but I will not write down *where* – a great secret is hidden. I shall come to that in due course. A time for everything, and everything in its time, as my grandfather the bishop used to say. (He was a martyr to the pox for the last 20 years of his life.) Suffice it for now that I tell you that this secret of mine consists of all that remains of a play of Mr Shakespeare's that is otherwise lost.

Here's a riddle for you: it's not *lost*, for the *lost* one you have already. This is the lost *un*lost one.

No need to bruise your brains unduly on such wit-work.

It is my plan to include this play in my book!

That's a good warm word that GALLIGASKINS which I used in my last chapter. Some say it came over fom the French, but I reckon that far-fetched. It's a sailor word – from the galleys, do you see? I don't think it necessary to salvation to believe that such thoroughly English breeches were ever worn in Gascony. I believe they must just be gallant gaskins – good bold pairs of breeks.

I could do with some Shakespeare breeches myself as I sit here and write this morning. The brass monkeys outside the pawnshop in the alley below just gave a high falsetto shriek.

I'm sucking a pickled mulberry I picked long ago from the tree of that astringent fruit which Mr Shakespeare planted in his garden. I like the taste of mulberries. It is like my own.

---

[*] *The Most Excellent and Lamentable Tragedy of Romeo and Juliet*, Act I, Scene 3, line 23.

Chapter Eighteen

The Man in the Moon, or
Pickleherring in praise of country history

Talking of the famous play of Pyramus and Thisbe, that most lamentable comedy, Mr Quince, the carpenter, gives due directions, as follows: 'One must come in with a bush of thorns and a lantern, and say he comes to disfigure, or to present, the person of moonshine.' And this order is realised. 'All I have to say,' concludes the performer of this strange part, 'is, to tell you, that the lanthorn is the moon; I, the man i' the moon; this thorn-bush, my thorn-bush; and this dog, my dog.'

Who is this *Man in the Moon*, this person of moonshine? I will tell you. He is the annalist or chronicler of what I call country history. More of that in a minute. For the moment, gentle reader, prove to yourself your gentleness by not despising him. Be like Duke Theseus, and acknowledge that *never anything can be amiss, / When simpleness and duty tender it.* Remember that while Mr Shakespeare ridicules those entertainments and interludes which were presented by the rustic amateurs before great people, yet he, at the same time, furnishes the best and most generous defence of them. He teaches us how such simple-minded if ridiculous efforts should be treated by all persons of good breeding. *The kinder we*, as the Duke says, *to give them thanks for nothing.*

So then: THE MAN IN THE MOON, who is he?

It is, I agree, sir, a familiar expression, to which few persons attach any definite idea.

Many would be found – yes, madam – under a belief such as yours, that it refers merely to that faint appearance of a face which the moon presents when full.

But those, dear friends, who are better acquainted with natural objects,

and with folk matters, will be aware that the Man in the Moon – the thing referred to under that name – is a dusky resemblance to a human figure which appears on the western side of the lunar luminary when she is eight days old, being somewhat like a man carrying a thorn-bush on his back, and at the same time engaged in climbing, while a detached object in front looks like his dog going on before him.

It is a very old popular notion (or so my mother taught me), that this figure is no less than the man referred to in the Book of Numbers (chap. xv, v, 32 *et seq*) as having been detected by the children of Israel in the wilderness, in the act of gathering sticks on the Sabbath-day, and whom the Lord directed (in absence of a law on the subject) to be stoned to death without the camp.

One would have thought this poor benighted stick-gatherer sufficiently punished in the Biblical history. Nevertheless, the popular mind has assigned him the additional pain of a perpetual pillorying in the moon.

There he is with his burden of sticks upon his back! See how he is continually climbing up that shining height with his little dog before him! Observe that he never gets a single step higher! And so it must be while this world endures. . . .

Yet I say that the Man in the Moon is an historian.

Or, at least, the patron of a certain sort of history.

Consider: there are two ways of looking at the moon and the sun. Of the moon, you can see her as the satellite of the earth, a mere secondary planet, or you can see her as a deity, the queen of tides and poets. Of the sun, when it rises, one man might say he saw a round disc of fire somewhat like a guinea, while another man might say he saw an innumerable company of the heavenly host crying 'Holy, Holy, Holy is the Lord God Almighty!'

The second way is the way Mr Shakespeare saw the world. (Though he understood the other way of seeing it, or he would not have made a playwright.)

The second way is the way that I see his life's story. (Though I do my best all the same to be true to the things in my black boxes.)

Reader, just as there are two ways of seeing, so there are two ways of historizing.

Reader, there are, in truth, as I would now make clear for your better understanding of this sorry mad book of mine, two kinds of history, as different from each other as chalk and cheese.

There is *town* history and there is *country* history.

Town history is cynical and exact. It is written by wits and it orders and limits what it talks about. It relies on facts and figures. It is knowing. Dry

and sceptical and clever, it is ruled by the head. Beginning in the shadow of the law courts, at the end of the day your town history tends to the universities – it becomes academic. Town history is believable and reliable. Offering proofs, it never strains credulity. But sometimes it can't see the Forest of Arden for the trees. And it falls probably short of the mark when it comes up against Mr Shakespeare.

Your country history is a different matter. Country history is faithful and open-ended. It is a tale told by various idiots on the village green, all busy contradicting themselves in the name of a common truth. It exaggerates and enflames what it talks about. It delights in lies and gossip. It is unwise. Wild and mystical and passionate, it is ruled by the heart. Beginning by the glow of the hearth, at the end of the night your country history tends to pass into balladry and legend – it becomes poetic. Country history is fanciful and maggoty. Easy to mock, it always strains belief. But sometimes it catches the ghostly coat-tails of what is otherwise ungraspable. It is the only possible way of accounting for Mr Shakespeare.

Town history is quickly written down and printed.

Country history is told for years, passing from mouth to mouth before anyone bothers to write it down. And when it *is* written down, it loses something. Publishing stops it.

Town history rests on the premise that facts tell the truth.

Country history, on the contrary, knows that facts can obscure the truth. Your country historian, your Man in the Moon, your servant Pickleherring, allows for the fact that the facts can prove anything, that they prickle and point in all directions, like the twigs on a tree that's still growing. The truth of the tree is its life. That's the green blood that springs, like a fountain, from the roots to the stars.

This book you read is mostly country history. It consists of tales I have heard told about Mr Shakespeare.

Our hero was a country-man who took the town by storm. He set the Thames on fire with what he knew from the Avon. But he remained in his heart a man of the country. And he went back to his origins to die.

I have collected most of my tales about him from people who knew him. In Stratford, in Warwick, in London. The wheres do not matter. You can be a good country historian in Paternoster Row.

What matters is that it's told tales I am telling you. Tales told me. Twice-told tales. Tales, tales, tales, tales. Here there are Canterbury tales, and old wives' tales. Here there are tales of tubs and of roasted horses. One tale is good until another's told. All are the tales of every common tongue. Tales, idle tales, fictions.

And if some of my told tales are tall, that's because in the minds of the tellers the late Mr William Shakespeare was a giant.

Town history is mostly written. Country history is all in the telling.

Town history begins and ends in the mind. Country history begins and lives in the tongue, and it can have no end while the Man in the Moon keeps on climbing.

I am, like Mr Shakespeare, motley-minded.

I have, like Mr Shakespeare, a peasant heart.

Chapter Nineteen

*Positively the last word
about whittawers*

To be a poet is to be one thing. Not so John Shakespeare. He was *on the make.*

So he did different jobs at different times. Then, in the end, he didn't do much at all. He diced. He drank. He told stories, but nobody listened. He mortgaged his wife's lands, and he passed his days in law-suits (which he lost). He became just a huge hill of flesh always warming his buttocks by the fire. He went about Stratford, where once he had been Chief Alderman in scarlet robes, wearing a ragged leather jerkin and an old torn pair of breeches, with his hose out at his heels, and a pair of broken slip shoes on his feet. He wore a greasy cap on his white head.

I like John Shakespeare. His life was chequered with vicissitudes. For a man on the make, he ended as an honourable failure.

Many instances of his benevolence are recorded. When not hiring it out at interest, he gave away his money freely. A broken gamester, observing him one night win five guineas at cribbage, and putting the money into his pocket with indifference, exclaimed, 'How happy that money would make me!' John Shakespeare, overhearing this, turned and placed the guineas in his palm, saying, 'Go, then, shog off and be happy!'

His gambling made him notorious even in those improvident days. I like him also for his philosophy to justify his gambling – that a man ought to have a bet every day, else he might be walking about lucky and never know it. Similarly philosophical, his excuse on one occasion, when his horse was beaten shortly, that the horse's neck was not quite long enough.

And his extempore wit was sharp enough in his prime, lending credence again to the thought that his son found Falstaff in him. As when once, at

the market in Warwick, on seeing the wife of the Puritan divine Thomas Cartwright go by riding on a pony, he remarked that no doubt it was the first time the lady had ever had 14 hands between her legs.

The truth is that there was a wild streak in the Shakespeares. In John it took some years for it to come out, but when it did it took control of his life. His father, Richard Shakespeare, the poet's grandfather, had a bad name all his days for cantankerousness. He refused to ring his swine and he let his stock run loose in the Clopton meadows. He was a husbandman, and lived by tilling the soil.

Richard Shakespeare lived at Snitterfield, to the north of Stratford, but he was not born there. The wildest Shakespeares came first from Balsall and Wroxall (where the prioress showed us her leg in the apple tree), and from a couple of other villages in the Forest of Arden. I mean the hamlets of Rowington and Baddesley Clinton. Dick Shakespeare came from one of these – I am not sure which. When he died he left an estate that was valued at £38 17s. It is said that he bequeathed five shillings in his will specifically for his sons to get drunk for the last time at his expense.

Dick Shakespeare's other son was christened Henry. He farmed at Ingon in the parish of Hampton Lucy, staying on the land after his father's death (unlike his brother John). There's plenty of evidence that Henry ran wild all his life. When young he was fined for brawling and drawing blood in an affray against the Constable. Then in his middle years he was fined again for wearing a hat to church instead of a cap. As an old man, he went to prison twice for not paying his debts. He was also involved in disputes over tithes and sued his own brother John. But after he died it was found he had money enough in his coffers, as well as a fine mare in his stable, and much corn and hay in his barn. This was our poet's Uncle Henry, always known as 'Harry' or 'Hal'.

I weary of these wild Shakespeares—— But, note well, they had spunk in them. Also they were hardy men, makers, masters and sons of the soil. If you think poets do not descend from such strong lines, madam, then I have to beg to differ. I believe Chaucer's father was a vintner. (True, Dante's was a lawyer, but we'll forgive that.) In any case, consider William Shakespeare's total craft and trade. He was not just a poet. He was a playwright. And a playwright is a wright, or maker, like a boatwright or a cartwright or a wheelwright. Where they make boats and carts and wheels, he makes his plays. He leaves his mark, as they do, on the work.

Since I weary of the subject of this chapter, and swear it will be positively the last word about whittawers in my book, permit me a little note

concerning that earthquake which Mr Shakespeare must have remembered from late in his fifteenth year.

There have not been so many earthquakes in England that a boy would ever forget one he had felt with his own feet.

Not that the dead rose from their graves in Trinity churchyard, but on that evening of Easter Wednesday, 1580, the whole of the south of England felt the shaking of the ground. In London, the great clock bell at Westminster struck two with the shock, and the bells of the churches in the city were all set jangling. It is reported that the playgoers rushed out of the theatres in consternation, and that the gentlemen of the Temple, quitting their suppers, ran out of the Temple Hall with their knives in their hands. Part of the Temple Church was cast down, some stones fell from St Paul's, and two apprentices were killed at Christ Church by the fall of a gargoyle during sermon-time.

This earthquake was felt pretty generally throughout the queendom, and was the cause of much damage in Kent, where many castles and other buildings were injured; and at Dover a portion of a cliff fell, carrying with it part of the castle wall.

So alarmed were all classes, so I've heard tell, that Queen Elizabeth thought it advisable to cause a form of prayer to be used by all householders with their whole family, every evening before going to bed:

ALMIGHTY *everlasting God, who lookest upon the earth, and makest it to tremble: spare them that fear thee, be merciful to them that call upon thee; that whereas we are sore afraid for thy wrath that shaketh the foundations of the earth, we may likewise feel thy mercy when thou healest the sores thereof.*

O GOD, *who hast laid the foundations of the earth that they shall never be moved, receive the prayers and oblations of thy people: put far from us the present perils of earthquake, and turn the terrors of thy divine anger into a wholesome medicine for the safety of mankind; that they who are of the earth and shall return to earth, may rejoice to be made citizens of heaven by holy conversation.*

Through CHRIST, *Our Lord. Amen.*

But you hadn't said a word about whittawers in this chapter . . . .

That, madam, is the point if you will take it.

What I'm really doing is avoiding my *next* chapter – the subject or ruler of which I introduced some few paragraphs above. I need more than a prayer against earthquakes to undertake with impunity what I have now to tell you.

Chapter Twenty

*What if Queen Elizabeth
was Shakespeare's mother?*

Well then, now then, William Shakespeare, the matter of his mother, his real mother and was she Mary Arden. Some say she was not. Was she Juliet then, the miller's daughter? That is not likely. The mother of William Shakespeare could not have been a woman who lacked conversation. Given that John Shakespeare was a huge heavy bull of a man, she must have been a woman of unusual capacity. Yet William Shakespeare's mother would be very pale and haughty. She would have hair that was yellowish-red, and beautiful hands. Her face might be pitted by small-pox, but her body would be sensuous and royal. No woman would ever have possessed to a greater pitch than William Shakespeare's mother that great feminine capacity for identifying her personal desires with righteousness and her personal needs with the justice of God. No woman could have been of higher degree. So then, now then, what if Queen Elizabeth was Shakespeare's mother?

The Queen spoke six languages. She hawked and she hunted and she played the virginals. She danced high and disposedly. Also, the Queen played at chess.

Elizabeth had in her life a kind of kinship with the method of Shakespeare's genius. You might say that in her reign three kinds of mind were evident in England – the Roman Catholic, the Protestant, and that third kind of mind which may be called Shakespearean, neither Catholic nor Protestant, capable of holding two quite different beliefs in balance at the same time. What better mother for the living embodiment of that mind than the Queen herself?

The babe must of course have been fostered. There's no problem with

that. The Queen could do anything she liked, but she would not have wanted to keep by her at Court the product of a moment's passion in the Forest of Arden with a piece of rough trade. On the other hand, her agents might have assisted with the boy's education, and seen to it that the way was smoothed for him when he came as a young man to make his fortune in the capital. She took a lively interest in his plays. It is well-known that *The Merry Wives of Windsor* was written (in a fortnight) at her express command, she having sent word to Mr Shakespeare that it was her sovereign fancy to see 'Sir John Falstaff in love'. The play was first done for the Court revels at Christmas, 1598.

I saw Queen Elizabeth for the first time then. She had very blue eyes and a queer sort of smile. Despite her age and her wig, I noticed at once the resemblance to my master. With both of them you saw their upper teeth gleaming when they smiled, and in fact they always reminded me of an animal's teeth – a fox's teeth, perhaps.

But to the logistics. If the deed was done, how was it done? and when? Supposing Queen Elizabeth to have been Shakespeare's mother, how could his great begetting have come about?

Plague touched the edges of the Court in the summer of 1563. Elizabeth had been on the throne for just five years. She was 30 years old, and in her prime. Already the character of her heart was evident: chaste yet promiscuous. She entertained many suitors, but would marry none. There was not as yet a particular favourite in her affections, such as Lord Robert Dudley would become, or (later) Hatton and then Ralegh and then Essex. But that she would never submit to be married was quite apparent. As Burghley told her, 'I know your spirit cannot endure a commander.'

It was Burghley, then plain William Cecil, who suggested Kenilworth to her as a haven from the plague. The Queen accepted his suggestion with alacrity. She knew that her principal Secretary of State had only her best interests at heart. He was uneasy lest her health should succumb to the foul distemper which presently laid London waste. So she went into the country.

Queen Elizabeth, at thirty, was a lively piece. In the phrases of John Harrington, translator of Ariosto and the privy, quoting Hatton: 'The Queen did fish for men's souls, and she had so sweet a bait that no one could escape her net-work.' She was a perverse and wanton kind of virgin. Her Court hummed with lust. Ben Jonson (who had the intimation direct from Sir Walter Ralegh) said later that she had a membrana on her, which made her incapable of men, though for her delight she tried many. She wore a girdle made of kidskin under a foam of petticoats.

Lord Burghley prepared her escort. He was the sort of Secretary of State who judges the truth of metaphysical principles by their moral consequences; in short, a rat. Twelve Maids of Honour accompanied Elizabeth from Westminster, and 30 Lords of the Royal Bedchamber. Having seen her safely dispatched, Burghley, with his principal catamites, retired to his own palace at Theobalds in Hertfordshire, where, isolated from the rest of the people, he remained until the plague had passed.

The Queen, meanwhile. The incidents of her progress were not auspicious. On the first night, at Windsor, she was so cold despite the midsummer weather that no less than ten of the Lords of the Bedchamber fell by the way. This might be thought appalling, madam, yes, but if Pickleherring uses that word then what is he to say of the completion of Elizabeth's second day's progress, when another ten noble gentlemen went under?

A score of defaulters, however, did not prevent Queen Elizabeth from continuing her journey, and she swanned on through England, shedding men all the way, until at last she arrived at Kenilworth, in safety, but with only one male attendant left to warm her.

This valiant gentleman was spent by morning. Then Queen Elizabeth, great Harry's daughter as well as daughter of the Essex witch Anne Bullen, went out for a walk on her own in the Forest of Arden, and while she is walking meets up with no less than John Shakespeare.

Now John Shakespeare, as your author trusts he has already made clear, was a bit of a man in his own right. By one blow of his fist he'd flattened a thunderbolt once, which he kept in his waistcoat pocket, in the shape of a folded pancake, rolled up, to show his enemies, if they felt like a fight.

When he sees Queen Elizabeth wandering, her hair so long, her breasts so high, he marches straight up to her in the bluebells and offers her the hilt of his sword.

His monarch looks him up and she looks him down.

She likes what she sees.

'What is your name, my man?' says she.

'John Shakespeare, if it pleases your majesty,' says John Shakespeare.

'Well, Mr Hotspur,' the Queen says, 'I will take you on, and you'll be well rewarded on one condition.'

Aha thinks John, but it isn't aha at all, for Queen Elizabeth adds: 'The condition is that you must never employ any low or dirty words in our regal presence. I can't abide a dirty word,' she explains.

True enough, it suits her character, sir, you will admit, for isn't she the great ice-maiden, the winter doxy, with snowflakes on it and the north wind

blowing hailstones down her slot. Do not forget the thirty Lords of the Royal Bedchamber. Fallen. Not to speak, madam, of the twelve Maids of Honour skewered on that exceptional clitoris.

However, dear friends, John Shakespeare is nothing if not adventurous, and there are few adventures he prefers to those which test his verbal resourcefulness – and Queen Elizabeth's person, as your author has presented it, would seem to offer hope of those few too.

So John agrees to the Queen's condition, and is made her man.

They walk on side by side through the Forest of Arden.

As they come out of the oak trees above Stratford what should they see but an old white sow, with a boar aboard grunting away so vehemently that the foam is flying out of his mouth and hanging on the summer breeze like spindrift.

Queen Elizabeth turns to John Shakespeare. She lays her lovely hand upon his sleeve. 'Mr Cockspur,' she says, 'Mr Cockspur, what do you make of that?'

John Shakespeare thinks for a bit, and he thinks how his monarch has forbidden him to use any low or dirty words in her presence and also how her grotto is said to be so particularly icy, and in the end he says, 'What do I make of that, majesty? Well, it's staring you in the face, isn't it? The one underneath is a kind relation of the one on top, some sort of aunt I should imagine, and her nephew isn't feeling well, and she's carrying him home.'

Queen Elizabeth looks at Mr John Shakespeare sharpish. Then a laugh begins to tickle in her throat. 'Yes, Mr Cockspur,' she says, 'I think that must be it, my gentleman.'

They wander on. And as they come into Clopton Meadows what should they see but a herd of cattle, and the bull just making himself at home on one of his favourites.

Queen Elizabeth touches John Shakespeare's wrist with a long sharp blue fingernail. 'Well, Mr Prickspeare,' she says, 'well, Mr Prickspeare, what's that then?'

John Shakespeare doesn't have to think so much this time. He's getting the hang of the game. 'Majesty, I'll tell you exactly what it is,' he answers. 'The poor old cow is pathetically short-sighted, and she's eaten all the grass that she can see. So the bull, who looks after the cows, is just giving her a gentle shove on her way towards some fresh pasture.'

Queen Elizabeth laughs again. 'Indeed, Mr Prickspeare,' says she, 'I think you must be right, my gentleman.'

They wander on some more. And as they're coming along through the

Welcombe cuckoo-flowers what should they see but a herd of horses, and a stallion busy working on a mare.

Queen Elizabeth fondles John Shakespeare's sword hilt. 'Tell me, Mr Sexpure,' she says, 'Mr Sexpure, tell me what's that then?'

'That,' says John quickly, 'is no doubt on account of the fire.'

'The fire?' says his mistress, her left eyebrow raised.

'Yes, majesty,' says John Shakespeare, and he points to a house with a blazing chimney in the Gild Pits below them. 'The stallion wants a better view of it,' he explains, 'so he's climbed up on the back of the mare, just to have a good look.'

'I do believe you're right, Mr Sexpure,' the Queen says, though she can't stop her giggling, 'I do believe you're right, my gentleman.'

They wander on. At last they arrive at those warm springs by Tiddington Mill which feed the River Avon. Secretary Burghley has recommended to his monarch that she should bathe here, for unspecified purposes, but no doubt as a prophylactic against the plague, so she offs with her clothes, kidskin girdle and all, and into the water with her high mightiness.

John Shakespeare stands watching at a respectful but attentive distance, under some willow trees which afford a green veil between him and what he should not see.

Queen Elizabeth splashes sportive in the springs.

Then she calls out very sweetly, in a little girl's voice: 'Is it hard, Mr Ramrod?'

John Shakespeare can't believe his furry pointed ears. 'Is what hard, O my sovereign liege?' says he.

'Is it hard standing under those trees, Mr Prickley, while I'm in the water?' enquires Queen Elizabeth.

'Well,' honest John answers, 'yes, majesty, I suppose it is, somewhat.'

'Some what?' asks the Queen, splashing him.

'Somewhat,' says John Shakespeare, and puts his hat over it.

Queen Elizabeth splashes about some more, and then she says softly: 'If you want to bathe with me, Mr Upstart, you had better undress yourself, hadn't you?'

'Undress myself?' John echoes foolishly.

'Strip off, my gentleman!' says the peremptory Queen.

So John Shakespeare takes off his green shirt, and his green boots, and his green breeches, and he enters the warm springs by Tiddington Mill.

As her new attendant comes into the water, Queen Elizabeth notes to herself with approval the length and apparent usefulness of his tool. Her breasts pout like pigeons. As a child she was teased and tickled, mentally

and corporally rolled and spanked by her wicked step-uncle, Lord Seymour of Sudely. Times like these, she remembers it.

Now they are wading about together in the warm clear bubbling water, Queen Elizabeth and John Shakespeare, and it's soft and salt and lovely where they are. The Queen's mind goes flowing back. She remembers her step-aunt Parr holding her down, legs kicking, while big Seymour cut holes in her night-dress with a pair of silver scissors. So she puts her fingers to her lower lips and parts them, and she shows herself to this new man and she asks him, 'What's this then, Mr Shagbag?'

'A well,' John Shakespeare answers, as quick as you like. 'It's a wishing well, madam.'

'Yes, yes,' agrees the Queen, and she reaches down with her hands and makes a deft grab for him under the water. 'And what's this then, Mr Shakespout?' she demands. 'What's this thing between your legs here?'

'That,' says John Shakespeare, gulping, 'is called a donkey.'

'A donkey!' exclaims Queen Elizabeth with delight. 'And does your donkey have to drink then, sometimes, Mr Spigot, my gentleman?'

'He does, majesty,' answers John, as dignified as you could expect him to be, with the hands that rule all England on his creature. 'But only when he's thirsty,' he explains.

Queen Elizabeth's clever fingers move up and down the length of Mr John Shakespeare, and round and round the width of her royalty. Her one long pearl-pale hand is warming his member, while with her other long pearl-pale hand she is warming herself, and she thinks of the manhood she first felt concealed in the yellow magnificence of her father's lap, King Harry's great sceptre, and the water is warm, and the air is warm, and warm is her heart, and she sings as she plays, and she plays as she sings, and the hot springs bubble up incessantly, and the pool by Tiddington's full of good warm currents, swirling all about their naked limbs as she fingers him, and herself, and then both of them, and there's a sweet rich scent of apricocks on the air, and purple grapes, green figs, and mulberries, and her thighs are white as wax through the clear water, and the Queen's fingers work upon him like sucking fish, and the day is warm, and the Queen's fingers pump, and the blossoms fall down, and the water frets and bubbles, and there's a smell of dewberries,* and John Shakespeare's lucky member gets bigger and bigger, swelling and lengthening under the royal command, lengthening and swelling and thickening until he is half-scared that it might burst, but the Queen's other hand is equally busy, and just as good about its

---

* The fruit of the dwarf mulberry or knot-berry. So-called by the Warwickshire peasantry, and exceedingly plentiful in the lanes between Stratford-upon-Avon and Aston Cantlowe.

business, tickling and diddling, and stirring and stretching, and preparing and opening, though she needs no lubrication, what with all the warmth and the water, and the swooning airs of summer, and her womb turned inside out, and the skylarks high above them, and the flood and the fire, and the oxslips on the bank, and the warm warm warming water, and the whispering violet currents, and so:

'O,' Queen Elizabeth wonders, 'O Mr Cockburn, Mr Cockburn, is your donkey thirsty now?'

'He is,' John Shakespeare answers, between gaspings. 'Yes, he is, madam, quite.'

'O,' Queen Elizabeth expostulates, 'O Mr Frigspear, Mr Frigspear, and would he like a drink then? A little drink in my well, my gentleman?'

'He would,' croaks John Shakespeare. 'He would enjoy that, madam, I believe.'

'Then come in, darling donkey,' Queen Elizabeth invites. 'Only don't go in too deep or you'll drown and then be nothing, my poor thing.'

The Queen means, of course, that the extreme glacial coldness of her fissure will be the death of the interesting beast, and she is a-weary of her men's men dying on her. But as for sturdy John Shakespeare, like the angel of the Apocalypse he now has one foot on the known and the other on the unknown, and he's past counsel or caring. He can't hold anything back now, so he enters her quick, smooth, and hard.

Reader, all her long life Queen Elizabeth delighted in cerebral adoration, and the stronger the hint of corporal madness the more she delighted in it.

But now it is something else that pleases her.

Now it is something immediate.

Now it is something hard and very simple.

She forgets old Harry's lap and bad Seymour's fingers. She has no room for memory any more.

John Shakespeare has her. The father of William Shakespeare is up her. And the larks sing, and the choughs rise, and the wild thyme blows, and a donkey is braying over by Clopton Bridge, and the warming water, and the circling currents, and the bubbling springs, and the midsummer morning, and the weeping willows, and the great summer sun, and all the sweet blandishments and entreaties of all these little natural miracles make Elizabeth Tudor open her white royal legs wider and wider, make the Queen of England open her legs as she has never opened them before for any other man, so that John Shakespeare flows in, and William Shakespeare flows in, and the water flows in, and the warm flows in, and

England flows in, and the world flows in, and it is all flowing warm flowing and flowing flowing warm until——

'O Mr Spermspear!' cries Queen Elizabeth. 'O Mr Shakespunk! Mr Shakespunk! Mr Shakespunk! O Mr Fuckster, O make your donkey go in deeper, my gentleman!'

So John Shakespeare does.

He does what the Queen tells him.

He does Queen Elizabeth thoroughly.

But——

'Deeper!' the Queen cries, 'Deeper yet! And harder! O my dear donkey! Do it! Do it! Do it!'

So John Shakespeare does.

He does what the Queen commands him.

He does Queen Elizabeth thoroughly all over again.

Until——

'O Warwick!' cries the Queen. 'O Warwick! Warwick!'

And the donkey finds that the well is very deep. And the donkey finds that the well is very very deep. But the donkey does not drown. And nor does the donkey freeze. On account, in part, of the warm springs and the other natural circumstances already mentioned.

John Shakespeare was very sorry to leave the water. He always came back to drink sack by Tiddington Mill. In his last years he would sit there, all under the willow trees, a fat man alone, and a drunkard, abusing the swans.

Few knew why he did it.

Queen Elizabeth was sorry to leave the water, too. In her dreams, in her later years, she would sometimes murmur and cry out *'Warwick!'* Which thing caused more than one row with Lords Leicester and Essex.

Mr John Shakespeare and Queen Elizabeth met thus and parted the same day. You will find their son's version of it in his play called *A Midsummer Night's Dream*.

Nine months after the sweet encounter in the water, to that very day, to that very hour, so they say, the poet William Shakespeare came into this world. His mother, knowing a bastard prince might bring civil war, returned home to the Palace of Westminster in London without him. The babe was left with John Shakespeare, who by that time was long married to Mary Arden. Mary had a good heart, and she brought up the child as her own.

Chapter Twenty-One

The Shakespeare Arms

Assuredly, madam, yes, if Queen Elizabeth was indeed our hero's mother then it makes Mary Shakespeare's games with him less reprehensible. Well, a mite so. A moiety. A shadow of a shade.

But no, sir, emphatically, I don't believe it either.

That's a nice word, that MOIETY. The late Mr William Shakespeare was at all times very fond of it. He was even its coiner, so far as I know, in its sense of being the smaller or lesser portion of anything. He employs it thus in the dedication to his *Rape of Lucrece*, and then again in *The Winter's Tale*, I think. Yes, I just looked it up for you – Act Two, Scene 3, Leontes: *Say that she were gone . . . a moiety of my rest/Might come to me again.* That's how I felt about Jane. But she's no part of the story. I'm telling you the Life of William Shakespeare.

A shadow of a shade less blameworthy, yes, that business of Mary Shakespeare's hand on the young William's balls and pintle, *if* Queen Elizabeth could be thought to be the boy's mother. I, friends, cannot believe it, all the same. Even though you might think that the source of the story's impeccable.

The source of the story?

John Shakespeare!

He told it me, directly, in his cups. I met him once, the time he came to London. Rainy autumn it was, of that year when I first met Mr Shakespeare. We did *Hamlet* at the Swan, with Mr Shakespeare taking the Ghost's part. His own little son had died that year, and now here was this play full of father and son stuff, and then his own father in London.

Not that John Shakespeare saw *Hamlet*. He'd come to town for

something much more important than that. He'd come to get a coat of arms from the College of Heralds.

He was granted it, too, thanks largely to his son. The late Mr William Shakespeare had many talents, and one was the art or craft of pulling strings. The Heralds' Office was lax in bestowal of the honour, and a little influence and a liberal use of money went a long way to secure the coveted dignity. Several of the players became gentlemen this way. It was a sign that you weren't just a common actor. Augustine Phillips, Thomas Pope, Richard Cowley, John Heminges, and Richard Burbage – all sooner or later secured this right to display arms. In Mr Shakespeare's case, there was the added incentive that his father had already applied for the honour some thirty years earlier, at the height of his civic dignity in Stratford, but the arms had not been granted. Now he was old, and fallen on hard times, and his son seized this chance to redeem him. He made up some fiction about John Shakespeare's antecessors and how they had provided 'valiant and faithful service' to King Henry the Seventh. He pulled, as I say, the right strings. He went in person to see the Garter King of Arms, Sir William Dethick, in the College of Heralds which lay just across the Thames from his Bankside lodgings.

I remember he showed me the draft. He had it all roughed out in his own hand on a great yellow scroll which he tucked under his oxter as he stepped into the wherry. I was hugely impressed. Remember, I was only thirteen, an impressionable lad, and the ways of the capital were new to me.

The coat of arms had, across a black incline, in its field of gold, a silver-tipped spear, the point upward, while for the crest or cognizance it displayed a falcon with out-stretched wings. The motto was *Non sans droict*. Not without right. Which Mr Ben Jonson mocked two years later in his *Every Man out of His Humour* as 'Not without mustard'.

Not without right. And a falcon shaking a spear. It was all very suitable, in my humble opinion. And the College of Arms thought so too. They granted the petition, and my master came back happy in the wherry.

My job, meanwhile, had been to keep tabs on Mr John Shakespeare, the gentleman being ennobled. He had rolled in from Stratford as drunk as a lord, and when his son saw him he remarked that the day's main task would be to keep the potential arms-bearer as far away as possible from the arms of the Heralds themselves.

So little Pickleherring was appointed to amuse the man. Which meant that I danced along behind him, keeping John Shakespeare company as he trundled and trolled through the taverns.

I have the list that I kept of the places he drank in. The Boar's Head, the Poultry, the Rose, the Three Cranes, the Mermaid, the Mitre which was next door to the Mermaid, the Nag's Head at the corner of Friday Street, the Razor and Hen, the Leg and Seven Stars, the Eagle and Child, and the Goat in Boots.

What did John Shakespeare drink? He drank beer made of hops, and also cider. He drank claret, muscadine, and charneco. But mostly he drank sherris sack in very great quantities – which is to say, canary, white Spanish wine.

I had never seen a man drink so much before. He held his drink well, I must say, until by mid-afternoon it started to flow out of him from his ears, mostly. By then I had equipped us with a wheelbarrow, in which it was my joy to wheel him on from one beer-boltered sack-soaked cellar to the next. He kicked his boots in the air as he lay in the barrow. I sang *O Polly Dear* and he belched hubbubs in my face for a refrain. To tell you the truth, that day I regretted ever going on the stage. An actor's life no longer seemed such a fine thing. Not if it meant humouring and placating Mr William Shakespeare's father while he got a coat of arms by not showing his face.

Somewhere in the course of our pilgrimage – I believe, at the Rose – Mr John Shakespeare confided to me what he called 'the Reason for the Falcon'. It had been Anne Bullen's device, he said, and her daughter Queen Elizabeth had adopted it in turn. This information he imparted with a wise nod and a wink. Many winks and nods later, and many cups of sherris sack, he told me the whole story of his alleged amorous encounter with the lady who was then our sovereign. I did not believe him then, and I do not now. But that night I wrote it all down, and when I was writing my last chapter I fished those notes out of one of my black boxes and I used them. If there was some ardent lyricism in that chapter put it down to Mr Shakespeare's father and his wine-loosened tongue, and not to Pickleherring. You will have noticed, madam. Eros is not my style.

When John Shakespeare had finished, and sat staring into space and breathing heavily, I said (just for something to say, which I used to do in those days): 'All suddenly you saw the Faerie Queen, then?'

But Mr Shakespeare's father didn't know what I was talking about.

'Elizabeth was no fairy,' he said shortly. 'She was warm as toast.'

Not wanting to lose my head, I was glad when he dropped the subject, going off on a long and complicated tale about some people called Lambert and how he had sued them for cheating him. (This story is very boring, and I'll try not to tell it, if I can.) Whether John Shakespeare believed his own

drunken fantasy concerning the Queen is difficult to say. Nor does it matter. Interestingly, perhaps all the incident really afforded me was a glimpse of the crude rude origins of what had become imagination in his son. That there *was* some link between father and son let *A Midsummer Night's Dream* testify, for reasons already mentioned. I am sure John Shakespeare never heard of Bottom. But William must have heard some such story from him as I heard.

In short, John Shakespeare was a fantast. And the only people who'll credit his story, and want to believe it, are snobs. That is, the sort who want all Shakespeare's works to be written by Lord Verulam, Francis Bacon, or Edward de Vere, Earl of Oxford. Because those lads were nobles, don't you know, while our hero was only a clod.

At least my listening to John Shakespeare's story helped to keep him out of trouble while his son got his coat of arms for him.

It was the only time I ever saw Mr Shakespeare senior. He was a vast man. I remember his nose like a baby's backside in the middle of his face, and the sweat forming crystal pustules on the crags of his forehead. I remember he had white tufts of hair growing out of his nostrils. I remember he struck the board with the flat of his hand and he said very quietly, almost as if whispering a secret, 'The Lord God Almighty is angry with Elizabeth Tudor.' I remember he said that his bunions were killing him. I remember him farting. He stood on one leg and he farted, and then shook his foot. 'Another Spanish galleon sunk!' he bellowed triumphantly. A second time, when he did the same, he did not shake his foot, but said sweetly, holding up one finger: 'Hark! Hark! The cry of an imprisoned turd!' Despite such grossness, there was something almost delicate about him. He was like a big fat dancer, a ruined sprite. You could see he was proud of his son, but they didn't say much to each other. He spent a long time just stroking the scroll, when William came back with it ratified.

A falcon shaking a spear. I suppose it makes sense.

I never ever saw Mr Shakespeare's mother, not having travelled to Stratford until later days when she was dead. Unless, of course, she *was* that woman in the flame-red wig for whom John Falstaff made the wives of Windsor merry.

Chapter Twenty-Two

Pickleherring's Song

I think it is high time that I gave you that ballad which has now been sung three times in the course of this book – by my mother to me to get me to sleep, by me to Mr William Shakespeare when I was sitting on the wall of the yard of that tavern when I first met him, and again by me in the last chapter to amuse Mr John Shakespeare in his cups.

Here are the words, then, of *O Polly Dear*:

> *Oh how I wish that I was there*
> *With my dear Polly at the fair!*
> *O Polly dear*
> *Why aren't you here?*
> *We were so happy at the fair!*
>
> *About my feet the grass grows green –*
> *Greener grass I've never seen!*
> *O Polly dear*
> *Why aren't you here?*
> *How happy we were at the fair!*
>
> *Above my head the night is black –*
> *O my lost love, come back! come back!*
> *O Polly dear*
> *Why aren't you here?*
> *How happy we were at the fair!*

Oh how I wish that I was there
With my dear Polly at the fair!
O Polly dear
Why aren't you here?
We were so happy at the fair!

This is the saddest song I ever heard. I think it has something to do with the sound of the rhyme changing from *there* to *here* and then back to *fair*, and perhaps also with the little variation of rhythm in the last line of the two middle verses, but I'm a comedian not a poet, and I don't really know.

Here it is with the music:

A—bove my head the night is black— O my lost love, come
back! come back! O Po—lly dear why ar—ent you here? How
ha—ppy we were at the fair!

Oh how I wish that I was there With my dear Po—lly
at the fair! O Po—lly dear why ar—ent you here? We
were so ha—ppy at the fair!

Chapter Twenty-Three

About the childhood ailments
of William Shakespeare

I have outlived my own life. So I'm writing Mr Shakespeare's.

The childhood of our immortal bard was not without the usual diseases. It fell to the Reverend Bretchgirdle to cure the little man.

The parish priest was a great believer in natural nostrums, balms, treatments, and remedies. He suffered himself from the ague. He cured it, not by wrapping a spider in a raisin and swallowing it, as you might think, sir, nor by eating sage leaves seven mornings running, madam, as you might hope, but by going out at night alone to the Church Street crossroads and as the Guildhall clock struck midnight turning round on his heels three times and driving a large iron nail into the earth up to the head. Then he walked away backwards from the nail before the clock had completed its twelfth stroke. The ague left him, passing into the tax collector who was the next person to step over the nail.

William Shakespeare caught the measles. The Reverend Bretchgirdle cured William's measles by cutting off his cat's left ear and persuading the boy to swallow three warm drops of cat's blood in a wineglassful of water.

William Shakespeare caught the jaundice. The Reverend Bretchgirdle cured William's jaundice by making the boy eat nine fat lice on a piece of bread and butter. The other cure – twelve earth-worms baked on a shovel and reduced to powder to make a philter to drink every morning for a week – had failed to shift it. Ditto the tench tied to William's bare back.

William Shakespeare had a rupture. The Reverend Bretchgirdle cured it by going to the ash grove above Shottery and cutting a long sapling longitudinally and getting the lad to climb, naked, in and out of the fissure three times at sunset on St Valentine's Day, after which the fat priest bound

up the tree tightly and plastered over the crack with dung and clay. As the hole healed so did William. The other cure – the snail stopped up in the hollow oak – did not work.

William Shakespeare had the whooping cough. The Reverend Bretchgirdle cured William's whoopers by taking a saucerful of brown sugar and encouraging a slug to crawl over it until the sugar was good and slimy. He then got William to eat the sugar. The muslin bag full of spiders, worn round the neck, and the hair from the boy's head stuck between two bits of buttered toast and fed to a dog, had both failed to do the trick.

William Shakespeare had the toothache. The Reverend Bretchgirdle cured that by chasing him widdershins round Holy Trinity Church and making him bite from the frosty ground the first fern to appear in spring on the banks of the Avon.

William Shakespeare had the pneumonie. The Reverend Bretchgirdle cured it by tying a bullock's milt to the sole of the lad's left foot, and burying the milt when young Will had walked a league upon it.

William Shakespeare immediately contracted the thrush, with a terrible hick-hop. To cure him, the Reverend Bretchgirdle captured a duck from the pond by Tinkers Lane and placed its beak in the boy's mouth so that when he tickled the duck's throat and it opened its beak it breathed into the boy. The cold breath of the duck cured the thrush and the hiccup. The other cure – reciting the Emerald Table of Hermes Trismegistus over the victim three times three days running – did not work in this case.

Chapter Twenty-Four

*About the great plague
that was late in London*
(Christmas Eve, 1665)

It is Christmas Eve. It is snowing. The plague seems passed, at last, thanks be to God.

So far I never mentioned the plague in this book of mine, for I wanted to keep my pages clean of all pestilence. But now that the worst is over it is time that I spoke of it.

Strange to tell, I began the present narrative just three months ago, in the week ending the 19th of September, 1665, which was the week in which (they are now saying) this memorable calamity reached its greatest pitch of destructiveness.

The infection came in from Holland in the spring. The first official notice announcing that the plague had established itself in the parish of St Giles in the Fields appeared in an order of council back in April.

During the months of May and June, the infection spread. People began to hurry out of town in great numbers, until the strictest measures were enforced to prevent the spread of the plague to the rest of the country. The King with the Court fled in July, taking refuge so I heard in Salisbury, leaving the care of London to the Duke of Albermarle. (It's wonderful what news you learn from whores.)

The circumstance of the summer being unusually hot, and with few breezes blowing down the Thames, the disease was nourished all the days of August. London might well be said to be all in tears. As the plague raged, and families under the slightest suspicion were shut up in their houses, the streets became deserted and overgrown with grass. It was the necessity of going out of the houses to buy provisions which was, in great measure, the

ruin of the city. People caught the vile distemper, on these occasions, one from another, and even the provisions themselves were often tainted. I heard that the butchers of Whitechapel, where the greatest part of all flesh-meat is killed, were dreadfully visited by the pestilence, to such a degree that by midsummer few of their shops were kept open, and those that remained of them were killing their meat at Mile End and further, and bringing it in to market upon horses.

It is true that people used all possible precautions. The pie-maker in our basement told me that when anyone bought a joint of meat in the market they would not take it out of the butcher's hand, but took it off the hook themselves. On the other hand, the pie-maker said, the butcher would not touch the money, but have it put into a pot full of vinegar, which he kept for that purpose. The buyers carried always small money to make up any odd sum, that they might take no change. They carried bottles of scents and perfumes in their hands, as if to drive off death with a whiff of sweetness.

Even up here in my attic I witnessed the most dismal scenes. Sometimes a man or a woman dropped down dead in the street below. Many people that had the plague upon them knew nothing of it till the inward gangrene had affected their vitals. They died then in a matter of moments. I saw one man who had just time to run to the porch of the little Quaker meeting house opposite and put on his hat to sit down in the doorway to die. By the end of the summer, such things were commonplace, and one no longer noticed them. Dead bodies lay here and there upon the ground. People stepped over them quickly, or went the long way round. By night the bearers attending the dead-cart would take up the bodies, and carry them away. I watched it by moonlight from my window. Nor did those undaunted creatures, who performed these offices, fail to pick the pockets of the dead, and sometimes strip off their clothes if they were well dressed.

The pain of the swellings in this plague was in particular very violent, and to some intolerable. I saw a woman break naked out into the street and run directly down to the river, plunging herself into the water. Nobody cared to haul her out, for fear of infection. Others just ran up and down, not knowing what they did, till they dropped down stark dead. The worst cases were where people exhausted their spirits but did not die instantly, so that they fell down in the street and lingered on for perhaps half an hour or an hour. What was most piteous was that they were sure to come to themselves entirely in that half hour or hour, and then to make most grievous and piercing cries and lamentations. I never heard such horror before in my life. It was worse than the horrors one heard in the late Civil

Wars. Worse because so inward and so intimate. In time of plague the enemy is inside you. And no one can be sure that they haven't got it.

The tale of the blind piper I had from Pompey Bum. (I will tell you all about Pompey Bum another time.) He had the story from one of the men who carted the dead to the burial places, whose name was John Hayward, and in whose cart the accident occurred. The fellow was not blind, in truth, but a simpleton so clumsy and vague that he gave that impression. He commonly went his rounds about ten o'clock at night, when he went piping along from door to door, and the people would take him in at public-houses where they knew him, and give him drink and victuals, and sometimes farthings. In return, he would pipe and sing, and talk simply, which diverted the people, and thus he lived.

The plague was no time for a piper. Yet the poor fellow went about as usual, though he was all but starving. When anyone asked how he did, he would answer, 'The dead-cart hasn't taken me yet, but they've promised to call again next week.'

It happened one night that this poor fellow, whether somebody had given him too much to drink or no, laid himself out all along upon the top of a bulk or stall, and fell fast asleep, by a door in the street near London Wall, towards Cripplegate. And upon the same bulk or stall, the people of some house in the alley, hearing the bell, which signified the coming of the dead-cart, laid out a body dead of the plague close by where the piper lay, supposing he was another corpse set out for collection. Accordingly, when John Hayward with his bell and cart came along, finding two bodies lying upon the stall, he had them taken up with the long shovel they used, and thrown into the cart. And all this while the piper slept soundly.

From hence they passed along, and took up other dead bodies all laid out beneath the moon, until, as honest John Hayward told Pompey Bum, they must almost have buried the poor fellow alive in the cart. Yet all this while the piper slept soundly on.

At length the cart comes to the place where the bodies are to be thrown into the ground – which, as I remember, is at Mountmill – and, as the cart usually stopped some time before they were ready to pitch out the melancholy load they had in it, as soon as the cart stops, the piper wakes up, and he struggles a bit to get his head out from under all the dead bodies, but at last he sits upright in the cart and he cries out in confusion, 'Hey! Hey! Where am I?'

This frighted the wits out of the other attendants, but stout John Hayward turned never a hair, but said: 'Lord bless us! Here's somebody in the cart who's not quite dead!'

So one of the others calls out to the piper, and says: 'Who are you?'
'I'm the poor piper,' the fellow answers. 'Where am I?'

'Where are you!' says Hayward. 'Why, you are in the dead-cart, and we are going to bury you.'

'But I ain't dead, though, am I?' says the piper.

It was a question, not a statement, that's the point.

So he played them a tune on his pipe, and John Hayward and his men judged that he was not dead. And they helped the poor fellow down, and he went about his business.

That's what I'm doing, reader. I play my pipe to prove I am not dead.

I began in a week when upwards of ten thousand were reported dead. My Life of Mr Shakespeare was conceived first as an answer to the plague. Yet I was determined that the pestilence should leave my memories unscathed, which is why I never mentioned it when I started opening my boxes and writing up their contents at the height of it.

No doubt the piper played a merry tune. For certain he never piped any dirge on that dead-cart. No more do I. I knew that the late Mr Shakespeare would be my living companion, dancing me out of doomed London. And so it has proved.

The weather began to change when I began writing, and the air became cooled and purified by the equinoctial winds. That's why I praised the snow, of course, in chapter 17. It has fallen like a blessing on the city. It has cured the great plague that lay upon the streets.

Pompey Bum says (I know not on what authority) that more than a hundred thousand persons have perished by this terrible visitation.

But not Pickleherring, my lily lords and ladies.

At last the bells ring out tonight for a birth and not for burials. Christmas Eve, snow falling, and bells ringing. If I were not so old then I might almost be happy.

Listen, I beg you. Harken to my tales, friends.

When I was young I lived to dream, and now I am old I have to dream to live. This Life of William Shakespeare is my life now. He dreamed me up that afternoon in Cambridge. My life has been a nightmare since he died. Christmas Eve 1665, snow falling, and bells ringing. How much of my long existence has been a dream then? As in the old old story, am I the man dreaming he is a butterfly or the butterfly dreaming that he is a man?

Chapter Twenty-Five

Bretchgirdle's cat

Although the Reverend Bretchgirdle cut off his cat's left ear in the interests of curing the boy Shakespeare's measles, he was still very fond of the creature.

Bretchgirdle never did anything by halves. He baked a cake once in honour of the Virgin's lying-in. His friend Brownsword wouldn't eat it. No such ceremony should be observed, he pointed out, because Mary suffered no pollution, therefore needed no purification.

So these fine scholars passed their days in Stratford.

Bretchgirdle, in all truth, was a sentimentalist. It would not be too much to say that he leant towards Rome. One summer he told two of his choirboys that Lady's Thistle gets its name from the fact that Our Lady, walking near Nazareth with aching breasts, shook or squirted drops of milk upon it, to relieve the tension. The lads were kind not to report this opinion to the Bishop. It's true that the leaves of the plant are diversified with white spots. But I doubt if it ever grew in the Holy Land.

Bretchgirdle was always going on about Jesus's mother. Whether it was her virginity, her sinlessness, or her peculiar closeness to the Godhead, the present writer is not sure, but something about the woman appealed to him greatly. He wouldn't even have it that the brethren of Our Lord were Joseph's children by a former marriage. Their mother was quite another Mary, Bretchgirdle said, Mary the wife of Clopas or Alphaeus, the Virgin's sister.

Brownsword, on the other hand, was a Latinist only in the classical sense. He argued that the colourlessness of Mary's character, not only in the gospels but in the apocrypha too, makes it fatally easy to imagine her and to imagine that one understands that imagination.

Bretchgirdle ignored this thorn.

The parish priest bought a kitten in the Rother Market and christened it Dulia. When the schoolmaster heard him calling it, he said, 'What do you call that cat?'

'Dulia,' said Bretchgirdle.

'After the martyr?' said Brownsword.

'No, not Julia – Dulia,' Bretchgirdle explained.

'I hear you now,' said Brownsword, and added, 'I thought you had a cold.'

When the cat got bigger Bretchgirdle started calling it Hyperdulia.

It was a fat cat, kink-tailed, tabby in colour, forever shaking its head as if it wanted to lick its ear, a nasty sort of creature by all accounts. It had fleas and the fleas gave it worms. The flea-larvae swallow the eggs of the worm along with the organic matter in the bottom of the cat-box. The worm-larvae hatch from these eggs in the midgut of the flea-larvae, penetrate the midgut and arrive in the stomach of the flea-larvae. They stay there during the pupal and adult stages of the flea, growing all the while. An animal becomes infected or re-infected by swallowing such fleas when, for example, licking its coat.

(I learned all this from Dr Walter Warner, true discoverer of the circulation of the blood. Of course, the facts were not known in the ignorant century gone, when Bretchgirdle and Brownsword busied themselves with aspects of Mariolatry, and suchlike.)

Dulia was always licking her coat, so she was forever eating her own fleas and giving herself worms. According to Warner's *Artis Analyticae Praxis* (1631), his only book, this would have constituted a vicious circle or at least circumlocution – cat licking, cat chewing, fleas going down, worms breeding in the swallowed fleas, cat having worms, flea-larvae eating the eggs of the worms along with the organic matter in the bottom of the cat-box, cysticeroids hatching in the midgut, and so on, and so on, adult fleas copulating a few hours after their emergence from the cocoon and before having had a blood meal, the females laying a batch of fresh eggs after a day or two, but needing a blood meal before each batch.

Bretchgirdle liked his cat. Perhaps he did not love it, but he liked it.

Chapter Twenty-Six

*Of the games of William Shakespeare
when he was young*

In this box there is a top and a ball. The top is many-coloured. The ball won't bounce. But once the ball bounced – when the boy William tossed it against the wall of his father's house on Henley Street, catching it on the tricky spin as it came back.

I have made a list of all the games the poet played when he was young. The ball he gave me himself, not long after we first met. Joan Hart, his sister, made me a gift of the top, when I was in Stratford much later pursuing my researches. The other games I infer from the plays and the poems. Perhaps we should more truly say that our man had knowledge of them all, rather than claim that he played them. But with Mr Shakespeare knowing was nearly always doing.

Many times in his writings there is mention of *marbles* and *bowls*. As well as the *top-spinning* already mentioned, he tells also of *hoop-rolling*, of *hide-and-seek*, and of *blind-man's-buff*.

That he knew how to *fence* and all the language of *fencing* and *sword-play* could be proved from a score of his plays. And he was a *toxophilite* – well able, like old Double as recalled by Justice Shallow, to draw a bow and clap you an arrow in the clout at twelve score, even if he couldn't on horse-back hit a sparrow flying, any more than could that sprightly Scot of Scots, Douglas, according to scornful Prince Hal.

Of course, he played *tennis* – real tennis, I mean – for besides the Dauphin's tennis-balls there are a dozen allusions to and terms drawn from that game. But this was not a pastime of his childhood. There was no tennis-court in Stratford. Mr Shakespeare learned the game later, in London, on the Earl of Southampton's private tennis-court.

And he played *football*   that's in *Lear*. And at *push-pin*, like Nestor in *Love's Labour's Lost*. And at *more sacks-to-the-mill* (see Berowne's reference to this 'old infant play' in the same piece).

Swimming, of course. He did that in the Avon. And *skating* on the ponds when they froze in winter. *Jumping* and *wrestling, hand-to-hand fighting, wielding the lance* and *greyhound-racing* were all things the boy Shakespeare saw done at Mr Robert Dover's Olimpick Games upon the Cotswold Hills. Nobility and commoners came from many miles around to this annual event. 'How does your fallow greyhound, sir? I heard say he was outrun on Cotsall,' says Abraham Slender, in *The Merry Wives of Windsor*.

But the real sport in the Forest of Arden was *hunting*. Mr Shakespeare certainly hunted, but I think on foot. What sort of hounds were those of Duke Theseus in *A Midsummer Night's Dream*? Basset hounds? Spaniels? The poet had in mind a memory of the Stratford beagles, I suspect. I have no doubt that he *coursed hares*, running afoot with them when he was a boy or a young man.

Add to the list that he was a *fowler*, and went out with a gun and shot wild geese and choughs. *Cards* he played too; with me, sometimes, for kisses. There are not many allusions to card-playing in the plays, when you come to look for them, though there's a game going on in Act V Scene 1 of *King Henry VIII*. *Primero* was the late Mr Shakespeare's favourite card-game, though like Falstaff he was inclined to get too excited and foreswear himself when he saw good cards in his hand. In all honesty, Mr Shakespeare's face was always too much the index of his heart and mind for him to be any good at bluffing card-games. Yet he loved to play them – *gleek, brag*, and *post and pair* were others that he liked.

Let me tell you why I think William Shakespeare knew little about *chess*. It is not just that I never saw him play a game of it in the Mermaid tavern, where Mr Beaumont and Mr Fletcher were always locked in combat of wits, blond head against black, above the checkered board. Nor is it that to the best of my knowledge he employed no chess-terms in the course of his imagery. No, sir, I think Mr Shakespeare knew little or nothing about chess because in *The Tempest* he has Miranda say that Ferdinand is cheating – and it isn't easy at all to cheat at chess.

It was at the Mermaid that I first met Dr Warner. He was one of those poor fellows who do good and original work, only to find reward and credit for it go to other men. A thin little person, almost fleshless, with a withered left hand which he always kept hidden in his sleeve, the first time I saw him he was taking a frog from his pocket to demonstrate on the table among the tankards that heart-beats could only be explained by the circulation of the

blood. The honour for this discovery went some twenty years later to Dr William Harvey, who had also been present when Warner produced that frog from out of his pocket.

So the world wags, and fame is a foul strumpet.

As for the doctrine which made Harvey famous, Mr Shakespeare accepted it long before it was made public in that great anatomist's *Exercitatio anatomica de motu cordis et sanguinis in animalibus* (1628). Witness Biron in Act IV, Scene 3 of *Love's Labour's Lost*, where he speaks of *the nimble spirits in the arteries*. Witness King John in Act III, Scene 3 of the play of that name, where he talks of *blood thickened by melancholy*, and then goes on:

> *Or if that surly spirit, melancholy,*
> *Had bak'd thy blood, and made it heavy-thick,*
> *Which else runs tickling up and down the veins,*
> *Making that idiot, laughter, keep men's eyes. . . .*

All of which tells you that Mr Shakespeare was also paying attention to Dr Warner and his frog that night at the Mermaid.

But Pickleherring has wandered somewhat (as is his wont and manner) from the subject of this chapter – which was the boy Shakespeare's GAMES. O dear O simple long-lost days of childhood.

And how I wish I had left to drink some of that Scorbutick Ale which Mr Shakespeare's son-in-law, Dr John Hall, once prescribed for me. It was a truly excellent stomach drink, and John Hall was another wise doctor of the kind unsung by history, even though all his ministrations failed to save Mr Shakespeare when it came down to it.

That Scorbutick Ale helped digestion, expelled wind, and dissolved congealed phlegm upon the lungs. It was therefore sovereign against colds and coughs, as well as scurvy. Being drunk in the evening, it moderately fortified Nature, causing good rest, and hugely corroborating both the brain and the memory.

Yes, I could do with a deep draught of Scorbutick Ale to help me to write my Life of William Shakespeare. In the absence of the reality, I will drink the remembrance. And boil and eat this egg which a whore just fetched me.

Chapter Twenty-Seven

The midwife Gertrude's tale

The midwife Gertrude was a great teller of stories.

Every Wednesday evening – Gertrude's Wednesdays, they used to call them – would find her seated in her rocking chair in the marketplace at Snitterfield, the breeze blowing sweet in summer from the groves of the Forest of Arden, her bottles and her boxes spread at her feet. (Yes, madam, in winter she would do her stuff indoors.)

First she would eat a spoonful of this. Then she would drink a mouthful of that. Then she would blow her nose, clean out her ears with a knitting-needle, rub her eyes on a dockleaf, gargle, spit, clear her throat, take William Shakespeare on her knee, and begin a story.

The boy William's favourite was the tale of the monk and the nightingale. It went like this.

There was once a monk who was a good man but not a good monk. He did not like praying in church with the other monks. He liked walking in the green wood in the cool of the evening, and listening to the voices of the wind, and the streams, and the birds.

One night when he should have been at prayer the little monk wandered out into the dark and sat down under a willow tree. He chose the willow because its trailing branches made a screen around him, and he wanted to be alone to think.

He was thinking that he was not a good man because he was not a good monk when all at once a bird began singing in the tree above him.

It was a nightingale. Its song was so beautiful the monk wept for joy. Yet the song was not only a flow of joy. There was sadness in it too. It was sweet and sad, laughing and crying, merry and melancholy, all in one. The

bird poured out its heart and the monk listened in a trance of delight, caught up in the music, pressed close to the heart of it.

On and on the nightingale sang, as if in rapture. In fact its breast was pressed against a thorn, which was why it sang. Its music told no story, least of all the story of the thorn, but it cast such a spell of melody everywhere in the dark around, the thronging notes echoing among the other trees, that the stream seemed to stop to listen, and the night breeze hold its breath.

'*Tiouou, tiouou, tiouou, tiouou,*' sang the nightingale, '*lu, lu, lu, ly, ly, ly, li, li, li, li.*'

When the bird stopped the monk was so exhausted with delight and gratefulness that he sat quite still in the dark for a little while, calming his heart. Then he hurried back to the church.

He saw the Abbot and went up to him. 'Father,' he said simply, 'I have heard the nightingale——'

'Who are you?' broke in the Abbot crossly.

The monk looked closely at the Abbot in the gloom. He did not recognise him. It was a new Abbot. But how could that be?

'I do not understand,' he said. 'I went out into the night and I sat a moment under a willow and listened to the nightingale. Oh, Father, it was so beautiful I have no words for it. I wished that moment could have lasted for ever.'

The Abbot seized his arm and stared into his eyes. 'Are you telling the truth?' he demanded.

'Of course I am telling the truth,' said the monk. 'The nightingale sang——'

'I know nothing of the nightingale,' said the Abbot, 'but a hundred years ago a monk went out from this church into the night – it is written in the records of the monastery – and he never came back again. The Abbot of the time searched and searched, and the monks searched, but the man was never found. It was thought that he had fled away because he was a bad man.'

'I am not a good monk,' said the monk, 'and I would not claim to be a good man, but if I was a bad man I do not think I would have heard the nightingale.'

And then there was only dust in the Abbot's hands. For in listening so attentively to the song of the nightingale the little monk had heard a moment in eternity – which may take a hundred years of time.

This, as I say, was William Shakespeare's favourite from among the many stories told by the midwife Gertrude.

She was a woman too much given to allicholly and musing. Tiny, rather

plump, voluble, and obliging, with grey hair and a narrow mouth, she wore eyeglasses and a black hat pulled square across her forehead. She used to sing to herself a lot. *'Oh tennis,'* she sang, *'oh tennis is the finest game and boy and girl believe / The game they love is just the same that Adam played with Eve.'* This woman spoke often to William Shakespeare also of crickets – with results that you may see in *Romeo and Juliet*, Act I, Scene 4, line 63, and in *Cymbeline*, Act II, Scene 2, line 11, and in *Pericles* where at the start of the third Act Mr Shakespeare announces that he has taken over the writing from Mr Wilkins by having Gower speak of how *crickets sing at the oven's mouth*. There is also a good bit about being *as merry as crickets* in the first part of *King Henry IV*, and in *The Winter's Tale* where Mamillius promises Hermione and the ladies a tale of sprites and goblins and goes on thus:

> *There was a man. . . .*
> *Dwelt by a churchyard. I will tell it softly;*
> *Yond crickets shall not hear it.*

But the best line of all with crickets in it was given to me, of course, in my role as Lady Macbeth. Which fateful play, should you be interested, was actually written in Scotland and then first performed there – but I'll be coming to that when it's time for it.

I cannot believe that the midwife Gertrude knew as much about crickets as Dr Walter Warner. From him I learned that the wings of crickets when folded form long thin filaments, giving the appearance of a bifid tail, while in the male they are provided with a stridulating apparatus by which the well-known chirping sound is produced. The abdomen of the female ends in a long thin ovipositor. House crickets are greyish yellow marked with brown. Field crickets are bigger and darker. It burrows in the ground, the cricket, and in the evening the male cricket is to be seen sitting at the mouth of its hole noisily stridulating until a female approaches, when the louder notes are succeeded by a more subdued tone, whilst the successful musician caresses with his antennae the mate he has won. The cricket's musical apparatus consists of upwards of 130 transverse ridges on the under side of one of the nervures of the wing cover, which are rapidly scraped over a smooth projecting nervure on the opposite wing. The mole cricket is different. Its front legs are like hands.

The midwife Gertrude had a soft, animal nature. She loved to be happy like a sheep in the sun. And to do her justice, she liked also to see others happy, like more sheep in the sun.

Chapter Twenty-Eight

*Of little WS and the cauldron
of inspiration and science*

Some say that in the corner of Mary Shakespeare's kitchen there stood a cauldron of inspiration and science. It was a giant cauldron and the brew it contained was dark and thick. Those who believe this say that as soon as the boy William was strong enough his mother set him the task of stirring the contents of her cauldron for a year and a day.

Bretchgirdle died, and Brownsword went back to Macclesfield. But Mary had learned from the fat vicar before he died most of the magical virtues and vices of the flowers and ferns that grew in the fields about Stratford and in that green forest which bore her maiden name.

For instance, she knew of the heart-shaped wood-sorrel which warms the blood, and of moonwort which waxes and wanes with the moon and turns mercury into silver and will unshoe any horse that treads upon it. And she knew of the yellow juice of the celandine which will cure jaundice, and of liver-wort which is good for the liver. Also, you can take it that Shakespeare's mother was familiar with polypody which grows on old oaks and stops the whooping cough rather more effectively than the slug-slimed brown sugar Bretchgirdle had favoured. Certainly she would have known that the simple marigold is sovereign against melancholy, and that herb-dragon (speckled like a dragon) is the perfect antidote to adder bites.

Some of these plants, and many others that were stranger, went into the giant cauldron. Those who believe that Mary Shakespeare was a witch report that often she would be away from the house on Henley Street for weeks on end, searching in far and desolate places for rare herbs – for cassia out of Egypt, to the Transylvanian mountains for the purple-flowered hellebore, or getting aloes from Zocotora.

Was Mary Shakespeare a witch, then?

I do not know. I do not care to think so. Yet Mr John Shakespeare — in his cups, in London, that only time I met him — spoke darkly of a woman he knew well who had only to whistle for the wind to rise, and only to sigh for it to fall again. However, he did not say this woman was his wife. He implied that she was young, so he might have meant Mrs Anne Shakespeare, his daughter-in-law. Assuredly there was something witchy about *her*. But then so there was about all the women I ever met who were in any way close to the late Mr Shakespeare. Lucy Negro once claimed she could keep lightning in a bottle. Mr Shakespeare's sister Joan was invariably surrounded by black cats. And I admit that on that delicious occasion when Mr Shakespeare's widow drove me (dressed in her petticoats) from New Place, she clapped her hands thrice and a star fell out of the sky.

I prefer not to dwell on such things.

And stars fall down anyway.

Back to the cauldron, then. Those who believe in it say that Mary Shakespeare knew that when the brew in it had boiled for a year and a day then three precious drops of Inspiration from it would be sufficient to make her daughter Joan a poet. Joan was ugly and stupid and Mary had resolved, therefore, to confer poetry upon the new-born child, so that her wit and wisdom would gain her honour, and make up for her lack of grace.

As for the boy William, it is said that he never *meant* to taste the magic brew himself. It was an accident that he did. This is how it happened.

On the very last day, the day of the year and a day that the cauldron had to be kept boiling in the Henley Street kitchen, he was at work early, as usual, stirring with the huge wooden ladle. Perhaps he was excited by the thought that the moment had nearly come when the brew would be ready, according to his mother, perfected, for whatever reason, and his long labours ended. Perhaps he was just worn out by his mother's attentions.

Whatever the cause, the boy William Shakespeare was not stirring his mother's cauldron as steadily as he should have been. He splashed the gummy surface of the brew in dragging the ladle through it and three drops flew out of the cauldron and fell on his finger. They were so hot that — without thinking — the boy popped his finger in his mouth to suck it cool.

In that instant, as the three precious drops of Inspiration melted on his tongue, William Shakespeare was made a poet. It was as if a window had opened in his head. He looked out of the window and he saw a star so bright and clear that the light of all the other stars was swallowed up by it,

and then there was only one star, giving so much light that the light seemed alive.

Then the night was gone and William Shakespeare saw a new country, just like the country around Stratford he had always known but everything in it looking fresh and strange and early, as though the world had just begun that minute. The grass in this new country was greener than any grass he had ever seen, and buttercups grew there in the green grass so gold that they hurt his eyes, bringing tears to them. Gold-belted bees made merry from flower to flower; butterflies with green-veined and gold-spotted wings dabbled in the sunlight; the trees stood like delicate green steeples; the lakes were peopled by silver swans; the rivers ran over snowy pebbles with a sound that made WS smile; the breeze smelt deliciously of new-mown hay. It was all good enough to eat. And the strange thing was that WS felt he *could* eat it. He had only to open his mouth and he would bite the new day to the core, taste its sunlight on his tongue, feast on the green and the gold, drink the perfect country.

But even more strangely, *William Shakespeare did not want to eat it.* He knew it would be wrong to. He felt good, and he was content to look at the good things around him, without feeling any greed to have them.

Then it began to rain in the perfect country. The rain fell as rain, but when it had fallen it was little sapphire men and women who ran about hand-in-hand, singing.

As he listened to their song, trying to make out the words of it, William Shakespeare's head began to spin.

He saw wars and warriors and fires that flashed through the air.

He saw ships ploughing the sea without sails or oars.

He saw other ships – like silver pencils – sail through the clouds and leave dewy snail-wakes down the blue.

He saw empires rise and fall, castles crumble and new castles rise in their places.

He saw a chicken pecking its way out of an egg – only the egg was the moon.

He saw a tree growing upside-down, its branches touching the ground, its roots in the sky.

And all the while words he could not understand burned holes in the boy Shakespeare's thinking. His mind could hardly contain all the crowd of things in it, and he clutched his head in his hands.

Then, clearer than anything else he had seen so far, WS had a sudden vision of his mother as she was at this moment, gathering the last plants for her cauldron in the land that lies at the back of the North Wind. Even as

William watched her in his head he saw her hand freeze as it stretched to pluck a mandrake out by the roots and her eyes turned, as it seemed, towards him and she screamed with anger and cursed him.

Shakespeare fell down in his fear. Then, pulling himself together, he realised that his best hope was to use his new-found powers to protect himself against his mother's vengeance.

He fled from the house in Henley Street.

The cauldron seethed behind him in the kitchen. Purple bubbles burst from the magic brew. Hot ooze began to spill down its brazen sides.

Then the cauldron cracked in two, with a melodious *twang*.

This was because all the liquor it contained except the three drops of Inspiration was poisonous, and now the pure poison rose up and had its way. The cauldron split from side to side and the terrible brew flowed in a hissing snake-like stream over the floor, and out of the house, and down the streets and lanes till it came to the River Avon. Some swans on the river were poisoned instantly and fell dead in their own reflections.

Mary Arden went after her son like a fury.

When little William looked over his shoulder and saw his mother coming his heart swelled with fear so that he thought it would burst inside his chest.

Then he remembered the magic powers he had gained from the three drops of Inspiration and still running he changed himself into a hare.

But Mary had powers and wiles to equal his. Her blue eyes flashed when she saw what her son had done. She stamped her foot and changed herself into a greyhound, chasing after the hare and snapping at it with long lean jaws.

Then WS came to the Avon and plunged into it, changing himself into a fish and diving down, down, down into the cool and deep and safety of the dark.

But Mary Arden followed quickly after him there in the shape of an otter-bitch, lank and sleek, with teeth like scissors, and she would have caught him if – in leaping down the weir at Alveston – he had not suddenly changed himself into a crow and flapped away into the air.

Seeing this, his mother flicked her otter's tail and followed after as a long-winged hawk, harrying the crow and giving him no rest in the sky.

Then, just as she was about to fall on him and tear him to pieces with her beak and talons, WS saw a barn below, and a heap of winnowed wheat on the floor of the barn, and he dropped down like a stone among the wheat, and changed himself into one of the tiny white grains.

Then Mary Arden beat her long black wings and turned herself into a

high-crested black hen and scratched in the wheat until she found William, and swallowed him.

And no sooner had she swallowed him than she changed back to a woman again and went home to the house on Henley Street.

Now, madam, no doubt this was a dream, or never happened. Yet Mr Shakespeare spoke more than once as if it had. I remember the tears in his eyes as he told me of the raindrop men and women.

The poet Jack Donne, later Dean of St Paul's but in early days a great visitor of ladies and a great frequenter of plays, had a pet theory that every writer leaves somewhere in his work a portrait of his mother. I asked Mr S where his was. I have never forgotten his sly smile as he answered: 'The witch Sycorax, in *The Tempest*.' (Sycorax, Caliban's mother, does not, of course, appear in *The Tempest*. But as I hardly need to point out, her broomstick shadow lies darkly across all the action.)

As for the notion that Mr Shakespeare's sister was the one who should really have been the poet, I recall that song at the end of *Love's Labour's Lost* with its refrain

> *Tu-whit, to-who,*
> *A merry note,*
> *While greasy Joan doth keel the pot.*

My wife Jane told me that where she came from 'keeling the pot' is adding water or other cool liquor to it to save the brew from boiling over as you stir it. The reference to the cauldron is quite clear.

What happened to the swallowed wheat-grain Shakespeare?

Why, sir, returned home, his mother Mary shat little Willy out some nine hours later, and all went on as merrily as before.

Chapter Twenty-Nine

Some tales that William Shakespeare
told his mother

Now that if only for a moment the boy Shakespeare had held the future in his memory, he was no longer content to listen to the tales told by the midwife Gertrude.

Instead, he had his own stories to tell. On winter evenings, once a week, Mary Shakespeare would sit sewing shrouds by the fire and little Willy was allowed to stay up late to entertain her while his father was busy fulfilling himself at the alehouse. As a reward, when they heard the chimes at midnight, if John had not come home, his mother would take the lad to bed with her, and play sweet tricks upon his person. But that is not the point.

What tales did William Shakespeare tell his mother?

He told her who set the sun on fire, what poppies dream, and where breath goes when it is breathed out on a frosty morning.

He told her of a great bird called a Ruck, that could carry a man on its back.

He told her of a floating island that danced in the sea to the sound of music made by sunlight on the waves.

He told her of a spindle that caught fire for love of the queen's fingers who used it at her spinning.

He told her of cities at the bottom of the sea, and of rusty anchors that had been found fixed in the tops of mountains.

He told her of a baker who thought his body was made of butter and who would not sit in the sun or near the fire for fear of melting.

He told her of the worlds that were inside each flake of the falling snow.

He told her the story of the two swallows that were lazy in love and so missed the flying of the other swallows South. How the two birds could not

think what to do when winter came, so flew down under the waters of the River Avon and held their breath. And how the Avon froze over, and when the ice broke a fisherman found the two swallows in a block of ice, locked beak to beak where they had breathed into each other, kissing to keep alive under the water. And how the fisherman took the birds in the ice and warmed them on his stove, and when the ice fell away as water hissing on the stove, the swallows flapped their bright blue wings and flew out of the window.

He told her of the werewolves of Meath, and the tale of the white raven.

He told her how Launcelot fought with the demon cats.

He told her of Richard Sans Peur and the unquiet corpse.

He told her of Merlin and Vivian, and of the fly with the wooden leg.

He told her of Hamlet in Scotland, and of True Thomas and the Queen of Elphame.

He told her of the widow who wore horseshoes, and the tale of the mouse, the bird, and the sausage.

He told her of fairy rings,* and of how he had danced in them with men wearing silver shoon and green pantaloons that were buttoned with bobs of silk.

All this, and more, the boy William Shakespeare told his mother Mary, by the fireside, according to some.

But others say that he never said much at all.

I have learned from sources outside the family that the boy was in fact at first mistaken for a dunce. These neighbours report that Shakespeare was slow to read and slower to write, and that far from pouring out stories by the glow of a winter fire he was a moping and miserable child, taciturn in the extreme, who never spoke unless he was spoken to. He would shut himself up in his bedroom, and cared for no companions. Sometimes he would burst into tears for no reason that anyone could understand. At other times, he would stare into someone's face for many minutes together, without appearing to observe them or acknowledging who they were. There were neighbours wise enough to see madness in these peculiarities, but none who discerned the self-absorption of beginning genius.

This uninspired version of the childhood of William Shakespeare would have it that he learned his letters finally from an old illuminated manuscript. Then, according even to his detractors, a sudden change took place in the boy, and at seven years old, it is said, he would read without

---

* Circles of rank or withered grass, often seen in the Stratford meadows, once said to be produced by fairies dancing, but according to Dr Walter Warner simply an agaric or fungus below the surface, which has seeded in a circular range, as many plants do.

urging, and read anything and everything, from morning to night, if his mother would let him. She, for her part, only worried at this development, lest her son go blind.

He was a handsome child, all seem agreed. His eyes were blue, flecked (when he was excited) with the wild burning colour of bracken in autumn. At other times (when he was thoughtful) they were as deep and inscrutable as a forest pool cobbled with leaves and shadows that do not move. His features were fine, yet delicate. His forehead was slightly out of proportion to the rest of his face. His hair in those days was gold – not the colour of common straw, but the kind of pure firy gold you find hidden in strange amber. His lips were red and full, if a touch ascetic. His nose was straight and long, very wide at the nostrils. His hands were large, with long tapering fingers which he was fond of waving about as he talked, and making shadow-pictures with on the wall. Everyone praised the gentleness of his manner. The number of times WS has been described as 'gentle', man and boy, is indeed remarkable. Sometimes I wish he had been less so. Had he not been so gentle it might have been easier to know him, or to remember what one encountered apart from the gentleness. But I do not think he was gentle through and through. When I seek to find an emblem for the heart of William Shakespeare the image that comes most readily and indelibly to mind is of a snow-gentled hawthorn. There was always something sharp at the core of his sweetness. Yet he was, as even Ben Jonson admitted, a very lovable spirit; and, indeed, he was honest, and of an open and free nature.

This was the boy William Shakespeare who at the end of August, 1571, being then seven years and four months old, was admitted into the Grammar School at Stratford.

Chapter Thirty

What Shakespeare learned
at Stratford Grammar School

Here's Shakespeare's hornbook. The handle, pierced with a round hole, has lost the piece of string which once attached the little primer to his girdle. A single leaf of yellow parchment is set in the gnawed oak frame, with a slice of transparent horn protecting it. This went with him every day when he went to school.

Here is Shakespeare's alphabet, both large and small, followed by a barbaric regiment of monosyllables: *ab eb ib ob ub/ba be bi bo bu.* (I read the chant straight across at the second line. See where Holofernes comes from, with his baaing and his bleating?)

Here is Shakespeare's Lord's Prayer, his *Paternoster* cut out in black-letter, with above it his *In nomine*, in Gothic script: 𝕴𝖓 𝖙𝖍𝖊 𝖓𝖆𝖒𝖊 𝖔𝖋 𝖙𝖍𝖊 𝕱𝖆𝖙𝖍𝖊𝖗, 𝖆𝖓𝖉 𝖔𝖋 𝖙𝖍𝖊 𝕾𝖔𝖓, & 𝖔𝖋 𝖙𝖍𝖊 𝖍𝖔𝖑𝖞 𝕲𝖍𝖔𝖘𝖙.

This pellucid horn, cool to the touch, was what saved these letters from Shakespeare's inky fingers as he pored over them. I hold in my aged hand what he held once in his young one, reciting in the big schoolroom, at the top of the stone stairs, under beams of chamfered oak, the master enthroned on high at his desk before him, his assistant behind, rod ready for the boys who had not learned their lesson.

Ben Jonson sneered that the late Mr Shakespeare knew 'small Latin, and less Greek', but I say that the education he received at the King's New School at Stratford was not to be sniffed at. Learning was highly thought of there in Shakespeare's youth, and the magister got £20 a year (which was more than a master at Eton). The school itself was free to the sons of notable citizens. John Shakespeare was certainly that in the year that William entered it. That was the year the butcher served as bailiff to the

town. That year and the next Will was in what they called 'petty school', sitting down with the other boys, but learning the rudiments. In fact he never studied the *quadrivium* – arithmetic, music, geometry, astronomy. His lot was the *trivium* – the first or 'trivial' part of the medieval curriculum, still then in vogue. In other words, Shakespeare learned the essentials of all knowledge: grammar itself, and logic, and rhetoric. He left before he got to the second stage.

Why did he leave?

I'll be coming to that, as my grandfather the bishop used to promise his choirboys.

So what did Shakespeare learn from this trivial schooling?

He learned an educated disbelief. I think he learned above all how to take what he needed from his studies, how to leave the rest.

And what exactly did he study?

Latin, some Greek, more French than you might think likely in the provinces (in *Henry V* the dialogue in that language is grammatically accurate if not idiomatic). History. Biblical bits and pieces – I've counted more than two hundred references to things in the Bible in his plays, nearly all of them of an unmystical cast, thank God; for instance, he seems to have been especially impressed by the story of Cain and Abel, the treachery of Judas, and the parable of the Prodigal Son. Then, of course, he studied the major Roman poets and historians and orators. And how to parse a sentence. And how to scan.

Which authors in particular did he read there?

Ovid (I have his copy, with his signature), Virgil, the comedies of Plautus, and the tragedies of Seneca. Prudentius, Boethius, Livy, Sallust. But all such education comes out only in his prentice work. There he can't help letting us know what he knows, like a bright boy forever raising his arm in the classroom. Later, Mr S stopped showing off. He forgot what he had read, and he wrote without reading. But even then the occasional memory from that room at the top of the open stone staircase came in useful. Palingenius, for instance, whose *Zodiac of Life*, running to 9000 Latin hexameters, he'd had to parse, memorise, and translate at the rate of one hundred lines a week, gave him one remembered line: *All the world's a stage*. Horace came in handy when he was writing the sonnets, so it seems, and in *Titus Andronicus* you will find an aphoristic villain who has read him also, 'in the grammar long ago'.

Would you make William Shakespeare a great scholar?

Not at all, sir. Not like John Selden, or Ben Jonson. Not even like

William Smith, his exact contemporary, who went on from Stratford school to matriculate at Oxford.

Wasn't he fancy's child?

Madam, I perceive you know your Milton! But Milton never knew our man at all. Leonard Digges, stepson to one of his executors, got it better in another of those prefatory poems in the Folio, where he says, *Nature only helped him.* By her *dim light* Mr Shakespeare made his way. No scholar he, yet his scholarship was profound. What he learned in the King's New School was from the *method* of what was done there in the name of education, where every side of every question was considered, and different voices encouraged equally to express opposing views. In place of dogmatic definition, versatility of presentation was in favour. No bad training for a future dramatist.

Which book left most mark on him, apart from the Bible?

William Lyly's *Grammar.* He quotes it in his plays ten times or more.

Does that mean he admired it?

I'd say not. I think it only means he remembered it. I have seen Shakespeare's desk in the Stratford schoolroom. In the lid of it he carved the words *Nulla emolumenta laborum* ('There is no reward for work'), which is Lyly turned upside-down. In fact, sobersides Lyly is often comical, though of course he didn't mean to be. His *Grammar* is full of saws that cut no ice for William. For instance, '*homo* is a common name to all men.' Mr S has Gadshill, a sententious thief, recite this schoolboy wisdom to impress his partners in crime. They are duly impressed. But the Bailiff's son wasn't. The *Grammar* also promotes a Calvinistical morality, which Mr Shakespeare always found amusing. For instance, it claims 'it is most healthful to get up at dawn.' This sounds more plausible in Latin, and Sir Toby invokes that Latin in *Twelfth Night.* A drunkard, in truth he goes to bed with the sunrise, like John Shakespeare.

Do you make Shakespeare out a cynic, like yourself?

Madam, you flatter me. I know nothing of Antisthenes, nor Diogenes neither. As for Mr Shakespeare, what his Stratford education gave him was the start of a way of understanding human nature in all its complexity and contradictoriness. That understanding, though, was never anybody's but his own. Consider: Ben Jonson had much the same sort of schooling, at Westminster, under Camden, and applied himself much more thoroughly to the curriculum. His *Catiline* is a fair example of the result – a classical construction, good warring against evil, all clear as cold. But if you take Shakespeare's version of the same material in *Julius Caesar* what you find is a hero who is in part a villain, and a tyrant who is heroic. Which is more

true to life, the truer poetry? WS, by the way, never got his due from Jonson, and he knew it. He was responsible for getting Jonson's first plays put on, and his rival resented that. If you look at everything Jonson said about Shakespeare there is always some barb concealed in there amidst the praise. He knew that Shakespeare was the better dramatist, and it choked him. He was always a praiser of himself, and a contemner and scorner of others. As for Mr WS, he never went in much for criticising other writers. But he made one pun sending up Jonson's classical pretensions, when he stood godfather to a son of Ben's, and gave the boy a dozen latin spoons (that is, spoons made of latin, a kind of brass). These, he said, were for Jonson to translate. Shakespeare himself never needs translation, nor does his verse ever sound translated. Ovid I know he loved. But he remembered him mostly from Golding's English version – though he did employ a Latin couplet from the *Amores* as epigraph to *Venus and Adonis*. You could say he got his five-act structure from Terence and Plautus. But what he filled it with is pure impure English hodge-podge.

Who were William Shakespeare's teachers at his school?

First, Simon Hunt. Then, Thomas Jenkins. Last, John Cotton.

Do we know much about them?

Enough, perhaps. Hunt and Cotton were both Catholics. Hunt had to see down a little rebellion among his pupils, following the St Bartholomew Massacre. They smashed some windows and threw a few books about. I can't see Willy having any great stomach for this, even at eight years old. Hunt was a man of parts, evidently. When his religion forced his resignation, he went off abroad, where he became a Jesuit, and died in Rome. Cotton was probably a good teacher, too. He was a graduate of Brasenose College, Oxford.

What about Thomas Jenkins? Was he a Papist?

No, sir. He was some sect of Puritan. Shakespeare makes fun of him, I believe, in the character of Sir Hugh Evans in *The Merry Wives of Windsor*, where there is a schoolroom scene in which he makes fun of himself too, as a recalcitrant pupil called Will. Quite evidently this Welsh Jenkins was far from possessing a powerful brain. What is certain is that right in the middle of one school year, when Shakespeare was fourteen, the governors got rid of the teacher suddenly. He was given £6 to relinquish his duties and hand the cane over to Cotton, a competent master of the old type, lately down from Oxford.

Do you say Shakespeare was taught well? By two Papists and a Puritan!

I say nothing of the sort. I say he learned from their extremes a *via media*, a middle way.

Which master had the greatest influence upon him?

Jenkins, in my opinion. He taught him something about foolishness. And remember that he was a Welshman, and that he seems (judging from his caricature as Hugh Evans) to have abused the English language thoroughly. It is just possible that he was the person who first gave William Shakespeare some notion of the possibilities that lie in stitching Latin and Saxon words together to make new compounds, and of playing off the one strain in our tongue against the other. The portrait of Evans is not without affection. And someone such may well have served to set the boy Shakespeare off on the love-affair with language that lasted all his life, finding new terms for new times, setting fire to English!

How did his school day go? Do we have any details?

He lived close by the school – about a quarter of a mile away. The bell started ringing at a quarter to six every morning in summer, an hour later in winter. On the stroke of six the pupil was supposed to be in class. So Will would rise and say his prayers and wash his morning face until it shone and sometimes comb his hair and greet his parents and always collect his books and then shoulder his satchel before creeping like a snail unwillingly down Henley Street and Chapel Street to the corner of Chapel Lane where the school was situated just behind the Guild Chapel. There were thirty desks in the room beneath the long rafters. Everyone chanted 'Good morning, sir' to the master, then lessons would begin with choral singing. (Will's favourite, as I have reason to know, was the 24th Psalm, especially verses 7 to 10.) This morning session lasted until eleven. Will would then trot home to help his mother with the housework. You can suppose from what he has to say about schools and schoolboys in his plays that he always went out a good bit faster than he came in. If he was lucky then his father might be in a jovial mood and allow him to draw ale from the cask and pour it into a pitcher and say grace for the family before they all sat down to dinner at noon – this was a privilege of being the eldest son. After dinner he would go back to school at one o'clock, and stay there until five, with just fifteen minutes' recreation. Thursdays and Saturdays, he had half-days, school finishing at noon. Sundays there was no school. Then he went to church.

Were the boys flogged?

Soundly, sir, when they were obstinate and ungovernable. Moral advice would also be given to complete their punishment. 'God has sanctified the rod,' as Seager says in his *The Schoole of Vertue and the Book of Good Nourture for Chyldren*, the last word on the subject, published when William Shakespeare was just thirteen. 'Thus it must be used as the instrument of God.' I knew

myself a schoolmaster who in winter would ordinarily on a cold morning whip his boys over, for no other purpose than to get himself a heat.

When are you going to tell us some more about the Misses Muchmore?

Fie, madam! Shame upon you! Do you want *your* pretty bottom smacked, or what?

Chapter Thirty-One

About Pompey Bum

+

Pickleherring's Shakespeare Test

I have this garret above a whorehouse which I rent. My landlord is the pie-maker, Pompey Bum. Some of his pies – the sweetest, of course – are tarts. I like cold custard ones, myself, with nutmeg sprinkled on them.

I have this bed, which is not entirely straw. I have this to sit in that was once a chair. I have this worn-out body, and this crust to eat, of which the rats have eaten only part.

Last week, as I recall, one of the girls from below gave me a fresh-laid speckled hen's egg to boil. Such treasures in heaven! No rage, no remorse, no despair. I have this soul in pawn, and this delirious heart.

Now, not for the first time, the plague has passed me by. Pickleherring has been spared to complete his great work. I live on just to write my Life of Shakespeare.

It is a lack of teeth compels me to eat only eggs, fish, hash, and other spoon-meats. I eat when I am hungry, at any hour of the day or night. I drink when I am thirsty, but only water. And I go to bed or arise just as I feel inclined, without any reference to a clock.

It is years now since I gathered my precious data. I drank too much and I slept too little in those days. Then I would rather have broken my neck rushing downstairs than miss getting a story about Mr Shakespeare from a departing guest. The rush remains – but only in my pen. Now I commit my stories all helter-skelter to the page. Haste and muddle were always my middle names. I write, madam, tumultuarily, as these things come into my head, or as I go fishing memories out of one of my boxes. All may easily be reduced into order at your leisure, sir, by numbering my subjects with red

ink, according to time and place, *et cetera*. Your cochineal paste is to be recommended for the office.

I write to prove that I am still alive, and that so is Mr Shakespeare. It is much to be deplored that people nowadays find it convenient to look down their enlightened noses at him. I know the modern taste calls him vulgar and crabbed, an uncouth spirit. I say his day was good, and that it will surely come again when the French fashions that swept into England with King Charles II have gone out again.

I predict that one day Mr William Shakespeare and his works will be so popular and so revered that children will be required to study the subject in schools and universities. You find the notion crazy, sir? Preposterous, madam? Well, it is not important. Humour an old man's whim; his maggot, even. I cannot imagine, for the life of me, that Mr Shakespeare himself would ever have wanted any such fate. But certainly one day his plays will all be staged again, properly, in their entirety, and not in tidied-up and 'corrected' versions to suit a newfangled classicalism. And when they are it won't be with women in the cast!

Meanwhile, here, gentle reader, just for fun, and to eke out a box with nothing in it, is an Examination Paper which I have prepared for your testing:

1.   What happens in *Hamlet*? And why?
2.   How many children had Lady Macbeth?
3.   Who and/or what is Silvia? (Give examples.)
4.   Are people murdered in tragedies or aren't they?
5.   What was Puck's average speed when flying? And Ariel's? How do we know that Puck was probably the better flyer of the two?
6.   Whose bawdy hand was on whose prick in *Romeo and Juliet*? (Discuss.)
7.   In which play does William Shakespeare name me, and wish a plague upon me? In which other play does he also name me (twice) in the first three lines of Act II (well, almost), and then go on to prescribe the exact procedure that I am employing in the writing of this book?
8.   What is the effect of the word DUCDAME?
9.   Is this a duck or a rabbit?

10.   Where is fancy bred?

Chapter Thirty-Two

*Did Shakespeare go to school
at Polesworth?*

I had a friend among the younger players who could never believe that Shakespeare was taught in Stratford. He insisted that the poet went as a boy to the old school attached to Polesworth Abbey, deep in the Forest of Arden.

I have found no actual evidence that would support this. All that is certain is that in 1571, John Shakespeare, as bailiff, entertained Sir Henry Goodere of Polesworth at the Bear Inn in Bridge Street. Sir Henry was in Stratford to give judgement in an arbitration case. I have consulted the Corporation accounts, and they twice mention payments for his horse-hire.

A year later, according to my friend, John Shakespeare somehow persuaded Sir Henry to take Will into his household. There, in the rambling manor house at Polesworth, the lad served as a page. The place was quite a nest of singing birds. The poet Michael Drayton, one year older, was already a page there. Thomas Lodge (whose story *Rosalynde* provided Mr S with the plot for *As You Like It*) seems to have kept popping in and out. Ralph Holinshed lived in the parish, and might even have taught history at the school.

If you ask me, it is all just a bit too convenient. Especially when you add the detail that this Goodere was also friends with the father of Shakespeare's future patron, the Earl of Southampton. Of whom more anon, as my grandfather the bishop used to say.

Anyway, madam, if you can credit it, perhaps it was at Polesworth that William acquired his Latin, and got introduced in due course to polite society.

Speaking of which, there is always Goodere's daughter. (I say 'always'

119

advisedly, since her monument still leaves a space for the date of her death. I have seen it at Clifford Chambers, which is not far from Stratford.)

Well, sir, this girl's name was Anne, and she was by all accounts remarkable. If Shakespeare ever lived under the one roof with such a creature, then I think we would have heard. Drayton was most certainly in love with her. She was the first inspiration for the figure of 'Idea' who appears throughout his work. The marvellous sonnet beginning *Since there's no help, come let us kiss and part* was addressed to her. When her father died, she married Harry Rainsford, who was knighted at the coronation of James I. Drayton himself never married, but continued to spend his summers in her company. In later years, so they say, Anne was still straight-backed and beautiful. It was impossible to tell whether she was young or old. I had this information from Mr Shakespeare's son-in-law, John Hall, who was her doctor. He was a sober fellow, not given to romance.

There is symmetry, of course, in having William Shakespeare go to school with Michael Drayton. They were certainly good friends in the London years. And some say that it was after a drinking bout with Drayton and Ben Jonson that Mr Shakespeare contracted the fever that led to his death.

Also there is this music: Shake-*spear/Poles*-worth.

All the same, when it comes down to it, my friend had not a jot of hard evidence for his theory. It rests entirely on the fact of Drayton's career as a page at Polesworth, and the way it won him patronage, and a wish that Mr S might also have enjoyed some similar start in life.

I repeat the story now because I liked the player who first propounded it. His name was David Weston, a fine steely Hal when young who then took over as Falstaff after John Heminges got the stutters. He played the old boy with fire and love, making the part his own for ever after. I shall never forget the way he used to cry *Banish plump Jack, and banish all the world!* It sent a shiver down my spine, and the thought of it does so still.

Chapter Thirty-Three

Why John Shakespeare liked
to be called Jack

John Shakespeare always liked to be known as Jack among his cronies. He said that John was no name for a fortunate man. By way of example of what he meant, he would cite all the Popes who had used that name:

John I died in prison.

John II and *John III* were complete nonentities.

John IV was accused of heresy.

John V spent most of his pontificate in bed.

John VI and *John VII* were even bigger (or smaller?) nonentities than *Johns II* and *III*.

John VIII was held prisoner in St Peter's by Lambert, Duke of Spoleto. When he was released he adopted a young man called Boso as his son, and tried to get himself crowned as King of Italy. He did deals with Charles the Bald and Charles the Fat, giving them both the imperial crown, when this failed too. His last years were spent chiefly in hurling vain anathemas against his enemies. A transvestite, according to the annalist of Fulda he was eventually murdered by members of his own household.

John IX had matted hair and fang-like teeth. He had to put up with a rival Pope called Sergius III. In any case, he spent most of his two-year reign inducing the council to determine that the consecration of all future Popes should take place only in the presence of the imperial legates. He was, in other words, a politician.

John X only became Pope through the wiles of Theodora, wife of Theophylact, the most powerful noble in Rome. This Pope was really a soldier. He took the field in person against the Saracens, slaughtering many with his own hands when he gained a famous victory on the banks of the

Garigliano. All his hopes of a united Italy were dashed by the death of Berangar, and he pontificated over four years of increasing anarchy and confusion, before perishing through the intrigues of Marozia, Theodora's daughter.

John XI was the bastard son of the Marozia just mentioned and that papal pretender Sergius III who had made *John IX*'s life such a religious misery. He was made Pope at the age of 21 only through the influence of his mother. He remained the mere exponent of her wishes until he was imprisoned with her in the Lateran by his half-brother Alberic, and died there.

John XII was Alberic's son. He succeeded his father as Pope at the age of 16. His original name was Octavian, but when he assumed the papal tiara he adopted the name of John – the first example, it is said, of the custom of taking a new name with elevation to the papal chair. This pseudo-John lacked all vigour, save in bed. His union of the papal office with his civic dignities proved a source of weakness rather than of strength. His scandalous private life made the Pope's name a by-word of reproach. In order to protect his own position he called to his aid Otto the Great of Germany, to whom he granted the imperial crown. Even before Otto left Rome, however, *John XII* began to conspire against him, fearing his creature's power might now overshadow his own authority. His intrigues were discovered by Otto who returned to Rome and summoned a council which deposed John, who was hiding in the mountains of Campania. Leo VIII was elected in his stead. *John XII* returned to Rome at the head of a formidable company as soon as Otto had left, and caused Leo to seek safety in immediate flight. Otto determined to make an effort in support of Leo, who had blue eyes, but before he could reach the city John was assassinated.

John XIII, Leo's successor, was Otto's pawn. His submissive attitude towards the imperial power was so distasteful to the Romans that they expelled him from the city. On account of Otto's German threats, they permitted him shortly afterwards to return, upon which, with the sanction of his master, he took savage vengeance on those who had opposed him. He gave the imperial crown to Otto II in assurance of his succession to his father. He also crowned Theophano as empress because he liked the look of her.

John XIV was imperial chancellor of Otto II before his elevation to the papal chair. Otto died shortly after and John was deposed and placed in prison. He died incarcerated at the Castle of St Angelo, either by poison or starvation, no one knows.

(The Pope John who ruled for four months after *John XIV* is now omitted by the best authorities.)

John XV was entirely in the hands of the Empress Theophano. When she let him go, this Pope, whose venality and nepotism made him famous, died of fever before the arrival of Otto III, who elevated his own kinsman Bruno to the papal dignity.

John XVI was a Greek with five gold teeth, and a favourite of the Empress Theophano. His original name was Philagathus, which is no name for a Pope, but God knows why he took the name of John, given the terrible track record. He was wily and ambitious, but his treacherous intrigues aroused the wrath of Otto III. He died immured in a dungeon after enduring cruel and ignominious tortures at the hands of the emperor, whom he had cuckolded.

John XVII lasted only four months in the office.

John XVIII, a cross-patch, was during his whole pontificate the creature of the patrician John Crescentius. Ultimately he abdicated and retired to a monastery, where he soon died.

John XIX only took holy orders to enable him to ascend the papal chair. He spent the whole of his pontificate taking bribes. He died in full possession of his dignities, and was succeeded by his nephew, who was twelve years old.

John XX was only Pope for eight months before the roof of the palace he had built for himself at Viterbo fell down on his head.

John XXI was a magician.

John XXII was a tax collector, and was being tried for heresy when he died.

John XXIII was only antipope, but he was found guilty of enough deeds of immorality, tyranny, ambition, and simony to be deposed even from that pseudo-office. Before becoming antipope this John had been a pirate. His abilities were mainly administrative and military, although he did repent when at last caught out. He died on the 22nd of December 1419, and all visitors to the baptistery at Florence now admire, under its high baldacchino, the sombre figure sculptured by Donatello to the dethroned pontiff, who had at least the merit of bowing his head under his chastisement, and of contributing by his passive resignation to the extinction of the series of Popes which sprang from the council of Pisa, and the extinction at the same time of the series of Popes called John.

After that, Popes got the point of the name's unluckiness, and not a single one has taken it on.

My late wife Jane was once fucked by a fellow named John Pope. She never could resist a papal pizzle.

John Shakespeare used to say that one day there would be a Pope called Jack. Jack was a name he liked. Jack Straw. Jack Sprat. Jack and the Beanstalk. Jack the Giant Killer. That time in London, in the Nag's Head at the corner of Friday Street, he told me England's christian name was Jack.

As for Pope Jack – Jack Shakespeare would have wagered on the possibility, he said, with his friend Fluellen, only he knew he wouldn't live long enough to collect.

Chapter Thirty-Four

What Shakespeare saw when he looked
under Clopton Bridge

My friend the player Weston used to say in support of his Polesworth conjecture that Shakespeare never mentions Stratford in any of his writings. But that's not true.

If you stand on the eighteenth arch of Clopton Bridge (the one nearest the point where the road goes off to London), and if you watch the River Avon below when it is in flood, you will see a curious thing that Shakespeare saw.

The force of the current under the adjoining arches, coupled with the curve there is at that strait in the riverbank, produces a very queer and swirling eddy. What happens is that the bounding water is forced *back* through the arch in an exactly contrary direction.

I have seen sticks and straws, which I have just watched swirling downstream through the arch, brought back again as swiftly against the flood.

The boy Will saw this too. Here's how he describes it:

> As through an arch the violent roaring tide
> Outruns the eye that doth behold his haste,
> Yet in the eddy boundeth in his pride
> Back to the strait that forc'd him on so fast,
> In rage sent out, recall'd in rage, being past:
> > Even so his sighs, his sorrows, make a saw,
> > To push grief on and back the same grief draw.

That's from *The Rape of Lucrece*, lines 1667–73. How many times must he

have watched it, perhaps with tears in his bright eyes?

You can see the river behave like this at Stratford even on a calm day, but if you want to observe the full force of that saw-like eddy then choose a day with a violent roaring tide. At all events, here, my dears, we have something very particular and peculiar and right in the heart of his home town that William Shakespeare noticed.

Chapter Thirty-Five

About water

Water and all its ways pleased William Shakespeare. You might almost say he was enchanted by it.

I think the Avon proved his best and sweetest tutor, and that the boy Will learned more about poetry and the workings of the minds of men from watching that river in its different moods than he was taught by all his schoolmasters put together.

In summer he sauntered by on the river banks, observing the green current gliding with white swans upon it. In winter he watched it rage, and must often afterwards have noticed *meadows not yet dry, / With miry slime left on them* as he reports in *Titus Andronicus*.

The Avon knows flooding, in fact, both in winter and summer. Sir Hugh Clopton built his bridge at Stratford, towards the end of the fifteenth century, because before it people were refusing to come to market in town when the river was up, for fear that they might drown, and their cattle with them. Even this solid stone structure could not always hold against the fury of the flood. In July of 1588 – during that wild, wet, and windy summer provided by God to assist England in the defeat of the Spanish Armada – the bridge was broken at both ends by the roaring tide, imprisoning in the middle three men who were in the act of crossing it.

Water in flood is an image you will find all over Shakespeare. Sometimes these images are simple, picturing an irresistible force which will suffer nothing to stop it, but *engluts and swallows* all in its way, as he says in *Othello*. At other times he makes of the flooding river an emblem of rebellion, as when Scroop in *Richard II* (Act III, Scene 2), speaking of the uprising, compares things to

> an unseasonable stormy day
> Which makes the silver rivers drown their shores,
> As if the world were all dissolv'd to tears,
> So high above his limits swells the rage
> Of Bolingbroke.

I don't think you will find as many river similes in any other of the dramatists, either Elizabethan or modern. But then I never acted much in other men's plays. I did once take the walking-on part of Helen of Troy in Marlowe's *Dr Faustus*, though, and I heard old Alleyn in *Tamburlaine* at the Rose, and I can tell you that I doubt if there's a river image in the whole of Marlowe. The sea was more in his line – there's plenty of that. As for Ben Jonson, all his river stuff is most perfunctory and of a general nature; it shows no sign of any direct observation.

I imagine the mills on the Avon were Shakespeare's delight. There is a great mill at Barford, and another at Alveston, and two at Hampton Lucy. All these lie upstream from where he lived. Then there is Stratford mill, just below the church where he was baptised and now lies buried. And downstream there are mills at Luddington and Binton and Welford and Bidford. There are also two mills on the Stour, which runs into the Avon about two miles below Stratford. And on the fast-flowing Alne that runs by Henley-in-Arden there's a mill at every mile, just about. No doubt the boy Will found a fresh mill-pond to bathe in every week of the year. No doubt but he also carved toy boats and floated them down the mill-leats.

There's not a lot to suggest that Mr Shakespeare liked fishing. His references to the sport are all rather ordinary – Claudio saying *Bait the hook well; this fish will bite,* that sort of thing. I think he preferred to stand and stare at the waters, without disturbing them with his own ambition.

Swimming's a different matter. I know he could swim. As a boy I like to imagine him plunging into the angry waters of the Avon, as did Cassius once with Caesar in the Tiber. Only a practised swimmer could have written, as he does in the second scene of the first act of the Scottish play:

> *Doubtful it stood;*
> *As two spent swimmers, that do cling together*
> *And choke their art.*

I don't claim he could swim like a fish like Ariel. But I was with him one night by the Thames when he tore off his clothes. 'Be contented,' I told

him. 'It's a naughty night to swim in.' He liked that well enough to put it straight into the storm scene in *King Lear*.

Chapter Thirty-Six

Of weeds and the original Ophelia

I want to say a word about Shakespeare and weeds. Not the word WEEDS, mind you. When the poet uses that it is nearly always in some negative moral context – talking of evil as weeds, of weeds as faults in human character, of souls or gardens choked with weeds, and so forth.

No, I mean Shakespeare's liking for certain wild or at any rate out-of-garden plants that few others either note or celebrate. Not the word but the things, sir, that's what I mean.

Many poets tell you plenty about flowers. Mr Shakespeare does too. And unlike some poets what he tells you is usually true. When he mentions a flower you know that he has seen it often, growing. He makes you feel that he has plucked it with his own fingers and stroked it across his face. He was, after all, a country boy before he became a great poet. He knows every mark and spot and stamen of whatever he's talking about.

Contrast his flowers with John Milton's, gentle reader, and you'll see what I mean. I respect Mr Milton, of course, but I can't say I love him. He will bid you bring the rathe primrose, the tufted crow-toe and pale jessamine, the white pink and the pansy freaked with jet, the glowing violet, the musk-rose, and the well-attired woodbine, with cowslips wan that hang the pensive head, to strew the laureat hearse where Lycid lies, and all that. But apart from the fact that they couldn't all have been in flower at the same time of year, doesn't it sound rather as if he is giving poetical orders to his gardener? His epithets aren't too good, either, when you think about it. Violets don't glow. Honeysuckle is more untidy than well-attired. Madam, have you ever seen a cowslip looking pensive? As to amaranthus, I doubt if Milton ever saw one in his life. It is not so much a flower as a lovely quadrisyllable.

With Shakespeare, it is quite a different matter. He never drags in any flower just because of its name, and what he says about the look or the scent of it will always prove true. At his best in this matter, he doesn't even *describe* the flower at all; instead, he presents you with the essence of its nature. For example, Perdita in *The Winter's Tale* conjuring up daffodils and what they do in just 16 simple words, not one of which is in any way remarkable, but the whole is breath-taking:

> *golden daffodils,*
> *That come before the swallow dares, and take*
> *The winds of March with beauty.*

And then, to give one other example, camomile. He only mentions once this creeping herb. It has downy leaves and flowers that are white in the ray and yellow in the disk. But none of that's to Mr Shakespeare's purpose. I'm sure he knew exactly what camomile looked like, but like any true countryman (not to speak of true poets) he knew also that what counts about this humble plant is its perseverance, its obstinacy, its prolifical keeping-on no matter what. So he has Falstaff say, when speaking to Prince Hal in the style of his father, the King: 'Harry, I do not only marvel where thou spendest thy time, but also how thou art accompanied: for though *the camomile, the more it is trodden on, the faster it grows*, yet youth, the more it is wasted, the sooner it wears.' That seems to me, in its truth not just to nature but the heart, about the opposite of the way that flowers are used in Milton.

But it's Shakespeare's knowledge of *weeds* that I want to stress. It's something peculiar to him. It's right at the core of his spirit. It's vital to his genius, I think. No other poet I know is so curious of weeds or so familiar with them. A man might learn the names of flowers from an after-dinner stroll in his lady's garden. Weeds he learns otherwise, and bitterly, and not because he wants to, nor because there's any profit in it. Weeds a man learns from intimate acquaintance with wild places, from walking abroad in the sun and the wind and the rain, from personal experience of ploughing land, from lying in a ditch after a hard night's drinking.

Whether Shakespeare ever ploughed I would not know. But I know he knows his weeds like no one else. Take, for example, that moment when Cordelia meets mad Lear:

> *Crowned with rank fumiter and furrow-weeds,*
> *With hardokes, hemlock, nettles, cuckoo-flowers,*

> *Darnel and all the idle weeds that grow*
> *In our sustaining corn.*

(You'll find it in Act IV, the fourth scene, sir, right at the start, if memory serves me right.) Or take, again, the Duke of Burgundy in *Henry V*, bemoaning the sorry war-torn state of the French countryside, and seeing:

> *her hedges even-pleach'd,*
> *Like prisoners wildly overgrown with hair,*
> *Put forth disorder'd twigs; her fallow leas*
> *The darnel, hemlock and rank fumitory*
> *Doth root upon, while that the coulter rusts*
> *That should deracinate such savagery;*
> *The even mead, that erst brought sweetly forth*
> *The freckled cowslip, burnet, and green clover,*
> *Wanting the scythe, all uncorrected, rank,*
> *Conceives by idleness, and nothing teems*
> *But hateful docks, rough thistles, kecksies, burrs . . .*

(Yes, madam, I confess I had to look that up in my faithful Folio: Act V, Scene 2, lines 42 to 52.)

You won't find any KECKSIES in the works of Mr John Milton. They're the dry and hollow stalks of cow parsnips or wild chervil.

Pickleherring's point, sir? (How kind of you to presume I may even have one!) Pickleherring's point is that no one but a country boy could have written that. Yes, and one who had probably held a pruning hook in his hand and pleached a hedge.

Don't forget that gardener, either, who knows all about the ways of weeds and caterpillars in *King Richard II*. And (my trump card, this) there's Imogen proving the things had equal honour in our poet's mind by strewing the supposed grave of her Posthumus 'with wild wood-leaves *and weeds*'.

Pickleherring's point (and it is not just the point of this chapter, come to that) – Pickleherring's point is that the late Mr Shakespeare not only knew the names and the nick-names and the dirty names of all the things that grew in Mary Arden's garden by design. The late Mr Shakespeare knew just as much if not more about the plants and shrubs and flowers that grew unwanted there. And about whatever grows wild outside all our garden walls. In a word, WEEDS. And he knew your honest weed is not the worst thing in the world. *Lilies that fester smell far worse than weeds*, remember?

It was either my dear Jane or the playwright John Webster who once remarked that the death of a beautiful woman is unquestionably the most poetical topic in the world. I think that it was probably Mr Webster. He was much possessed by death. (In view of how things turned out, it would have been strange if it was Jane.)

Whatever, whichever, whomever, there were two deaths of females in Stratford-upon-Avon while William Shakespeare was young which, I have reason to believe, haunted him at some deep level at least until they found outlet in his work.

The first occurred, in fact, in the year he was born, so that it was only by repute that he could ever have heard of it. But the sad tale was current in Stratford for many years after, and in its horror seems just the sort of nightmare that would make Will's blood run cold.

What happened was this. In the early summer of 1564 there was a sudden outbreak of plague in Stratford. ('*Hic incepit pestis,*' scribbled Bretchgirdle in the parish register – and I don't think he was talking about the birth of baby S.) Corpses get buried hurriedly and without fuss at such times, and a young girl who was believed to be dead was buried so. But when the family vault was opened again later for the coffin of another victim, the body of the unfortunate girl was found on the floor with her shroud torn off. She had been buried alive, come to her senses in her coffin, then crawled from it and scratched vainly at the door of the vault before she perished.

It is this that Mr Shakespeare was remembering, in my opinion, when he has Juliet cry, before venturing into the tomb of her ancestors:

> *Shall I not then be stifled in the vault,*
> *To whose foul mouth no healthsome air breathes in,*
> *And there die strangled ere my Romeo comes? ...*
> *O, if I wake, shall I not be distraught,*
> *Environed with all these hideous fears?*
> *And madly play with my forefathers' joints?*
> *And pluck the mangled Tybalt from his shroud?*
> *And, in this rage, with some great kinsman's bone,*
> *As with a club, dash out my desperate brains?**

This particular nightmare vexed the boy William all his childhood time in Stratford, I suspect, and fed into his fears of the charnel house.

* *Romeo and Juliet*, Act IV, Scene 3.

The second death was the death of Katharine Hamlett. This took place in February of 1580, when Shakespeare was not quite sixteen. The girl was found drowned in the Avon, at a spot where the roots of a great willow tree dam up the current and make a deep pool in the river bed.

Katharine Hamlett's death was the subject of a coroner's inquest. The jury was inclined to believe that it was a case of suicide. The girl's family, asking for Christian burial, claimed that her death had been accidental, and that Katharine had slipped when leaning over the bank to moisten her flowers. The inquest went on for eight weeks before a verdict of accidental death was brought in. But people still talked. And Shakespeare listened.

He was always a very good listener, Mr S.

At all events, madam, you will recall what he made of this when he came to write *Hamlet*, where he has Queen Gertrude thus describe the sad death of Ophelia:

> *There is a willow grows aslant a brook,*
> *That shows his hoar leaves in the glassy stream;*
> *There with fantastic garlands did she come,*
> *Of crow-flowers, nettles, daisies, and long purples,*
> *That liberal shepherds give a grosser name,*
> *But our cold maids do dead men's fingers call them;*
> *There, on the pendent boughs her coronet weeds*
> *Clambering to hang, an envious sliver broke,*
> *When down her weedy trophies and herself*
> *Fell in the weeping brook.*

(It's in the seventh scene of Act IV, of course. By the way, 'long purples' probably refers to purple cuckoo-pint or pintle rather than purple loose-strife. I never heard of loose-strife having a grosser name, while cuckoo-pintle is so called because it looks like a little prick in a state of erection.)

The death of poor Katharine Hamlett seems to have provided Mr Shakespeare not only with that passage about the death of Ophelia, but also with much of the lugubrious conversation among the gravediggers about the right of a suicide to rest in consecrated ground. That was precisely the topic which exercised the wits and wagging tongues of Stratford for eight weeks.

Consider. Here is a poor girl probably drowned by mischance as she dips her flowers into Avon pool where Tiddington brook flows in. Up jumps vicar Heicroft (Bretchgirdle's dead) and refuses her body burial. The laymen then decide to try to fine the corpse for felony. Her family's grief is

compounded by all this debate. It's the town scandal until – with a touch of true Christian charity – the coroner elects to suppose that Katharine Hamlett never meant to drown, that her death is and must for ever remain a mystery, *'per infortium et non aliter nec allio modo ad mortem suam devenit'*, as it kindly says in his report.

This, sir, is that I mean by country history. An item in the chronicles of local gossip, madam, a tale told over the punch-bowl by a roaring fire.

Perhaps it is not so surprising that Mr Shakespeare remembered Katharine Hamlett when he came to kill off poor Ophelia. Her name would have floated back into his mind with his play's title. And a boy of fifteen could not have been indifferent to a young girl's drowning in that river that flowed right through his own mind.

What *is* surprising is the way the talk of those gravediggers in *Hamlet* echoes the words of the inquest. I have put them side by side. The resemblance is remarkable.

Only a laureate of weeds does something like that.

Chapter Thirty-Seven

The revels at Kenilworth
9th July, 1575

They're going to the revels at Kenilworth. Who's going to the revels at Kenilworth? We're going to the revels at Kenilworth. Shakespeare and son.

This is the way it was. Everywhere there was something for him but today at Kenilworth Castle there would be everything. Everywhere would be somewhere for one day. Everything would be something at Kenilworth Castle.

Everywhere on the roads there are fathers riding. And everywhere in the roads there are sons running. Fathers and sons, riding and running, they're all going to the revels at Kenilworth. We're going to the revels at Kenilworth. Who's going to the revels at Kenilworth? Shakespeare and son.

John Shakespeare wears his bailiff's butcher's best. His flat velvet cap, plum-coloured, is plumed with a great cockfeather, more bailiff than butcher. But his slashed butcher boots are made of the finest whitleather. Will, rising twelve, runs the road in his father's fat shadow. It goes like that. It goes along. He wears a laced and embroidered shirt just like his father's. His mother Mary sewed it when she was not sewing shrouds. He runs, he's elated, he runs, he's cock-a-hoop. Your merry heart goes all the day. (Your sad tires in a mile-a.) As for John Shakespeare, bold butcher Jack, on this hottest day in living memory he's sweating like a pig. Father and son in peaked doublets with scarlet silk trunk hose reaching down to their bald knees.

It's John Shakespeare who is singing as he rides. John Shakespeare has a song for each occasion. A great voice among the basses, and he always sings

in tune, even when drunk. John Shakespeare's singing now as he rides the Queen's highway. Who's going to the revels at Kenilworth? We're going to the revels at Kenilworth. Who's going to the revels at Kenilworth? Shakespeare and son.

That is his song.

As for young Willy, he runs.

Riding, a man can sing, but running no.

Will does not sing but his father's song runs in his head. We're going to the revels at Kenilworth. In Will's head, though, the song is differently sung. His feet ring on the road. Shakespeare and father.

It's far too hot for all their finery. Running, Will's nose runs, and he has to wipe it with his arm, and the snot runs down his sleeve. Riding, John Shakespeare, plump Jack, already has a firkin of best canary refining his blood.

The sun is up and the larks sing on Stinchcombe Hill.

The world is for fathers to lead and their sons to follow.

So John Shakespeare sings. Who's going? We're going! Who's going? He sings as he rides the way the gentlemen ride and he sings. At Kenilworth, to Kenilworth, in Kenilworth. This is the way, a-gallop, a-gallop, a-gallop.

And this is the way, lark, that gentlemen wait for their sons. So he has another swig and he sings in the sun as he waits. Who's going to the revels at Kenilworth? I'm going to the revels at Kenilworth! He's (hurry up) going to the revels at Kenilworth! Shakespeare and son.

Will found it best to maintain an even gait. Too fast and you stumbled, too slow and you wanted to stop. Will wanted anyway to stop but he did not for he wanted more to see the revels. The revels at Kenilworth he wanted to see more than all in the world. He wanted above all else to see the Queen's pageant at Kenilworth Castle. Will found it best to think of anything except his running feet.

He did things together with his father but they did not sing songs together. Will had his own song. He did not sing a song for each occasion. Will had one song. This is what he sang:

> *My name is Will and Will is my name.*
> *I will be Will whatever my fame.*
> *I will be Willy always the same.*

That was his song.

You could sing it without full-stops or even commas. You could make a

catch of it, or a round, or a ballad. You could change the spelling and punctuation and change the meaning.

For instance:

> *My name is? Will! An Will is my name,*
> *I will be Will. Whatever my fame,*
> *I will be, will I, always the same?*

That was amusing. But best of all he liked just to add one beat to each line to turn song into speech:

> *My name is Will and Will is my true name.*
> *I will be Will whatever my false fame.*
> *I will be always Willy, and the same.*

That last line, though, was perhaps a bit bathetic. Meaning what you said was sometimes not quite enough in poetry. You had to sound as though you meant it, which was harder. You had to get words and meaning to make the one tune.

Will's side hurt but his heart would keep him running. He always stopped singing his song if he thought that anyone could hear him singing it. Everything excited him. Anything made him blush.

My name is Will. . . .

It was a large claim, when you came to think about it. Once, before he ever came to think about it, when he was singing his song by the river, a girl had overheard him. Her name was Rose Bradley. She lived three doors away, in Henley Street. Rose stopped rolling her hoop and she said, 'That's a silly song.'

'So it is,' he said. 'That's why I sing it.'

Rose Bradley did not understand this, but from then on she called him Silly Willy. So now he waited until it was dark and sang his song only to himself under the covers at home in his bed.

Rose Bradley's father was a glover. He had a wart between his eyes. They said Rose had a wart as well but no one had seen where.

Will kept on running.

His father moved off as soon as he caught up, setting spurs to his nag. Who's going to the revels at Kenilworth then?

Will did not care for the stars, but he liked the moon.

It is ten long miles from Stratford to Kenilworth Castle. (As the upstart crow flies.) No doubt it seems further to a running boy whose father is

riding the horse. They had started out with the sunrise, and Mary clucking and fussing that the run would prove too much for her dear darling boy. To which John invoked stuff and bloody nonsense. Nothing to it, in a father's honest opinion. He'd run further than that for *his* father when he was half the age. Such trials are what start to make a man out of a mother's boy. On the way home, besides, Shakespeare senior promised that he would let young Will ride too. But on the way there, to Kenilworth, it was only right and proper that a bailiff should take precedence. A bailiff rides solo, with his son running after him like a squire.

So they're coming to the revels at Kenilworth. Who else is coming to the revels at Kenilworth? Everyone who's anyone, that's who. Everywhere there are fathers and sons and more fathers out here on the roads. (There are bachelors, even.) Not all the sons run, but not all of the fathers are bailiffs. Not all the sons read, but not all the fathers are butchers. Some journey on horse-back, on mule-back, on donkey-back, but most come in carts or on foot. Everywhere on the Queen's roads coming to Kenilworth there are runners and riders and walkers and jokers on stilts. Everywhere at the revels there are merchants and soldiers and tinkers and minstrels and girls. There are lords and there are ladies. There are priests and there are publicans. Up hill and down dale they have come. They have all come to Kenilworth.

Who does John Shakespeare recognise? Whose face does he see that he knows in that great crowd?

John Addenbrooke, Richard Barton, Gilbert Bradley, Frank Collins, John Combe, Richard Hathaway, John Horder, Richard Lane, Anthony Nash, Adrian Quiney, John Richardson, John Robinson, Hamnet Sadler, Fulke Sandells, Derek Stanford, Abraham Sturley (servant of Sir Thomas Lucy of Charlecote), Ralph Tyler, William Underhill, Thomas Whatcott, Tom Whittington the shepherd, and Victor Young.

No doubt that John Shakespeare thinks it will be good for his business to be here. In addition to the revels, it will be good to be seen in such good company. Quite apart from the Queen and the Earl of Leicester, when they should come, it is good to see customers and friends, at Kenilworth.

As for Will, he thinks nothing. He has stitch.

Never such splendour before this. Never such feasting in Warwickshire. They say that it's costing Lord Leicester one thousand pounds a day. They say this great castle has a dozen kitchens. Besides which, what you can see with your eyes, if you stop feeling sorry for yourself, and take a look. Here, eat this crackling off the hog-roast, and consider it: towers, courts, battlements, fountains, gardens. A man might go a whole lifetime and

never see the like. They say this castle encloses full seven acres *within* its walls, and that some of those walls there are twenty feet thick, so that a column of soldiers can march seven abreast a-top of them. And the Queen gave all this to her Lord Leicester. They say that the rooms inside are of ivory and gold. And they say that those rooms of great state are carried upon pillars of freestone, carved and wrought. As for that lake as wide as the eye can see, it wasn't there last week, and when the revels are done it will be gone. The Earl dammed up a river to make that lake. He's made that lake for the revels before the Queen.

All day they're watching the great revels at Kenilworth. They're at the royal revels at Kenilworth. It's the Queen's pageant they have come to see. Shakespeare and son. To see magnificence.

But where is the Queen? Will the Queen come to Kenilworth? When will the Queen be here so we can see her? How can the Queen's pageant be without the Queen?

She will be here anon. My son, have patience. She will be here in her good time, and Lord Leicester besides.

Over the party, pagan deities preside. Bacchus pours out full silver cups everywhere, every hour, here at the revels at Kenilworth, of all kinds of wine, and of ale and beer as well. They must have a lake of wine beneath the castle. Jack Shakespeare likes that. He likes to drink the wine and think the lake.

More to young William's taste, the thought of fish. Not to eat them, just to see them, just to smell them. That here, at the revels at Kenilworth, inland, and far from the sea, a man dressed gigantically as Neptune, with trident and horn, offers fresh sea-fish of every sort in the ocean – mullet, salmon, conger-eels, and oysters. Fresh herring too, and none of your pickled variety! Will was always a boy for the thought of the fish in the sea.

All day until darkfall they're watching the revels at Kenilworth. Bears dance. Bands play. Clowns tumble. Men said to be from Egypt swallow swords and snakes. But when will the Queen be coming?

Now then, when darkness falls, at least comes Jove. If great Jove comes, can the Queen be far behind? Here's the great father of the gods, a-shooting of his thunderbolts. See how each one is handed up to him for firing by his lame son Vulcan. So, Vulcan is the firemaster. But does Vulcan have to run?

People could see those fireworks some twenty miles away. The night sky was filled up with flowers of fire. At half that distance, his mother Mary stood in her garden and watched them, wondering, blessing herself and her

stars, at home in Stratford. And mildly damned the pealing cannon which woke up Joan.

But those cannon and then these trumpets were for the Queen.

She came riding on a horse as white as snow. She came riding out of the woods and the night, and down to her lake. And more trumpets sounded as the crowds parted and cheered, and Queen Elizabeth rode to her revels here at Kenilworth.

Suddenly there were fairies all round the lakeside, green and golden. Suddenly, also, witches, magicians in black. A mermaid riding on a dolphin appeared in the torchlit lake. Then another, and another, another, another, until a quire of mermaids riding on dolphins was greeting the Queen's arrival, all singing of Cynthia.

And the Queen came on through the crowds, riding down towards where he stood. Lord Leicester rode there at her side, as the fanfares sounded. But she came towards Will as she came to her revels at Kenilworth.

And now the poet Arion appeared upon a dolphin. Not all the crowd would understand this part. To Will, though, it was his own image out there in the lake. He knew about Arion, son of Cycleus, of Methymna in Lesbos. This poet, connected with the birth of tragedy through the invention of a choral kind of dithyramb, spent most of his life at the Court of Periander, but was once thrown overboard by sailors and rescued from the sea by being carried to land on the back of a dolphin who was enchanted by his music.

The thought of a poet on the back of a dolphin had pleased Will from the moment he first heard of it, he did not know why. So here, at a high point in the revels at Kenilworth, was Arion on a dolphin, harp in hand, and ready to make court to the Queen herself.

But as the Queen approached him, it all went wrong. The man on the dolphin, who had been busy among the wine-pots most of the afternoon, got his lines wrong. He stuttered his speech of welcome. He stammered. He forgot. At last, flinging his harp in the lake, he leaped to dry land. He ran to Queen Elizabeth, and tore off his mask, and he cried:

'I am none of your Arion, madam, no, no, not I, but your plain and honest servant Harry Goldingham!'

Sweet bully Bottom was conceived that minute.

It was a midsummer's night. But it was not a dream.

The Queen, on her high horse, coming nearer and nearer.

Will standing then, eyes agog, fists clenched, holding his breath, now almost a living part of the revels at Kenilworth, watching the pageant as the

Wild One, the woodwose, hair matted like Pope John the whichever's, fang-toothed, unaccommodated man and no mistake, face caked with filth, Tom o' Bedlam, all overgrown with moss and ivy, like a walking tree, meaning to abase himself before Her Majesty, comes striding from the woods, Caliban, in one hand another tree, a young oak sapling, plucked up by the roots, which he waves overhead as he comes.

'Beauty and the Beast,' mutters John Shakespeare. But he's sprawled out where he watches, and Willy's pretending to himself that he is not with him, not Shakespeare and father; *I know thee not, old man.*

The Wild Man breaks his tree as the Queen rides by. He breaks his tree in two and he casts it towards her. It is meant as a gesture of abasement, but again it comes out wrong. A half of the tree, looping through the torchlit midsummer dusk, just misses hitting the Queen's white mare across the head. Footmen rush to the horse and its rider.

'No hurt, no hurt!' quoth the Fairy Queen, an affable laughing guest on this first night of her visit to her favourite, this night of her own revels here at Kenilworth, and then – so near to Will she could almost have touched him – she leans across the neck of her horse and she touches Lord Leicester. Like one of the gypsy girls who'll go with you behind the stalls in Rother Market for a penny, the Queen of all England leans across to tickle the Earl of Leicester's chin and his cheek, and then to fondle the great pommel of his saddle, a leer on her lips.

A high point of the revels here at Kenilworth, for which he ran half the morning, and waited in the sun all afternoon. Hard to surpass a thing like that.

Even the Kenilworth doorkeeper, got up as Hercules, mercifully with no speech to say so nothing to go wrong with that, leading a bear in chains, and the bear behaving civilly, offering the keys of the castle to this Elizabeth. Even Merlin the wizard leaving his island in the lake and breaking his wand in two and on bended knee renouncing his magic art in favour of Her Highness. Even Proteus, the mutable god, already our Will's guardian, casting himself into many forms and fashions to crawl on the ground to please his sovereign lady.

Impossible to surpass that unprecedented moment in the revels here at Kenilworth when the Queen pulled off her gauntlet, embroidered with seed pearls, and with her naked fingers kittled her favourite's neck.

Impossible to surpass the way she stroked him. She played him like a fiddler playing a fiddle.

'Pretty Robin!' she said. 'Ah, my pretty Robin!'

And she laughed to herself, and moved her fingers on his pommel, up and down.

Queen Elizabeth's face was hard, as though cut out from white wood or tallow wax. If such a thing had been imaginable, Will would have sworn that the great cloud of soft red hair about her head had never grown there. He remembered the tales he had been told of how in certain prisons the jailers cut their captives' locks and sell them to be fashioned into curls to suit court ladies, and how some even said that fresh graves have been robbed when girls with long golden hair are buried. Could it be that the Queen of all England was wearing a wig?

Of course he said nothing about the matter to his father when they were riding home, John Shakespeare slumped in the saddle, relying on the nag to know the way, and Will half-asleep himself, worn out with enchantments and disenchantments, with a surfeit of delight, too warmly pleased. And he said nothing about it either to his mother when they got home, and his father fell down in a puddle, and he burst into tears. He told her, instead, the next morning, at their breakfast, of a boy he had seen riding on a dolphin, whose poem seemed to please Her Majesty.

They had been to the great revels at Kenilworth. They had seen the royal revels at Kenilworth. Their revels now, our revels now, are ended. That is the way it was. Never before had England witnessed such splendour.

But what Will remembered was the Queen doing that rude thing to Robert Dudley.

Chapter Thirty-Eight

More about Jenkins

Pompey Bum was just at the door, demanding his rent. Being dunned makes me feel quite the author. I told him I would pay him some, and, as most debtors do, promise him infinitely. But I fear the man is no playgoer, and this reference to the Epilogue to the second part of *King Henry IV* was misspent on him.

It is true that I am a shiftless little person, roving and maggoty-headed, and sometimes not much better than crazed. But it is not true what Mr Anthony Wood told Mr Aubrey – that I was ever exceedingly credulous, stuffed with fooleries and misinformations. That insufferable recluse of Postmaster's Hall does not comprehend my method. He is no amateur of country history. He does not understand me.

I pride myself somewhat on not wasting time over things which everyone knows – which you know, sir, and you know also, madam – but that I prefer rather to select the small, the forgotten, detail.

Singularities: that's what I'm after.

And I work through metaphorics, not metaphysics.

Of course, no one *knows* what Shakespeare's life was, even one who knew him as well as I did. It occurs to me today, with just half the rent paid, that every attempt to find out the truth of another man's life, and to write his Life, throws light on the person who makes the attempt, as much as on the man biographied. There, I have even invented a new verb. In the main, though, I protest I am not an inventor.

Inventories, however, are quite a different matter, and much to my liking, and here in this box I have one such which I trust will interest the reader. It was compiled by Emma Careless, wife of that Reverend Henry Heicroft already mentioned, vicar of Stratford from 1569 to 1584.

I have this feeling, do you see, that there is more to say about Jenkins – that Jenkins is peculiarly important to Mr Shakespeare's story. Where else might the poet have picked up certain tricks of his diction than from the verbal habits of a Welshman? I mean such characteristic locutions as his way of balancing two contrasting adjectives on the sea-saw of an 'and', and having both of them qualify a third word, always a noun. For example:

A beauty-waning and distressed widow.

That's from *Richard III*. And then, from *The Tempest*, some twenty years later:

To act her earthy and abhorred commands.

I contend that what we hear on these sea-saws of sense is a development of what Shakespeare heard from the lips of Thomas Jenkins in his Stratford schoolroom. He makes fun of Jenkins and his mispronunciations in *The Merry Wives of Windsor*: 'What is the focative case, William?' But if Jenkins, like Evans in that play, made fritters of English, still Shakespeare fed on those fritters, for a purpose all his own.

Pickleherring suspects that Jenkins brought a touch of Welsh wizardry to Stratford too, perhaps telling his pupils tales drawn out of a book called *The Mabinogion* which collects such myths and legends. How else explain the way that notion of the cauldron of inspiration and science survives in local gossip as representing something that bubbled in the corner of Mary Shakespeare's kitchen? Such a cauldron figures in Welsh stories about the poet Taliesin, so I have heard. Other elements from those tales seem remembered in *The Tempest*.

Alas, having promised you 'more about Jenkins', I have to confess that the 'more' which we really require – if my thesis has truth in it – is to hear how he spoke, and what young Will heard. That's where Emma Careless comes in. For some reason (probably for amusement), the vicar's wife drew up an inventory of the goods and chattels of the Welsh schoolmaster, writing it down in a manner which makes a burlesque of the sound of Jenkins' voice. It is the nearest we'll ever get to hearing what Shakespeare heard. You may judge for yourself if the poet learned anything from it.

Han Infentory of the Couds
of Thomas Jenkins ap Hughes
(B.A. 1566), Schoolmaster

Imprimis, in the *Wardrope* – One Irish rugg, 1 buff frize shirkin, 1 sheep-skin tublet, 2 Irish stocking, 2 shooe, 6 leather point (two proken).
Item, in the *Tary* – One toasting shees, 3 oaten-cake, 3 pints of cow-milk, 1 pound of cow-putter, eggs.

Item, in the *Kitchen* – One cridiron, 1 fripan, 2 white pot, 3 red herring, 9 sprat (for hur own eating).

Item, in the *Cellar* – One firkin of wiggan, 2 gallon sweet sower sider, one pint of perry, 1 little pottle of Carmarden sack, alias Metheglin, wort, and malmsey.

Item, in the *Study* (hur was almost forgot hur!) – One Welch Pible, 2 almanac, 1 Seven Champions, for St Taffy sake, 12 pallat, one pedigree, one most capricious Ovid.

Item, in the *Closet* – 2 sorrow-struck and mortal hat, one pouse, 4 napkin (one for hursulf, one for hur wife Shone, two for cusen ap Powell when was cum to hur house).

Item, in the *Yard*, under the wall – One fickle wheel, two pucket, 1 ladder, 2 frantic and forsaken rope, one mouse-trap.

Item, in the *Carden* – One ped of carlike (for to mend hur kissing), 9 honourable onion (hur eyes smell hem), 12 leek (for heating upon St Davy's Day), 12 viperous and surprising worm, 6 frog.

NB: *A Note of some Legacy of a creat deal of Coods*
bequeathed to hur Wife and hur two Shild, and
all hur Cusens, and Friends, and Kindred, in
manner as followeth:

Imprimis – Was to give to hur teer wife, *Shone Jenkins*, all the coods in the ped-room.

Item – Was to give hur eldest and digressing sun, *Plack Shack*, 40 and 12 card to play at Whipper-shinny, to sheat hur cusen.

Item – Was to give to hur second sun, little *Jenkins* ap *Jenkins*, hur short ladder under the wall in the yard, and 2 rope.

Item – Was to give to hur Cusen *Lewellin Morgan* ap *William*, whom was made hur executor, full power and puissance to pay awl hur tets, when hur can get sum money now at usance.

> *This Infentory taken Note (ferbatim) in the*
> *Presence of Emma Careless of Stratford-upon-Avon,*
> *in 1579, upon the Ten and Thirtieth of Shun.*
> *The above-named Thomas Jenkins then quit the*
> *parish.*

I say that Jenkins served William Shakespeare in the same capacity as Holofernes served the young Gargantua. He taught him his ABC backwards.

Chapter Thirty-Nine

John Shakespeare when sober

When sober, John Shakespeare taught his son the spartan vices. When a gentleman has had his arms and legs broken, he used to say, and two slow sword-thrusts through his belly, then, and not till then, he may say, 'Really, I don't feel well.'

Once when William was thirteen he fell and broke his arm when walking in the Forest of Arden. His father told him not to tell his mother because she had been looking peakish and the news might put her off her food.

Yet there was the occasional unexpected paternal gentleness in William Shakespeare's upbringing also. His father did not approve of children being wakened too abruptly, for instance, and he would wake his son by singing to him, softly at first, then getting louder and louder until he had called the boy back to the waking world.

Perhaps it was when he was sober that John Shakespeare took William to witness the Coventry plays. These mysteries were presented each Corpus Christi Day at Coventry by the trade guilds on waggons moving in procession through the streets from station to station. Father and son stood there in the street, watching one waggon after another as it rolled up, delivered its story, and then rolled away.

I think that the Coventry play which made the deepest impression upon our Shakespeare was the one acted by the Guild of Shearmen and Tailors, in which Herod of Jewry takes the leading role. Why so, sir? I will tell you why. Because in that play there is a stage direction which says that Herod is to leap off the pageant-waggon and into the crowd of spectators: 'Here Herod rages in the pageant, and in the street also.' We may well suppose that the vainglorious braggart was costumed in red cloak and red gloves and that to punctuate his anger he carried a big club stuffed with wool

(don't forget that these were shearmen). Further, we might well suppose that he employed this club to belabour all who came within his range (don't forget that these were rude mechanicals). Is it beyond supposition, then, to imagine an enthusiastic actor bearing down with all the terror of this club upon the future dramatist?

Shakespeare never forgot the scene. Among the references to it in his plays I have noted the following:

What a Herod of Jewry is this! (*Merry Wives*, II, 1, 20.)

It out-herods Herod! (*Hamlet*, III, 2, 16.)

To whom Herod of Jewry may do homage (*Antony and Cleopatra*, I, 2, 28.)

Herod of Jewry dare not look upon you

But when you are well pleased (*Ibid.*, III, 3, 3.)

Another scene in the same play that must have deeply affected the boy William is the slaughter of the children by Herod's soldiers, when the women fight with pot-ladles to repulse them. He refers to it in *Henry V: As did the wives of Jewry at Herod's bloody-hunting slaughtermen* (III, 3, 41.)

Was John Shakespeare sober when he summoned real actors to Stratford? Perhaps, madam. But we may doubt if he was sober when they left. Performances took place in the yard of one of the inns – either the Bear, or the Swan, or the Falcon. I have seen from the corporation records that it was during John Shakespeare's time as high bailiff that companies of London actors came to town for the first time – the Queen's Players, the best in the kingdom, and the Earl of Worcester's Players, not quite so good. (The first got 9 shillings from Stratford by way of reward, the second only one shilling.)

Then, in 1577, the Earl of Leicester's Players came, under the direction of Mr James Burbage, complete with anchor on his thigh and other accoutrements. Don't get me wrong, gentle reader. Old Burbage was a perfectly sufficient actor in his day, though not a patch on his son Richard. The plays were all piss and wind in those early times, of course, compared with what was to come in the Nineties, and a lot of the early players won their reputations merely from an ability to strut and shout and point their codpieces in the general direction of the audience.

Still, no doubt little Willy was impressed. He may even have thought that his dreams were coming to town. Dressed in satin and lace, the players would enter Stratford by Clopton Bridge, advancing up Bridge Street. You can be sure there was a trumpeter. (In those days there were always trumpeters.) Picture that trumpeter, then, as the boy Shakespeare must have seen him: all in scarlet embroidered with gold, wheeling his horse

about where Wood Street and Mere Street converge, whilst the drummer beside him beat his drum at the run.

The play was an anti-climax after that.

Sober or drunk, or somewhere in between, we can be sure that John Shakespeare showed the actors such courtesies as he could. And that both he and his son found their performances preferable to what otherwise passed for public entertainment in Stratford-upon-Avon – namely, the royal proclamations read and the sermons sometimes preached at the High Cross which stands at the north end of Bridge Street. (Stocks, pillory, and whipping-post are set near by so that the ears of those undergoing punishment might also be edified.)

I say that the play was an anti-climax after the drama of the procession, but that leaves out of account the fact that the least and crudest play has *words* in it, that plays indeed are made of words all through, and that language must already have been food and drink to the boy Shakespeare. Turn up the prologue to *The Taming of the Shrew* and you will see instantly how excited he would have been at the arrival of a troupe of travelling players. To read it is to be transported back to Stratford at the point where Leicester's servants must have turned his mind towards the theatre in its infancy. (Madam, I mean his infancy *and* the theatre's, for they shared a common period of nurture.) That prologue, by the by, brings us straight into the very neighbourhood where Shakespeare's mother was brought up. The characters are local men and women he knew well, and who are still remembered in Warwickshire: Marian Hacket, the fat ale-wife of Wincot, her servant Cicely, and the famous village drunkard, Christopher Sly. Sly describes himself as 'Old Sly's son of Burton Heath'. In fact, Burton Heath is Barton-on-the-Heath, the home of William's aunt Joan (one of those Lamberts I want to keep out of the story). For all I know, Peter Turf and Henry Pimpernell were real people too. They sound as if they might have been. John Naps certainly was. You'll meet him in my next chapter.

I wonder what age William Shakespeare was when bored by bombast he conceived the great idea of one day there being a play that has a man in it who simply wanders on stage with his dog, and sits down on the ground, and takes off his shoes, and scratches his feet, and starts to tell us stories about the dog and his shoes and his troubles? 'This shoe is my father,' he says. 'No, this left shoe is my father,' he says. 'No, no, this left shoe is my mother,' he says. And it's all about as far away from out-heroding Herod as anyone could imagine. Friends, no one before the late Mr Shakespeare put real true things like Launce and his dog on the stage.

Forgive an old man his whimsey. Pickleherring likes to think that WS

first entertained such dreams of the waking world with his father warm beside him in the press, perhaps at Coventry, perhaps at Stratford, but in whichever place with John Shakespeare sober.

Chapter Forty

Jack Naps of Greece:
his story

It was in the early summer of 1578 that Martin Frobisher, that great mariner, set sail on his third quest for the North-West Passage. Life must have seemed fair and full of promise for Shakespeare then, too. He was fourteen years old, and the star of the grammar school. He might well have expected to benefit by being awarded one of the scholarships which bridge-building Clopton had established for the students of his town. The gates of the University of Oxford would then have been open to Will. But now something happened which dashed such hopes on the rocks. John Shakespeare fell.

The fall of Mr John Shakespeare is no laughing matter. All the same, here are two stories his daughter told me, with a wild laugh. (She was an odd woman, Mrs Hart, but yet there is no reason to disbelieve her testimony, and there was as I've said a wild streak in all the Shakespeares.) These stories demonstrate more vividly than the fines I could otherwise cite from the municipal accounts just how addiction to strong drink brought about the father's downfall.

John Shakespeare falls asleep outside the ale-house. He's drunk and his little mate is hanging out. Two of Heicroft's choirboys come by and tie a red ribbon on it. When John Shakespeare wakes up and sees the ribbon he says to his prick: 'God knows where you've been or what you've been up to, but I'm glad you won first prize!'

Second story. John Shakespeare's drunk, as usual, and passing by Holy Trinity Church, when who should he meet but Emma Careless. Quick as a flash, he's got his John Thomas out, and he's showing it to her. 'Half-a-crown,' he says, 'if you rub this for me.' 'Rub it yourself,' says the vicar's

wife, 'for nothing.' John Shakespeare thinks this over, and concludes that it sounds reasonable. So he performs the bargain while she watches.

After these, and other misadventures, it is no wonder the butcher's business collapsed. He no longer paid his tax for the poor of the parish. 'I *am* one of the poor of the parish,' he said, and withdrew his son from school. Will would have been asked to leave anyway, when Mrs Heicroft told her husband.

All hopes of university gone, William Shakespeare had now to complete his education in the rough school of life. Some say he ran away from home, ashamed of his father, and worked for a man in Warwick who made fireworks and squibs. William Shakespeare's part was the selling of these fireworks. He was a good salesman too, quick in phrase, apt in gesture, not averse to disputation but stinkingly polite. We may imagine that he made his customers feel better than themselves with a little Ovid; doubtless that's the trick of it.

One day Will was hawking his fireworks as usual, in the market-place, on a flat stone under the town clock, which probably stood at five to eleven, it usually did, in those days, the sun spilling on the cobbles, white as salt, and quite a crowd gathered to watch him, from the bull ring, when the constable approaches. 'Are you selling?' says the constable. 'I am selling,' says William Shakespeare. 'Do you have a licence?' says the constable. William Shakespeare shows it to him. The constable barely looks at it. He flicks it back at our poet as though he's frightened it might scratch his eyes if he holds it too close. 'Those fireworks,' he declares, 'are wicked things, calculated to assist thieves in the night.' 'Fiddle de dee,' says young master William Shakespeare, pedlar.

Fiddle de dee is not the right thing to say to any officer. 'I pronounce them an abomination,' the constable shouts, putting his face down next to Shakespeare's. 'Sixpence,' says Will, 'to you, comrade.' The constable seizes him by the scruff of the neck, kicks his squibs into the gutter, and hauls him off before the magistrate.

This magistrate, whose name was Sir Thomas Lucy, will figure again in our story, so I'd better describe him. He was a silly short man who always powdered his cheeks. He's not pleased to see Shakespeare, having seen more than enough of his father (though not in the sense that Emma Careless had, of course). The beak's temper does not improve when he hears what the boy has been up to. 'Those fireworks,' he opines, 'ought not to have been invented. You are a scoundrel, sir, to be endangering life and limb by selling them in a public place. How would you feel,' he adds, 'if a

child took it into his head to play with one of them, and caught fire, and burned to death?'

Shakespeare thinks carefully. He likes riddles. He is not good at them, but he still likes them. He stands on his head to warm his wits in the corner. He hums and he haws a while, playing on his lips with his forefinger.

'Come, sir,' Lucy the magistrate thunders (or, more probably, squeaks). 'My question is clear enough, is it not? How would you feel if a child burned to death because of one of your wicked fireworks?'

'Regretful,' says Shakespeare.

'How dare you!' cries the beak.

Shakespeare supposes that he has made (and not for the first time) an incorrect response. 'Mortified,' he suggests, while the beak's face grows longer and blanker, and flakes of powder peel off with his sweat. 'My heart would cool with mortifying groans,' adds Shakespeare, placatingly, or so he trusts.

'The lad's a monster,' says the constable. 'He ought to be in jail, the dirty incinerate, and that's the long and short of it.'

'Hold hard,' protests Shakespeare. 'All I have done is sell a few squibs and dragons at a bob a nob.'

'Trmph,' troats Sir Thomas, 'then you plead guilty, do you? A month!'

Shakespeare goes green. 'Are you sending me to prison?' he enquires.

'That I am, sir,' the magistrate confirms. 'A month's worth. To mend your ways. I hope you see, by the grace of God, their error.'

'It's you that's full of error,' Will says. 'I am sound.'

'Two months!' says Thomas Lucy.

Will shuts his mouth.

In Warwick Jail young William Shakespeare associated with the rest. If he had been inclined to turn thief, he once told me, he had plenty of opportunities and offers of instruction. The separate or silent system was not then in vogue. Will worked on the tread-wheel. Most of the men who worked with him had nothing to say, the labour being arduous. But one day a new man worked with him, and this one proved different.

'Good morning,' says this stranger. 'Sir, here is my prescription for a long and happy life: Be bold, be bold, but not too bold.'

Will Shakespeare intimates by a grunt and a shake of his beardless chin that he does not understand this. The stranger marches beside him on the tread-wheel. As he marches he talks. He tells from the side of his lopsided mouth the following story:

'There was once a young lady called Lady Mary who had two brothers called Forbes and Edward. My name is Forbes. I was the elder brother!

The Lady Mary, rest her soul in paradise, for she was my very sister and never a sweeter girl pulled on a pair of stockings! Attend, sir, to my tale. Our parents had been killed in the wars, for this was in a foreign country, but the new King was kind to us children and we were rich, owning houses in the north, the south, the east, and the west also. When we grew up and came of an age to know our minds we chose to spend a little of each year in each house. Thus, in spring we went to the house in the north. In summer, we went to the house in the east. In autumn, we went to the house in the south. And in winter, sir, in winter we went to the house in the west. Each house was adequate in its season. Lady Mary and my brother Edward and I were happy to travel and pleased to have four places to stay. For when one has travelled then it is good to stay, and when one has stayed a while then it is good to travel. What a satisfactory arrangement life can be! Attend, sir. I have completed the preliminaries. The story proper begins.

'The house in the west was our favourite house,' the stranger went on. 'It stood on a blue cliff overlooking the sea. One winter, as soon as we were arrived there, we decided to hold some revels to which all the people round about could come. Lady Mary penned the invitations. My brother Edward and myself saw to it that there would be plenty to eat and drink, as well as minstrels for the dancing. The guests came, sir, and a merry evening began. Among the guests one man stood out. His name was Lord Fox. He was tall and dark, with a wit like a greengage. Nobody knew much about him. He was new to the west, they said. It was clear that he was not married, and that he took a great fancy to my sister. Well he might. He danced with her till dawn, and saved all his choicest epigrams for her ears alone. Those ears were like snowballs, sir, delicate whorls of intricacy, like sliced snowballs, or mushrooms opened for the inspection of an elf. They were surpassed only by the beauty of her navel, though I say it myself. Be that as it may, the Lady Mary, my sister, was charmed by the company of Lord Fox. She was charmed, sir, and Edward was charmed, and I, Forbes, was charmed also. We were all well charmed.'

The stranger trod the wheel in silence for a while. Then he went on. 'Lord Fox came back,' he said. 'Lord Fox came back again and again to the house on the cliff. It was a very strange thing, as my sister the Lady Mary soon noticed, but we never needed to send him an invitation. I had only to mention his name to Edward, or Edward had only to say something to me about him, and there he would be, strolling towards us across the lawns in sunlight peeling off his elegant black mittens or leaning in the doorway toying with the hilt of his sword, nodding and smiling and wishing us good day. As for my sister herself, she had only to *think* of Lord Fox, and

lo, he appeared. He dined with us, hunted with us, sailed with us in the bright bay and went with us for long walks on the shore looking for shells and starfish, which latter he likened I remember to the dropped gloves of angels. His supply of amusing remarks was endless. He seemed to have been everywhere and done most things. For all that, he remained what one of your chapbook writers would call a somewhat mysterious personage. Edward and I never quite found out from his conversation who he was or where he came from – and he avoided our questions on points like these by telling us new stories, always so interesting and extraordinary that we quite forgot he had not answered us until later, when we began to feel unsatisfied and uneasy that we knew so little about him. But our sister, the Lady Mary, did not let such matters bother her. She found Lord Fox the most enchanting person she had ever met, and she was always asking him to visit our house on the cliff.'

The stranger spat, and trod, then resumed his story.

'One evening,' he said, 'towards Christmas, when Edward and I were busy in the armour room, Lord Fox turned to my sister and remarked that it had been so pleasant all these times, visiting her here in her house, that he felt he would be delighted if she permitted him to return the compliment. He had this rather cavernous way of speaking, which Lady Mary considered perfect in a gentleman. "Why, sir," my sister said, "what do you mean?" "I mean," says Lord Fox, smoothing his black moustaches, "that you should come one day, my dear, and visit me in *my* house." "That would be most agreeable," my sister said. But when she suggested that Edward and I might accompany her, Lord Fox said quickly: "Oh no, not Forbes, splendid fellow though he is, nor Edward, though I like to think of him as my own brother. Just yourself, dear lady." "But I go everywhere with my brothers," my sister pointed out. "Just so," says sly Lord Fox. Then he's smiling his most extreme smile and my sister felt her heart begin to melt. "You should do some things on your own, my dear," he said. "You aren't a child any more, you know," he reminded her. Well, Lady Mary felt there was some truth in these remarks, but she promised nothing. "Where is your house anyway, Lord Fox?" she said. "It's called Bold House, isn't it?" (She remembered sending his invitations there, but she did not think she had ever seen the place.) "Bold House," acknowledges Lord Fox, his black eyes sparkling, "that's right, my dear." "Well," said Lady Mary, "where is Bold House?" "Oh, you can't miss it," Lord Fox assures her, waving his vague white hand gracefully in the air. "Nobody who comes to visit me ever misses it," he added. Lady Mary was puzzled. "But which direction is it from here?" she asked him. "North of the north," says

Lord Fox, "east of the east, south of the south, and west of the west." "That sounds a long way away," the Lady Mary says. "Not at all," replies Lord Fox, "in fact you'd be surprised how near it is, my darling." Well, sir, just at that moment Edward and I returned and Lord Fox said no more to my sister about visiting his house. But the next time he came, and the next, he asked her again to visit him. He always waited until they were alone before suggesting it, and he always gave the same mysteriously vile directions. Lady Mary said nothing to us, her brothers, about any of this.'

Shakespeare and his fellow prisoner worked the tread-wheel in silence for a while. Then the fellow went on.

'Christmas Day came,' he said. 'My sister found herself left on her own while Edward and I went out flying hawks that had been given to us by our aunts. She was bored and she was lonely, was the Lady Mary, and she falls to thinking about Lord Fox and his invitations. How agreeably sinister they seemed! Her cockles quivered in her marrowbone! Alas, but my sister decided then and there that she would go and visit him. She put on her best dress and hat, and she set out alone. Really, she did not expect to arrive anywhere. It seemed so hard to find a house that was north of north, east of east, south of south, and west of west. But the mystery was a challenge, so she tried. As it happened, sir, she found Bold House in no time at all. It was quite near, just as Lord Fox had said it was. Lady Mary could not understand how she had never noticed it before. It was a big house, and it had a black door. Lady Mary went up to the door and she knocked. No one answered. Lady Mary knocked again. The doorknocker was cold in her hand. There was still no answer. Lady Mary noticed that over the portal of the door some words were written. She read them. The words said: *Be bold, be bold, but not too bold.* She knocked a third time. This time, sir, the big black door swung slowly open. There was nobody there. Lady Mary thought to herself that the door could not have been properly locked or bolted, which meant that perhaps Lord Fox was at home but had not heard her knocking. So she went in. The hall was long, and as cold as a tomb. Lady Mary passed down it, along it, thorough its cold length. She drifted past the wafting tapestries. Those tapestries had a life of their own. They moved, they writhed. The carpets were like snakes. My sister glided down the twilit corridors, pale, white as salt, like a ghost with a lamp in its hand. She passed the portraits of other sisters. She sped down carpetless corridors, by bare whitewashed walls. She was in an hospital interior, its dead veins leading towards a pumped-out heart. Her slippered feet were quaint on the chilling tiles. Her toes were benumbed, her ringless fingers aching each by each. At last she came to a spiral stair. As far as she had

fallen through the house, so many levels had she now to climb. Over the spiral stair some words were written. The Lady Mary read them. The words said: *Be bold, be bold, but not too bold.* "Lord Fox?" called Lady Mary. " 'Tis I, Lady Mary. 'Tis myself, the Lady Mary. Halloo, halloo, loo, loo! Anybody home, Lord Fox?" There came no answer. Lady Mary went slowly up the stairs. Her dress was spread, so, on the ivory steps. They were long steps, alternate black and white, like the keys of a harpsichord, save that the keys of a harpsichord of course are not alternate. Well, sir, neither was that spiral ivory stair. It was arranged even as a keyboard is arranged, or even as a keyboard has been arranged since the Ruckers got to work on it. The Lady Mary climbed three octaves towards silence. Her trailing dress ascended through the dusk. Her train was a relentment, her golden hair a coruscation. There was music where she was. At the top of the stair, sir, she came to a gallery. It was roofed I think with ice, like the inside of a wolf's mouth. The gallery was like a mouth, in any measure, a wolf's mouth agape. Over the entrance, above the entrance to the gallery, some words were written. The Lady Mary read them. The words said: *Be bold, be bold, but not too bold.* "Clotpoll," thought Lady Mary, "can he really have the same idiot inscription written all over his house?" Then she called. "Lord Fox," she called, "where are you, Lord Fox?" There came no answer. The listening house stood still. My sister the Lady Mary went on through the gallery. The walls glistened with frost. Her skirts made a swishing sound. At the end of the gallery she came to another door. This door was also black. But it was very small. There were some words written on it. Lady Mary had to kneel to read them. Her spectacles slipped down her nose. Her garters twanged on her plump white thighs. The words said: *Be bold, be bold, but not too bold – lest that your heart's blood should run cold.* My sister the Lady Mary was not a person to be frightened off now that she had come so far. She turned the key in the tight lock. She opened the door. She stuck her head and shoulders into the tiny room. The tiny room was full of tubs of blood. Skeletons hung from hooks in the rafters. Skulls grinned at her from every shelf. The floor was thick with coils of human hair. Lady Mary did not scream. She shut the door. She stood up. She went to the window for air, and saw Lord Fox. He was coming towards the house across rank lawns. It had begun to snow and his figure, dressed all in black, loomed like a devil in a mist of whirling white flakes. He snowed towards my sister. He carried in his left hand a long thin sword. With his right he dragged a young girl by the hair. The girl screamed. But Lord Fox said nothing. The Lady Mary sprang back from the window. She snatched up her skirts and she ran through the gallery. She tried door after door after door after door

after door after door after door after door after door after door after door after door after door after door after door after door after door after door after door after door after door after door for a place to hide, but all were locked. She hurried down the spiral stair. She flew. She spun. She fell. She glided. Her face was the colour of mushrooms. Down the black and white, white and black stair she went, note after note after note after note. What was the tune, what was the melody of the Lady Mary's fall? It was the opening bars of that song which is called *Heart's-ease.*[*] It was the sound of a snowflake falling, the world in the evening, the witches of regret that shout "All hail!", the end of it all, minutest quickening conclusion. As Lady Mary fell the last act rose to meet her. They met. They merged. They melted. Her hair streamed. Her shadow was a gleam on gleaming ivory. She could hear Lord Fox coming. She hid herself under the staircase. Lord Fox entered the hall. Lord Fox and his victim. My sister's heart was beating like a drum. "A goitre like a bladder of lard, a goitre like a bladder of lard, bladder of lard, bladder of lard, bladder of bladder of bladder of lard," cried the heart of the Lady Mary. Her heart thought she must be caught. But Lord Fox did not see her. No, sir, yes, sir, so bent is he on his own cruel business that he does not see my sister where she lies huddled in the blue pool of her dress. He begins to drag the poor girl up the stair. The girl does not go easy. She screams. She kicks. She plunges. Begging for mercy, she catches hold of a knob at the turn of the bannisters. Lady Mary, peeping up from her hiding place, sees the girl's hand tighten. The girl wears a silver bracelet round her wrist. As Lady Mary watches, Lord Fox raises up his sword and cuts off the girl's hand. Cut. Hand and bracelet fall in my sister's lap. She hears Lord Fox going down the gallery, and the dragging sound of the girl behind him. The harpsichord of the stair was silent. My sister ran, sir, ran ran ran from Bold House, ran through the snow, and she did not stop running until she reached the safety of our house on the cliff.'

They had reached the end of their afternoon stint on the tread-wheel. Shakespeare turned to his companion. 'A most strange story,' he said. The teller turned away. He said nothing. He went to his cell.

All the rest of that day, and all night, Will thought over the story the stranger had told him. He considered it one of the best stories he had ever heard. The next morning he looked for the man in the file to the tread-wheel, to tell him so. But the man was not there.

The next day Shakespeare looked for him again. Still this particular prisoner did not appear among the others. It was a week from the day

[*] An anonymous Elizabethan air later employed by John Dowland for his setting of 'Come away, come away, death' in *Twelfth Night.*

when William Shakespeare first heard the names of Lord Fox and the Lady Mary before he encountered the storyteller once more. The man was already in position on the tread-wheel. Nobody else seemed keen to share his company, so Will found it an easy matter to go and work beside him.

'I wanted to tell you,' he said, 'how good I thought your story.'

'But I didn't finish it,' the storyteller said.

Chapter Forty-One

Jack Naps of Greece:
his story
concluded

'You mean that there is more to it?' asked William Shakespeare.
'I mean that there is more to it,' the storyteller said.
And he began to tell the more to it, as follows.

'Lord Fox,' he said, 'had been invited to dine with us on New Year's Day. My sister did not cancel that invitation because of what she now knew about him. So Lord Fox came, and was his usual self, the heart of charm, the soul of wit. Ted and I were ready to fall in with his pleasantness, just as we always had been. But the Lady Mary was not. She sat stroking spoons until after dinner, when Lord Fox turned to her with a sudden smile and said, "You are very quiet this evening, my dear." My sister did not look at him, but she answered him sidelong: "It is because of a strange dream I had at Christmas." "Dreams," said Lord Fox, "always make me wake up feeling hungry." "I do not think that you would like this one," said Lady Mary. But Lord Fox insisted that he would like it, and Ted and I said that we were curious to hear it too, so Lady Mary began telling it, and this is what she said: "I dreamt that I visited your house, Lord Fox, just as you invited me to. I set out north of north, east of east, south of south, and west of west, and in no time at all I found it: Bold House. I knocked on the door, Lord Fox, but there was no answer, so I went in, and down the long dark hall, and up the turning stair, round and round, until I came to the gallery. That gallery I went down, Lord Fox, and at the end of it I found a door. And on the door some words were written," my sister said. Lord Fox was frowning at my sister, sir, frowning, frowning, as though he would think her out of existence. "Really?" he said. "Really," said Lady Mary. "Oh, but in

my dream," she added. "Strange dream," said Lord Fox. "Tell me, dear lady," he pursued, "what did the words say?" "They said," said Lady Mary, *"Be bold, be bold, but not too bold — lest that your heart's blood should run cold."* She did not look at our guest as she said this. "But remember," she added, "that this is only a dream, and of course it is not so in your real house, Lord Fox, is it?" "It is not so," agreed Lord Fox readily. "Nor was it so," he added. "Of course not," said Lady Mary. "Well," she went on, "I opened the door of the room at the end of the gallery and looked in, Lord Fox, and there I found, all in my dream, of course, skeletons on hooks, and tubs full of blood, and subtle skulls galore. And the floor, Lord Fox, the floor was strewn with coils of human hair. But, of course, it is not so in your real house, is it?" Lord Fox bit his tobacco pipe in half. "It is not so," he muttered, "nor was it so." "Of course not," said Lady Mary. "Well," she went on, "I did not stay to look long at that room. In my strange dream, that is, Lord Fox. But looking from the window, looking from the little diamond-shaped window, leaning to look across the sill of that little window with the leaded panes in shapes of hearts and diamonds, I saw you, Lord Fox, coming through the snow across the lawns, and you had your collar up, Lord Fox, and your drawn sword in your left hand, naked naked sword, naked naked hand, your naked sword in your naked hand, those nakednesses touching, and with your right hand, also naked, you dragged a poor shrieking girl by the hair." "Angels and ministers of grace defend us!" cried out Ted. "This was the work of the night-mare," I added. "Why, Lord Fox, if any of this dark dream of my sister's were the least bit true, you would be a monster, sir, a devil in disguise." "That's right," said Lady Mary, "but it is not so, is it, Lord Fox?" Lord Fox was sweating now. His eyes went to and fro. His hands shook. He pulled on his gloves. His fingers played with each other, touching through the skin of the gloves. They were fine yellow gloves, made of kidskin.* Lord Fox opened his mouth. "It is not so," he said, his voice like dead leaves rustling together on the ground. "It is not so," he said, "nor it was not so, and God forbid it should be so." My sister ignored him. "I hid myself under the stair," she went on. "You came in, Lord Fox, and you did not see me. You came in and you did not see me there. You dragged that poor girl down the hall. She was kicking and fighting and begging you, Lord Fox, begging you most piteously to let her go. But you had no pity, Lord Fox. You started to drag her up the stair." "Enough!" cried Lord Fox. "It is not so," he cried. "Nor was it so," he cried. "And God forbid it should be so," he added. My sister ignored him. "That poor girl caught hold of the bannister to try to stop you," she

---

* My poor dead father left me a dictionary bound in the same substance.

went on, "and you struck at her hand, which had a silver bracelet about the wrist, you struck at her hand, Lord Fox, and you cut her hand off, Lord Fox, you cut her hand off. Cut. Cut." "No, no, no," cried Lord Fox, "no, no, no, no, no. It is not so, nor it was not so, and God forbid it should be so!" "Be calm, Lord Fox," said Edward, moving his hand up and down his sword-hilt. "Be calm, be calm, sir, for my sister merely tells her dream." "Her Christmas dream," said I, fingering my own good sword. "No dream," said then the Lady Mary. "No dream at all, Lord Fox," she cried, "for it is so, and it was so, and here the hand I have to show!" And my sister snatched the hand and its silver bracelet from where they lay hidden in her lap, and she threw the bloody bundle in Lord Fox's face. That devil roared with rage. He ran to the door. But we had locked the door. Then Lord Fox was at the window, clawing, clawing, but not before us. For we had known, Edward and I, known from the start, sir, that our sister Mary's dream was not a dream. We met him with our swords, sir, that wicked Lord Fox, and we fell upon him, sir, and we cut him into a hundred little pieces. And we threw the hundred pieces into the sea, where they boiled and hissed and turned the water black as pitch before they sank from sight and were seen no more.'

The stranger stopped treading on the tread-wheel. His eyes were mild as milk as he blinked in the gloom.

'That, sir,' he said, 'is the end.'

'A good story,' said Shakespeare. 'I do not know,' he added, 'which half I liked the better.'

The storyteller looked at him, then he stopped looking at him, then he went away. His work on the wheel was not done, but then he went away.

'Come back,' mouthed William Shakespeare, without speaking.

The man did not come back.

Nor did Shakespeare see him again during the remainder of his spell in Warwick Jail.

On the day of his release he asked a jailer what had happened to the fine fellow with the white hair who had worked beside him betimes on the tread-wheel, the man the other prisoners seemed to shun. Had he gone home? Had he escaped? Had he been moved to another prison?

'Not him,' said the jailer. 'That was Jack Naps the murderer.'

'Murder?' said Shakespeare.

'Didn't you hear all about it in Stratford?' the jailer said, mockingly. 'He cut up his sister with a carving knife. She'd been making the beast with two backs with a tinker from Greete moor. Just enjoying a bit of luxury, poor girl. You know how it is, some brothers are that jealous.'

'What happened to him though?' demanded Shakespeare.

'He went for a long walk,' the jailer replied.

Shakespeare asked no more questions. He had been in prison long enough to know what that meant. The walk in question is done with a hank of hempen rope about one's neck. It does not end in sights.

Chapter Forty-Two

Flute

When William Shakespeare was in Warwick Jail, to pass away the gloomy hours he took a rail out of the wooden stool belonging to his cell and, with the knife he had for cutting of his meat, he fashioned it into a flute.

The keeper, hearing music, followed the sound of the music to Shakespeare's cell. But while they were unlocking the door, the ingenious prisoner replaced the rail in the stool, so that the searchers were unable to resolve the mystery.

Nor, during the remainder of Shakespeare's residence in the jail, did they ever discover how the music had been produced. And, on his last day there, Shakespeare managed to fall on the stool so that all the rails were broken and the thing was thrown away as useless.

Thus William Shakespeare was remembered in Warwick Jail as the prisoner who had been attended by music, but it was never discovered how the music had been there for Shakespeare, or if he had made it himself.

I like this story.

Chapter Forty-Three

The speech that Shakespeare made
when he killed a calf

There are those who say that William Shakespeare never sold fireworks, and so was never in Warwick Jail with a phantom flute.

Mr John Aubrey, for instance, will have it that when Shakespeare was a boy he exercised his father's trade of butcher, but that when he killed a calf he would do it in a high style and make a speech.

Now, there is some truth in this, but like all the things that Mr Aubrey tells his friends it is spoiled by carelessness, as well as by a complete failure to give any tangible examples in proof of what he says.

It could not have been for his father, in fact, that young William ever worked as a butcher's apprentice. By the time that he had to leave the grammar school to earn his living, his father's butchery business was forspent.

It was probably to his neighbour, Thomas Giles, established as a butcher in Sheep Street, or perhaps to Ralph Cowdrey similarly established in Bridge Street, that jolly Jack Shakespeare offered his son's services. The families of Giles, Cowdrey, and Shakespeare were already linked by the skin and leather trade. And when Jack stopped butchering he didn't stop drinking with other butchers.

So when William came back from Warwick and returned home like the prodigal son, it was a neighbour's fatted calf that he had to kill. And it would have been either in Giles's butcher shop, or (at a pinch) Cowdrey's, that he made that high style speech still remembered in Stratford.

But what was that speech?

You might well ask, sir.

What did Shakespeare actually say?

That, my dear madam, is a very good question.

Mr Aubrey does not tell us.

Mr Aubrey may not know, indeed. But Mr Robert Reynolds does.

Here then, gentle reader, from Pickleherring's 43rd box, carefully copied down nearly half a century ago after Mr Shakespeare's funeral from the tear-oiled lips of a fellow mourner (Lucy Hornby, widow of the blacksmith Richard Hornby) is the speech that Shakespeare made when he killed a calf.

The bard's famous calf-killing speech, never before published.

Mrs Hornby told me she heard it twice. She had never been able to forget the boy William standing there in the sawdust, cleaver in hand, eyes rolling, apron cross-hatched and boltered with blood, nor the words that came pouring forth in a red torrent as she waited with some impatience for her joint.

This is what Shakespeare said:

> *I am the butcher takes away the calf*
> *And binds the wretch, and beats it when it strays,*
> *And bears it to the bloody slaughter-house.*
> *Hark how his dam runs lowing up and down,*
> *Looking the way her harmless young one went!*
> *She can do naught but wail her darling's loss. . . .*
> *I am the butcher,* & etc., & etc., & etc.

That is, old Mrs Hornby claimed that Shakespeare repeated what he had said. He would say the lines over and over, she insisted, rather than get on with the job in hand, and actually cut up the calf.

(I must say that I doubt this repetition. Mr Shakespeare in my experience never repeated himself. More likely that my informant was disguising her own failure to remember more.)

Some of the other customers, the widow Hornby told me, made complaints to the management. They appreciated neither the tenderness of the sentiments expressed in the verse nor the toughness of the steaks carved out by Shakespeare.

The way in which the apprentice reminded his audience just what the meat on the end of their forks really is cannot have been much good for business either. But I think it took more than a few dissatisfied customers to put an end to William Shakespeare's too brilliant career as a butcher, and to drive him forth again from the bounds of Stratford.

It took, my dears, a death, and a birth, and an earthquake.

Chapter Forty-Four

In which there is a death, and a birth,
and an earthquake

The death, first. The death was that of Shakespeare's sister Anne.

All the Annes in this book are important, and I suggest you mark them well with your red ink, sir – even those, like Lady Anne Rainsford (Michael Drayton's 'Idea') who play no real part in the story. Soon we shall be meeting Mr Shakespeare's future wife, Anne Hathaway. And a very elusive lady called Anne Whateley, who may never have existed except on a page in a book. Early and late, our poet's life was riddled with women called Anne. Sometimes I even wonder if the so-called Dark Lady of the sonnets could have been another one, although as you will see for yourselves when we come to that mystery so far there are no Annes among the suspects. As for Anne Shakespeare, Will's sister, she was important to him both in the matter and the manner of her death.

Little Anne Shakespeare was only a child when she died. Those who remembered her spoke of an angel-like creature. She was frail as she was fair, with golden hair so long that she could sit on it. Her surviving relatives referred to her always with a wistful mixture of awe and affection, as if talking about a beautiful spirit that had come briefly to visit them, and found this world intolerable, and gone back therefore to that realm of light which was its true home. For years after Anne's death they kept her tiny wicker chair in the corner of the kitchen by the stove. None of the other children would ever have presumed or dared to sit in it.

Anne Shakespeare died in the springtime of the year, as well as her own springtime. She was just seven years and six months old. Mrs Shakespeare, the bard's widow, used to say that Anne was eight, but she was not. With a creature so evanescent, it seems vital to get the one or two facts right, and I

have consulted both the register of the parish church of Holy Trinity (for her birth) and the chamberlain's accounts Council Book A in Stratford (for her death).

Here is the entry for her baptism:

'28 September, 1571, christened Anna filia magistri Shakspere.'

And here is the entry for her burial:

'April 4th, 1579, 8d paid for the bell & pall of Mr Shakspeare's dawter.'

So, you see, the poor soul never reached the age of eight.

But facts break down now, and we pass into a misty shire of pure superstition, for Mrs Shakespeare always used to repeat the versions of little Anne's death which she had heard from Mary Arden, her mother-in-law, old wives' tales that had for their moral burden the insistence that the child perished as a direct consequence of bringing hawthorn blossom across the threshold of the house on Henley Street.

There is a saying amongst country folk, many centuries old, that you must never bring the hawthorn into the house when you go gathering it to celebrate the coming of the spring, which they call going a-maying. If you cross the threshold with the may, it means a death. The hawthorn is the may, the blossom of life, but to fetch it into the house is to ask death in.

Mrs Shakespeare told me this herself, with every appearance of perfect sincerity, and I respected her. You hang hawthorn in the front porch, she said, and you hang it round the doorposts. You may even decorate your sills and windows with it, outside. But you never, never, never bring hawthorn across the threshold, and into the body of the house.

Anne Shakespeare did.

In her innocence that pretty child came running into the house on Henley Street with her arms full of blossoms, and she crowned herself Queen of the May with a fatal sprig of hawthorn.

She died a few days later, no one knew how. There was no fret or fever. She simply died.

Let us hope that Anne Shakespeare was buried deep in flowers. Larded with sweet flowers, madam, yes. With rosemary, pansies, and fennel. With columbines, daisies, and rue. Like Ophelia, she wore her rue with a difference. (And observe that there is no hawthorn in Ophelia's list of flowers.)

Anne's death doubtless provided John Shakespeare with another reason to be drunk and neglect his business, and I'm certain it left its mark on William too. He never directly referred to it, but then there was no reason why he should, not in my company. But the boy was not yet fifteen when his sister perished, and such things go in deep at any age.

I cannot think of Anne Shakespeare running innocently into the house in Henley Street with her little sprig of flowering hawthorn in her hand without the tears welling up in my eyes. I confess it, reader. To shed a few tears for the death of a girl you never knew is unquestionably the mark of some foul sentiment, but there it is. I have to live with such discomfortable things.

And here is a song for her, which song I found on a bit of yellow vellum, three centuries old, in the great public library founded at Oxford by Sir Thomas Bodley:

> *Of everykunē tre —*
> *Of everykunē tre —*
> *The hawthorne blowet suotes*
> *Of everykunē tre.*

> *My lemmon she shal be —*
> *My lemmon she shal be —*
> *The fairest of erth kinne*
> *My lemmon she shal be.*

EVERYKUNE is every kind, with the mark over the e to show us how they said it; BLOWET SUOTES is bloweth sweetest; LEMMON is leman or lover.

Nice poem.

A year after Anne's death, there was a birth in the family. I quote again from the parish register, the entry I found:

'3 May, 1580, christened, Edmund sonne to Mr John Shakespeare.'

Was there an odour of hawthorn about the new baby's cradle? Had John and Mary tried in their grief to call poor lost Anne back? This last offspring of their union, Edmund, was certainly a late child, an afterthought, six years younger than his nearest sibling, and some sixteen years younger than William, their eldest.

Here, if I give you a table of the Shakespeare children, you will discern the pattern:

Born 1564, William
1566, Gilbert
1569, Joan ('greasy', married Hart the hatter)
1571, Anne
1574, Richard
1580, Edmund

All lived to maturity, except the unfortunate Anne, though Edmund was only 28 when he died, of brandy-wine, a player, but not one of the King's Men.

We may well suppose that William, as the eldest, was required to help to care for the smaller children. Discounting the indignity felt by an adolescent pressed into such a role, perhaps this might be considered positively as his earliest training for his work as a dramatist, in that it gave him some of his insight into the warring elements not just of family life but of human nature as a whole.

But look again at my table.

And remember that William, a disappointed scholar, brimming with poetry, either with or without the brief taste of the wide world provided by his adventures as a fireworks salesman, was now back at home in a household where there was first the sudden death of a child full of promise, and then a new baby, another mouth to feed, an infant rival, with him having to work at a trade which by no stretch of the imagination can he have found congenial, while his father (who *was* a butcher) preferred to work at nothing much but the indulgence of his paternal belly by the satisfaction of his infernal thirst.

Anne's death and Edmund's birth, in the circumstances, would have been enough, I think, to make young William restless.

But then, to cap it all, there was an earthquake.

It was only a small earthquake, as befits England, as we know, but all the same the good earth moved and trembled. On the evening of Easter Wednesday, 1580, in that very month when his brother Edmund was hatched, the solid Warwickshire countryside threatened to dissolve beneath the feet of William Shakespeare.

Such things do more in the mind of a poet than they do to the world as a whole.

Of that earthquake's physical effects in Stratford-upon-Avon there is report only of chimneystacks twisted anti-clockwise, and the like. There was one fatality – a stone fell from one of the arches in the south transept of Holy Trinity Church, killing a field-mouse.

But who can say what that small earthquake did to Shakespeare?

Consider, reader.

We know, from *Romeo and Juliet*, that he never forgot it.

We know, indeed, as I pointed out in my 7th chapter, that like the Nurse in that play, he even measured the years from the date of it.

So the earthquake was plainly of some importance in his life.

How could it not be? An intimation – however slight or minor – that the

world might end, that the world *will* end, that the fabric of the earth can crack and perish, could hardly fail to make a lasting impression on anyone who suffers it. It is one thing to think (as young poets do) of identifying yourself with the force that through the green fuse drives the flower. It is quite another to feel the spear of your own being shaken by it.

There is a little wind before an earthquake.

Everyone knows that, even Pickleherring who was never in one.

There is always a little wind before an earthquake. (God knows why.)

The late Mr Shakespeare spoke more than once to me about that wind. But of the earthquake itself, the 'quake' of which he felt beneath his own feet, he said little and that little belittling, even disparaging.

He said he had been sitting by a dove-house in his mother's garden, and that the earthquake was no more than the shaking of the dove-house as the doves prepare to fly. In its homeliness, as in its precision, the image tells us much of the shock of the tremor. In all this, of course, his experience matches that which he gives to Juliet's nurse.

What else happened?

A mirror cracked from top to bottom in the hatter's shop of young William Hart, just starting to make his way in Mere Street; some copies of Lyly's *Grammar* were spilled from a shelf in the King's New School; six bricks fell down the chimney and into the men's dormitory at the poorhouse.

A small earthquake, but sufficient.

Sufficient, that is, to make William Shakespeare shake the familiar dust of Stratford from his shoes once the earth stopped shaking under them.

Chapter Forty-Five

Pickleherring's peep-hole

I've this hole in the floor of my room. I'm not complaining. I cover it with my Ovid, so no one knows. That's not the Ovid that Mr Shakespeare gave me, with his signature on the flyleaf. Just Golding's English translation, you understand.

The hole's not big, but it's big enough to see through. I have a perfect view of the bedroom below.

I like watching the whores through my peep-hole.

My greatest interest is not to watch them being fucked, but to watch them dressing. I like to see their tricks before the mirror. It's all their little secrets I want to know – the faces they turn on themselves, not the faces they make up for others. Their primping, their pricking, their painting, that's what I enjoy.

I snuff out my candle and I settle down to watch them. The hole's half-hidden by a rafter. They don't suspect a thing.

There's one girl in particular I like watching. She's the one who fetched me up the speckled egg. She has long dark hair and a little snub nose like a button. She's not beautiful at all, though her figure's good and slender. Small white bubbies, nicely rounded, very firm, like those eggs hard-boiled and warm with the shells just peeled off and a sort of dew upon them.

This dark one's my favourite. I think that she's new to the game. She's very young, and sweet. If I press my nose into the hole I can almost smell her perfume. But I don't do that much. I prefer to look.

Why I think she's new to the game is not just because she's so young. Some of these girls start very early – before they're fifteen. I'd not be surprised if this little tart is about the same age that I was when I jumped down off that wall to meet Mr Shakespeare. But, as I say, it's not only

youth that makes her seem innocent. There's this awkwardness about the way she moves. She's much more shy and tentative than the others.

When I watch her at work on her face in the glass, my favourite, you can see her trying to imagine what she does to men. She turns her head this way and that, and pulls and twists her hair across her cheeks. She throws her head back, and gives little gasps. She's showing herself what she looks like when they fuck her. Sometimes, her mouth made up, she kisses her own image in the mirror, leaving a carmine smear and a cloud of breath. She likes to flirt with the girl in the glass, hiding her eyes with a fan or with her fingers and then peeping. It's all very provocative, I can tell you; not least because she's like a little girl trying on her mother's things.

There's something that maddens my senses about this one girl. I don't know what it is, but she seems shy and gentle. She has little blue veins just over each temple. Her nostrils are like those of an animal that finds its way by scent. I'd love to press my thumbs to her eyes when they're shut tight, just to feel her heart beating and the secret thoughts that leap there. But I don't want to hurt her. I would never hurt my beauty. There's something exquisitely virginal about her, although she is a whore. Like Marina in the brothel in *Pericles*.

Last night I saw her strip off her clothes to look at herself in the mirror. She was all alone, so she thought, but old Pickleherring was watching. She looked at herself in the mirror, my little egg girl. It was plain she is in love with what she sees.

Why not? Who could blame her?

She played with her own nipples. I watched them harden. They pricked out from her bubbies like tiny pink thorns. You'd think a whore would be weary of hands on her breasts, but not this girl. She smiled at herself in the glass, and she sighed with self-enchantment.

Some whores will wear their night-rails in the street. Not my little favourite. Last night she tried gown after gown just to see what best suited her mood.

I knelt in a trance of delight, my eye pressed to the peep-hole. I saw her dress herself in silks and damasks, thin tiffanies, newfangled cobweb lawns. I watched her take each garment off again. I could hear the crisp crackle of some of them, as she put them on, as she took them off, and the soft swish of others.

Nothing satisfied her, quite, when she consulted the effect of it in her pier glass.

My favourite's final choice was a boisterous foamy farthingale. It made her look for all the world like a little mermaid coming up from the depths

of the sea. She rose up and down on the balls of her feet, though, once she'd got it on, and trotted about to listen to it rustle on the floor-boards.

She looked perfectly adorable in that.

Her dress on, my girl goes and changes her stockings. She's always a goose-brain, doing silly things like this, back-to-front things, all draggle-tail arsy-versy. But, of course, I adore her the more for such ways. And it was delicious seeing her legs with that dress rucked up.

She sat down on the side of the bed to adjust her black garters. Then, with a squeal of vexation, the vixen tore them off. I was pleased to see her go and select a white pair from her drawer. And my pleasure was complete when she stretched out each leg in turn to draw them on up her plump little thighs, smoothing her sheer silk stockings as she did so, patting and pampering the garters in place, with a thrilling little wriggle of her haunches.

Madam, you're wrong if you think I want to fuck this sweet delightful creature. Just to watch her, myself unseen, that is enough. In fact she's far too exquisite to be fucked. There is something infinitely gentle about her, and what I feel for her is the kind of tenderness and wonder one might feel for a spiderweb all sparkling with morning dew, an intricate simplicity not to be touched without destroying it.

Only, of course, this favourite young whore of mine is also infinitely more appealing to the senses than any spiderweb!

I love watching her when she doesn't know I'm there. I love watching her when she doesn't know *anyone*'s there. When she thinks she's quite alone, and so perfectly natural.

All I want is to be as close to her as possible.

I would like to be her comb.

I wish I was her dress.

Best of all, how I'd love to be my child-whore's silk stockings!

Well, reader, there you have it – the secret erotic life of Robert Tiresias Pickleherring Reynolds.

Old Mr Pickerel: his wholesome whoreson pleasures.

I never meant to put that in my book but now I have I shall not cross it out.

And having put it in, it occurs to me to observe that my watching the young whore through this peep-hole is perhaps a perfect emblem of this art of biography in which I am involved for the rest of the time. What is the biographical act but a species of spying? You participate in a life you cannot share. You take part offstage in a play that is none of your making.

Besides, it is only fair that if a biographer tells you the unpalatable and

the disagreeable things about the life of his subject (as, in the name of truth, he must), then he ought to be prepared to tell you about his own unpalatables and his own disagreeables. I make it a rule for all who follow me in this new art. Procopius and Suetonius should have done no less. When a man wants to spit at life, he should spit in his own face, first.

Watching my perfect little whore at her toilet is like writing about Mr Shakespeare. It's her private face I want to know, not the tricks that she turns for others.

I have never yet watched her being fucked, though sometimes I have listened. It sounded as if she was laughing. I stopped up my ears.

If I ever do watch while she's fucked, I'll tell you about it.

There has been, at all events, a moral outcome. Feeling good after last night's rapt observance of my darling, I stumped up this morning and paid Pompey Bum the rest of his rent. I used a guinea that was in today's box, a guinea given to Mr Shakespeare by a whore. It was Lucy Negro who gave Mr Shakespeare that guinea. Why she gave it to him I do not know. So I have no story to tell you about that guinea. I cannot tell you a tale I do not know. (Other biographers, please copy.)

Having been moral, and paid the money I owed, I had my reward not in heaven but here on earth immediately. That whore must be my good angel. A good angel in dainty white garters! Whatever she is, Pickleherring's day was made when Pompey Bum called out to the girl, addressing her by name as he passed her on the stair.

She is called Anne.

Chapter Forty-Six

About silk stockings

So you think it strange that Pickleherring wants to *be* a young whore's stockings as she's putting them on?

There have been stranger desires at the Court of Queen Venus.

King James I (of England) and VI (of Scotland) used to come off paddling naked in the entrails of just-slaughtered stags.

Veronica Juliana, a nun, beatified by Pope Pius II, always slept with a lamb, kissing it and letting it suckle on her breasts.

The philosopher Aristotle liked to be ridden by a courtesan of Athens with nothing on his person but a saddle and bridle.

Philip Massinger, the playwright, once told me that the only interesting part of a woman was her shoe. Laced boots with high black heels especially charmed him.

Guy Fawkes collected girls' handkerchiefs.

Francis Bacon, Lord Verulam, perished in the act of intercourse with a hen. He had stuffed its little love-hole full of snow.

Some of these people had excuses.

The nun, for instance, claimed that she took the lamb to bed in memory of Jesus. And Bacon's genitals were very small.

Pickleherring's excuse would be that this is the price he has to pay for all the women's parts he's had to play. He fell in love with the clothes he wore to do it.

His real name as he has told you is Nicholas Nemo. Nobody can say what Nobody is capable of.

But perhaps there was always much of a woman in my own innermost nature. And Mr Shakespeare saw that right from the start.

So he re-named me, and my name has been:

Portia	Juliet	Ophelia
Hermione	Silvia	Cordelia
Cleopatra	Jessica	Desdemona
Rosalind	Beatrice	Cressida

My many parts. So many a time I ended with an A. Why I don't know. You'd have to ask him, and I doubt if he could answer. Perhaps because A stands for Anne. And now I've an Anne of my own.

But I need no excuses. Silk stockings are very nice and sweet and voluptuous, and no justification should be required for their worship.

It was the Virgin Queen herself who set the fashion. In the second year of her reign, her silk woman, Mrs Montague, presented Elizabeth with a pair of black silk stockings for a new-year's gift. They say that wearing those silk stockings pleased the Queen so much that she sent for Mrs Montague, and asked her where she had these silk stockings from, and if she could help her to any more of the lovely things.

'I made them very carefully for your Majesty,' said the silk woman, 'and of purpose only for your Majesty. But seeing these silk stockings please you so well, I will presently set more in hand.'

'Do so,' quoth the Queen, 'for indeed I like silk stockings so well, because they are pleasant, fine, and delicate, that henceforth I will wear no other stockings.'

And from that time to her death Queen Elizabeth wore only silk stockings. No doubt she was wearing them at the time of her revels at Kenilworth. And perhaps at her earlier revels in the Forest of Arden.

(I don't always cite my sources, any more than a good cook will give you his recipes, since the craft is in the cooking not the ingredients. But in this case – just to prevent you from discrediting yourself with the suspicion that I might be making it all up to justify or aggrandise my own passion – I advise you to consult John Stow's *Chronicle*, the 1631 edition being the one I have open before me, and look at page 887.)

I confess I like silk stockings linking Queen Elizabeth and my little tart Anne. Confess it, now, all you lechers: Any woman wearing a pair of silk stockings is much more desirable than one with nothing on. I think even your most hardened modern rake – that young Earl of Rochester, say – would agree with Pickleherring in this matter.

As for me, when I was in female costume for my parts, crossing my legs or walking in silk stockings was always the sweetest of pleasures, what with the little intimate sounds your legs make, rubbing and rasping, kissing each other through the webs of silk.

And no, madam, I did not mock at women thus. On the contrary, I worshipped Woman.

With my silk stockings on, the very word WOMAN would bring my young man to attention.

Thereby hangs, as the bishop used to say, another tale. But it's not time for that yet. It's time to ponder the 'lost years' of William Shakespeare.

Chapter Forty-Seven

*How Shakespeare went to teach
in Lancashire*

In this box I have kept two extracts from a will. It is the will of a Papist gentleman of Lancashire. His name was Alexander Hoghton, Esq., of Lea, near Preston. Lea Hall was not his principal residence. That was Hoghton Tower. Mr Hoghton, who seems to have been the same age as his century, died in 1581. He was by all accounts a wealthy fellow.

He was in fact something of a provincial Maecenas, this Hoghton of Hoghton Tower, a patron of the arts, for here in his will (dated 3 August 1581, and proved one month later) we find him bequeathing his stock of play-costumes and all his musical instruments to his brother Thomas, or, if brother Thomas does not choose to keep players, to his neighbour Sir Thomas Hesketh.

There follows this sentence: 'And I most heartily require the said Sir Thomas to be friendly unto Fulke Gyllome and *William Shakeshafte now dwelling with me* and either to take them into his service or else to help them to some good master, as my trust is he will.' (Pickleherring's italics.)

Later, Hoghton names William Shakeshafte twice as among his 'servants', and bequeaths him forty shillings (Fulke Gyllome gets the same).

After that earthquake in southern England, did Shakespeare go to work in Lancashire? It is not impossible. I have heard Mr Aubrey saying that our author worked when young as a schoolmaster in the country. If Shakespeare and Shakeshafte are the same, then he went to work for Hoghton at Hoghton Tower, first perhaps as a Latin tutor to the grandchildren or great-grandchildren in that rich man's large household, then perhaps as a player in Hoghton's private company of actors.

I don't know if this is what happened, but I do know that it is arresting to

see a William Shakeshafte being mentioned in a play-acting connection as early as 1581.

I know too that John Cotton, the boy William's last teacher at the Grammar School, the one who superseded Taffy Jenkins, came originally from Tarnacre, in Lancashire, and that Tarnacre is only about ten miles away from Lea. John Cotton is also remembered in Hoghton's will.

Might this Lancastrian school-teacher have recommended his brightest ex-pupil to his old friend the master of Hoghton Tower? And might Shakespeare then have found playing rather more to his taste than tutoring?

The answer to the second question is yes.

To the other one, maybe.

Chapter Forty-Eight

*How Shakespeare went to sea
with Francis Drake*

In this box I have one remainder biscuit. It's there to provide me with tangible and tasteful evidence of another theory to account for those undocumented 'lost years' in the life of William Shakespeare.

Could he have gone to sea as a sailor with Francis Drake?

Was our Shakespeare a cabin-boy in the crew of the *Golden Hind* when she circumnavigated the globe?

Pickleherring brings to your notice, friends, the high incidence of *shipwrecks* in the plays collected in the Folio. There's one in *The Tempest*, there are two in *Pericles*. *Twelfth Night* starts off with Sebastian and Viola having been shipwrecked, and *The Comedy of Errors* starts off with a shipwreck too. Even Antonio's ships in *The Merchant of Venice* get wrecked one after another. Shakespeare, in short, was obsessed with shipwrecks, perhaps in the way that only a man who has nearly perished in one at an impressionable age might be. He also exhibits in his works a considerable knowledge of seas and storms, as well as deploying several familiar terms that sailors use when they're speaking of seas and storms or of their ships.

Above all, there's this fear in him of drowning. Remember poor Clarence's dream in *Richard III*:

> *O Lord! methought what pain it was to drown!*
> *What dreadful noise of waters in mine ears!*

You don't write like that without first-hand experience of the matter. (I should know. I once fell off a jetty at Yarmouth.) Notice there is no nonsense in Clarence about seeing your whole past life in a flash, or of

drowning being an easy way to die. Mr Shakespeare, I say, had either once nearly been drowned himself or he had listened carefully to somebody else who suffered and survived the same fate – which somebody was not me, because I kept my mouth shut.

Now then, let us consider Milford Haven.

Why does Shakespeare drag Milford Haven into *Cymbeline*? It was never a famous or mighty sea-port, Milford Haven. Yet Posthumus sails from Milford Haven on his way to Italy – rather than from Bristol or from Plymouth, either of which would be more likely. And he writes to Imogen to meet him at Milford Haven on his return.

If you look at the map, sir, you will see that Milford Haven is in fact the nearest port to Stratford. That is not to say much, I grant you, since the bard's birthplace is about bang in the heart of England, and the farthest you could get inland from the sea. But if you marched due west from Stratford, looking neither to left nor to right, with the idea of running away to sea in your young head, then Milford Haven is the port you'd reach.

My friend the player Weston loved this theory. He liked the notion of Shakespeare at sea as a cabin-boy with Drake, in buckle shoes, with a feather in his cap. He would quote in support of it the King's sea-sickened invocation of Sleep in Part 2 of *Henry IV*:

> *Wilt thou upon the high and giddy mast*
> *Seal up the ship-boy's eyes and rock his brains*
> *In cradle of the rude imperious surge,*
> *And in the visitation of the winds,*
> *Who take the ruffian billows by the top,*
> *Curling their monstrous heads, and hanging them*
> *With deaf'ning clamour in the slippery shrouds ...*

My dears, you don't write stuff like that if your only experience of sea-faring is crossing the Thames from Westminster Stairs to Southwark in a wherry. Nor do you learn the ropes – witness all that language taut with sea-knowledge in the first scene of *The Tempest* – from punting about between weirs on the River Avon.

But (and this was David Weston's clinching argument, with which with portly sails he brought his argosies of speculation home) there is one thing in Shakespeare, one remarkable thing, which makes it almost certain that

---

* The Folio has *clouds*. But I remember it as *shrouds*. Bob Benfield had the part. He always played old kings. Benfield had six teeth missing by that time, so *clouds* could possibly have come out as *shrouds*. But I think *shrouds* the ship-shape word, in context, as well as making more exacting sense.

at some point in his life he had gone not just on a voyage, and not just on a long voyage, but that he had sailed the five oceans of the world on *a very long voyage indeed*, and that thing comes, of all places, in a completely land-locked scene, back at home, in England, in the Forest of Arden, when Jaques, in the 7th scene of the second act of *As You Like It*, speaking of the fool he has met in the forest remarks that the fool's brain is '*as dry as the remainder biscuit after a voyage*'.

Search all the works of Marlowe and Chapman, madam. They are full of sea-imagery, awash with it, their pages salt-stained. They speak much and sing more of tall ships and high seas, of tides and masts and spars and sails and stars and storms and all the windy rest of it. But in neither of these writers, nor in the work of any other writer I can think of, no not even in great Homer, is there a single mention of REMAINDER BISCUIT.

Only your true Elizabethan long-distance mariner would know of the existence of such biscuits. Drake's crew was reduced to living on them at the end of their round-the-world voyage.

How on earth (and I mean this literally), how on earth could William Shakespeare have conceived that extraordinary similitude unless he had himself been on the voyage and, yes, had himself cracked his teeth on just such a biscuit as this one, after shaking the wretched weevils out of the thing?

Chapter Forty-Nine

*How Shakespeare went to work
in a lawyer's office*

There is another story (there always is). This version has Shakespeare passing his 'lost years' in a lawyer's office.

I never knew a soul that wanted to believe this story true, perhaps because lawyers are not poetical figures. But then the late Mr Shakespeare was not a poetical figure either – go and look at the bust his widow and daughters had erected to commemorate him in Trinity Church, if you should doubt me; that bust is a pretty good likeness of the man in his later years, yet fitting not at all the common notion of a poet. With pork-filled face and portly torso, and with quill in fist, it might be taken for the portrait of a lawyer. Did Shakespeare ever go to work as one?

There is no evidence to support the theory. All that it rests on, when you get down to brass tacks, is the plethora of metaphors drawn from the legal profession to be found in his plays and in his sonnets. I turned up no decrepit litigants who remembered his service when I went looking for my items of country history in Stratford-upon-Avon. Nobody spoke of young Shakespeare as a clerk in the office of any of the town's attorneys of the time – not that of Thomas Russell (his mother's kinsman), not that of William Court, not that of the principal lawyer, Henry Rogers.

Absence of *anecdota* does not quite disprove the case, though. Your finest lawyers are invisible men. Shakespeare might have slaved away, head-down at his parchments, dealing with dozens of those minor legalities which call no attention to themselves, do not disturb the world by their redress, and which then disappear from the minds of men leaving no more trace than the dust blown away from an ancient writ. He might have worked thus for some years, I say, without anyone remembering him. And,

in favour of the theory, since we must suppose that no poet could *enjoy* such labours, there is the heart-felt cry he puts in the mouth of Dick the Butcher, rebel Cade's right-hand man in *Henry VI*, Part 2: 'The first thing we do, let's kill all the lawyers!'

But, pardon me, I did not mean to bring this up. Nor do I intend to summon as witness to the crime of Shakespeare's lawyerhood each and every reference to 'quillets' and 'fee simples' and the like which we find in the plays. That Parolles, trembling and sweating under the examination of his captors, vomits up phrases from the deed-box, is not so very interesting. Nor is Hamlet's disquisition to an imaginary jury on the possibility of one of his disinterred skulls being that of a corrupt solicitor.

No, no, your worships, what I would prefer to draw to your attention is something that could never be anticipated – not a knowing reference to the law in a context where the action of a drama requires it, but a usage of legal terminology where it's not required at all. That Portia is a legalist proves nothing. That Silvia and Mrs Page are is a very different matter.

What I am driving at is the oddity of the way certain images drawn from the law keep cropping up in Shakespeare where we least expect them. I take it I do not need to quote sonnet 18? But if it is strange to find a poem in praise of a loved one's beauty suddenly prattling like any lawyer's clerk of 'leases' and 'dates', how much stranger to find Romeo (in the tomb with his heart breaking) pause above the body of Juliet to bid his lips:

> *seal with a righteous kiss*
> *A dateless bargain to engrossing Death.*

The last six words are very legal-minded. Not as persuasive or conclusive, perhaps, as REMAINDER BISCUIT. But since there is not a shred of evidence that Romeo was a lawyer then circumstantially at least those six words point back to the man who wrote them as the only other suspect who could have committed such an offence.

And there I would rest my case, were it not for NOVERINT.

This useful word derives, your honour, from the Latin. In that language it is the Third Person Plural of the perfect subjunctive tense of the verb *nescere*, to know. In English it occurs as the opening phrase of writs. Thus, *noverint universi*, 'let all men know'.

Now then, by extension this English word NOVERINT has come to be applied not just to a writ but to the man who writes it – in short, to any member of the tribe of legal scriveners.

And here I call to the stand the writer Thomas Nashe, dramatist and

satirist, and author incidentally of the greatest work in English in praise of the red herring.* For in Nashe's epistle to the *Gentlemen Students of Two Universities*, printed in 1589, he writes scornfully of 'a sort of shifting companions' who 'leave the trade of *Noverint*' in order to 'busy themselves with the endeavours of art'. Such a one, he goes on, 'will afford you whole *Hamlets* – I should say handfuls of tragical speeches'.

Does Nashe mean Shakespeare? If he does, it means of course that a version of *Hamlet* existed some years before the one we first did at the Curtain. That is not impossible. For all that Mr Shakespeare (as Heminges and Cundell remarked) never blotted a line, he often reworked his own early plays, always improving them, and I have told you how he augmented the part of Juliet just for me. If you compare the versions of those plays published in Quarto form with the final texts of the same plays as they appear in the Folio you will see how Mr Shakespeare worked over the originals even after his retirement to Stratford. What Heminges and Cundell meant, I think, was that his fair copies for the theatre were always written out in a neat and legible hand – a noverint's hand, indeed, with its straight or gothic letters. Not like Ben Jonson's scrawl.

Taken at face value, Thomas Nashe's testimony does seem to intimate that he knows of a new writer coming up who has written something called *Hamlet* and that this writer formerly had employment in a lawyer's office. In tone and temper, it's worth pointing out, Nashe's little attack has something in common with the rather more notorious libel which was to be perpetrated three years later by Robert Greene, a drunken disappointed hack who as he lay dying accused his young rival Shakespeare of being a thief and a plagiarist, 'an upstart crow'.

Greene was killed by pickle herring.

I'll be coming to that.

* *Lenten Style* (1599).

Chapter Fifty

How Shakespeare went to the wars
& sailed the seas (again?)
& took a long walk in
the Forest of Arden
& captured a castle

O R – (and sometimes I think that OR should be this book's sub-title, not that there is much should-ness* in my spirit) – *or*, some say, Shakespeare turned soldier and went to the wars in Holland, seeking reputation even in the cannon's mouth. Well, perhaps not quite its mouth, but somewhere in the vicinity of a cannon. Since every able man in England between the ages of 16 and 60 was liable for military service at that time, it is unlikely that our Willy eluded the net.

Here is Corporal Shakespeare reporting for duty, sir. He served under the Earl of Leicester, in that brigade of poets led by Sir Philip Sidney, the hero of us all. Shakespeare was not a hero. Auctors aren't. Shakespeare escaped being mentioned in dispatches. But perhaps he carried them, for Sidney does mention, as the messenger bearing home to his wife a letter from the Netherlands, a certain Will whom he calls 'the jesting player'. Shakespeare the regimental jester? Will the wag of the mess-room? Who knows? There is an authentic whiff of gunpowder to the stuff about small sieges in the history plays. It makes you think that their author knows what it's like to be under fire. Best of all, when Talbot speaks with scorn of 'Pucelle or puzzel, dolphin or dogfish' you hear the voice of an English soldier in foreign parts, mocking the natives and making himself at home by pronouncing their words as English words. The men who went to

---

* Like Claudius in *Hamlet*, I tend to think *this should is like a spendthrift sigh,/That hurts by easing.*

187

Agincourt always put a T on the end of it, and called Ypres 'Wipers'. So we can take it that Shakespeare knew his pack-drill. Unlike belligerent Ben Jonson, though, he never killed a man in single combat.

After military service, WS went off again to sea. This time he sailed in a merchant vessel called *The Tiger*, bent on making his fortune, or some of it, only to be shipwrecked off the sea-coast of Bohemia. Shaking the brine from his hair, he made his way to Italy where he rescued the young Earl of Southampton, who had been set upon by thieves while travelling on vacation from St John's College, Cambridge. The grateful boy arranged for his saviour's passage back to London after a brief idyll in France where Shakespeare met the Countess of Rousillon and picked up the ingredients for the syllabub which is *Love's Labour's Lost*. (Remind me to give you *Love's Labour's Won* when it's time for that.)

OR perhaps he never went abroad at all? Perhaps he never crossed the Channel in his life? Perhaps WS just lost his 'lost years' by getting lost himself – at home, in England, going for a long walk in the Forest of Arden, picking flowers, stealing birds' eggs, writing sonnets, climbing trees, spitting with the wind, pissing in the ditches, forgetting the way out of the woods. Lost in a green dream, he was turning into 'Shakespeare'.

He went for a long walk, if he did, like many another likely lad, under shady boughs, in dewy dells, where no doubt he came across maidens, and others who were no longer in that condition. He explored the Cotswolds, and the wilds of Gloucestershire, and the hinterland of his own heart. He hawked and he hunted. It was at this time in his life that he got to know Will Squele and Old Double the archer, drinking small beer with them in country taverns where they were served at their benches outdoors by maids in sprig muslin with holes in their stockings. Perhaps he drank with his father too, larger and more various potations, and slept all night under the crab tree with him at Bidford, intolerably intoxicated, both of them, too drunk to crawl home and face Mary Arden. The furthest he ventured from Stratford might well have been Daventry, where he perceived through the dregs of his dissipation the red nose of the innkeeper. Then he wandered on again, lost again, in the Forest of Arden again, until he met a fool, a fool in the forest, and the fool was him, and young Will found himself, a motley fool, and came sober out of the trees as WILLIAM SHAKESPEARE.

Bit neat, that.

Bit too neat for me, madam.

The truth in it would be that if nobody knows where Shakespeare lost his 'lost years' then perhaps it is because Shakespeare did not know himself where they were spent.

But Nobody does know.

I'm Nobody, Nicholas Nemo, and I know.

That's why I put 'lost years' in inverted commas.

I, nobody, Reynolds, Reynolds, good Reynaldo, your fool, your zany, your Jack Pudding, your clown, my own buffoon, I know and now I will tell you, ladies and gentlemen.

Am I not your accredited, true and original *Engelische Comedien und Tragedien sampt dem Pickelhering*?

So they say in Germany, which is I think germane.

I am he, *mein herr.*

Gnädige frau, it is Singing Simpkin at your service here. Take down your drawers and prepare for action.

In France, of course, they call me Jean Pottage.

In Italy, Maccaroni.

I am that droll whom every nation calls by the name of the dish of meat which it loves best.

So, in good round English, I am known honestly, which is without salt or mustard, as your simple Pickleherring.

Did I not tell you this at the outset – before I ever fell like Humpty Dumpty off the wall, and met our Mr Shakespeare?

I did.

And have I not at all points been concerned to explain to you, gentle reader, that what you are holding in your hands is in no known sense a work of literature?

It is, in fact, what all the king's horses and all the king's men could not put together again.

Herzchen, let there be no doubt about it.

This book consists of what my German audience used to call (in my latter hey-day) a series of *Pickelhärings-spiele.*

Me, madam?

I call it plain pickery.

So, little students of OR-atory, no need to rack your brains or stew your wits with wondering which is the true or more favoured as the probable account – land-locked Willy in Lancashire as private tutor to little Papists with a taste for amateur theatricals, or barnacle Bill the sailor all at sea and munching horrible biscuit with the (eventual) Member of Parliament for Bosinney, Cornwall.

No call for a Corporal Shakespeare either, nor even a Lance-Corporal Shakespeare (ha! ha! not among the trumpets).

Best of all, most devoutly to be wished, abolish and expunge from the

tables of your memory, ladies and gentlemen, all trivial fond records of the truly abominable thought of William Shakespeare at work as a provincial lawyer's clerk.

I, Pickleherring Pickle-Bottle, can tell you exactly where our man was and what he was doing in those 'lost years'.

I, Pick-Purse Pickleherring, *will* tell you precisely where William Shakespeare was and what he was doing in those years which were not lost at all.

There is no mystery.

Here are the facts of the matter.

He went away.

He went away to a far-away island.

There Mr Shakespeare studied certain works on magic until abjuring the mystic art he proceeded to Naples, and thence to Milan. Here he fell into the hands of brigands who, pleased by his gentle address and ready wit, made him their chief. At the head of this band, Shakespeare captured the castle of Mondragon, which became then the base for his many expeditions of plunder and looting. In his lust for treasure (or, as he called it, finance) the outlaw WS dispatched his enemies with a 'disembraining spoon'. He would gather his loot into an enormous sack, which it was his pleasure to drag behind him. This sack he called his 'bombard', presumably because of its resemblance to a primitive type of cannon.

Surrounded at last in his castle by a superior force of brigands which had crept up disguised as trees, Shakespeare made his escape in a large basket of soiled linen – leaving, alas, his bombard behind him.

Then he came home to England.

And the rest is history.

Chapter Fifty-One

Pickleherring's confession

My father left me almost nothing but debts, and my mother likewise, and my whole inheritance came to a green shirt, a pair of lugged boots, three or four pieces of crockery, and a kidskin dictionary. The Misses Muchmore volunteered to adopt me. I grew up half their son, and half their mannikin. By the time I went to London with Mr Shakespeare I was accustomed to obedience. Possessing a clear voice, an unusually sturdy constitution, and a retentive memory, I made a good actor.

So much for 'childhood memories'.

Truth to tell, I have no childhood memories. I made that up about the Misses Muchmore. They did not beat me. And I cannot even remember what the sisters looked like. The first thing I truly remember is jumping down off the wall and meeting Mr Shakespeare.

The real story is my own story, which I can't tell. It is not obviously innocent. I am like a child playing hide-and-seek, who doesn't know what he fears and wants more – to stay hidden, or to be found. Besides, what if this book where I conceal myself should be like that bridal burial box in the old story? There was a princess who played hide-and-seek on the day of her wedding. She climbed into an ornate box and shut the lid above her. By the time her bridesmaids found her and prised the lid open she had suffocated. They buried her in that box in her white wedding-gown.

I am not writing this book to say that I have nothing to say. I am writing this book to tell you all I know about the late Mr Shakespeare. I knew him well, which is also to say that I knew him well enough to know that I know nothing. There's little to know, but there is much to tell. He covered his traces as no other human being has ever done before. His best mask was his

plays. By writing them he made himself many men and no one. The play's the thing. Let the author alone.

The plays, indeed, are perfect. They manifest omniscience, omnipotence, and the loftiest of mortal intentions. They must have been written by a god. And I trust that I have told you enough about the late Mr Shakespeare for you to be sure that he was not at all like any known kind of a god. Not that I come to bury him.

My purpose is to postpone and even exorcise my own death by writing the Life of Mr Shakespeare, and by certain 'magical operations' with words to make him live again before your eyes. There is a pleasure of playing with vocabulary, also. It cannot delay the fatal issue by one minute, but one can act as if it could.

Every man writes what he is, and I am a player. I see now that not just this Life of Shakespeare but all Lives of Shakespeare will be peculiar autobiographies. The sublimity of the subject ensures empathy and the impersonality of the life-record teases speculation.

I am a player – which is to say, a man speaking words that are never his own, an actor of word-works, talking because he is on stage and it is demanded that he should talk, and because he is afraid of the dark and the silence that will fall with the final curtain. Suppose such a man eager to find an audience, even of one or two, fit though few, if only they will take him with the seriousness with which he takes his task, himself, and them. He will weave you a taut web of words whatever he is talking about, a web of authenticity, of truth, plain dealing. Such a man am I, reader, despite my player's hide, your honest plain dealer.

Imagine a writer who is unable to make one clear statement without yards of equivocation, rambling on and on in a thrasonical prose which is forever clearing its throat, making its points twice over, three times, four, only to deny their validity altogether a page or two after.

Such a fellow could make an art of beating about the bush. Yet if you accused him thus, then might he not protest – hand on heart, but with his eyes averted so that you could never be sure that he was not lying when he told you he was telling a lie – that the reason he needed to beat about the bush was because there are no birds in it? This pretence of foregoing artifice would be itself an artifice, and one far more artful than the play-making art.

I was a player once. I dealt plainly in artifice. What did I play? I played parts, sir. I was a man of parts. But what did I play as a whole? Madam, I played all and everything, as I do now: comedies and tragedies, histories, interludes, morals, pastorals, and farces. You name it, I played it. And

others we cannot name. All for your recreation, friends, as for your solace and your pleasure. Tragedy, comedy, history, pastoral, pastoral-comical, historical-pastoral, tragical-historical, tragical-comical-historical pastoral, scene individable, or poem unlimited. I'm sure you know your *Hamlet* as well as I do.

Is my writing then no more than what that prince said he was reading in his book? Words, words, words? A man is his words. But I am a player, and my words are not my own. How could they be, when I am writing the Life of the man who made me live? This book is the player's revenge. So it is not all play.

Yet I say of this writing of mine what Mr Shakespeare has his Holofernes say in criticism: 'He is too picked, too spruce, too affected, too odd, as it were, too peregrinate, as I may call it.' Peregrinate Pickleherring, that's the name for me. I draw out the thread of my verbosity finer than the staple of my argument. I have lived too long on the alms-basket of words. I am a poor old man.

When I was a player I was a man of quality. I had favour even at the hands of the Queen herself. So did Mr Shakespeare.

The distillation of Mr Shakespeare's quality as a man is to be found now in the works which he left behind him. They are more really *himself* than anything that can be recorded about the person who produced them. Perhaps I have now got to the root of the matter. A writer should be judged not by his extravagances, meannesses, intoxications, sobrieties, quarrels, loves, vagaries, constancies, shames, honours, shortcomings as a husband, lapses from being a perfect gentleman, kindnesses towards his cat, and so forth, but solely by the extent of his achievement in what he has written.

Does it matter in what position the poet sat when he began to write 'To be or not to be'?

Yet this world matters, madam. The mind of Shakespeare, when it ceased from *Hamlet* and *The Tempest*, did not forget to use reasonable means to recover his proper dues from his debtors at Stratford.

Mr Shakespeare was a play-maker, and undoubtedly a man of many parts. He put on different masks for different people. I think sometimes that he felt he had no identity of his own and could only exist by adopting the identities of others. But despite the many faces of the man some continuities emerge. He was a man obsessed – obsessed by the pen, obsessed by private terrors. Perhaps it is only in its contradictions that the real meaning of his life is to be found. But no doubt that is true of any life.

One thing is certain: This is not the end of the story.

Of the late Mr Shakespeare what I remember is the innocence withal,

the mirth, the sheer *abundance*. For (as Mr Jonson said) I loved the man, and do honour his memory, on this side idolatry, as much as any.

He was always very gentle, delicate, and polite. 'Sweet Mr Shakespeare' – several said that. And they were right, all of them. He was a sweet little rogue.

Yet sometimes he seemed a lost soul and his pintle was certainly in the back row. It was a little tiny thing that disgusted Lucy Negro to such a degree as to frustrate her into the most impolite abuse. I'll be coming to that.

He was always good company, though, and of a very ready and pleasant smooth wit. He was not like Mr Jonson. He did not live much before the public, and he did not love to take them into his confidence. He was a handsome well-shaped man. He was no great company-keeper, and would not be debauched. If invited to, he would send down a note saying he was in pain.

I remember a story my mother told me that I never heard anywhere else. It concerned a merchant who returned from the market and brought his youngest daughter a silver saucer and a transparent apple. All day long the girl spun the apple in the saucer, gazing upon it until she beheld the cities of the earth, the rivers and the seas, the flocks and the distant markets. As a child, then, I spun the world round in a silver saucer. And so do I now, with this Life of Mr Shakespeare. It spins and spins till I am frightened by the story. It is a world I cannot hope to understand. I remember at the end of the story my mother told me the girl's sisters were jealous and killed her with an axe, and took away the transparent apple and the silver saucer. When she was dead they buried her under a birch tree and a single reed grew from her grave and a shepherd made a pipe from it and the pipe played with the voice of the merchant's daughter. That's all. That is all that I remember.

I like stories to be in books, and I like books to be full of stories, but while I like the thought of a never-ending story I like books to have a middle, a beginning, and an end, though not necessarily in that order. This bit will be the middle. I daresay I should have begun with it, but it's too late now.

Chapter Fifty-Two

In which Anne Hathaway

Here is Anne Hathaway walking down Henley Street. She goes down one side, she comes up the other. She is wearing a white gown with a crimson sash of velvet, a hat of plaited straw, long fine silk gloves to her elbows, new sandals on her feet. It is when she is crossing the road outside the butcher's shop that she has suddenly to stop and step aside to let a cart go by.

When Anne tries to move again, it seems that she cannot. She stands stock-still in the middle of Henley Street. She is a handsome woman, 26 years old, well-versed in country matters, with a decent little dowry, but so far none of her suitors has asked for her hand in marriage. This might be because of her tongue, which is known to be sharp and shrewd. Besides, it is said that her hand can be had without benefit of clergy. Like Perdita, a queen of curds and cream, she is willing to use it to milk her importunate swains when their needs grow too much. Unlike Perdita, Anne Hathaway now appears to be transfixed in Henley Street.

Her flat wooden sandals seem stuck fast, in fact, in a deep heap of dung. It is summer, and the dung is thick and warm.

Miss Hathaway's father, a farmer, died last year. Her home is at Hewlands Farm, Shottery, about a mile away. There she lives, the eldest daughter, with a stepmother she detests, and her senior brother Bartholomew who is married and who brought in his wife to help him run the farm. Anne's four younger brothers also live at Hewlands, all aged between four and 13, on purpose (she often surmises) to make her life less than the joy it might otherwise be.

Miss H, in short, is in quest of a husband. At the moment, however, you might think she has a more pressing problem that requires to be solved.

Anne Hathaway seeks to ease up her right foot within her sandal where it is embedded in the dung, keeping her instep pressed against the thong of whitleather.

The sandal does not budge in its sticky bed.

Anne Hathaway shifts her weight and tries to ease up her left foot, this time pressing with her ankle against the thong at the back of the sandal.

Still no go, apparently.

The maiden now stuck in the midden is fond of these sandals. They cost her two shillings and sixpence at Evesham Fair.

Here she stands, in distress, as it seems, in the middle of the road. And the more that she struggles to pull her sandals free without removing her feet from them, the deeper those sandals are sinking in the soft, sticky dung. Flies start to buzz about her. The day is very hot.

Quite a predicament, reader, I think you'll agree.

Presumably Anne Hathaway cannot just slip out of her sandals and walk barefoot in the street. Her feet would get dirty, or they might perhaps be cut. A farmer's daughter in quest of a husband has in any case at all times to behave like a lady in public, and ladies do not go barefoot on the Queen's highway.

Should she then remove her gloves and remove her sandals and then replace her sandals on her feet?

She could, sir, yes. But a lady does not remove her gloves out of doors, no, quite so, madam.

Should she then retain her gloves and still remove her sandals and then replace her sandals on her feet?

I think not, madam, no. For if she does that then her gloves will get covered with dung, yes, indubitably, sir, and they are fine gloves, silk gloves, also purchased at Evesham Fair.

With gloves on or off, gloves retained or gloves sacrificed, we might also suppose that Anne Hathaway's predicament is compounded by knowledge that whichever course of action she should decide upon, assuming she cannot simply lift feet complete with sandals out of the dung, then she will have to stoop and bend over in Henley Street in order to accomplish it. Again, here is something a lady would prefer not to do, if she can possibly avoid it.

So, Anne Hathaway stands, Anne Hathaway is standing there, all of a dither. She flaps her hands about in the long silk gloves. She emits little mewing cries, as the flies go buzz about her, in what she trusts no doubt is a distressed manner. In fact she sounds more like a buzzard that hovers high above its prey.

What is Anne Hathaway doing? She is looking for a husband. Why should she look in a dunghill? Because it is there.

Do we know that she has not planned this? We do not. John Shakespeare's *sterquinarium*, if not exactly a trysting-place, is something of a landmark in the district. And where the dung is there the flies are found. Anne knows all such proverbs.

Besides, she has known William Shakespeare since both of them were children. But that six-year difference in their ages has not enchanted her in his eyes, or so she suspects. She has seemed to him, perhaps, too much of a bossy-boots. So it could be with some cunning that she has devised the present accident.

Here is Anne Hathaway, standing right outside the house where William Shakespeare lives, apparently vulnerable and undecided in the street, fixed in a nasty predicament which might be blamed in part upon his father, and in a posture that calls out for firm over-riding male action on the part of the son.

She is seeking to seem inadequate, frail, and clinging. She has placed herself in a position where he must sweep her off her feet.

Now a small crowd has gathered to watch her. Children laugh, and the town idiot pelts her with cherry stones.

Anne Hathaway's big blue eyes fill up very fetchingly with tears.

So along comes William Shakespeare on his white horse. It's a shuffling nag, actually, spavined, old, and with a touch of stringhalt, but it serves well enough for a young man of eighteen with no fortune.

William Shakespeare draws rein. He tries to spin his horse, but the creature's not having that. Mr Shakespeare dismounts with a leap, after standing bolt-upright in his stirrups. He tethers his steed to a tree, though there's probably no need since the creature falls asleep as soon as it stops.

William Shakespeare approaches Anne Hathaway where she stands in distress.

William Shakespeare plucks off his bonnet and bows as he comes to the lady.

With a courteous 'By your leave', William Shakespeare gallantly lifts Anne Hathaway up and out of her stuck sandals.

He carries her in his strong arms to the pavement just outside his father's shop.

Then he sets her down very gently in a patch of grassy shadow. Anne wriggles her pretty little toes in the grass as she stands there barefoot. Shakespeare's eyes observe the gesture. Anne gives him a smile of thanks. He bows again, low.

Then young Mr Shakespeare strides back to the middle of Henley Street, holding up his left hand modestly to acknowledge the applause of the spectators, and he tugs Miss Hathaway's wooden sandals out of the dung.

Even the town idiot cheers.

In fact, he cheers loudest.

Now this, as I have already intimated, was not of course the first meeting of William Shakespeare and Anne Hathaway. But it was certainly the first time William lifted Anne up and carried her in his arms.

By Christmas of that year the pair were married. The licence was applied for at the end of November. It was a special licence, since there was now some haste. Their first child, their daughter Susanna, was born the following May.

I must have been conceived about the same time as Susanna Shakespeare. I doubt, however, if the circumstances were anything like the same. My father made love to my mother in a confession-box.

We may suppose, I trust, that Mr Shakespeare gave his Miss Hathaway a green gown. That is to say, the lovers slipped out from a dance into the night, and by the time they returned to the dance the back of Anne's dancing dress was stained with tell-tale green grass. I like these rural euphemisms. The world would be a more brutal and a less poetic place without them. You can find a use of this 'green-gown' phrase, in the explicit sense of 'giving a girl a green-gown', somewhere in the works of the poet and parson Robert Herrick, but I'm not able to recall the poem by name. Herrick, I think, is one of the few decent and authentic modern poets. Mr Shakespeare might have liked him, had he lived long enough to read him.

I have in my possession one stanza of a very early poem which Mr Shakespeare wrote about Anne Hathaway. That poem was remembered for me, in conversation, by his sister, Mrs Joan Hart. The stanza runs like this:

> *Thou knowest, my heart, Anne Hathaway!*
> *She hath a way,*
> *Anne Hathaway,*
> *To make thee smart, Anne Hathaway!*

Mr Shakespeare's sister was in her older years when she recited this for me from memory, but we can assume that her powers of recollection were undiminished. If the tone of the poem is indicative of mixed feelings then the cause will be made clear enough in later chapters. While I have some reason to believe that Mr Shakespeare loved his wife, I also have every

reason to suspect that he sometimes regretted his marriage, seeing it as not so much a love-match as a wedlock forced upon him because he had got Anne with child. Possibly there were moments when he felt that Anne had 'caught' him, and the story which he told me about her misadventure with her sandals in Henley Street was emblematic of his feeling this. Certainly there is nothing of the conventional love-song about the verses remembered by Mrs Hart, and plenty of suspicion concerning Anne's charming 'way' evident in his punning on her surname.

Mrs Hart told me that there were further stanzas in which her brother addressed his own mind and eyes and other parts accordingly. Alas, these (she said) were gone beyond recall. Judging from the manner in which the quoted stanza works by internal rhyme to make Shakespeare's *heart* to *smart*, we can well suppose that Anne had a way to make his *mind* either *blind* or *kind*, and his *eyes* perhaps *wise*. The way she had to please his other parts might be readily inferred, but we cannot deduce by rhyme what that condition was in which she left them. The refrain would have been the same, in any case.

Mrs Hart also said that her brother told her that Anne Hathaway had fleas in her drawers. I confess I do not know what this means. A country saying, perhaps, like that 'green gowns'? There were no fleas present in the pair of Mrs Shakespeare's drawers which I once had the pleasure of inspecting, as you will in due course hear.

Shakespeare did not marry his Anne in Stratford. The ceremony took place in one of the neighbouring villages, but which one I don't know. Despite strenuous searches, I have been unable to turn up the record. Mrs Shakespeare made clear to me more than once that she did not want to speak about the matter. His sister replied, in answer to a direct question of mine, that it was *not* Temple Grafton – the significance of which will be made apparent in my next chapter, where Anne Whateley will be considered as rival bride.

In this box I have kept one other piece of verse which is something of a mystery. I shall insert it here although there is no reason for supposing that it really belongs here. Indeed, it may not belong at all in my Life of William Shakespeare.

I include it because I feel it to be of some interest, all the same. I found the verses tucked between the pages of a prayer book in Trinity Church. (It was in the middle of the marriage service, perhaps that's what struck me.) The scrap of thin white paper had been neatly folded and refolded into a tiny square. The handwriting is not Mr Shakespeare's, but I do not know whose it is. Some say that there was a second butcher's boy in Stratford, at

the same time as Shakespeare, who also made poetical speeches over the slaughtered calves. Perhaps this little piece of versification is his work. That other butcher's boy died young, so I heard tell, but they are fools who claim that if he had gone on, and run away to London, then he would have turned out to be another William Shakespeare, or even greater.

Shakespeare's sister, when I showed her these verses, insisted that she knew nothing about them. However, when I pressed gently, she did confirm that the subject of the lines would almost certainly have been that Emma Careless already noticed in this book as being the lively wife of John Heicroft, the vicar, the object of some unwelcome attention on the part of Shakespeare's father, and the recorder of the speech-ways of the schoolmaster Jenkins.

Here are the verses:

> *Careless by name, and Careless by nature,*
> *Careless of fame, and Careless of feature;*
> *Careless of love, and Careless of hate,*
> *Careless if crooked, and Careless if straight;*
> *Careless at table, and Careless in bed,*
> *Careless if maiden, and Careless if wed——*
> *Were you Careful for once to return me my love*
> *I'd care not that Careless to others you'd prove;*
> *I then should be Careless how Careless you were,*
> *And the more Careless you, still the less I should care.*

I suppose it is just possible that the lines are by the first butcher's boy, but I doubt it. Emma Careless, incidentally, was a native of Stratford, who married the Reverend Heicroft two years after his arrival in succession to Bretchgirdle. Five children were born to the Heicrofts while they were in Stratford, though three of them died in their cradles, whether due to Emma's carelessness or to some other cause I know not. Heicroft is recorded as having preached special sermons for Lent in 1583 and it was on Trinity Sunday of that year – a red-letter day in the calendar of Trinity Church – that he baptised Shakespeare's daughter, Susanna. A year later he moved with Emma to the richer living of Rowington, some ten miles away as the upstart crow might fly.

Chapter Fifty-Three

Shakespeare's other Anne

But what of William Shakespeare's other Anne?

In the episcopal register of the Bishop of Worcester, John Whitgift, under the date of 27th November, 1582, is the following record of a grant of a licence for marriage:

> *'Item eodem die similis emanavit licencia inter Willelmum Shaxpere et Annam Whateley de Temple Grafton.'*

Yet one day later the same source lists 'William Shagspere and Anne Hathwey of Stratford' as being able, since sureties have been provided, to marry with only one reading of the banns instead of the usual three. Since these sureties amounted to the not inconsiderable sum of £40, it is quite obvious that the couple were in very great haste to marry. Since they were provided by two farmers, John Richardson and Fulke Sandells, who had been friends of the bride's late father, it is equally obvious that the Hathaway clan was pressing for William to make an honest woman of the pregnant Anne.

But are Anne Whateley and Anne Hathaway the same woman? And if they are, and the bishop's clerk simply made a slip of the pen when he wrote down 'Whateley' for 'Hathaway', why did he say on one day that the bride resided at Temple Grafton, only to say on the next day that she came from Stratford like the groom?

My friend the player Weston believed in Anne Whateley. He said she was the true love of Shakespeare's life. She was a nun (said David), a sister of the Order of St Clare, beautiful, witty, and chaste. She lived at Temple Grafton, in seclusion, and young Will lost his heart to her when he came to

do odd jobs in the convent garden. Sister Anne returned his love, but because of her vow of chastity had to deny him what Dr Donne (in his Jack Donne days) once called 'the right true end of love'. Shakespeare was thinking of this woman when he wrote that line in his poem *A Lover's Complaint: My parts had pow'r to charm a sacred nun.* He also celebrated their 'married chastity' in *The Phoenix and the Turtle.* But he was eighteen years old, in the full grip of the force that through the green fuse drives the flower, and when Anne Hathaway offered him what Anne Whateley withheld, why, Will went for it. Miss Hathaway's farmer friends then escorted him to the altar, at the double, as soon as the lass proved pregnant. But Will's heart belonged to Whateley.

This is romantic stuff. I cannot wear it.

Apart from that name and address in the register, there is not a shred of evidence that any Anne Whateley ever existed, let alone in the unlikely guise of a beautiful nun.

Yet nor can I believe in a mere slip of the pen on the part of an episcopal noverint.

I suggest that 'Anne Whateley' came just for an instant into this world, like that, in inverted commas. In short, that she was an alternative Anne, a sweet fiction conjured up by the young Shakespeare's imagination as he stood there, no doubt frantic with mixed feelings, giving details of his Intended to the clerk with the quill and the book. For a moment, in his fancy, it was not the Anne he had wronged that he would have to marry, but another Anne, an Idea or Ideal of Anne, the Anne of all Annes he would choose in a perfect world.

There is an old English word WHATE, meaning fortune, fate, or destiny. I think that in a desperate moment of inspiration, confused before the clerk, Shakespeare reached into his heart and came out with the name of that Anne who would have been his choice, his fate, his destiny. She was no more than a sweet breath of hawthorn across the early hedges, but he had glimpsed her, and seen the way other flowers sprang up whitely where she went. And because this uncreated woman was so real to him, so he blurted out a name for her, and she entered the bishop's records. The ghost Anne Whateley, Shakespeare's other Anne.

But why Temple Grafton? I confess I can find no reason – save that it's a very pretty village, with an abundance of hawthorn in May, some seven miles west of Stratford, on the north bank of the Avon, and that there's a green hill there where you can readily imagine the young Shakespeare standing, since it affords a magnificent prospect to the south out over the Cotswolds. On a clear day you can see as far as Cheltenham.

The day I climbed it I heard a voice singing. It was someone in the distance, whether a man or a woman I could not tell, but the words by some freak of the landskip came clearly upon me:

> *On yonder hill there stands a creature*
> *Who she is I do not know*
> *I'll go court her for her beauty*
> *She must answer Yes or No*
> *O No John, No John, No John No.*

Last night I watched my whore-child sipping chocolate through a straw. This is the very latest beverage, which some call the Indian Nectar. It is made from the seeds of a tree that grows in Mexico. I know what was being consumed downstairs must have been this Mexican *chocolatl*. A man like Sir Walter Ralegh brought in my Anne a dish of it on a silver tray.

I watched her drink that chocolate. Then she brushed her long hair. She brushed it hard, till it glowed black as jet in the candlelight.

Then my little madam removed very carefully all the strands of her hair adhering to the comb, and held them out at arm's length with fickle fingers, dropping them one by one to flare up and blaze in the candleflame. She laughed the while, and sat licking her lips flecked with chocolate.

For some reason I cannot explain, this weird barber-work sent quicksilver running through my ancient veins. I had not thought I could be so enraptured.

I only put down my boot over the peep-hole when Sir Walter started removing his buckram breeches.

Then I read a page of Ovid and soon fell fast asleep. I don't think I have had a better night's sleep since Jane was killed.

Chapter Fifty-Four

Pickleherring's nine muses

I n these great decadent days that are upon us, they are allowing women to
act upon the stage. The first was Mrs Margaret Hughes, Prince Rupert's
mistress. She took the part of Desdemona. If she was any good, I do not
know. I did not go. I said I was in pain.

In my day women's parts were of course played always by boys. Some
moderns affect to believe that this must have taken from the excellence of
the performance. But permit me to assure you to the contrary that it added
much to it. Even if it had not, this was the way it *was*, and Mr Shakespeare
wrote those parts for boys to play. Would you hear a tune for the flute
performed on the sackbut? It will sound different. The music will not be the
same.

The restriction (if you want to call it that) was one, in any case, that our
playwright accepted, and he made the best of it in all kinds of ways. You
might even say that the fact that Shakespeare knew that it would be a boy
who would be playing the parts he wrote for a woman brought things out
of his imagination that might otherwise never have seen the light of day. It
was an inspiring constraint. It enabled him to enact the confusions in his
own heart. Besides which, the prevalence of boy actors was in my view no
drawback to the stage in general. Nearly all boys can act, and some boys
can act extremely well. There are few men and women who can act at all.

It pertains to quite a different order of seriousness to admit that the
playing of women's parts by boys may have limited not Mr Shakespeare's
art as a whole but the shape of the parts themselves. His women are kept
within a range of thought and feeling likely to be understood by boys. This
probably accounts for their pure animal spirits. There is no trace of the idle
woman in her megrims in any Shakespeare play. But then both men and

women alike in his work are alive. They never forget that they are animals. They never let anyone else forget that they are also divine.

In Mr Shakespeare's comedies, the women dominate. In his tragedies, they do not. Forget Ophelia and Desdemona – they are helpless victims. What catches and enflames our author's imagination, usually, is a young woman of a different kind – one who by her wit and energy manages to control events in the world around her. A bright young woman. A woman with spunk in her. He had a model for such a woman at home in Anne Hathaway. He had another to hand in the person of picklesome me.

'Acting a part' – that's the thing of it. At the heart of Mr Shakespeare's comedies there is frequently a female character who is acting a part, whether disguising herself as a boy or pretending in some more subtle fashion to be something or someone she is not. (And here I am, sir, doing it all again.)

Believe me, it is not difficult for a boy to play the part of a woman in comedy, especially when like Rosalind, Portia, Viola, and Imogen he takes the part of a girl pretending to be a boy. Nor does the unsexed Lady Macbeth present many more difficulties. But it gets a bit harder when it comes to the tragic parts of Juliet, and Desdemona, and above all Cleopatra.

Mr Shakespeare helped me by not making the love passages get ridiculous. There is no passionate kissing in his plays. Better yet, have you ever noticed how his lovers use words to hold each other at arm's length? Rosalind and Orlando are like a pair of fencers. The same could go for Beatrice and Benedick, and Kate and Petruchio. This device, which works well in comedy, he had to abandon when disposing his tragic lovers. He then found different solutions in different plays. Othello has wooed and married Desdemona before the play begins, and is most intimate with her when he kills her. Cleopatra and Antony are never left alone together, so that unlike the holy priests the audience never sees the queen when she is riggish. In the most passionate scene of *Romeo and Juliet* the lovers are kept apart by the height of Juliet's balcony.

When lovers come together on stage in Shakespeare it is always to die, and not just to make love. Thus he avoided a certain ludicrousness inherent in such situations, given that the woman on stage is really a boy. You might laugh at two same-sex lovers, but not if there's death in their caress. All the same, when the boy playing the woman has to be the active partner there can be a little trouble, as in that moment when Cleopatra takes Antony in her arms and kisses him, perhaps the most difficult scene in all Shakespeare for a boy to play. (I always found it so.)

Talking of Cleopatra, Mr Shakespeare even has her remind the audience of the fact that she is being played by a boy, when in Act V, Scene 2, imagining possible indignities, she says:

> *I shall see*
> *Some squeaking Cleopatra boy my greatness*
> *I' the posture of a whore.*

This was a daring remark, when you come to think about it, in that it was tempting the audience to laugh at me. And thereby hangs a tale. For although Cleopatra was perhaps in theory the greatest part that Mr Shakespeare wrote for me, by the time I came to play it my voice was going. The top of my performance had been Rosalind. I had now begun to croak like any raven. When I first read those lines he was making me say, I protested. Mr S would not have it. 'If *you* say it then they will not,' was all he said, meaning that my self-criticism would disarm our audience. He was right. All the same, I *did* squeak and croak a bit as Cleopatra, and the play was never the success he knew it should have been.

I don't know if it proved a success for Prince Rupert's sackbut. Had she asked my advice I would have told her (or any woman) to begin her study of how to play a woman's part in Shakespeare by first of all imagining herself a boy. It is a perverse paradox, no doubt, madam. And yet I do assure you that it holds a truth.

There are nine Muses, but don't ask me to name them. I forgot all things like that long, long ago. But there are also nine great woman's parts in Shakespeare, female roles which correspond in some degree to the nine Muses, only because they are women not immortals they are more interesting. Those parts are these: Cleopatra, Desdemona, Juliet, Lady Macbeth, Ophelia, Portia, Beatrice, Viola, and Rosalind. (I leave out Cressida because that's actually a smaller part than everyone seems to remember, and I never cared for that scene in which she has to kiss the Greek generals in turn.) I played all those parts for Mr Shakespeare. O yes, I, Pickleherring, was his nine muses.

Let me try now to recall for you a few of the details I put into them – in common with my method throughout this book, the sort of things you will never learn anywhere else. I wore, of course, different wigs for the different women. Ophelia had hair like barley; Desdemona was gold; Beatrice was auburn; Viola was dark; Rosalind had red hair – but then I used the same wig for Lady Macbeth, with the late Mr Shakespeare's approval, he liked little tricks like that.

As Rosalind, I used not just to strut, but to jump about. I played her as not so much a character as the characterisation of a mood, an exquisite poetic 'essence'. Impetuous starts and headlong darts, provocative pouts and charming – well, I almost said 'shouts' for the sake of the rhyme, but I don't think I ever shouted in the part of Rosalind, nor in any other part save Ariel. (By the time of *The Tempest* I was too antique and venerable for women's roles, being 28 years old when we did it first at court.) So let us say that I spoke the part of Rosalind in much the same voice that Lear approves in his dead Cordelia when he remarks: *Her voice was ever soft,/ Gentle, and low – an excellent thing in woman.* It made a good contradiction: soft voice and boyish gestures. That proved much to our author's liking.

I think that's what he liked in me from the start, my voice. For the voice I employed for Rosalind was really my own voice. Once I asked Mr Shakespeare what it was he liked in me that day when I first met him. 'Your boots,' he said. But when I frowned and pouted (as I daresay I did) he said that my thought that day had been sweet-voiced and quick as a singing bird's. That pleased me very much. That he thought that I thought.

Anyway, I remember that I could always enchant him, on stage or off, with that simple phrase of Rosalind's to Celia, after she has got rid of Orlando: 'O coz, coz, coz, my pretty little coz.' I could make that sound soft and intimate and sleepy, like the murmur of a ring-dove.

What did Mr Shakespeare teach me as an actor? He taught me principles of grace and sweetness. He taught me to say my lines and to listen with my eyes as well as my ears when I was on stage while others were saying their lines. He instructed me not to knock over the furniture or trip in my gowns. (I had in those far-off days a waist that suited a stomacher, and I had sufficient agility to manage the Elizabethan farthingale, more cumbrous than girls' skirts you see today.) He encouraged me to be myself, whoever and whatever that might be. He gave me lessons in expressing the infancy of knowledge, in which he said I had to learn to read with the eye of a bird, and to speak with the tongue of a bee, and to understand with the heart of a child. These were not easy lessons, but I was a willing pupil. Give me leave to wonder if Mrs Hughes went to school like this.

Mr Shakespeare, my master, did not care for mannish women. Boyish ones, yes, they were a different matter. Bold ones, sharp-tongued ones, disarming ones: they were to his liking. Slim ones, and fashionable. I cut a fashionable figure, let me tell you, when I was playing any of those girl-into-boy-into-girl transformations of which he was so fond. He liked to get me out of my dress and into doublet, cloak, and trunk-hose – and then back

again, once I'd strutted my stuff for a bit. All this cross-dressing suited some secret theatre he kept in his head, where all his plays came from.

I think that Mr Shakespeare wanted me not just to be a heroine who put on masculine apparel, but one whose speech had always a slightly ambiguous, indefinably hermaphroditical cast. Not that I was an in-between, you understand. He did not want that. He could never abide (nor I) a masculine whore. He wanted me to be first the boy playing the woman, then the woman being the girl, then the girl playing the boy, then the boy turning back into the woman, then at last the woman coming out of the play to be a boy again. The differences and the extremes, that's what he liked. And I think he liked nothing better than the thought of the male phallus under the petticoats. Unless it was the fact of the male phallus under the petticoats.

Chapter Fifty-Five

In which John Shakespeare plays Shylock

Here is John Shakespeare busy taking his ease in a tavern. Except he is not. He is drunk, but he's busy at work. See that orange tawny bonnet on his head? It's a sign, a badge of office, a wink to the wise. The men who drink with him know by this what they're dealing with. His eyes are shrewd above that Cain-coloured beard. His greedy grin.

Say John Shakespeare's bonnet was not orange tawny, what colour would it be?

Your straw colour. Your purple in grain. Your french crown colour. Or your perfect yellow.

Those be the colours the clients of John Shakespeare would recognise. Consult Bacon's *Of Usurie*, if you doubt me. That chicken-stuffing essayist knew his groats when it came down to the low trade of lending at high interest.

I don't want to make too much of this, believe me, dear reader. I met John Shakespeare once and did not dislike him, despite the way he stood next to me pissing in the jakes and kept clucking his tongue. But the fact remains that the man did rank bad business as a usurer. No doubt butchery is too much like hard work when you're well-oiled, and the glover's scissors and compasses require too steady a hand. Hence the orange tawny bonnet, and the big bag of gold coins under the perfect yellow cloak. If you sit in the tavern all day, then why not let your money work for you?

It was somewhat of an open secret in Stratford, but I found no one who was prepared even many years later to talk much about it. At the time when Shakespeare's father practised his money-lending, all forms of such activity were illegal.

So severe a view of the crime was taken by the government that

informers were rewarded by a grant of a half-share of the penalties imposed upon offenders. Thus, John Shakespeare faced at least two prosecutions before the Exchequer which I have turned up.

In the first, one Anthony Harrison of Evesham, Worcestershire, accuses John Shakespeare of having lent out the sum of £100 to John Mussum of Wulton in Warwick, over a one-year period, at a rate of 20% interest. The transaction is reported to have taken place at Westminster. (JS travelled and traded more widely than you might think who think he was just a country yokel, sir.)

The second case arose at the instigation of one James Langrake of Whittlebury, Northamptonshire. He accused 'Shagpere *alias* Shakespeare', 'glover' of 'Stratford upon Haven', of lending out £80 over a term of one month, to be repaid with 20% interest – an extortionate annual rate of interest of some 242%!

(Usury at 10% was the highest rate ever permitted in the last century, and then only at exceptional times or in exceptional circumstances. No usury at all was lawful when jolly Jack Shakespeare was caught.)

A writ was issued to bring 'Shagpere' (*alias* Shylock?) to court. He complied of his own volition, and was heavily fined.

Shakespeare's father was also found guilty of illegal wool-dealing. He had purchased 200 tods of wool (5600 pounds) in conspiracy with another illegal dealer, and 100 tods on his own account. He had no licences for any of this.

In fact, all his long life, John Shakespeare was embroiled in legal disputes. I refuse to tell the tale of the boring Lamberts. Suffice it to say that it involves his relentless pursuit of certain of his wife's relatives for sums of money owing to him, or allegedly owing to him. William himself was dragged into this by his dad.

Enough to say that by my calculations (after researches which by no means exhaust the matter) John Shakespeare was involved in no less than 25 legal suits or disputes over a 40-year period. Some of these were no more than cases of tradesmen collecting their debts. But some, as I've just shown, were a deal more shady.

Where does this leave young William?

Well, gentles, it is possible that he had employment for a while drafting bonds for his father's trading transactions. And it is certain that following his marriage to Anne Hathaway, the couple had to lodge in the Henley Street house. Susanna was born there, and the twins Hamlet and Judith two years later.

This, then, readers, was the world in which William Shakespeare was

living – with a wife and three small children to keep, a mother perhaps unnaturally jealous of her daughter-in-law, and a father who was creeping about playing Shylock when not busy cavorting as Falstaff.

It is no wonder that our Shakespeare now turned briefly to a life of crime himself, as you shall quickly hear.

Chapter Fifty-Six

In which Lucy is lousy

The story is soon told. Shakespeare fell in with bad company, a misfortune common enough to young romantic fellows. Amongst them there were some who made a frequent practice of deer-stealing, and these engaged with him more than once in robbing a park that belonged to the magistrate Sir Thomas Lucy of Charlecote, near Stratford. On moonlit nights they killed rabbits as well as deer. Worse, when Lucy threatened the poachers with prosecution, Will wrote a ballad upon him, which he then went and hung on the gates of Charlecote Park.

Pickleherring has in this 56th box the first stanza of that ballad, put down in writing for him by one of Shakespeare's accomplices in crime, the amiable Mr Thomas Jones of Tardebigge. It is all that Mr Jones could well remember. It goes like this:

> *A parliament member, a justice of peace,*
> *At home a poor scarecrow, in London an ass,*
> *If lousy is Lucy (as some volk miscall it)*
> *Then Lucy is lousy, whatever befall it.*
> > *He thinks himself great,*
> > *Yet an ass in his state*
> *We allow by his ears but with asses to mate.*
> *If Lucy is lousy (as some volk miscall it)*
> *Sing O lousy Lucy whatever befall it.*

Apart from the rhythm (which I count a pleasant rollick), there are several points of interest to this stanza.

First, we might learn from it what Mr Shakespeare's voice sounded like

when he was young, before he came to London – *volk* being the way he pronounced the word *folk*. Old Mr Jones was insistent upon this spelling – both that *volk* is the way Shakespeare wrote it, and also the way that he said it. 'It is the way, besides, that King Alfred would have said it,' he told me, with a great air of triumph. (A hit for my country history! A very palpable hit!) Yet I should in fairness add that the mild-mannered gentleman might have been missing the point, since by spelling the word *volk* Shakespeare could be extending some criticism of those among his fellows who pronounce the name *Lucy* as *lousy*. Already he is standing at a little distance from the crowd. They say Lucy as lousy. He doesn't. He says Lucy *is* lousy.

Second, we might observe that the lampoon is scurrile. Lucy's ass's ears are similar equipment to a cuckold's horns, and in lines 6 and 7 what is being suggested is that the man has to submit to buggery to achieve his sexual satisfactions. (I have even wondered whether Mr Jones modified the seventh line for what he took to be my maiden ears, and whether the fifth word in that line should not properly if improperly be *rear*.)

Third, there is a triple (if trivial) pun being made upon Lucy's coat of arms – 'three silver pikes gasping'. A pike is a luce is a louse.

Fourth, last, and most important, we can take pleasure in the way this whole tiny constellation of wit appears again years later in *The Merry Wives of Windsor*, where foolish Shallow is Lucy, with 'a dozen white luces' in his coat of arms.

Reminiscing for me, Mr Thomas Jones remarked that Will had never been much of a poacher. He was 'a cack-handed tradesman with a snare', and much too tender-hearted – once they had taken a hare alive, and Will had let her go before they could 'dacently' club her. Mr Jones also described, unbidden, the hated magistrate, saying that while Lucy was very thin and queer, he was 'lecherous as a monkey'. He had never heard of Falstaff's description of Justice Shallow:

'Like a man made after supper of a cheese-paring: when a' was naked he was for all the world like a forked radish, with a head fantastically carved upon it with a knife.'

When I quoted this to him, my ancient informant clapped his skinny yellow hands together and cried, 'That's Lucy to the life!'

I see Mr Shakespeare in his role of poacher as one like Fenton in the *Wives*, who himself confesses to his 'riots past, my wild societies', and who capers and dances and has the eyes of youth. He does not just go out, a thief in the night, to rob a rich man of his deer (and his rabbits). He is Alan a' Dale as well as bold Robin Hood. He writes verses, he speaks holiday, he smells April and May. Stolen venison tastes sweetest, and Will's offence has

a ring of high spirits to it, as well as youthful daring. As he asks in *Titus Andronicus*: 'What! has not thou full often struck a doe and borne her cleanly by the keeper's nose?' Some say he not only took the game but seduced the gamekeeper's daughter.

But, alas, this Lucy was the same louse who had already had Shakespeare imprisoned for selling those dragons. The prospect of another term of imprisonment, or of a public whipping at the post by the High Cross, for the theft and for the libel, made up Will's mind for him.

One night in the summer of 1587, Shakespeare kissed his wife and bairns good-bye, and slipped out of the back door of the house on Henley Street, and down across Clopton Bridge, and out of Stratford, taking the high road to London.

Chapter Fifty-Seven

Shakespeare's Canopy, or
Pickleherring in dispraise of wine

It is also probable, if you ask me, that alcohol played a part in William Shakespeare's decision to get away from Stratford. I do not mean pride, intense selfishness, the alcohol of egotism, no, madam. I mean alcohol of wine, the pure or rectified spirit, that impure intoxicating element which possesses your fermented liquors.

What a weird word it is, this ALCOHOL. In my father's kidskin dictionary it says that it comes from the name of a certain black powder of lead ore which the ladies in Barbary once put upon their eyelids: AL-KA-HOL. How that glamour relates to the power of sherris-sack is beyond my knowledge.

What I do know, as I have said, is that in London the late Mr Shakespeare lived for the most part an abstemious life. My point is that no one save a Puritan takes such care as he did to avoid most occasions of debauchery unless they have suffered in its toils at some earlier stage. Since Mr William Shakespeare was no Puritan, I suspect that in his hot youth in Stratford he may have drunk with his father until he sickened himself. His going to London was his turning his back on such things.

Some interesting silences on the part of his widow – in response to this suggestion – only tended to confirm the idea in my mind. There is, besides, the matter of Shakespeare's Canopy.

Shakespeare's Canopy is the name given to a giant crab-tree in the village of Bidford, seven miles south of Stratford. I was shown this tree by Mr Thomas Jones, the ancient poacher. He told me the poet slept under it one night. The story goes as follows.

Shakespeare was a mighty drinker in those days, his old friend said, and he had come to Bidford with a band of fellows from Stratford (Tom Jones

among them) to try his skill against the men of Bidford, who were famous throughout all Warwickshire as topers. Asking a shepherd for the Bidford drinkers, he was instructed that they were absent, though the Bidford sippers, who might be sufficient for him, were still here at home.

Shakespeare and company had no choice but to do battle against the sippers. They were defeated, hands down and bottoms up, and had to sleep off their drink by making their lodging under the tree for the night.

In the morning, said Jones, some of the Stratford men wanted to resume the contest, but Shakespeare refused. He declared he had drunk with:

> *Piping Pebworth, dancing Marston,*
> *Haunted Hillborough, hungry Grafton,*
> *Dadgeing Exhall, Papist Wicksford,*
> *Beggarly Broom, and drunken Bidford.*

(I do not know what 'dadgeing' is, and Mr Jones would not enlighten me.) In another version of the same story, already referred to, it is Shakespeare's father who spends the night with him under the crab-tree, both of them hopelessly drunk.

I do think that Shakespeare's crimes – his poaching expeditions – may well have been committed in his cups. There are several powerful but unnecessary passages in the plays about the abuse of alcohol, most notably in *Hamlet*, where the father/son relationship is plumbed most deeply. I owe this observation to the poet's daughter Susanna, who also remarked to me that *Hamlet* is full of things which strictly speaking have nothing to do with the story, unless you suppose some larger and untold story that lies at the back of it. I think this is true.

As to the date of Mr Shakespeare's departure from Stratford, I will tell you what makes me sure that it was 1587. In *The Winter's Tale*, when the shepherd finds the child Perdita, he says this:

'I would there were no age between ten and three-and-twenty, or that youth would sleep out the rest; for there is nothing in the between but getting wenches with child, wronging the ancientry, stealing, fighting.'

Now this passage has nothing to do with the play, nor the shepherd's occupation. What's more, nor does it ring true to the life of a shepherd boy, whose years between 10 and 23 are likely to be hard. I think the speech expresses WS's own youth, when he had nothing better to do than steal, fight, drink, wrong the ancientry, and get wenches with child. It is Shakespeare's confession. And it was in 1587 that William Shakespeare turned the age of 23.

One word more concerning AL-KA-HOL, and I am done. I am now myself a water-drinker, as I have told you, but be sure that such abstinence is the outcome of my sins. I would not have you think that I am one of those who teach others to fast, and play the gluttons themselves – like watermen, that look one way and row another.

Here, then, is Pickleherring's observation, which he trusts you, reader, will find of use and interest. It is this:

That the paradise of AL-KA-HOL is achieved with the first three glasses. After that, you drink more and more with just the one purpose: to get back to that paradise of the third glass – and you always fail. Why? Because the alcohol transforms you, so that the person who drinks the fourth glass is not the one who drinks the fifth. Nor can you stop at the third glass, in paradise, since like all paradises you do not know you are in it until you have lost it. It is a paradise always lost, and a paradise never to be regained. You might say it is also a hell, and I would not deny you.

Chapter Fifty-Eight

Pickleherring's Poetics
(some more about this book)

Sir, no man's enemy, forgiving all (even Will, his negative inversion), please note that again I have not done the obvious thing.

Namely, I have not claimed that our hero 'ran away' from Stratford-upon-Haven or whatever you feel like calling the wretched place just because he did not get on like a bed on fire with his wife.

I know that there are those who have said and will say this.

And I know well what they get up to in their sly attempts to prove it.

Their trick is to take certain bits and pieces from Mr Shakespeare's plays and to press these passages into service as if they could be made to illustrate Mr Shakespeare's private life.

For instance, such literary gossips seize on that line given to Parolles in *All's Well That Ends Well* (what a lovely title that is, madam, yes): 'A young man married is a young man marred.' And then they hop from there to the character of Adriana in *The Comedy of Errors* and they argue that because she is a nasty nagging scold it must follow that Shakespeare intended her as a portrait of his wife. Ergo, his married youth was marred by Anne Hathaway's tongue. Ergo, he quit Stratford.

Reader, I say this is wrong.

What is wrong with it is that Parolles's cynicism suits Parolles, and Adriana belongs in her play. In other words, these things fit where they are supposed to fit, they belong where they are, and they tell us nothing about the man who wrote them save that he was a good craftsman as well as a good observer of human character. The fact is that if you take the work of a dramatist with such a wide range as Shakespeare then you can find within

it items which when extracted could be used to prove anything at all if applied to his biography.

My method in this book is different in kind.

I only use those bits that do not fit.

For example, that shepherd's quite irrelevant personal outburst about the significance of attaining the age of 23.

For example, the land-locked philosophical Jaques suddenly introducing REMAINDER BISCUIT into his account of the fool he has met in the Forest of Arden.

For example, Prince Hamlet on the very great perils of drunkenness.

For example, Juliet's nurse counting the years from the time of an earthquake that killed a mouse and rattled some dove-cotes in *Stratford*.

For example, the mistaken idea that you can cheat at chess.

These things do not belong where our playwright puts them.

They neither sit well in context, nor can it be claimed that they are alien remnants left over from the sources behind their plays. (You will find no old sea-biscuits in Ralph Holinshed.)

Your author picks up on such items because he believes that because they do not belong in their plays then they must belong to something else.

And the something else they must belong to is the life of the man who wrote those plays, the late Mr William Shakespeare.

Pickleherring is writing the Life of William Shakespeare for you now. So he snaps up all these previously unconsidered trifles that do not fit in the works where they occur, and he seeks to show where they fit in the drama of the life.

Thus, as the well-spurred Aristotle would say, the *Poetics* of this book that you are reading.

What do you mean, madam – you feel that you will have to take a bath?

Chapter Fifty-Nine

*What Shakespeare did when
first he came to London*

There are those who say we do not know what Shakespeare did when he first came to London. But I say we do. Lie back in your bath-tub, madam, and Pickleherring will tell you.

The best information comes always from the enemy. Never trust a man's friends to give you the plain truth about his life. It is those who would deny or decry his way in the world who can invariably be relied upon to provide the clearest notions of what he has been doing.

So – Let us speed forward some five years from the time of Mr Shakespeare's coming to London. It is the night of the 2nd day of September, 1592, and here in this garret in Eastcheap a man is dying. The plague rages through London, but it is not the plague that is killing him. He sits at his table and scribbles. He clutches his guts. He has a long red beard tugged and twisted into a point, and on his head he has crammed two caps, one Oxford, one Cambridge, the only things that remain in his life to remind him that once he had his Master of Arts degree from both those universities. His name is Robert Greene.

He has at his elbow a penny pot of malmsey. The shirt on his back is the shirt of his mistress's husband, borrowed for him to wear while she scrubs out the lice from his own shirt. Tomorrow morning, when she finds him dead, this good kindly woman, Mrs Isam, will crown Greene's poor head with a garland of bays. Then she will sell his sword to pay for his winding sheet (four shillings). The charge for his burial in the new churchyard near Bedlam will be borne by her husband (six shillings and fourpence).

Robert Greene is a writer, a man of letters. But writers live on hope, and he has none left. Once, this unhappy hack was almost famous. His

Menaphon, published three years ago, was even reprinted. He called it *Greene's Arcadia* that second time around. Before that, he wrote a novel called *Pandosto*, which will one day provide the plot for *The Winter's Tale*. He has written plays as well, but now no one will put them on, even though he offers each one to two companies at the same time. His *Friar Bacon and Friar Bungay*, once popular, would get laughed off the stage in these more sophisticated days. At 34 years old, Greene's considered a has-been, an umquhile man.

Like many in his case, Robert Greene has turned to religion. Now, in this last night of his life, he is at work on a diatribe, cast in the form of a letter to his 'fellow scholars', in which he intends to expose the villainies of the contemporary literary world. He can yark up a pamphlet like this in a day and a night. All it takes is a little self-righteousness and a great deal of alcohol, for Greene is an evangelist. The name of his final evangel is *A Groatsworth of Wit bought with a Million of Repentance*. (No, not a catchy title, I agree.)

Mr Greene has a good word for actors. He has four good words, in fact, each of them prompted by our reluctance to do his plays. He calls us 'apes' and 'peasants'. He calls us 'painted monsters'. But the main targets for his wrath are his fellow writers, especially those young rival dramatists whose successes he blames for his own failure. Amongst these there are two who fill him up with a particular angry vitriol. The first is Mr Christopher Marlowe, although Greene cannot bring himself to name his name, soundly berated on account of his notorious atheism. The second is another un-named fellow, an even viler villain, who inspires our dying moralist to an apoplectic outburst of disgust.

Pass me that sponge, madam. I will do your back.

What does Greene say? Here is what he says:

'There is an upstart Crow, beautified with our feathers, that with his *Tyger's heart wrapt in a Player's hide*, supposes he is as well able to bombast out a blank verse as the best of you: and being an absolute *Johannes fac totum*, is in his own conceit the only Shake-scene in a country.'

He then goes on to call this arch-enemy of all that is good a 'rude groom', after warning his fellow writers not to acquaint him with their intentions lest he should steal them.

Yes, madam, Shake-scene is Shakespeare.

Of course I am sure. That bit about his heart being *wrapt in a Player's hide* is a parody of a line in the third part of his *Henry VI* – all Greene has done is substitute the word *Player* for the word *woman*. What he is saying is that Shakespeare is an animal disguised as an actor. What he is saying is that

Shakespeare is also a thief – in Horace's third epistle, the crow is the symbol of plagiarism. What Greene is saying is that this hated creature has tricked his way into the confidence of the other actors and writers, in order to mimic their styles and appropriate their works.

Some unguents? Mmm, assuredly.

Yes, madam, Greene is saying that Shakespeare is a conceited little upstart. But he's telling us more than that. He's telling us, more or less, exactly what Shakespeare has been doing since he came to London. Unpick each of his insults and it gives you a job.

Take, first, that *rude groom*. . . . Well, in the time of Elizabeth, coaches being yet uncommon, and hired coaches not at all in use, those who were too proud, too tender, or too idle to walk, went on horseback to any distant business or diversion. Many came on horseback to the play, and when Shakespeare fled to London from the terror of a criminal prosecution, I have had it from no less an authority than Sir William Davenant, our Poet Laureate, his own godson, that the great man's first expedient was to wait at the door of the playhouse, and *hold the horses* of those that had no servants, that they might be ready again after the performance. In this office he became so conspicuous for his care and readiness, indeed, that in a short time every man as he alighted called for 'Will Shakespeare!' and scarcely any other waiter was trusted with a horse while Will Shakespeare could be had. This was the first dawn of a better fortune, madam. Because our Will was always his father's son, with an eye to the easier way and the better profits, and in no time at all, finding more horses put into his hand than he could hold, he hired a team of boys to wait outside the theatre under his inspection, who, when 'Will Shakespeare!' was summoned, were taught to present themselves immediately, saying, 'I am Shakespeare's boy, sir!' Thus, our Will was not long a *rude groom* himself, but doubtless it was in that office that Greene first made his acquaintance. Besides, according to his godson, for as long as the practice of riding to the playhouse continued, the waiters that held the horses retained the appellation of *Shakespeare's Boys*.

Soap of Alicante? Yes! Yes! Yes!

Now then, once he got a foot inside the theatre, Shakespeare lost no time in becoming an actor, even though he was a rude untutored country boy in the estimation of a university wit like Mr Robert Greene. That, surely, is one of the things Greene means by calling him an *upstart Crow*? Never forget, madam, that as I think I may have told you, your Mr Shakespeare was a handsome well-shaped man, and of a smooth and ready wit, and as you might readily imagine (lying there in your spindrift of frothy oils) he made a very tolerable player, though he rarely appeared in the main parts

in his own plays – Prospero being the exception which proves my rule. However, able as he was at *bombasting out a blank verse* in this next profession of actor, it was not long again before our Shakespeare managed to convince Mr James Burbage that he would be even better employed as a play-patcher, a reviser and refurbisher of old plays, Mr Greene's no doubt among them. Just picture it for yourself: The young actor protesting, 'I can't say this stuff! How about if I said this instead?' and going on to transmute Greene's verbal base metal into pure Shakespearean gold as he stood on the spot. Imagine the great Mr Robert Greene, M.A. of two universities, having to submit to the indignity of finding his plays improved and his scansion corrected by this upstart he had first but half-noticed as he chucked him the reins when he found time to pay a visit to the playhouse! No wonder he calls Shakespeare *an absolute Johannes fac totum*, a horrible Jack-of-all-trades, groom turned actor, actor turned play-patcher, play-patcher turned play-maker, play-maker who *in his own conceit* is now reckoned *the only Shake-scene* in the country – which is to say, by this summer of '92, as Greene sits a-dying, the top playwright, the new man, the one who has stolen everyone else's thunder, and replaced Mr Greene and his friends in the favour of the audiences. Perhaps the most bitter pill is that Greene knows in his guts that it is true, and that this *Shake-scene* is his better in every way?

Well, yes, madam, I agree that Robert Greene's prose is turgid stuff. I did not mean to spoil your lovely bath. Some fellows used words like soap in those far-off days. Euphuism, they called it. You employ a lot of rhetorical devices, such as antithesis and homocoteleuton and paranomasia. You make elaborate comparisons and stir it all up with far-fetched metaphors without regard to any canon of verisimilitude. It is a highly analytical style, madam, which ceaselessly dissects and catalogues, compares and contrasts. It aspires thereby to represent the polite discourse of urbane and elegant persons.

Urbane, madam, and elegant, that is what I said. It was what we would call 'all the rage', then. It made thin thought seem of substance, so its writers believed. Even Mr Shakespeare tried it briefly, in his early days, though by the time of *Love's Labour's Lost* he is satirising such affectations. He soon pared himself of any tendency in that direction, and spared us all. The more you have to say the plainer you say it.

Right. From Greene's *Groatsworth* we learn that when Shakespeare first came to London he was first a groom, and then an actor, and then a Jack-of-all-trades about the theatre, and that by the summer of 1592, when he was 28 years old, he was already popular enough to be considered an

enviable rival by at least one other dramatist. Greene died, and his pamphlet was published. Evidently Shakespeare and his friends complained, for Henry Chettle, who had prepared the *Groatsworth* for the press, then offered a handsome sort of apology, saying that he had now met Shakespeare, and found him not like Greene's libels, but an amiable gentleman altogether, and——

No, madam, I did *not* say I had murdered Robert Greene.

I do assure you, madam, I claimed no such thing!

Look again at that conclusion to Chapter 49, then. You will see that what I say—— There, you have it! Pickle herring killed Mr Greene. A great surfeit of the buggers.

A week or so previous, do you see, he had sat down with his friend Thomas Nashe and their acquaintance William Monox to a terrible banquet of my little namesakes, washed down with tankards of strong Rhenish wine. At once Greene fell sick. That was too rich a diet for his diseased kidneys, all poisoned as they were by his jealousy of Shakespeare. (A thing which Dr Walter Warner deemed well possible – that men have been rotted away within by their own hates.)

Greene never recovered from those pickle herring. I claim no credit for the poor hack's death. I was but nine lamb-like years of age when all this happened, and still in the tender care of the Misses Muchmore, living as you may remember by a far fen.

Now, with your permission, madam, let me rub your breasts dry with this nice big fleecy white towel——

Chapter Sixty

*In which Pickleherring eats an egg
in honour of Mr Shakespeare*

Today was St George's Day, which day I always keep. This particular St George's Day I had especial cause to honour. It was 50 years ago today – 23rd April, 1616 – that the poet William Shakespeare breathed his last.

Anne brought me another egg, and she dressed my chamber! She fetched also a pitcher of cold fresh water, plus a little bowl of suckets. When I asked her if this was in honour of St George or Mr Shakespeare, she simply shook her head and stamped her foot. Our English patron saint, I fear, means nothing to this sweet witch. And I do not think she had heard of Mr Shakespeare.

For once, I nothing cared, to encounter such ignorance. I pinned a clean napkin before me, and I put on a pair of white Holland sleeves, which reached to my elbows. I ate my egg with relish, even the white part, and offered my guest a spoon of it, but she would not.

She had seated herself on a stack of my used boxes by the window. She showed not the least curiousness concerning their contents, nor in anything else in this room, for all that I could see. Yet how strange it must all seem to my whore-child's eyes! They are big and blue, by the by, with long dark lashes which she flutters prettily. Her ankles, when she sate herself, I perceived very neat and slender in her white silk stockings. (But your author knew that already, and so do you.)

She did not stay long, this dear sweet Anne of mine, but she left a perfume of herself across my room. While she was here, there was an illumination about her. Barely a word did she speak, once she came in, until her going out again, yet my poor old tired head sings with it.

'Sir,' – that's what she said, when I opened my door to her gentle knocking – 'I've brought another egg, sir. Would you like it?'

Ten words. Well, eleven, if I am allowed to draw out the contraction. And her voice is very beautiful, sweet and low. She called me *Sir*. She made me a delightful little curtsey. I did not let her know that I know her name.

What did they see, that pair of deep adorable blue eyes? What can their young owner have made of your ancient Pickleherring?

I keep no mirrors by me in this attic. I've allowed myself no looking-glass of any kind since my wife Jane departed this vain world. But of course I can remember what I look like. The memories are not all bad, sir, not all bad.

Pickleherring is of middle stature, with a fair complexion (remarkable I daresay for my extreme age), and of a pleasant countenance, open and cheerful even if somewhat cross-hatched with wrinkles. (*Beated and chopt with tann'd antiquity*, as Mr Shakespeare said of his own face, and still in his thirties when he said it.) My hair (by reason no barber has come near me for the space of several years) is much overgrown. My habit is plain and without ornament, for the most part – which is to say, when I am not dressed up in any of the ruins of my costumes, but no one ever sees me garbed like that. I favour a sad-coloured cloth, of a texture that will defend me against any machinations of the cold. Since Jane was killed, I say, there has been nothing to be found in my apparel which could be thought to betoken or express the least imagination of pride or of vain-glory.

As she was leaving my chamber, as she stood there in my doorway, I made this darling Anne the gift of one of my precious pickled mulberries.

'This is no common fruit,' I told her. 'It comes from the tree of the greatest poet and the dearest man who ever lived in England. And today is his day, little miss, as much as it is St George's.'

Anne inspected it most respectfully, before wrapping it up in her handkerchief. Then she dropped me another dainty curtsey, and scampered away. Watching her rush down the stairs I remembered her childishness. Perched on my boxes, legs crossed, she had looked something else.

Thus passed the most remarkable St George's Day I have ever known in my life, in which my only feast was on an egg. Blessed be the dear white hands that gave it to me. I ate that egg in Mr Shakespeare's honour. As I say, it is fifty years from the day that the poet died. I will not tell you how he bade farewell to me until it's time for that. Today, 50 years on, let me say only that William Shakespeare's purgatory must be past. His heaven will never end, be sure of it.

Chapter Sixty-One

In which Pickleherring speculates
concerning the meaning of eggs

Nothing in this box. And this nothing's more than matter to my mood. It fits my spirits, this box that when I tap it with my fingers sounds with hollow poverty and emptiness. I am a poor fellow, sir. I speak with nobody, and I do not answer. I am, again, Cordelia, am I not? 'What can you say?' 'Nothing, my lord.' 'Nothing!' 'Nothing.' And nothing will come of nothing, as Lear replied.

That was one of Mr Shakespeare's favourite words – that terrible NOTHING. He plays on it in every other play. It is no sort of a word for an old man like me.

Well, madam, there you have it, like as not. Pickleherring's down in the dumps this morning, after the high delights of his yesterday. Like a bear with a sore head, madam, O yes, indeed.

I lay awake and thought about those eggs last night. What can it mean – that twice now my bewitching whore-child has brought me an egg?

Reader, forgive me, for then various silly sayings concerning the meaning and significance of eggs came floating into my head where it tossed there, unable to sleep.

Does this Anne mean (thought I) to *egg me on*? Not likely, I thought. Why should she? How could she? There would be nothing for her in it, and while 'tis pity she's a whore yet a whore is what she is. (That strange image of *egg on* is a corruption of the Saxon *eggia*, to incite, according to my dictionary, consulted by candlelight in the dead vast and middle of the night. Madam, I *did* put my nightcap on.)

So then (thought I, safely back in my cot, and keeping that nightcap tugged down about my ears) does perhaps this dear sweet little innocent

mean to say without having to say it that we are *like as two eggs*, she and I? Hardly, I thought. We are in fact as different as chalk and cheese. And a broken white stick of dry-as-dust chalk is what I amount to, while a very tasty piece of parmesan looked that Anne, going down those stairs making cheeses with her petticoats.

But what if the cunning little vixen intends to laugh at me? How? Why, by *teaching her grandmother to suck eggs*? The naughty wicked scamp, if so, thought I, kicking off the bedclothes in my fury. For I should have to show the wench that Pickleherring is no grandmother but the veriest grand*father* under his red cotton nightshirt. And to achieve that office would I not need to take Anne across my knee, and have her drawers down, and attend to her posteriors. . . .

These final images brought me terribly awake, and confronted by my own base desires with regard to the girl. Yet I knew at the same time, even in my excitement, that she did not deserve this, not after her kindnesses to me, which might well have been performed for no motive but that they are the natural expression of a good and simple heart.

I determined then that I would myself have to *tread upon eggs* in regard to the creature – taking care not to frighten, not to startle, never to hurt her, but to go tenderly and gingerly in all, as if walking over eggs that are so easily broken.

Pickleherring calmed himself down from this unfortunate storm of passion by recalling the well-known anecdote of the silent man and the eggs. (This story, now I come to recite it for you, chimes with some of my procedures in this book – where there is often a delay between event and resolution, for no better reason than that being the way my comedian of a mind has always worked.)

The anecdote concerns as I say a man much given to long silences. One day, when riding over a bridge, this man turned about and asked his servant if he liked eggs, to which the servant briefly answered, 'Yes, sir.' Whereupon not a word more was spoken until a year later, when, riding over the same bridge, the man turned about to his servant once more, and said, 'How?' To which the instant answer came: 'Poached, sir.'

This fine example of intermission of discourse served me last night to take my mind off the matter in hand. I must then have fallen asleep, for the next thing I know I was watching a wonderful silver egg being laid by the joint labour of several serpents in the street below, and then buoyed up into the air above London by their hissing. I stepped out of my window and I caught the egg, and I rode off through the night at full speed astride it. I knew that I had to ride fast away from the serpents, to avoid being stung to

death. But I knew also that now I possessed the egg I was sure to prevail in my Life of Mr Shakespeare, and indeed to defeat all my enemies in any contest or combat that might befall me, and to be courted by King Charles and others in power. In my dream I then heard Anne's voice saying (as it seemed close by, and whispering, upon my pillow): 'Pliny says he has seen an egg just like ours, but it was only about the same size as an apple.'

Then I dreamt I wept, and woke. But why I wept, I knew not; yet I know.

Chapter Sixty-Two

About Mr Richard Field:
another ruminating gentleman

When William Shakespeare first came to London he lodged for some while at the sign of the White Greyhound in Paul's Churchyard. This place was not a tavern but a building that housed a printing works. It was owned by a friend who had been his fellow at the Stratford Grammar School, a young man by the name of Richard Field.

Richard Field was an enterprising gentleman. Son of a Stratford tanner, he had got himself apprenticed to a London printer when he was 18 years old. His second master was a Huguenot, Thomas Vautrollier, famous in his day for the beauty of his types and the excellence of his press-work. When Vautrollier died, young Dick married his widow, a Frenchwoman called Jacqueline. Thus, at an early age, he came into possession of one of the best printing establishments in England.

The house of Vautrollier had published some fine if heretical books. For example, the works of Calvin and Luther and Theodore de Bèze. For example, the works of Giordano Bruno. For example, new editions of Ovid and Plutarch. For example, *Campo di Fiore or Singing in four languages to aid those who wish to learn Latin, French and English, but especially Italian.* (I have this.) For example, that *Treatise on Melancholy*, by Dr Timothy Bright, which I have told you was of use to Mr Shakespeare when he was writing his *Hamlet*.

Under Field's control, the printing house became if anything even more distinguished. Having published Puttenham's important *The Art of English Poesie*, it went on to publish Mr Shakespeare's *Venus and Adonis* and *The Rape of Lucrece*, as well as Ariosto's *Orlando Furioso* in the translation made by Sir John Harington at Queen Elizabeth's request. But all this is to run ahead a

bit too fast. I just want to show you that our hero had a knack of falling on his feet even when starting out in a strange city.

At the time when Mr Shakespeare came to London, as it turned out, his old school-friend had just married the merry Jacqueline. She was a sportive piece, a black-eyed beauty. It cannot have taken much pity on Mr Field's part to bed her or to wed her, especially since it was only by inheritance or marriage that any newcomer could enter the close corporation of master-printers. The Fields' house was at the south end of an acre known as Little Britain – the printers' quarter. This meant that Mr Shakespeare had not far to go to do his first job of horse-holding at the theatres on the north side.

Later in life, Dick Field had an even better shop, the Splayed Eagle, in Wood Street, Cheapside, where his widow carried on the business after his death. It was in the back room of that establishment, over a dish of strawberries, that I once asked this enigmatic woman who *she* thought the Dark Lady of the sonnets might have been. She smiled into her fan. '*C'est moi*,' she said.

Field's printer's device (inherited, like the dark Jacqueline, from old Vautrollier) was an anchor surrounded by laurels and accompanied by the motto ANCHORA SPEI.

His other claim to fame, apart from his friendship with Shakespeare, is that like the Reverend Bretchgirdle, Mr Richard Field was a ruminating gentleman.

This human chewing of the cud is not so singular a thing as you might suppose, dear reader. Dr Walter Warner told me once that he had just had the satisfaction of dissecting a ruminant man, and proving the falseness of Bartholin's theory that such people possess double stomachs. So neither are they freaks in their anatomy.

Richard Field the master printer used to commence ruminating about a quarter of an hour after a meal, and the process usually occupied him for an hour and a half, being attended with greater gratification than the first mastication, after which he claimed the food lay heavy in his lower throat. He was obliged to retire from the dining table at his house beside the printing works, and to go into a little room, star-ceilinged, which he called his 'rumination chamber', where he could ruminate away to his heart's content. Often he declared in my hearing that this second process of mastication was 'sweeter than honey' and 'accompanied with a delightful relish'. His son by Jacqueline inherited the same faculty, but with him it was under better control, he being able to defer its exercise until any convenient opportunity, and so needing no star chamber for the purpose.

Mr Field seldom made any breakfast in his later days. He generally

dined about noon or one o'clock, eating heartily and quickly, and without much chewing. He never drank with his dinner, but afterwards he would sink a pint of such malt liquor as he could get. As I say, he usually went into his 'rumination chamber' and began his second chewing about fifteen minutes later, when he would claim that each and every morsel came up successively, sweeter and sweeter to the taste. Sometimes a gobbet might prove offensive and crude, in which case Richard Field would spit it out. The chewing continued usually about an hour or more. If he was interrupted in the act by a customer he found (alas) that he would be sick at stomach, and troubled with the heart burn, and foul breath. He could punctuate his second eating of the same meal by smoking a pipe of tobacco, and this was never to my knowledge attended by any ill consequences. It was not until a few weeks before his death, in 1624, that the faculty left him, and then poor Richard Field remained in tortures till the end.

I think it must have been one of the few sorrows of Mr Field's life that he parted with the copyrights of Shakespeare's narrative poems to a bookseller called Harrison. Both poems were extremely successful and went through many editions. Perhaps Field let them go because of his theological interests and because by then Mr S was getting big in the theatre. Field had no time at all for the world of the playhouse. He joined other residents of Blackfriars in signing a petition in 1596 – the year I came to London – against James Burbage's attempt to open a theatre there. The petition succeeded. I think that setback broke old Burbage's heart.

Chapter Sixty-Three

*About a great reckoning
in a little room*

I can never hear what they say but they haunt my mind's eye.

Look, there, as in a dumb-show, there are four of them. Four men come to a reckoning in a little room. Over and over, they act out for your delight the terrible scene. You always want it to be different, but each time the end is the same. The dagger thrust in the eye, the skull hacked open. Blood on the walls and the ceiling, the poet lying dead in a pool of his own hot blood on the floor.

From the start, from the moment when they meet together, you can see that two of these four men are ruffians, and one is not. It is none of these three, however, that you can't look away from. The fourth man, the victim, he is the natural magnet for your gaze. It is not just his sombre velvet doublet, his gold lace. It is not even that glittering ring hanging from his left ear, nor the gold buttons that seem far beyond his station. Neither is it, exactly, his sensual face, nor his dangerous smile. This is Christopher Marlowe, who is more than the sum of his parts. You can't take your eyes off a man like this.

The day has been hot. The place is a tavern in Deptford, three miles out of London, on the bank of the Thames. It's a low inn, and dirty, the house of a widow called Bull. There's a garden at the back of it, unkempt, full of thrusting May blossom, that runs down to the throbbing vein of the sunlit river.

These men met here this morning. All day they have been drinking and talking, and walking in the garden. They dined, too, at noon. Marlowe and the two ruffians have laughed a good deal – for the most part, you might think, at nothing. The third man, the gentleman, he does not laugh. His

name is Robert Poley. He's a government agent. He sits still in his cloak, hands folded, his face in the shadows, while the others fool about. You will have noticed that he drinks much less than they do. You may also have noticed that the ruffians provide Mr Marlowe with two drinks for every one of their own.

Now it is six o'clock, and the cool of the May evening has begun, and bats flap to the eaves, and all four men have come back into the tavern. Their glasses refilled, they retire to a little private room.

What causes their quarrel? We shall never know. Something that eyes cannot see, perhaps. Three of these men are liars, and the truth-teller soon lies dead.

Christopher Marlowe, poet and playwright, is stabbed through the right eye, quickly, by Ingram Frizer, in this small room in Deptford, after what seems to be a sudden quarrel over the bill or 'reckoning' presented for their food and drink. At the inquest, Frizer will claim Marlowe first attacked him, for no reason that he could guess, and unprovoked. He pleads he only killed the poet in self-defence. His fellow ruffian, one Nicholas Skeres, supports this story. Frizer will be acquitted by royal pardon.

What part Poley played I can never determine. I know only that there were those in high places who wanted Marlowe dead, and if he really died by chance as the result of a blow struck in a tavern brawl over who should pay the bill then it was certainly convenient for the Privy Council, before whom he was due to appear to answer charges of atheism and blasphemy.

As Marlowe wrote himself: *Cut is the branch that might have grown full straight.* Only it was not so much cut, my dears, as hacked to bits.

The son of a cobbler, he was just the two months older than William Shakespeare. His was a restless spirit, of an over-reaching ambition. Ben Jonson praised him for his 'mighty line'. You can hear this at its mightiest in *Tamburlaine*, the play of his which had the most success. The Lord Admiral's company first performed it in that same summer that Mr Shakespeare came to London, and I know that the newcomer stood three times among the groundlings to be intoxicated by its thundrous verbal music – he told me so himself. Marlowe fired both Will's fancy and his ambition. He said that hearing Marlowe opened his ears. He said that Tamburlaine was like Herod of the Coventry play made intelligent. He said that Marlowe, single-handed, had dragged the verse of the play-makers out of antiquity, and matched it to the sound of the speaking human voice, and made it modern and alive along every line.

He got to know the man, too, and I believe they were friends, despite deep differences of temper and of temperament. I believe that Marlowe

may have helped Mr Shakespeare in the drafting of the three *King Henry VI* plays, and that you can see some influence of Marlowe's *Jew of Malta* in the opening scenes of Shakespeare's *Richard III*.

That, though, is about the extent of it. There are those who suggest that if Marlowe had not been snuffed out in the blaze of his youth, then he would have gone on to be Shakespeare's equal. I cannot agree. Marlowe is all fine lines that stop the play – which may be poetry, but it is not drama. Also, Marlowe's scenes are brilliant, but they do not connect or cohere.

Michael Drayton once wrote of him: *His raptures were/All air and fire*. Which is true. But unlike Mr S he had not eaten of the earth and found it sweet. Nor had he any gift for comedy, in which Shakespeare is rich. Marlowe would have been incapable of creating a Falstaff. Look at the clown scenes in his *Faustus*; there's not a real laugh to be had. Some say Marlowe didn't write them, I know, that they were extemporised by the actors in the first place. If so, that's because he dared not even try in such a vein.

I say that Shakespeare and Marlowe were very different as men, and so they were. The epithet most often applied to Mr Shakespeare by his friends was that he was 'gentle'. No one would ever have dreamt of describing Marlowe thus. He was headlong, he was violent, he was like a little Lucifer. 'Intemperate and of a cruel heart,' said his friend and fellow lodger Thomas Kyd, but then poor Kyd was on the rack when he said that, as when he blurted out several of those 'monstrous opinions' which made Marlowe's name so hated by those in authority. There were supposed to be three sheets of paper which the cobbler's son had written denying the deity of Jesus Christ our Saviour – though if anyone ever read them, then I never met him. Then there was that report that he called John the disciple 'Christ's Alexis', meaning that Jesus had loved the man unnaturally just because he said of him that John was the disciple he loved best. In this, of course, Marlowe was simply attributing to Jesus his own predilections, as revealed on that other notorious occasion when he declared that 'all that love not tobacco and boys are fools'. His principal heresies, assembled, seem to be these:

That all Protestants are hypocritical asses;

That the woman of Samaria and her sister were whores, and that Christ had known them carnally;

That the archangel Gabriel, by his salutation to the Virgin Mary, was bawd to the Holy Ghost;

That all the Apostles were fishermen and base fellows, neither of wit nor worth, and that he could have written the Gospels better himself.

These are bold sayings. They are also rather silly. I think that Marlowe, had he lived, would have outgrown such schoolboy blasphemy. I think also that had Marlowe learned to believe it might have provided him with some release from the bondage of his intellectual pride. However, someone, in some high place – (and not God, I think) – decreed Marlowe should not have the chance to grow or to learn at all. Hence that dagger-thrust which penetrated his skull, making a wound of the depth of two inches and of the width of one inch, just above the right eye. He was 29 years old when they cut him down.

They say, some say, that Marlowe died blaspheming. I never heard him. When I watch that dumb show in the little theatre of my head I see nothing that makes me think that he dies blaspheming. Consider, it can only have been his murderers who ever claimed he did any such thing, and why should we believe them?

To be professed an atheist while bearing the name of Christopher must be an extraordinary burden.

Mr Shakespeare always spoke of Christopher Marlowe with tender affection. True, he was never like Ben Jonson, who put down his contemporaries. But Marlowe he went out of his way to praise. In his play of *As You Like It* he also pays his murdered friend the compliment of several backward glances, as when he had me (as Rosalind) mention how Troilus had his brains dashed out with a Grecian club, yet 'did what he could to die before'. (That was Marlowe to the life, as I have heard, a fire-eater who no one could ever have mistaken for a cud-chewer.) In the same play, Phoebe the shepherdess quotes directly from Marlowe's poem *Hero and Leander* when she invokes the dead poet on Mr Shakespeare's behalf:

> Dead shepherd, now I find thy saw of might:
> 'Who ever loved that loved not at first sight?'

And then Touchstone, to cap it all, recalls Marlowe's death by Frizer's dagger over the 'reckoning' in that Deptford tavern, when he says to Audrey: 'When a man's verses cannot be understood . . . it strikes a man more dead than a great reckoning in a little room.' That last allusion is the one that always brings tears to my eyes whenever I hear it. It is the more effective for being double: Mr Shakespeare means us to remember not only Marlowe's death, but one of his mightiest lines, from *The Jew of Malta*, where he speaks of 'Infinite riches in a little room'.

I have often wished I had met Mr Christopher Marlowe. He was surely the best of those spirits they called the Bohemians, the play-makers who

flourished between 1580 and 1590, the group which included George Peele and Thomas Nashe, and even (to be charitable) Robert Greene. Their plays were a great jumble of good and bad, a reflection in this of their own irregular lives. But at least they began that process which Shakespeare perfected. In their writing you see them start to take the ordinary common words and set them down in such a way that the verse sparkles and laughs at you, or then is sad and makes you want to cry. Before William Shakespeare, none of them did it better than Christopher Marlowe.

I wish I could hear what he says as he walks in the garden. I wish I could hear what he says when it comes to that reckoning.

Chapter Sixty-Four

More

These were William Shakespeare's earliest plays, all written and performed between 1587 and that terrible year of '93 when Marlowe was murdered and the plague caused the shutting of the playhouses:

The Two Gentlemen of Verona	*1 King Henry VI*
The Comedy of Errors	*2 King Henry VI*
Titus Andronicus	*3 King Henry VI*
The Taming of the Shrew	*Richard II*
Romeo and Juliet	*Love's Labour's Lost*

It will be seen that his rate of production ran from the start at about two plays a year – which is something I know he counted professional, unlike on the one side the torrent of thin stuff that was pouring from such as the amiable Thomas Heywood, and on the other side the costiveness of Mr Ben Jonson who seemed able only to squeeze out his 'humours' at long intervals and after much grunting and straining.

However, in these first years of Mr Shakespeare's industry there was more. Pardon me, gentles, I pun unpardonably. I mean that to this period we should also ascribe his original workings on that Hamlet play which haunted him a good half of his working life, growing longer and longer in the process, until some of our Company considered it unplayable; and also that other white elephant, the play they called *More*.

Before getting into that, though, a word about WHITE ELEPHANTS. Here is an image Mr Shakespeare would not have known, but which I find useful. I have it from a translation of *Pinto's Travels* published three years ago. It seems that the King of Siam makes a present of a white elephant to such of

his courtiers as he wishes to ruin on account of their obnoxiousness. Your white elephant, you see, being a huge and a delicate creature, costs so much to keep that none but a king can afford it. Thus, by extension, a man might beggar himself by wasting all his fortune on some pet article. For example, a person moving is determined to keep a rich and expensive carpet, so hires too grand a house just to fit the carpet. There are, as I say, such WHITE ELEPHANTS to be found among the works of William Shakespeare.

The *More* play (since this morning I feel like mixing my metaphors to spice my gruel) could also be said to have been a WHITE ELEPHANT which turned into a POISONED CHALICE. Several playwrights had a hand in it. It was a waste of all their time.

The idea was Anthony Munday's. He sketched out the plot. Henry Chettle then took over, taking out some of the religious polemic which had disfigured Munday's draft. The play was to be called *More* (more or less), and it was to chronicle the main events in the life of Sir Thomas More, King Henry VIII's chancellor, from his rise to favour, through his friendship with Erasmus and opposition to the King, to his fall and his death on the scaffold.

Frankly, I could have told them that this would not do. An historical drama in praise of her father's martyred arch-enemy was hardly likely to give much pleasure to Queen Elizabeth. As it turned out, the play was refused a licence to be performed. Most of it disappeared into the strongbox of Sir Edmund Tilney, censor and Master of the Revels, and was never seen again.

Here, in my own 64th little strongbox, I have William Shakespeare's contribution to this *More*, the only example I know to survive of his work as a cobbler and patcher of other men's plays. I am quite sure that the original idea could not have been his – religious and political controversy being a hurly (patience, madam!) which he always went out of his way to avoid. But at some point he was called in by old Mr Burbage to write the most difficult scene, in which More, as sheriff of London, uses his eloquence to quell the riot of the apprentices who wish to drive all foreigners out of the city.

The passage is passionate Shakespeare, a paean in praise of the necessity of respect for order and degree. It was a concept he worked out most completely in the great speech of Ulysses in *Troilus and Cressida.** The scene as a whole has much in common with another he wrote later – that scene where Menenius Agrippa calms the plebs in Rome in *Coriolanus.* As there,

---

* Act I, Scene 3, lines 75–137.

you can see him shifting sympathy from the rioters to the man who masters them by dint of just and reasoned argument. Not only the style but some of the words of *Coriolanus* are prefigured. Without law, says More, 'men, like ravenous fishes,/Would feed on one another'. Coriolanus upholds the rule of the senate who 'Under the gods, keep you in awe, which else/Would feed on one another'. The shouts of the rioters in *More* are identical with those later used in *Julius Caesar*, and Shakespeare begins More's speech with what sounds to me like a clumsy throat-clearing rehearsal for Mark Antony's *Friends, Romans, countrymen!* when he has the sheriff address the mob as *Friends, masters, fellow-citizens!*

If you look closer at the vocabulary which Mr Shakespeare deploys in this lost scene of the suppressed play *More* then there is even (forgive me) *more* that rewards attention. Here are to be found such phrases as 'in ruff of your opinion clothed', and 'stale custom', and 'unreverent knees', as well as 'self-right' and 'self-reason' – all expressions dear to WS and which he alone employed. His use of the word SHARK as a verb ('would shark on you') is a peculiarity which I have encountered nowhere else save in his own *Hamlet*.

Another idiosyncratic thing of interest here is that in the *More* manuscript fragment the word SILENCE is spelled as *scilens*. The late Mr Shakespeare always spelt that word that way. It is the old-fashioned way. (You will find it thus in Caxton.) Usually the printer corrected these ancient spellings when it came to setting the plays in type, but not invariably. In the Quarto of *2 King Henry IV*, for example, you will find Justice Silence called Scilens not once or twice but eight times!

Is this too bibliotic? I apologise. But the world is a book, sir.

I am citing all this, besides, because otherwise such information might be lost for ever, along with the whole play of *More*. The other plays, early and late, you can read for yourself in the Folio. Pickleherring seeks always to give you what you cannot get from any other source.

The lines being the draft of Mr Shakespeare's contribution as it stood before the whole went to the copyist, they tell us even MORE about his methods. It is plain, for example, that he was a careless contributor to the work in hand – he shows no respect for the play as a whole, distributing his speeches among the rioters with such titles as *Other*, instead of the name of a character. In one passage, where his usual fluency dries up, he leaves two and a half lines so tangled and confused that the book-keeper (Mr Burbage?) has struck them out and substituted a half-line of his own.

I mean that passage where Shakespeare first writes:

> *to kneel to be forgiven*
> *Is safer war than ever you can make*
> *Whose discipline is riot; why even your war*
> *Cannot proceed but by obedience.*

Then (perhaps observing that he has used the word WAR in two successive lines) he strikes out the second 'war' and substitutes the word HURLY, a favourite synonym of his to cover all forms of contention, which he uses in at least three other plays.* The lines now read:

> *to kneel to be forgiven*
> *Is safer war than ever you can make*
> *Whose discipline is riot; why even your hurly*
> *Cannot proceed but by obedience.*

That seems perfectly put to your author, but still it did not satisfy Mr Shakespeare, because he then inserts after the word RIOT, the phrase 'In, in to your obedience', perhaps wanting More to be more vigorous and direct. However, it is obvious that this pleases him no better, for he did not relate it to what followed, but instead gives up, leaving the passage a jumble as it stands. It is this that Mr Burbage, unable to solve the difficulty, has drawn his pen through, for there in quite another hand we see the tame and unShakespearean:

Tell me but this.

Now because these manuscript pages reveal much of Mr Shakespeare's method of composing, and the better to preserve them in context for a possible posterity, I intend to paste one of them into my book. Thus, if the two in the box are lost then this one may survive, and vice versa.

I will offer two general observations about them.

First, by their very carelessness (sometimes he even scribbles *Oth* and *O* to indicate successive speakers whose names he can't be bothered with) they suggest that Shakespeare already at the time of their writing held such a high place among his fellows that they recognised his superior talent by indulging him. They may have been so grateful that he deigned to contribute to the *More* play that they did not even complain when he scrawled *Moo* as a cipher for Sir Thomas More.

Second, with the one exception examined above, there are few alterations. You can see where he sometimes struck out a word, or the start

---

* *The Taming of the Shrew, King John* – and I forget the other.

of a word, almost as soon as he had written it, following on at once with his second thought. All this is evidence of Mr Shakespeare's quick hand and quicker brain, his fertility and his facility. You will see that sometimes his hand stumbled, but less often his thought – as when he starts to write the word NUMBER with *mu*, and then writes *in* instead of NO. As to actual corrections, all of them involve the substitution of better words within the lines: *watery* is changed to *sorry*, *help* to *advantage*, *god* to *he*, *only* to *solely*.

All this evidence of speed and ease in composition bears out, of course, what Mr Heminges and Mr Condell said in their address 'To the Great Variety of Readers' in the Folio – that Mr Shakespeare's mind and hand went together, and what he thought he uttered with such easiness that 'we have scarce received from him a blot in his papers.' Pickleherring can confirm this. When my master's mind was white-hot it was a wonder that the page did not catch fire beneath his hand, so fast his pen ran. He wrote the first two acts of *Macbeth* in a single day. (All the same, he went on writing *Hamlet* all his life.) Here, then, is the page from the *More* for you to see these things, dear reader, with your own eyes:

as mutynies ar incident, by his name
can still the rout who will obay a traytor
or howe can well that proclamation sounde
when ther is no adicion but a rebell
to quallyfy a rebell, youle put downe straingers
kill them cutt their throts possesse their howses
and leade the maiestie of lawe in liom
to slipp him lyke a hound; ~~sayeng~~ say nowe the king
as he is clement, yf thoffendor moorne
shoold so much com to short of your great trespas
as but to banysh you, whether woold you go.
what Country by the nature of yor error
shoold gyve you harber go you to ffraunce or flanders
to any Jarman province, ~~to~~ spane or portigall
nay any where ~~why you~~ that not adheres to Ingland
why you must needs be straingers, woold you be pleasd
to find a nation of such barbarous temper
that breaking out in hiddious violence
woold not afoord you, an abode on earth
whett their detested knyves against your throtes
spurne you lyke doggs, and lyke as yf that god
owed not nor made not you, nor that the elamentes
wer not all appropriat to ~~their~~ your Comforts.
but charterd unto them, what woold you thinck
to be thus vsd, this is the straingers case
and this your momtanish inhumanyty

---

all. fayth a saies trewe letts vs do as we may be doon by
linco. weele be ruld by you master moor yf youle stand our
freind to procure our pardon

moo. Submit you to theis noble gentlemen
entreate their mediation to the kinge
gyve vp yor sealf to forme obay the maiestrate
and thers no doubt, but mercy may be found yf you so seek it

Chapter Sixty-Five

A look at William Shakespeare

Imagine William Shakespeare in his prime. It is the April of 1594, say, and he is thirty years old today. He might be at his lodgings in London, though if he is there will be little enough for him to do here, the theatres having been shut down for over a year on account of the worst outbreak of the plague in living memory. (Fifteen thousand persons died of it in the last twelve months.) More likely, then, that he is in the provinces with his Company; or perhaps staying at Titchfield, the country house of his patron the Earl of Southampton; or he might even be at home with his wife and their three children. . . .

The place is not important. Where he is does not matter.

It is the face of William Shakespeare that I want you to look at.

It is a frank face, though it keeps many secrets. Fair-skinned, fresh-cheeked, it is a face that blushes easily to reveal its owner's heart. It is a good-looking face, with firm delicate features, and a gaze both calm and observant under brows set low.

It is a worldly face: sensual, sceptical, alert. The eyes are blue, and they dance with bright amusement most of the time. When they do not, the look they give you is straight and unwavering. He has a somewhat drooping lower lip.

That foolish hanging of his nether lip – I think he said he got it from his mother. His forehead, though, is splendid. Like the dome of an observatory.

The most singular feature, no doubt, is the poet's nose. It is broader at the nostrils than down the straight, solid bridge. It is tip-tilted (slightly), and those nostrils arch quickly at the least unpleasant smell. All Mr Shake-speare's senses are acute, but you can *see* his sense of smell at work, thanks

to that singular nose. He is most sensitive to dirt and evil odours. Put him in a room with a spaniel and a tainted bone and watch the way his eyes water and his nose twitches. His senses revolt from the way dogs are fed at table. But if he is your guest, he will say nothing. He is very polite. He is very 'After you'.

There is a small mole high on his left cheek.

I said his brow was splendid, and so it is. His hair, though, soft and brown, is receding from the forehead. Cheeks and chin are firmly moulded. He has downy moustaches and a small brown tuft of beard. Although the lower lip is more prominent than the upper, both are finely shaped. Their most characteristic expression is a faint ironic smile.

I only ever saw two portraits that came near doing this face justice. The first, the frontispiece of the Folio, that immortal piece of inferior engraving by Martin Droeshout. It *is* inferior, but it catches the man I knew. The other's that Stratford bust created by Gerard Jannsen, which (again) is no great work of art, but a pretty good likeness to how Mr Shakespeare looked in his later years. Note that both the Droeshout engraving and the Jannsen bust won the approval of those who knew him best – in the first instance, his fellow players; in the second, his widow and his daughters, and his sister. Two images of the Shakespeare I knew and loved.

In the bust, of course, the face has grown somewhat thicker, been a little bit coarsened. But the brow is still large and lofty, and the eyes do not leave you. He was always a well-built man, tall and lithe, his body nimble even when he put on weight.

I remember once we stood together by a haystack to shun a shower, and the rain ran down his face, and out of the corner of my eye I saw Mr Shakespeare's tongue slipping out slyly, this way and that, just the merest quick flicker, like an adder's, to get a taste of the raindrops on their way. I did not let him know I had seen him do it. But ever afterwards I have thought that the act was essential Shakespeare. He was a man who wanted to taste the sweetness and the bitterness of everything. He would eat each day to the core, and the dark night too. He smiled to himself as he feasted on those raindrops.

Chapter Sixty-Six

Pickleherring's list of
the world's lost plays

There are several lost plays in this careless world. Some went down to Cromwell, some were eaten by rats. Here, I will provide you with my list of them:

The Biter Bit

Rhodon and Iris

All and Everything

The Birth of Merlin

Amends for Ladies

Cardenio

Fair Em

The Way Things Happen

The Tragedy of Gowrie

Dogs, a Masque with Music

Love Lies Bleeding

The Elder Brother

Perkin Warbeck

Right You Are (If You
    Think You Are)

Mr Poe

Two Lovers Killed By Lightning

Arden of Faversham

The Devil's Jig

The Hog Hath Lost His Pearl

Queen Dido

The Bride Stript Bare

Whistle Binkie

The Bride's Maids Spankt

Every Man Erect

All to Bed

A Knot of Fools

When a Man's Single

The Chemical Wedding

Ninus and Semiramis

The Passionate Shepherdess

The Twins' Tragedy

Topcliffe, his Boots: or
    The Parsing of the Papist

Udolpho

The Incompetent Hawk, or In Two
    Fell Swoops

Locrine

Dramatic Eternity: Scene 666

Of these lost plays, only *Cardenio* was by William Shakespeare (writing in collaboration with Mr John Fletcher). We presented it at Whitehall, before the Duke of Savoy, quite late in Mr Shakespeare's lifetime, but that's all I can recall of the wretched thing. The player Thomas Betterton may have a copy of it, as he claims he has, in the handwriting of Mr Downes, the famous prompter. If so, why he has never yet ushered it into the world, I do not know. There is a tradition (which I will merely mention) that Mr Shakespeare gave the script of this play, as a present of value, to a natural daughter of his, for whose sake he wrote it, at the time of his retirement from the stage. I can only say that this daughter was not known to your humble servant.

Mr Betterton is in the habit of talking about three other plays which he claims were the work of Mr Shakespeare, namely:

> *The History of King Stephen*
> *Duke Humphrey, a Tragedy*
> *Iphis and Iantha, or A Marriage Without a Man,*
> > *a Comedy*

Frankly, I never heard of any of them, and Betterton's story that they perished when Mrs Shakespeare 'unluckily burned 'em by putting 'em under pie bottoms' speaks (in my opinion) for itself.

Love's Labour's Won, though, is a different matter.

Chapter Sixty-Seven

Love's Labour's Won

Love's Labour's Won is, in fact, the first version of the play now known as *All's Well That Ends Well*. It was one of Mr Shakespeare's earliest comedies, a companion piece in spirit to his *Love's Labour's Lost*.

I count this particular revision a spoiling and a pity. The trouble with *All's Well That Ends Well* is that you can see two hands at work in it. Both of them are Shakespeare, but the second is Shakespeare in a ruthless mood. Something about the froth of the original dissatisfied him. But in slashing out several key speeches he had given to Helena he removed, in my opinion, the heart of the thing.

As promised in Chapter Seventeen (the one where I first told you about the room where I am writing this book) I will now give you all that remains in my possession of *Love's Labour's Won*. As you will see, this consists entirely of Helena's speeches, as I remember them, and as I had written them out for my learning. Where they fit into *All's Well That Ends Well*, as it stands now, I cannot exactly remember. That play, to speak plainly, is a spatchcock. It was never popular with the public, nor was Helena a favourite part of mine.

As to the clever place where I conceal this treasure – would it surprise you, sir, to look under your nose? The best place to hide anything is out in the open. Therefore, I keep all that is left of *Love's Labour's Won* in that envelope there on the mantelpiece. Yes, madam, that one, propped beside my clock, which (as you say) you had not even noticed. Here, hand me the pages down, and I will speak them for you. . . .

First, Helena remembers her childhood in Narbonne, the hot south-land where her father was a physician:

'Twas ever summer in my dandled days
But sometime when the sky grew tired with heat
Slow thundry raindrops came, O it rained kisses
To cool my ear with whispers.
Then quickly flowers were jewels and moss was treasure
And long laburnam dripped like melting gold
And in the interstices of the stones
Small snails and lizards, spiders and black toads
Slid their wet scales against the cavern walls
Into the business of the flooded day.
First there was murmur in the tops of trees
Where the sky moved to ease the spate of rain,
Which though you could not see the branches tossed
To lay your hand upon the unmoved trunk
You knew the coming splendour of the storm,
And found the whole world water.
Great rivers grew where little trickles ran
And swans sat on them, cygnets in their wings,
And tall flamingoes beat against the wind
To find a higher perch above the surge.
All round me in the trees were watching eyes
As small things shivered for the wind and rain
And saw their masters ruffled from their lairs
Shake angry paws and pick fastidious ways
To proper earth where they could sit and lord it,
Letting the storm borrow their wilderness
And waiting for its idle strength to spend.
Which, when it had, the sun unburst his heat
And drew the vapours steaming from the ground
And with his stupid vapour hung the air
Till everything became itself again.
Among their drying stones the lizards lurked
And from the hill the lions swung their way,
Drooping their heads and blinking in a dream
As if the sky had never touched their peace.
Then, after they had passed, I saw a man —
A figure made of stone who stood whereat
That torrent had splashed down, sudden and strong.
Thinking I saw him move I held my breath
But he was stone and still and blind as silence.

And all around him in the working grass
The insects hummed, and birds' wings rushed again,
And all the noises heard themselves once more.

This next little excised passage came where Helena made her entrance in Scene 3 of the First Act, just after her guardian the Countess has spoken of love as 'this thorn' which belongs to 'our rose of youth'. No doubt the speech is too abrupt and not a little obscure, but (again) I think that its excision takes sympathy away from Helena who as she exists in *All's Well That Ends Well* lacks the essential dash of poetic feeling that's necessary to her deeds. Without lines like these, her pursuit of Bertram, and her use of the bed-trick, can strike the audience as repellent.

Anyway, picking up the image just expressed by the Countess of Rousillon, Bertram's mother, in *Love's Labour's Won* I had to say as Helena:

A counterfeit of silence is the rose –
For it's substantial fire, a patient palace
Listening to ghosts, a sorrow in sunlight.

Then there is this, which must come from Act IV, when Helena is in the widow's house in Florence, about to perform her trick on Bertram:

Far, far from such festivity of flesh
I dream in ignorance of sanctuary,
Night-compassed.
How may the swarming sun the hive of flesh
Exhaust our quintessential sense, madam?
All men are strangers! O rivers, rivers,
Solve in your too bright burden of reflection
The hubbub of an overhanging noon,
And by your volubility hush up
The synonyms of Echo.

Where this came in, God only knows, but I consider it a shame to have lost so much imagery of pretty fishes, which again adds beauty to the part of Helena:

Those rainbow waters vellumy
Are all the pages of my book:
A kind of prick-fish, stickleback,

And ticklish trout in the binding.
Rouch, bleak, loach, minnow, pickerel —
A perch voracious for her own blind eyes
In the frousty primer of my blindness.
Lavish as gudgeon, the dropsical carp
Came at my call, to troll the sun
Through nibbling nets of moss, or dusk,
Wounded with tench.
And — exhalations smouldering the far water —
The swans drift down on me with Lethe in their wings.

I have this written out as verse, but it may be prose. Here, with your permission, I might mention a private theory of my own — namely, that there are several passages given to female characters in Shakespeare which have been taken for prose but which sound, in fact, quite new and original verse-rhythms. The later speeches of Lady Macbeth, for example, which are printed in the Folio as prose, are to my ear really verse, and very fine verse at that. When I spoke them I delivered them always in measure, and Mr Shakespeare never stopped me. Those lines drawn out in monosyllabic feet seem to me as wonderfully effective as any he wrote. The speeches in the sleep-walking scene, for instance, if spoken as verse, have a very great majesty.

You have had enough of *Love's Labour's Won*, have you, friends?

Very well, then. But just one speech more, before I put the sheets back in the envelope. This must surely belong at the end, where in *All's Well* Helena never seems to have sufficient to say to Bertram to make it true in any sense that all ends well:

Helena (to Bertram)
> *Do not suppose I love you less because*
> *My heart beats words to cheat the meaning out*
> *Of love I cannot cheat so beat with words.*
> *I have had carnal knowledge of the night*
> *And move within the rose's jurisdiction.*
> *Because I lack wet willow's simple touch*
> *Do not suppose I love you overmuch.*

Chapter Sixty-Eight

Was Shakespeare raped?

Have you ever noticed how very queer Mr Shakespeare's two long narrative poems are?

I mean *Venus and Adonis* and *The Rape of Lucrece*, both published in this period when the theatres were closed down on account of the plague, both written therefore before his thirtieth birthday.

In the first a mannish woman rapes a womanish man, but he proves impotent.

In the second a man is excited by the idea of his friend's wife being chaste and rapes her, but the rape gets a bare eight lines out of the whole 1855. Before the rape, the poem lingers in a dream-like way over everything it invokes for our inspection: the doors and locks of the victim's house, the wind that blows down the corridors, Lucrece's discarded glove, her bedroom, her 'yet unstained' bed, her body's beauty – five gloating stanzas of the last, including a description of her breasts *like ivory globes circled with blue, / A pair of maiden yokes unconquered, / Save of their lord.* After the rape, the poem quickly enters the victim's mind and becomes her long rhetorical complaint before she kills herself. Although the presentation of the ravisher Tarquin is adequate, it is plain that the poet identifies more easily with the raped woman Lucrece.

I think that in both poems Shakespeare was looking back eleven years or so, towards that summer of 1582, when perhaps he played Adonis/Lucrece to Anne Hathaway's Venus/Tarquin in the fields of Shottery.

Was Shakespeare raped?

I think it not impossible. His Venus is not Ovid's Venus. She is not even much of a goddess. She is an older woman having her way with a country boy she has kidnapped.

Venus rapes Adonis, but she doesn't get what she wants. That much is made apparent at the climax:

> *Now is she in the very lists of love,*
> *Her champion mounted for the hot encounter:*
> *All is imaginary she doth prove,*
> *He will not manage her, although he mount her;*
> *That worse than Tantalus' is her annoy,*
> *To clip Elysium and to lack her joy.*

Tantalus was punished in Hades by being inflicted with a great thirst and placed up to his chin in water which receded whenever he tried to drink. The last line means there has been no penetration.

Did Shakespeare believe (like his beloved Ovid) that women get more sexual pleasure from the act than men do? Tiresias in the *Metamorphoses* is the type of those who say so. Juno rewarded him with blindness.

The lustful Venus certainly takes control from the start:

> *Backward she push'd him, as she would be thrust,*
> *And govern'd him in strength, though not in lust.*

Adonis, by contrast, is almost as chaste as Lucrece. Unwilling and obstinate, he takes another 521 lines to succumb in any sort to the blandishments of his ravisher:

> *He now obeys and now no more resisteth,*
> *While she takes all she can, not all she listeth.*

A couplet which suggests that their coupling gives her little pleasure, and him none. Notice, too, how the comic effect of such feminine rhymes as are employed (*encounter/he mount her*; *resisteth/she listeth*) is always to leave Venus looking more than a touch ridiculous.

Before and after the imperfect copulation, the imagery of the poem at many points suggests that fable of Shakespeare's childhood which had the boy Willy fleeing from his mother, both of them assuming different guises until she caught him. Venus is likened to an eagle, a wolf, a glutton, a vulture whose lips 'are conquerors', a milch doe 'whose swelling dugs do ache', and then to falcons (yes, in the plural). Adonis is severally a bird lying tangled in the net, a divedapper (a species of grebe common on the Avon) turning his head this way and that to escape unwanted kisses, a deer, a lily

prisoned in a jail of snow, a fleet-foot roe, a 'froward infant still'd with dandling',* a hare pursued by hounds, a bright star shooting from the sky, and (finally) a purple flower of which Venus 'crops the stalk', noting 'green-dropping sap' in 'the breach', which sap she compares to tears.

Ladies and gentlemen, I rest my case.

Venus and Adonis achieved an immediate and prolonged success with the public in general – 16 editions of it were called for during the poet's lifetime. But what was the nature of this success? Why, it was as a kind of aphrodisiac, a drug or preparation inducing venereal desire. It made people 'burn in love', as Shakespeare's disciple John Weever declared in an epigrammatic sonnet. Others spoke frankly of sleeping with it under their pillows, and nuns were said to be using it as an aid to manustupration.

Madam, Pickleherring is *not* making this up as he goes along! I call as witness John Robinson, who in his *Anatomie of the English Nunnery at Lisbon* – the second edition, of 1623 – tells us that he managed to get himself engaged as door-keeper of that convent to keep an eye on three cousins of the Earl of Southampton who had taken the veil, and that 'these ladies, although making parade of chastity, poverty and obedience possess licentious books and when the confessor feels merrily disposed after supper, it is usual for him to read from *Venus and Adonis* or the *Jests of George Peele*, as there are few idle pamphlets printed in England that are not to be found in this house.' It was no less popular at the Court of Queen Elizabeth. A mad soldier called William Renolds (no relation!) even claimed that it had been published to show the world that the Queen was in love with him. I doubt if she was; and it certainly wasn't.

None of this is said by way of disapprobation. Both *Venus and Adonis* and *The Rape of Lucrece* are sexually arousing, and it would be false to pretend that a part of Mr Shakespeare's first reputation was not as an erotic writer. Pickleherring is willing to confess that the first time he read these poems he came across passages that gave him a hard on, and he imagines they made those nuns feel warm and wet. There is nothing wrong with this. I wish a few more readers would admit it. (Thank you, madam! You advance in my respect.)

But, sir, I take your point. There *is* something reprehensible and disgusting about a man taking pleasure in the rape of poor Lucrece, and I *am* ashamed to have done so. At the same time, I insist that Mr Shakespeare's verse is by no means innocent of such pleasure itself. To say that Lucrece's breasts are 'unconquered' save by her husband is to be an

---

* An allusion to Mary Arden's playing with her son?

accomplice in the idea of ravishment. It feeds the doubtless horrible male fantasy that all sex is a game of conquest and possession. And I have not forgotten that the poem ends with Lucrece's suicide, no. As for that, the other one ends with Adonis gored to death by a wild boar, and Venus hanging over *the wide wound that the boar had trench'd/In his soft flank*, staining her face with the boy's blood, and confessing that if she had boar's teeth *With kissing him I should have kill'd him first.* Do you suppose that the author of *Othello* was ignorant of the fact that Love and Death are sisters, and pain and pleasure often close allied?

I set out to suggest in this chapter that William Shakespeare was not the dominant partner in his early sexual exchanges with Anne Hathaway, and to argue that in his identification with first Adonis and then Lucrece he might be telling us something of his own feelings with regard to what she may have done to him. Of course, it could be that like many men he found the very notion of a sexually predatory and aggressive female both disturbing and comical, and that he found this notion incarnate in the figure of Venus. All the same, working on my usual principle that what is interesting biographically in Shakespeare's work is what the subject does not demand he put there, I will maintain that in such an image as comes in the last line following we certainly do not see any Venus, any Goddess of Love:

> With this he breaketh from the sweet embrace
> Of those fair arms which bound him to her breast
> And homeward through the dark lawnd runs apace;
> Leaves Love upon her back, deeply distress'd.

That 'Love', deeply distress'd, left lying on her back in a Shottery meadow, might even be heard to drum her heels upon the ground in the well-known tantarum way of country girls unsatisfied by their swains. As to identifying Anne Hathaway with Sextus Tarquinius – I do no such foolish thing. Your author merely points out that William Shakespeare participates most keenly in the woman's role in this particular poem. Perhaps he was never raped. But he felt he had been.

The other thing to say about these two poems is that while both of them are dedicated to Henry Wriothesley, Earl of Southampton, there is an observable difference between the two dedications. The first is impersonal but not cold. The second is both personal and warm: 'What I have done is yours; what I have to do is yours: being part in all I have, devoted yours.' This difference in tone reflected the development in friendship between

poet and patron, but I'll keep that for my next chapter, which will be all about Southampton.

For the moment, suddenly, my mind is filled up by memory of Mrs Anne Shakespeare coming after me with that birch broom of hers, driving me from New Place and chasing me round the mulberry tree when she caught me in her black silk calimanco. All at once, the notion of her as Tarquin is not so foolish.

Chapter Sixty-Nine

All about Rizley

So here is the Right Honourable Henry Wriothesley, Baron Titchfield, Earl of Southampton, in a miniature painted by Nicholas Hilliard. He is twenty summers old – it depicts him at the time of *Venus and Adonis* and of Mr Shakespeare's first sonnets advising and exhorting him to marry. This is the face of Narcissus.

Under the exquisite arch of the brows the eyes look down, but not in any kind of modesty. They consider the rest of their owner, and are pleased with what they see. The gaze, you might say, is cock-sure. Who's a pretty boy then?

This is the face that launched a thousand quips, all of them complimentary. It is long and oval, with delicate features, the face of an aristocrat. The long thin nose is pointed, like a Russian dog's. It speaks of centuries of sniffing, as well as centuries of in-breeding. The hair is a cascade of love-locks, red-gold, curling. It dangles down over its grower's left shoulder, falling half-way to his wasp waist. It makes you want to swing him round the room by it. As for the mouth: two petulant petals pouting in complacent pride? That about covers it.

The lord and owner of this face has rings in his ears. He wears a white satin doublet. He has slashed and padded trunk-hose with, beneath his trunks, a pair of canions. Purple garters embroidered with silver thread hold up his white silk stockings. See, on the table beside him, his plumed helmet. One arm rests lightly on it. His other (gloved) hand rests on his padded hip.

To be honest, Pickleherring never much cared for the Earl of Southampton. You might say I was jealous, reader. Perhaps I was.

My main feeling, though, was straightforward dislike of the man. He was rich and he was a poet-fancier, that's all. I do not think he cared for poetry,

though at one point he was an ardent theatre-goer, spending his time merrily in going to plays every day. What he liked was being seen by the audience. He had his own stool which he perched upon, one leg thrust forward. His habit was to make much fuss with his hair, patting and primping, or powdering his cheeks as he sat. He never even pretended that he was listening. He liked to prop himself against a proscenium door, and kick aside his stool to show off the clock on his stocking. Did I mention that he was left-handed? A further token, if you like, of his aptitude for viciousness. Not that I have anything against left-handed people. But Southampton made a virtue of disconcerting you by holding out his left hand to be kissed.

The young Earl lived for his hair, I always thought. Poets and barbers were much the same to him. In fact, as Mr Shakespeare once told me in a rare unguarded moment, Southampton took an odd delight in having his hair combed in a measured or rhythmical manner. He would only have it done by dressers who were skilled in the rules of prosody. He claimed that while many take delight in the rubbing of their limbs and the combing of their hair, these exercises would delight much more if the servants at the baths, and all the barbers, were so skilful in the art of poesy that they could express any called-for measure with their fingers. Whether Mr Shakespeare provided his patron with iambic or trochaic combing, I know not. His dactyls may have caused no small delight.

Little or nothing in himself, Southampton wanted immortality through others. At Cambridge, his dissertation was on Fame. Mr Shakespeare claimed that some of the sonnets would give it to him. Alas, this is probably true, though they're not the best sonnets.

This golden youth was a Papist, and the heir of Papists. His father, a Mary Stuart man, had perished in the Tower. The boy was brought up by his mother, a more worldly creature who groomed him to marry Lord Burghley's granddaughter, the Lady Elizabeth Vere.

This marriage of convenience, which would have brought together two of England's greatest houses, never came to pass, despite Lady Southampton's plots and entreaties and then Mr Shakespeare's work in the same cause. I have always suspected, by the by, that those first 25 sonnets urging Southampton to marry were in fact *commissioned* by Lady Southampton, but I cannot prove it, and I never dared ask their author. (Notice how in the third one he flatters the boy's mother!) They did not work anyway. The young Earl did not feel like marrying.

He went for women as well as men, mind you. He liked both men and

women to adore him. Whether he loved anyone in his life, of either sex or none, I rather doubt.

Many writers sought Southampton's patronage, not just Shakespeare. It was known he would inherit a fortune on coming of age. (So he did, though Burghley contrived to dock it of £5000 on account of the young man's breach of contract in the matter of Elizabeth Vere.) Besides our hero, others who tried to tap Southampton for funds included Barnabe Barnes, Samuel Daniel, Gervase Markham, Henry Constable, Bartholomew Griffin, George Wither, Richard Barnfield, George Peele, Matthew Gwinne (whose 'comedy' *Vertumnus* once sent King James to sleep), Arthur Pryce, William Pettie, and George Chapman (who even tried to find a patron in his grocer). Thomas Nashe is known to have written obscene verses for the little charmer, excusing himself by saying that he was only following in Shakespeare's footsteps. Alas for Nashe, his verses were *so* obscene that they still remain in manuscript. Meanwhile, out in the published world, dedications rained on Southampton's head, and he got wet.

In Mr Shakespeare's case, money certainly changed hands. *Venus and Adonis* (or its fame, or its power when recited for a bit of barbering) must have proved sweet to the young Earl's taste, for by the time of its sequel Southampton was inviting its author to dine at Holborn House, his palatial London residence, and to stay with him at Titchfield in the country. Mr Shakespeare was always reticent regarding it, but I believe that his patron once made him a present of £1000 to enable him to go through with a purchase which he heard he had a mind to — enough to purchase a fine house in Stratford, a large number of shares in our Company of actors, and leave some change to spare for playing primero. Southampton played a lot of primero. Gambling of any kind pleased him. He once lost 1800 crowns at a tennis-match in Paris.

It has to be admitted that Shakespeare had something of a weakness regarding aristocrats. He liked them to like him. I could not say why. In Southampton, who was ten years his junior, he found, for a while, a powerful patron who seemed like a friend. No doubt he was flattered and excited to find himself invited into a circle that was like a little court. Here he was, accepted on his own merits by a set that put much store by wit — persons who were worldly wise as well as wealthy, all of them impressed by his gift for puns (I can put it no higher). You can see this reflected in *Love's Labour's Lost*, a comedy first written to amuse Southampton and his friends. Not all Southampton's friends were idiots, either. John Florio, the scholar, was his tutor. It was Florio who gave Mr S the seed for his mulberry tree.

Southampton's patronage of Shakespeare, then, developed quickly into intimacy. But this was a friendship that brought Shakespeare more torment than peace.

I no more want to speak of this than to tell the boring story of the boring Lamberts. Southampton is even more boring. Consider him apart from WS. All his life he sought 'praise and reputation' – his own words. He rose and then he fell with his flash friend Essex. He commanded in some fashion the *Garland* on the famous Islands Voyage of '97, and was even credited with the capture of a Spanish vessel. However (yawn, yawn), he aroused Queen Elizabeth's fury two years later by accepting the rank of General of the Horse under Essex in Ireland without royal permission. When Essex tried to capture the Queen and seize power, in 1601, it was Southampton's London house that was used as a base for the crazy insurrection. You could say this was the worst mistake of a mistaken life. Southampton was tried for treason with Essex, found guilty, and only escaped execution thanks to his Mamma pulling a few strings with Secretary Cecil. No doubt she persuaded him that so pretty a head could not be dangerous.

In his manners, the irksome Earl was always epicene. When he served in the wars in Ireland it is said that he saw most of his active service in bed with a Captain Piers Edmunds. Southampton would 'cole and hug' his captain in his arms, and 'play wantonly' with him – I quote from a report that was sent to Cecil. To COLE or CULL is to fondle, as in CULL-ME-TO-YOU, which as my wife Jane used to remind me is a country name for the pansy flower. WS may well have been thinking of Southampton and Edmunds when he wrote of Achilles and Patroclus in *Troilus and Cressida*. Something he said to me once led me to understand that Southampton is also Bertram in *All's Well That Ends Well*, that disagreeable hero, another reason why I do not like the play.

For the rest, I believe Southampton's part in Shakespeare's story to be negligible. True, when his patron toyed with studies of the law for a brief while, the poet obligingly fitted out a sonnet in praise of him with a few legal terms remembered from his own days as a NOVERINT. Then, when Southampton entertained day-dreams of serving the King of France, his Will-to-boot came up with comedies which transport the spectator to Nérac and the Louvre. Such things are not profound. They belong, like their begetter, to the surface.

This is not to say that William Shakespeare did not take Henry Wriothesley seriously. He did. Too seriously. And he suffered much pain as a consequence. You will learn of that when I tell you about the sonnets, the

story behind them, as that concerns Southampton. Not that he was the only one concerned.

For the pretty Earl's part, Pickleherring is sure that the sonnets were over his head. Beyond him. If he read them at all, that is, which he probably did not, except for the ones that are simply in praise of his beauty.

He died, in 1624, Henry Wriothesley, of a lethargy, having lived in one most of his life, if you ask me.

Oh yes, and Wriothesley should be pronounced as RIZLEY. That's how top people always say it. Rhymes with GRISLY.

Chapter Seventy

A Private Observation

I promised to tell you about it if I ever saw Anne fucked. Well, I have not seen Anne fucked, but I've seen her fucking.

Reader, I think it is time that you took yourself in hand. This matter's of some more than riddling interest, as I hope that you will presently agree. Pay heed to what I tell you, if you please.

Late last night I heard sweet noises coming from the room below. It was the sound of lechery. As I listened, I heard thumpings and bumpings, unmistakable in their import, and other intimate, disturbing noises. The summer night was full of provoking music.

Once thinking of Anne being fucked, I could think of nothing else. I snuffed out my candle. I sat still in the warm darkness, my heart beating hard against my breast bone. I was wrestling with my conscience, which instructed me not to look. Did I really want to see my dear little egg-girl under some sweating bull of a whoremaster who had purchased her body for a half an hour's business? Did I truly want to see that sweet young creature tupped?

I did indeed, sir! I wanted it more than anything in the world. My nerves cried out to watch it. And those noises continuing, louder, more urgent, with squeaks too, and squealings, and other indications of delight, I knew I had to watch what was going on below me in Anne's bedroom.

I removed my Ovid carefully, without a sound. I knelt down upon my knees, with my eye to the peep-hole.

What did I see?

I saw my lovely Anne, where she lay arse-upwards. She was naked save for those white silk stockings of hers. One stocking was held up by a black taffety garter. The other was tumbled, all anyhow, down round her ankle.

Her young limbs were busy in their lechery. I saw her back first, white and trim and lithe, with her plump little buttocks going up and down, plunging. She was wantoning, and revelling in the act. She has the most adorable dimple in her left bum-cheek.

So she likes to ride on top, thought I, the young harlot! What bliss! What joy! How the fortunate fellow below her on the bed must be pleasuring her! No doubt his cock is spear-hard, big, and thick, and my darling rides him now as not long ago she rode on her rocking-horse.

The chamber was illumined by a blazing thicket of candles. All round the bed they burned, like a fiery forest. Hot wax dripped down as the flames flickered straight in the gloom.

Anne's shadow on the wall made her look like a succubus.

But having feasted my eyes on my darling I saw then that the one below Anne was not a man as I'd supposed. It was another female, more mature, indeed voluptuous, with long blonde hair that shone bonnily in the candlelight. This woman was also naked, except for a band of black velvet she was wearing about her neck, with a cameo brooch on it. She looked vicious and lascivious, as she lay there with my whore-child in her arms. There was a proud patrician tilt to her ample breasts. Her hair streamed down, half-drowning both bodies as they twisted and threshed this way and that in their amorous disport. I saw that this older woman was clutching a red rose in her left fist. As I watched I saw her swivel her hips under Anne's downward thrusting, tightening the grip of her legs where they held her rider in place. She cried out some demand. I could not hear what. The effect, though, was immediate. Anne redoubled her thrustings. It was as if she was ploughing her companion.

I do not think this other woman was another of Pompey Bum's whores. I'd never seen her before, and I believe I have seen every woman employed in this establishment. Besides, there was something about her which spoke of power and money. Perhaps it was that cameo brooch. The tilt of her breasts and her chin. She had very blue eyes which blazed up at me as she lay there threshing from side to side, and her look was imperious. There was something matronly and aristocratic about her, and while it was plain that she was delighted with what little Anne was doing to her it was at the same time plain that she was really the one in command. Both of them seemed lost in their ecstasy, but the greater part of the pleasure was undoubtedly the blonde woman's.

As I watched, I saw her trail that red, red rose down Anne's white back. There was a blood-red ruby ring on the middle finger of her hand. It caught the blaze of the candleflames.

I watched Anne's bottom going up and down. It was white as snow, and the cheeks were firm and tight. Her whole body has a taut straight innocence, like an arrow.

Then that arrow hit the target, there on the bed in that magic Arabian cavern of candlelight under me. The ridden woman started bucking and screaming. She threw away the rose and grabbed hold of Anne by the ears. As for Anne, she was laughing, and kissing the woman as she rode her. But the woman did not laugh. Instead, she started slapping at her lover's arse with the open palms of her hands. Then she was bucking again, and screaming again, and scratching with her fingernails deep in Anne's bottom-cheeks, and crying out in her luxury: 'Yes! Yes! Yes!'

They lay still, these two pretty bed-fellows, for a long, long minute.

Then Anne rolled off her customer.

She had given her satisfaction.

My Anne rolled off the fair-haired matron and lay there on her back on the bed beside her.

And gazing down into my secret erotic theatre I saw that between her white thighs, over the faintest down of pubescent hair, Anne had strapped on a whopping dildo, both lifelike and terrible, shaped exactly like a man's prick, a black man's prick. It was with this artificial ebony phallus that my whore-child Anne had been fucking the older woman.

They lay there on their backs looking up at me.

One dark. And one so fair. The fair one fucked. The dark one her sweet fucker.

Amorously impleacht, the blonde hair and the black entwined on the pillow.

Their limbs gleaming with sweat in the candlelight. Their eyes wide with sensual surfeit as they gazed at me.

It was disconcerting, madam.

They were beautiful, both of them. They were lovely with the lineaments of satisfied desire. One blonde, the elder, one my dark young charmer, they lay there in the light of the candleflames, spread out for my inspection on the bed.

It was as if they knew that I was watching them, and they did not care. But I do not think they could see my eye at the peep-hole. They were too much involved with each other to know I was there.

Then, as I watched, the older woman (who for some reason to do with her air of assurance and self-possession I now began to think of as the Countess), this Countess began to run her long fingers up and down Anne's

dildo wonderingly, as if the thing was real, and now it had crossed her mind to play with it, to inspirit it into action once again.

Anne laughed at such sport. Then she jumped up, and strutted up and down. She walked about the chamber, in and out of the flickering circle of candlelight, her hands on her hips, and wriggling her bottom most wantonly. She was shaking the dildo, she was slapping it, she was waggling it up and down and from side to side as she strutted. She pranced. She pirouetted. Every joyful little gesture made the thing to dance as if it had a lewd life of its own. Anne looked so innocent with her dildo on. I know that's a strange thing to say, but I say that's how it was. You could see it was all such fun to her, such frolic, such forked excitement. She wagged her little tail as she walked with her black dildo on. She was like a child playing games, and her games the more exciting because adult and forbidden.

Then my darling jumped up on the bed, and smacked the Countess. She smacked the Countess, hard, across the breasts, with the black dildo. She did not take it off, but she made it do the smacking. The Countess screamed at the stings, but she seemed to like them.

Anne stopped.

She kissed the Countess lightly on the lips.

Then she kissed her again, most chastely, this time on her cheek.

Then she extricated herself from her bed-fellow's arms where they beseeched her, and rolled nimbly from the wide bed, and stood beside it.

Anne stood still. Trickles of sweat ran down her breasts. Her breasts are like little apples. She looked so lovely I could hardly bear it.

Then, as I watched, with bated breath, Anne slowly unstrapped the dildo from her thighs. She was taking her time. She was making her victim wait.

Suddenly, the dildo unstrapped, and clutched now in her right hand, Anne pushed the Countess back on the bed, and rolled her over, and with a squeal of glee began beating her with the dildo on her bare buttocks.

The Countess was wriggling her bum. She writhed beneath this punishment. I had no doubt at all but that she was enjoying it. She was crying out with the pleasure the pain was giving her. Her body arched up in long exquisite shudders from the bed.

Anne's response was to beat the proffered bottom yet more savagely. She smacked and she spanked till the Countess looked quite red and raw. Both were panting, and shouting out obscenities in their excitement. It surprised me to hear Anne shout out several words I would not have thought she knew. I mean words that I had hoped she would not have known on account of her tender years.

Then, eyes blazing, Anne strapped on the dildo once more, and in no

time at all the two women were at it again, at their amorous rites, first in this position then in that, like two sleek dolphins copulating in the foam. . . .

I could watch it no more.

I could stand it no longer.

I drew away from the peep-hole.

Pickleherring had seen enough.

I put Ovid back over the aperture.

This morning I don't feel much like working on my book. The day is hot. I have opened my window an inch or so. I can hear from the street below the sound of children playing. In summer this street is alive with the children of misery. Outside the grocer's a band of juvenile pickpockets will be absorbed in pitch and toss. At a short distance, a motley crew busies itself with games of barley-break, blow-point, loggats, marbles, muss. Oaths and idiot laughter mar their play. They spit and cheat. Osric is drunk and Mopsa adjusts her garters. Hal writes on Tybalt with a rusty knife. Pretty Lavinia farts. Lysander picks his teeth with the point of an arrow. It is still early, but the sun, who at this season takes only a nap, like myself, has got his chin above the level of the roof-tops opposite, where sparrows . . .

Enough of that.

It gets boring when you lie, and more boring when you accuse yourself of lying, when you wonder if the original statement was a lie, or the accusation of lying a lie, and then realise the pathetic flick at honesty implied in putting it all down, worrying your head over the whole thing, lie, counter-lie, truth, imbalance, balance, this whole damned trick of biography, of delicacy, of morality, this whole business or stamp of susceptibility, words, hesitations, qualifications, definitions, withdrawal, what the present writer is trying to get away from by writing the Life of Shakespeare.

In a word already said: sensibility.

Sensibility a curse.

Melodramatic, madam?

Try again.

Sensibility a nuisance.

That's enough.

But I tell you last night's love-scene was not what I expected.

And nor did I mean to write it out today.

Yet, having written it, I will let it stand. I can see that it forms part of my Life of Shakespeare, coming somewhere (as it does) after Venus and Lucrece and Rizley but before the Dark Lady of the sonnets. I cannot explain it. I will have to let it stand. Life sometimes gives you toads for your

imaginary garden. Not that my Anne is in the least like a toad. I mean just that she is real.

I am the toad, in fact. And she is the jewel in my head.

Last night's love-scene in my secret theatre of desire was not at all what I expected.

To have seen Anne like that disturbs me to the core. It has dismayed my spirit. This morning I am shaken, I am shattered. Where did my sweet child learn such things? For sure, they could not come naturally. But can she ever have been innocent? She must be wicked, yet she is so young.

Pickleherring, your servant, has lived a long life. I have seen most things, and I have done most things also, but never before have I seen a young girl fuck another female, a woman old enough to be her mother.

The terrible thing, of course, is that I enjoyed it.

Chapter Seventy-One

*In which Pickleherring presents
a lost sonnet by William Shakespeare*

The door to the room where Mr Shakespeare wrote his sonnets would not close fast again. Its hinges had been rusted up with the salt water of tears.

I call those sonnets William Shakespeare's spiritual and sentimental autobiography. In them he opens his heart.

Mind you, some of the sonnets were very obscure in their original form.

What would happen is that he would write one and then he would try it out on me, have me read it, or better still have me read it aloud to him, and then I would say I liked this line or that line, and he would strike out the others. Or he would learn what he needed to know about the sonnet from my reading of it, the hearing of his words spoken by another voice, and he would strike lines out himself, or add them to other lines. Sometimes he would end up with a completely new sonnet made from the lines I had liked. At other times, he would end up with several sonnets clarifying an obscure one, sonnets written by taking lines out and making sense of them by finding them new homes where they belonged.

Mr Shakespeare used to say that in a true poem the words make a truth of themselves. But unfortunately I do not know what this means.

To give you some small notion of what he was up against – the degree of confusion in his mind and heart – I am going to include in this book a sonnet of William Shakespeare's never before published. This was a first draft of one of the early ones. While this sonnet does not appear among the 154 eventually published by Thomas Thorpe from the manuscripts provided for him by William Hervey, Rizley's stepfather, and sold as a sixpenny volume in 1609, it contains within itself the germs of more than a

dozen which *are* to be found there, lines with which the reader may therefore be familiar.

Here, then, is

A LOST SONNET BY WILLIAM SHAKESPEARE

Shall I compare thee to a summer's day
That thereby beauty's rose might never die?
Though heavy sleep on sightless eyes doth stay
My heart doth plead that thou in him dost lie.
If I could write the beauty of your eyes
With means more blessed than my barren rhyme,
To find where your true image pictur'd lies
I would not count the clock that tells the time.
If I lose thee, my loss is my love's gain,
And yet love knows it is a greater grief:
Look what thy memory cannot contain
Th' offender's sorrow lends but weak relief.
    But thence I learn and find the lesson true,
    And all in war with Time for love of you.

Chapter Seventy-Two

Who was Shakespeare's Friend?

In general of Mr Shakespeare's sonnets it has been observed that there are many footprints around the cave of this mystery, none of them pointing in the outward direction.

Pickleherring will now try to clear a few things up for you, dear reader.

First, bearing in mind that at the present time this is the most difficult to obtain of Shakespeare's writings, and that the only recent edition was a catchpenny pirated job which tampered with the text to make lines addressed to a man read as though addressed to a woman, permit me to pen a few paragraphs in simple description of these sonnets. Sir, a connoisseur such as yourself can skip on down the page. Madam, please bear with me; I know that you know everything.

William Shakespeare's *Sonnets* were first printed in 1609, only seven years before their author's death, by George Eld for Thomas Thorpe, a fly-by-night publisher who died in an almshouse at Ewelme. The little volume is hard to get hold of because Mr S did not authorise its publication, and bought up copies where he could, and did his best altogether to suppress it, the reason being the private and indeed scandalous nature of some of the work it contained. It was his poetic diary, so to speak, much of it written for his own eyes only, and while he had every reason not to be ashamed of it, and in fact was not, at the same time I believe he would have preferred it if the poems had not been made available for public reading in his lifetime.

The volume, quarto-size, was dedicated by Thorpe to 'Mr W. H.' – William Hervey, Rizley's stepfather, who had provided him with copies of the poems. By that time, there was no love lost between Mr Shakespeare and any of the Southamptons.

The poems in the book fall into two sections – the first 126 being

concerned mainly with a Friend whom the poet addresses in terms of growing intimacy, first exhorting him to marry and beget children, then praising his beauty and promising to immortalise it by means of the verse, then upbraiding him for various acts of betrayal including the seduction of the poet's own mistress. The self-love of the Friend is at all points harped upon. Yet Shakespeare persists in loving him, and in forgiving him. The rest of the sonnets, from number 127 onwards, are concerned with the poet's relationship with his mistress, the Dark Lady, a *woman coloured ill* who is also described as a *female evil*, among other choice epithets. She is as skilled at playing upon men as she is skilled at playing upon the virginals. While from several physical descriptions we learn that she is in no way conventionally beautiful, yet she possesses a sexual magnetism which the poet cannot resist. Some would not use the word *love* to define their need for such a woman, but Shakespeare does. Several of the poems are bitter about this Dark Lady's infidelity with the Friend, and sore on the subject of her sexual appetites, and express the poet's self-disgust at his own lust for her – sonnet 129, for instance, describes *lust in action* as *th' expense of spirit in a waste of shame.* Yet by the strength of the truth in the poetry Shakespeare can be said in the end to forgive the Dark Lady as he forgives the Friend.

Now then, it ill behoves the present writer to say it, but in the final analysis poetry as good as this makes biography irrelevant. It does not matter who these people were. What matters is the truth that the poet has wrung from them. Was the poet sincere? The question is stupid. *The poetry is sincere.* That is all that there is to be said. Shakespeare's sonnets have a smell of unmistakable necessity. As my friend the poet Martin Seemore once remarked, they were written by a man who desperately wanted to exist well: 'to learn how to live and love truly'.

That is the real secret in the cave. Human nature being what it is, though, can I say anything about those footprints?

First, who was Shakespeare's Friend?

I hope you will not find it facetious if I answer that question by saying that the late Mr WS had several Friends. I will in any case add immediately that as I have already told you the Friend of the sonnets began as Rizley, with all those exhortations to him to marry, written at the behest of Lady Southampton, his mother.

But the Friend of the sonnets is not always Rizley.

Later, for example, it was me.

Yes, sir, I admit it. I was Shakespeare's boy, sir! On occasion, on dire or sweet occasion, and much against my will, I, Pickleherring, was the master-mistress of the great man's passion.

Madam, I do apologise, believe me. But, alas, I am not ashamed.

I had better tell you this, for your understanding. When I was playing all those female parts I had to watch my erections. I found the touch of the dresses against my genitals very provoking. I was a boy who was easily provoked. And of course my male protruberance was at all times something of a difficulty.

My skirts covered that well enough, of course, when I was wearing skirts. But there was the odd time, such as when Rosalind or Viola was swaggering about trying to look as butch as possible, when I had to mask or disguise the fact that I did indeed have a bulge between my legs.

I employed a tight wet bandage.

But then the trouble was that this bandage sometimes made me randy in itself.

So I used to have to wank a lot, offstage, spinning myself off, before going on, to keep my man small and amenable. Such are the secrets of the profession.

Forgive an old comedian his candour, madam. No doubt you have some secrets of your own?

What you must realise is what the Puritans (albeit in their foolish way) most assuredly knew: namely, that the theatre is a temple of Dionysus. The getting of hard pricks is to the point. Your subtle fellow might come off listening to *Romeo and Juliet*. At the ancient festivals, where all drama was born, the procession was led by boys dressed up as girls. Forgive me, I have smaller Latin and less Greek even than You Know Who, but I believe that dithyrambs come from Dionysus Dithyrambus, the ritual song of the god, where *di* + *thura* = DOUBLE DOOR. The god is born through two doors, one male, one female. Dressed in the part of a woman, I was an initiate in ancient mysteries. It is an honourable craft, this transvestism.

Well, then, I come to the point. Although my voice was years in the breaking, years during which I piped a between-times treble that Mr S pronounced ideal for such roles as Rosalind, in other respects I was soon more a man than a boy. I spoke with a reed voice, like that merchant's daughter buried by her sisters in my mother's story – the one who had the world as a transparent apple to spin on a silver saucer. But I had something between my legs which no merchant's daughter ever had.

Reader, I was well endowed. Not only that, but I got my erections at the drop of a hat, or the turn of an ankle, in those days, and I could in no wise *prevent* myself from getting them at inopportune moments. This proved an increasing embarrassment, though in a perverse way I reckon it added a

spice to my performance of certain parts. For instance, Lady Macbeth, when she has to call upon the spirits to unsex her.

Anyway, one evening, when we were doing *Hamlet*, and I was about to trip on stage for the final scene as Ophelia, scattering rosemary and rue and doing my mad bit, I found to my dismay that unseen I was yet crescive in my faculty. In other words, my cock was sticking up in my gown like a little truncheon. Worse, I had just burned my hand on one of the stage lamps and the skin on the palm was raw and giving my agony. There was no way I could jerk off in the usual fashion, to ensure the smooth performance of my role.

I was standing there, in misery, in the wings, with my Ophelia dress disfigured at the front by this throbbing erection, which seemed to get worse by the moment as I tried to will it down, wringing my hands together with a damp cloth, when Mr Shakespeare himself appeared beside me, still wearing his costume as the Ghost.

'You can't go on like *that*, boy,' he said, pointing.

'No, sir! Sorry, sir!' I said.

'So what are you going to do about it?' Mr Shakespeare demanded.

I explained, very quickly, my singular predicament.

Mr Shakespeare's face cracked into a smile through its heavy Ghost make-up. 'I see,' said he. 'Well, in that case there's only one thing for it . . .'

He took me in hand, sir. He cherished me. He stirred me up and tickled me. Then he disedged me.

That's right, madam. William Shakespeare proceeded to bring my erection down by his own manual ministrations.

It was after this little incident that he wrote sonnet 20, the one that begins

> *A woman's face with nature's own hand painted*
> *Hast thou, the Master-Mistress of my passion . . .*

In it, he goes on to say that I was first created to be a woman, till nature fell a-doting over me and added to my person 'one thing' (to his purpose nothing); in a word, my prick:

> *But since she prickt thee out for women's pleasure,*
> *Mine be thy love and thy love's use their treasure.*

Notice, if you please, that he says my penis is no use to him. And know from this that Mr Shakespeare was no sodomite, though some have said he

was. He played with my pintle when I was in female costume, that is all, for the play's sake. He tossed me off quickly before I went on stage.

I must admit that I do not know if it was altogether for the sake of art (or appearance) that he did the same thing to me when I was garbed in that doublet and hose in which I played Rosalind playing the part of a boy. Both my male and my female costumes in that role seemed much to his liking. Quite often, when we were doing *As You Like It*, he would unpack my prick from my doublet or my petticoats, and tease it and kiss it and fondle it and dandle it. Invariably, he brought me off like this. I never touched him, nor was I required to.

Much of this, as I have explained, was for professional purposes. But some (I must confess) seemed no such thing. He appeared addicted for a while to certain parts of mine – for example, Cleopatra and Juliet, as well as Rosalind. As for the last named, I have even wondered sometimes if that play's title should be seen as a private joke between us. *As You Like It*. It was certainly as he liked it. But I did too.

O my balls, O my little witnesses, William Shakespeare took you both in hand. He called us to a reckoning.

Ah well, friends, all that was long ago and (as Mr Marlowe would have said) in another country, and besides the wench is dead – or at least defunct.

Meanwhile, back in the world of the sonnets, Rizley was having carnal knowledge of the poet's mistress – the so-called Dark Lady, she whose eyes were nothing like the sun, and who had bad breath. And the tedious Earl was doing this not because he wanted her, but because he knew that Mr Shakespeare wanted her. *Thou dost love her, because thou knowst I love her*, as it says in sonnet 42. I doubt if Rizley was even excited by the triangle. Like Angelo in *Measure for Measure* when he made water his urine was congealed ice.

But who *was* the Dark Lady?

That is the question I shall answer next.

Chapter Seventy-Three

The Dark Lady of the Sonnets 1

Some say the Dark Lady of the sonnets was a woman named Mary Fitton.

This Mary Fitton was one of Queen Elizabeth's maids of honour, a coveted position she first assumed at the age of 17, though even by then she had little honour left and was probably not a maid. She owed her advancement to Sir William Knollys, a friend of her father's. Knollys, a married man, was besotted with this girl who was 30 years his junior. He made a laughing-stock of himself by his pursuit of her, even dyeing his beard in a pathetic attempt to look young.

Miss Mary had a mania for men. She was of good ancestry, highly cultured, sweet-natured, very modest-looking, and blushed easily. Yet she was always the terror of her family. It was said that from the age of twelve she had been in the habit of masturbating her brothers. The whole Court knew that she performed the same office for Knollys, since the fool boasted of it. She always wore a fur glove for the act, he said, and silver bracelets which he had given her for her 15th birthday. Her bracelets tinkled as she played the harlot with him. Old Knollys adored it.

Mary Fitton was not long at Court before making herself the cause of an even greater scandal. She fell pregnant by William Herbert, the Earl of Pembroke. It is said that she used to slip out of Elizabeth's chambers to meet her lover in the dead of night, disguised as a man in a long white cloak, with her lady-in-waiting's skirts tucked up. Pembroke had her regularly on a tomb in Westminster churchyard – Will Kempe, that lugubrious flea, once pointed it out to me, though God knows how he knew which one it was. The influence of the tomb could not have been good for her. Her unfortunate infant died soon after birth. Pembroke behaved

swinishly throughout, refusing to marry the mother of his child, even though the Queen in her usual fashion took this as a personal insult and packed him off to the Fleet Prison for a spell in an attempt to concentrate his mind upon the matter.

Miss Mary then became the mistress of Vice-Admiral Sir Richard Leveson, who took her to sea with him in the garb of a cabin-boy. After he died, worn out with voyaging, in 1605, she found a husband of her own at last, a retired sea captain called Polwhele, with one leg, and the rest of her life was Cornish and respectable.

Mary Fitton's claim to Dark Lady status rests on no more, in reality, than the fame and the scandal of the way men of all ages flocked to her like moths to a candleflame when she was young.

I never heard the late Mr Shakespeare so much as mention her, though he would have known her name, and she may have crossed his mind from time to time when he was not busy.

I saw this lady once myself, at a bear-baiting in the Paris Garden, when the great bear Sackerson was in his prime. She was eating tarts beneath the smoke-dried leaves. She had a slight, delicate figure, with a shower of curls falling on each side of her face under a shepherdess's hat. She had big bright eyes.

Unfortunately for history, those curls were soft and fair – not at all like the *black wires* which Shakespeare mentions as growing on the head of his mistress in sonnet 130. As for those eyes: in sonnet 127 the mistress's eyes are described as *raven black*, but the eyes I saw at the bear-baiting were not only bright, they were grey as squirrels.

All things considered, I do not think the Dark Lady was Mary Fitton.

Chapter Seventy-Four

The Dark Lady of the Sonnets 2

I stayed once at the house of the second candidate. She is rather more interesting.

Her name was Jane Davenant, and she was the wife of an Oxford innkeeper who became eventually the Mayor of that city. The Davenants kept the Tavern Inn, in Cornmarket Street. Shakespeare often stayed at this house on his journeys between London and Stratford – that is, when he took his preferred way through Woodstock and High Wycombe instead of riding via Banbury and Aylesbury, two towns he always avoided if he could. When we played before the Mayor and Corporation of Oxford on 9 October 1605 our whole Company lodged at the Tavern Inn, and I slept in a chamber the walls of which were adorned with an interlacing pattern of vines and flowers, and along the top a painted frieze which exhorted me to FEAR GOD ABOVE ALL THING, and I saw Mrs Davenant for myself, and she had dark hair.

But so do half the women in the world, and it is only because the Queen was fair that Mr Shakespeare ever pretended dark hair was out of fashion. Anyway, as we shall see, he meant something more when he harped upon his mistress being black.

Jane Davenant's claim to be the Dark Lady rests on the word of her son, Sir William Davenant, our present Poet Laureate, who decided some years ago to proclaim among his friends that the melancholy innkeeper (no one ever saw him smile) could not have been his father, and that William Shakespeare was. Please notice he said nothing of this until Shakespeare was dead. Please notice also that he was entirely silent on the subject until he had lost his nose as the result of mercury treatment for the pox. If he

ever looked like Shakespeare he assuredly does not now, though of course no one says any such thing out of pity for the fellow.

Davenant is to be blamed for the introduction of female players to the English stage, and other things including movable scenery. His *Gondibert* is unreadable, which I think it would not be if William Shakespeare's blood really flowed in his veins. You will say these are matters of opinion; so here is a *fact*. Davenant was not born until 1606, by which time the events of the sonnets were long past. I suppose that Mr S could have rekindled an old passion, and fathered his alleged bastard in that autumn when our Company played Oxford, but if he did then it was no more than an epilogue to the whole affair.

There is, however, a curious work called *Willobie his Avisa, or The True Picture of a Modest Maid, and of a Chaste and Constant Wife* which might be used to link Jane Davenant with the Dark Lady. This piece, a farrago of prose and verse, was published in 1594, and signed with the pseudonym Hadrian Dorrell. From a chance remark of Mr Shakespeare's, I know that its author was really a Henry Willoughby, a connection by marriage of Shakespeare's Warwickshire friend Thomas Russell, an overseer of the poet's will, in which he was left £5. In short, the thing was written by someone who might have heard some gossip about Shakespeare. I'd put it no higher than that. Whatever, the pamphlet gave serious offence to somebody with influence (Rizley?), even though it must always have been hard to understand. It was banned and burned before the last century was out.

That, friends, is why Pickleherring has a copy, here, in this 74th box. The thing is in essence a complicated libel upon the wife of an innkeeper. This woman is so beautiful that she draws to the inn a crowd of importunate gallants. But she is apparently so virtuous that she drives them all away, even threatening to murder one of them, a nobleman, rather than permit him to besmirch her honour. This perfect spouse is a rare bird (*rara Avis* or Avisa), but the author says a contrary meaning must be given to his epithets. Beneath the exterior of a Lucrece the reader is invited to see a wanton: *Let Lucres-Avis be thy name.*

Enter Henrico Willobego. He is conquered at first sight of Avisa, and begins to pine, until his friend WS, who has undergone the same torments, counsels him with wisdom born of experience. Amongst other wooden stuff, WS says this to his 'friend Harry':

She is no saint, she is no nun:
I think in time she may be won.

Awful crap, but I suppose it does recall two lines from *Titus Andronicus*:

> *She is a woman, therefore may be wooed;*
> *She is a woman, therefore may be won.*

Since WS is described as 'the old player', and Henrico Willobego quotes proverbs belonging to the collection made by Rizley's tutor John Florio, I suppose identification of these two men with Shakespeare and Southampton is not far-fetched. And Avisa might well be Mrs Davenant. After all, the nest of this 'Britain bird' that 'outflies them all', is clearly indicated: 'See yonder house where hangs the badge of England's saint'. The tavern kept by the Davenants had the red-cross shield of St George hanging outside its front door.

The allegory enacted in *Willobie his Avisa* is, all the same, much more obscure and difficult to follow than my summary may be leading you to think. Here, let me quote *verbatim* what seems the most relevant passage in it, and you can make up your own minds:

Henrico Willobego. Italo-Hispalensis.

H. W. being sodenly infected with the contagion of a fantasticall fit, at the first sight of *A*, pyneth a while in secret griefe, at length not able any longer to indure the burning heate of so fervent a humour, bewrayeth the secresy of his disease unto his familiar friend W. S. who not long before had tryed the curtesy of the like passion, and was now newly recovered of the like infection; yet finding his frend let bloud in the same vaine, he took pleasure for a tyme to see him bleed, & in steed of stopping the issue, he inlargeth the wound, with the sharpe rasor of a willing conceit, perswading him that he thought it a matter very easy to be compassed, & no doubt with payne, diligence & some cost in time to be obtayned. Thus this miserable comforter comforting his frend with an impossibilitie, eyther for that he now would secretly laugh at his frends folly, that had given occasion not long before unto others to laugh at his owne, or because he would see whether an other could play his part better than himselfe, & in vewing a far off the course of this loving Comedy, he determined to see whether it would sort to a happier end for this new actor, then it did for the old player. But at length this Comedy was like to have growen to a Tragedy, by the weake & feeble estate that H. W. was brought unto, by a desperate vewe of an impossibility of obtaining his purpose, til Time & Necessity, being his best Phisitions brought him a plaster, if not to heale, yet in part to ease his maladye. In all which discourse is lively represented the unrewly rage of

unbrydeled fancy, having the raines to rove at liberty, with the dyvers & sundry changes of affections & temptations, which Will, set loose from Reason, can devise, &c.

The part of this which rings most true to me is that WS does not leap to the aid of his afflicted friend, but rather 'took pleasure for a tyme to see him bleed'. The late Mr Shakespeare was not *always* gentle.

From my own observation at the Tavern Inn I can report that Mrs Jane Davenant was a woman of great beauty and a sprightly wit. Mr Shakespeare afforded her every courtesy in public, and the degree of their intimacy would have struck strangers as in no way improper, yet I admit that I can entertain without too much difficulty the thought that he might have shared her bed from time to time. Perhaps that's why her husband looked so miserable?

The truth is that William Shakespeare, when not at home with his wife in Stratford, did not live a life of perfect chastity. He was never debauched, but took pleasure where pleasure was offered. His couplings of this kind were mostly ephemeral. There is, for example, a story I picked up from John Manningham of the Middle Temple, which I can well believe because of the wit in it. This concerns a lady of some breeding who had seen Dick Burbage playing Richard III, and fallen enamoured of more than his bunch-back. She made an assignation with him on leaving the playhouse. Burbage was to call upon her that night, announcing himself at her door in the name of his part. Mr Shakespeare, overhearing their conclusion, went before, was entertained, and at his game before Burbage appeared on the scene. Then, message being brought that Richard the 3rd was at the door, Shakespeare caused return to be made: 'William the Conquerer came before Richard the 3rd!'

To be brief with Jane Davenant, as perhaps many men were, I can believe that she is Avisa, but I once heard her sing and she was deaf to tunes. It passes credence that she could have played well on the virginals. Believe me, reader, she was not the Dark Lady of the sonnets. Who was? Be patient. I shall give you my best suggestion soon.

Chapter Seventy-Five

The Dark Lady of the Sonnets 3

Before I do that, there is Emilia Lanier to dispatch. . . .

The delectable, the enigmatic Emilia is at first blush quite a plausible Dark Lady. Of Italian blood, it might be supposed for a start that her colouring was right. Then, as the illegitimate daughter of Baptiste Bassano, one of that famous family of Venetian musicians who have served the English Court since the reign of King Henry VIII, it can also be assumed that she knew her way up and down the keyboard of the virginals.

Emilia's talents did not end there. I have heard from several men with much experience in the matter that her accomplishments in bed were well out of the ordinary.

She always had to fight for her way in the world. Her father died when she was still a child, and she was brought up in the household of the Countess of Kent, becoming the mistress of Lord Hunsdon, who was old enough to be her grandfather. Falling pregnant by him, she was married off to Alphonse Lanier, another Court musician and one of a family of musicians from Rouen.

Hunsdon, who was the Queen's cousin, proved no Pembroke. He made adequate provision for Emilia, but her husband's extravagance was notorious and the family soon fell on hard times. Alphonse sought to repair their fortunes by taking service under the Earl of Essex in his expedition to the Azores and then in Ireland, having been instructed by the astrologer Simon Forman that his horoscope favoured such courses.

The astrologer, of course, was sleeping with Emilia. I doubt, all the same, if she let him fuck her properly. This lady preferred her soldiers to give her unconventional salutes.

From another of her lovers, Dr Walter Warner, I learned that Emilia

Lanier favoured sodomy to satisfy men's lusts. She would permit that little warp-handed physician to feel all the nooks and crannies of her body, and to kiss her, and to play with her bubbies while she was sitting naked upon his lap, but Emilia would never allow him access to her cunt. Penetration *via* the bum-hole, Warner told me, was much to her taste, however. She could not get enough of it, and sometimes had three or four men spending themselves successively in this fashion upon the altar of Aphrodite Steatopyga.

Warner reported that he had more than once heard Forman declare that Emilia Lanier was an *incuba* rather than a woman. I know that Biarmannus, and Wierus, and other doctors, stoutly deny the existence of such devils, but Austin and Erastus and Paracelsus say that it is possible. Philostratus, in his fourth book *De vita Apollonii* has a memorable instance of this kind, which I may not omit, of one Menippus Lycius, a young man going between Cenchreas and Corinth, who met such a phantasm in the habit of a fair gentlewoman. Taking him by the hand, she carried him home to her house in the suburbs of Corinth, and told him she was a Phoenician by birth, and if he would tarry with her 'he should hear her sing and play, and drink such wine as never any drank'. The young man, a philosopher, tarried with her awhile to his great content, and at last married her, to whose wedding, amongst other guests, came Apollonius, who, by some probable conjectures, found out the creature to be a serpent, a Lamia, and that all her furniture was like Tantalus' gold described by Homer, no substance, but mere illusion. When she saw herself descried, she wept, and desired Apollonius to be silent, but he would not be moved, and thereupon she, plate, house, and all that was in it, vanished in an instant. Many thousands, the good doctor says, took notice of this fact, for 'it was done in the midst of Greece'.

Now, let me speak frankly, friends, I do not believe a word of all this taradiddle, myself. I think your *incuba* is a nightmare all right, but she is a nightmare caused by eating too much cheese and sleeping upon your back. All the same, it is interesting that such particular fantasies were visited by men on the person of Emilia Lanier. Certainly there appears to have been about her a perfume of hot and perverse and mysterious eroticism which to some noses would suggest that here at last we are in the presence of the true Dark Lady.

Sir, I don't think so at all, and I'll tell you why. Emilia reformed during the latter part of her life, and turned poetess, and in 1611 she published a long religious poem called *Salve Deus Rex Judaeorum*, a sort of vindication of

the principal female characters in the Bible, from Eve to the Virgin Mary. I have not read it, but am told that it shows much learning.

My point is this: Had such a talented and articulate women ever been the mistress of William Shakespeare, I think that she would have told us so herself.

Consider, madam. If *you* were the Dark Lady of the sonnets, and you had now turned poet yourself, would you not publish it to the world that you had been in bed with Mr Shakespeare? And that you were (perhaps) not satisfied either by him or by those things that he had said you were? Would you not be filled by a desire to set the record straight, either in verse or prose, and to *get your own back*?

Emilia Lanier perished, in silence, having done no such thing.

She wrote about the women in the Bible.

But she wrote not a word about her own case, and she wrote not a word on the subject of William Shakespeare, who (had she been his mistress) would have been the love of her life.

Nor, in my opinion, did William Shakespeare write a word on the subject of her. He may have seen her in Lord Hunsdon's company, when she was very young, since Hunsdon was Lord Chamberlain and our Company of actors was then known as the Lord Chamberlain's Servants. Yet Hunsdon was more a patron than a playgoer, and I cannot recall ever seeing Emilia Lanier with my own eyes.

Latterly, so I heard tell, this lady kept a school for the children of gentlemen. Her own son (by Hunsdon) was musician to King Charles I. She lived to a grand old age, dying only about ten years ago, sustained in her last years by some pension she had succeeded in acquiring from the Crown.

What happened to the much-cuckolded Alphonse? He died about the time that his wife turned poet. Music and sweet poetry do not always agree, you see, sir. But I can't help feeling sorry for the fellow.

I feel sorry for Emilia also, yes, madam. She had indeed a miserable bitch of a life.

Poor Alphonse.

Poor Emilia.

Requiescant in pace.

I do not believe that this remarkable woman is the Dark Lady of the sonnets, and my clinching argument is that Dr Walter Warner told me her skin was white as snow and soft as swansdown. Those who claim that Forman described her body as 'very brown in youth' have simply misread the astrologer's handwriting. I have seen the passage in question. The word

is BRAVE. Emilia Lanier was very brave in youth, and no doubt very wanton. Later she was no less brave, and no doubt very religious. But the Dark Lady of the sonnets she was not.

Chapter Seventy-Six

The Dark Lady of the Sonnets 4

Now then, my dears, before I tell you the name of the Dark Lady, let's consider for a moment the sense in which there is *no* Dark Lady.

I mean, that sense in which outside the sonnets there is no Friend either, nor indeed a constant and unchanging (but strangely colourless) 'I'.

No Dark Lady.

No Friend.

No I.

These are not persons. They are patterns. While individuals went into their creation, giving substance to shapes in the poet's imagination, yet in the last and most serious analysis these figures have no existence save as the words they are, black marks on a white page.

Thus, I have already filled you in on how not just Rizley was the Friend. Pickleherring was in some small part Mr Shakespeare's Friend, also. And (who knows now?) there may have been others. There very probably *were* others.

Similarly, with the figure of the so-called Rival Poet who crops up in eight of the sonnets, who seems a rival not only in art but in the affections and perhaps the patronage of the Friend. I am half-convinced that Marlowe is implied here, especially when Shakespeare speaks of 'the proud full sail of his great verse'. The epithets suit Marlowe's verse as they suit no other of Mr S's contemporaries, and Marlowe as we have learned from the tender allusion to the 'dead shepherd' and the 'infinite reckoning in a little room' was the rival poet most liked and most admired by Mr Shakespeare. Yet I am equally half-sure that it is George Chapman who is sometimes thought of. There's all that stuff in Chapman about 'spirits'. While most people were doing their best to keep body and soul together, he was always

busy trying to separate them. Admittedly his verse is less like a proud full sail than it is like the *rush* of a game of football, where its subject is like the ball kicked here and there by opposing teams of thoughts. But Chapman was known to have claimed immortal if not divine inspiration in his own behalf, saying that one day when he was sitting on a hill near Hitchin, being still a boy at the time, he had been prompted to write by the spirit of Homer. Is it not likely that Mr S had this in mind, in his sonnet 86, when he goes on from the 'proud full sail' bit to ask the question

> *Was it his spirit, by spirits taught to write,*
> *Above a mortal pitch, that struck me dead?*

In short, this 86th sonnet provides a perfect paradigm of my thinking here. I believe that in it, within the space of a few lines, Shakespeare is invoking first Kit Marlowe then George Chapman. Both of them were rivals of his, envied and admired. Each of them figures here as Rival Poet.

Patience, madam. I agree that the Dark Lady is a far more intriguing conundrum. And I *do* still feel, as you do, that there is one woman who was (so to speak) *more* Dark Lady than all the other dark ladies who may or may not have put their shadows into her creation. I am *not* dodging the question. Pickleherring's next chapter will answer it, in fact, to the best of a comedian's ability.

But never forget that Mr Shakespeare's sonnets were not all written at the same time, nor even necessarily in the same period. They were like entries in a diary kept over several years. They may not even be printed in the correct order, for that matter.

What I am trying to impress upon you is that the three exterior personages – Friend (or Fair Youth), Dark Lady, Rival Poet – are real in Shakespeare's mind. Outside that mind there could have been several persons who contributed to each Idea or Image. For that matter, the 'I' of the sonnets is several persons too. WS was everyone and nobody. He did not stop being capable of dramatic characterisation when he started writing sonnets. Have you noticed that the first nine sonnets have no 'I' in them? And that even when the poet does speak in these sonnets in the first person singular he makes much less of an exhibition of himself than poets usually do?

Bear it in mind, sir: Mr Shakespeare was all his working life a playwright. The making of dramatic fictions was this man's trade. It was the air he breathed, the world he knew. Consider even further, then: What if the Friend and the Mistress, the Fair Youth and the Dark Lady, were in one

sense *parts* created by Shakespeare? And what if like parts in any play they were at different times played by different people? Thus Rizley played the Friend, but so did I. Thus several women were the one Dark Lady. Mr Shakespeare created the originals in his heart and his head, and then upon the page. Life copied them. Living can follow poetry in these matters. Ask any poet who is worth the name.

Reader, permit me to suggest that there is even an especial strange sense in which *I* served him later as the Dark Lady. I'll be coming to that, when it's time for such seasons in hell.

Meanwhile, entertain at least the possibility that both Fair Youth and Dark Lady are simple puzzles compared with the complexity of the identity of the 'I' that stalks and fleets through these sonnets.

Who is the Dark 'I' of the sonnets? That is the question. He makes his first appearance (in sonnet 10) declaring that he will change his mind, and he bows out of the action in sonnet 152* with a pun upon his 'perjur'd I' (or eye). In between, all that is constant is this elusive self's capacity for apparent truth-telling, made the more credible by the great number of occasions on which he accuses himself of lying.

There seems, indeed, an infinite number of selves of William Shakespeare who play that part of the 'I' in the drama of the sonnets. Even when we think we have grasped him, this shape-shifter escapes definition by reminding us that he is also an actor, and that motley is his business. His poems are not just love letters written to Henry Wriothesley, nor private jottings on the conduct of his mistress. They are the heart's truth of William Shakespeare. But who was William Shakespeare?

Understand old Pickleherring, please. I am trying to speak simply of something complicated. I am not saying that Shakespeare's sonnets were the artificial products of his fancy. To suppose as much (or as little) mistakes and misrepresents *all* sonnets, all poems and all poets, not just those Elizabethan artificers who are sometimes said to have written sonnets thus. When Shakespeare said that he had 'two loves', of 'comfort and despair', and that one of them was 'a man right fair' and the other 'a woman colour'd ill', believe me, gentle reader, *he was not kidding!*

But then the late Mr WS was (as I hope I may be proving by this Life) both many men and no one. Therefore be sure that all that is certain is that the sonnets were written by a man or men named Will. (There are sufficient puns on the name to make this more than likely.) As to the names

---

* The last two sonnets are plainly out of sequence. Either they are free translations of a 5th-century Greek epigram by Marianus Scholasticus, or they refer to a cure for the pox which Mr Shakespeare once took at Bath.

of the other apparent persons in them, though, nothing is certain. The Dark Lady could be all the ladies I have dealt with in the last three chapters, plus the lady I will canvas in the next, or she could be one or none. She could be a perfect fiction. Like Cleopatra. Like Shakespeare's mother. Or like me.

Talking of perfect fictions, here is another riddle for your delight. Who was William Shakespeare when he was playing Prospero? Was he Shakespeare playing Prospero, or was he Prospero playing Shakespeare? Remember the enchanter's last speech to the audience:

> I must be here confined by you,
> Or sent to Naples.

For Naples, try reading Stratford. And he goes on to say that he must remain spell-bound on stage until *we* (the audience) break the spell by our applause. In this speech Mr Shakespeare confesses the limitations of his own necromantic art, and craves our prayers, like any other sinner:

> As you from crimes would pardon'd be,
> Let your indulgence set me free.
>
> *[Exit]*

I say it is not just Prospero who exits then.

Who is the 'I' whose exits and whose entrances form the substance of the sonnets? That, as I say, is the question. It is the question I try to answer by this book. My method, friends, is to answer it indirectly by the asking.

Lady Southampton once referred to Mr Shakespeare as if he *was* Sir John Falstaff. 'Your friend Sir John Falstaff,' she wrote to Rizley. Think about it. That was a part that Shakespeare never even played when he was an actor. Yet I say there is a sense in which the lady got it right. That is the sense in which there is no Dark Lady.

Now then, at last then.

Enough metaphysics.

As my grandfather the bishop——

As *you* say, madam, and about time too, not to speak of providing a 'simple answer' to a 'simple question'.

The Dark Lady: who was she?

Chapter Seventy-Seven

The Dark Lady of the Sonnets 5

The last time I saw a dildo like the one young Anne was wearing when she fucked the Countess it was down at Lucy Negro's.

Lucy Negro, alias Lucy Morgan, kept a brothel in St John Street, Clerkenwell. She was known as the Abbess of Clerkenwell, head of the infamous sisterhood of the Black Nuns.

Her priory was amply provisioned, a palace of carnal delights. Once within its walls, the real world no longer existed. It was folly there to think of it, or indeed to think at all. The abbess demanded obedience, and she got it. Appliances of pleasure were everywhere. Here were women, here were boys, here were dancers, here were musicians, here was beauty in many strange forms, and here was wine. It was a convent sacred to amorous rites.

It was a soft-lit place, a maze of corridors. Each of her rooms held a different delight. There were pleasures here to match and satisfy each taste, no matter how outlandish or extreme. Sometimes I thought of that brothel as the very house of fiction. It was like the stories in the *Decameron*, one self-complete imagination leading into another, each particular pleasure foretelling the pleasure of the next room but only when you looked *back* (so satisfying each was in itself). I never exhausted it. Nor, I believe, did Mr Shakespeare, and he was certainly in more rooms than I tried for myself.

There were seven main rooms in the house of Lucy Negro – to mirror, no doubt, the seven deadly sins. None of the rooms had windows that looked out upon the world. Instead, in each of the rooms, to the right and the left, in the middle of each wall, a tall and narrow window looked back into the corridor which connected them. These windows were of stained glass whose colour varied in accordance with the prevailing hue of the

decorations of the chamber. That at the eastern extremity was hung, for example, in blue, and vividly blue were its windows. The second chamber was purple in its ornaments and tapestries, and here the panes were purple. The third was green throughout, and so were the casements. The fourth was furnished and lighted with orange, the fifth with white, the sixth with violet. The seventh apartment was closely shrouded in black velvet tapestries that hung all over the ceiling and down the walls, falling in heavy folds upon a carpet of the same material and hue. But in this chamber only the colour of the windows failed to correspond with the decorations. The panes here were scarlet – a deep blood-colour.

Now in no one of the seven apartments was there any lamp or candelabrum amid the profusion of golden ornaments that lay scattered to and fro or depended from the roof. There was no light of any kind emanating from lamp or candle within the suite of chambers; but in the corridors that followed the suite there stood opposite each window a heavy tripod bearing a brazier of fire that projected its rays through the tinted glass and so glaringly illumined the room. And thus were produced a multitude of gaudy and fantastic appearances. I thought once that I saw Helen of Troy in the blue chamber, and Dr Faustus in the purple; then, at other times, it was Merlin the magician that seemed to stalk before me as I entered the green chamber, and the enchantress Vivian was seen dancing in the orange; as for the white chamber, I saw Joan of Arc within it, and she was burning, with her henchman Gilles de Rais in the violet room. The seventh chamber I never went inside, but I can well believe what Mr Shakespeare once told me – that he found Othello therein, and Lady Macbeth. I believe that in that western or black chamber the effect of the fire-light that streamed upon the dark hangings, through the blood-tinted panes, was ghastly in the extreme, and produced so wild a look upon the countenances of those who entered that there were few bold enough to set foot within its precincts at any time, and fewer still who would stay there once they had got there.

In spite of these things, or because of them, the house of Lucy Negro was an enchanted place, and a home to magnificent revels. The tastes of its mistress were exotic and expensive, her imagination unparalleled when it came to any matter touching upon sensual gratification. She had a fine eye for all colours and effects. Her plans were bold and fiery, and her conceptions always glowed with barbaric lustre. There were some who would no doubt have considered her mad. Her followers, myself among them, felt sure she was not. It was perhaps necessary to hear her, and to see her, and to touch her – to be *sure* that she was not.

She had not always been a whore, of course. Come to that, I would not have dared to call her a whore in the days that I knew her. She was the Queen of Air and Darkness, to my young mind. I was only in her house a dozen times. I never even took my shoes off, though once (as you shall hear) I did perform in her clothes there. (I'll tell you of that when it's time, and not before.) It was a very strange place, and being in it was like being inside the mind of a very strange woman. So you'll see, sir, this is not at all what you may have been supposing.

There are two lines in one of the sonnets addressed to the Fair Youth which I believe might first have been addressed to the Dark Lady. They run as follows:

> *What is your substance, whereof are you made,*
> *That millions of strange shadows on you tend?*

That is Lucy Negro and her house.

Lucy means light, and Negro of course means black. Some say that her real name was Lucy Morgan. Those who can credit this put it about also that from March 1579 to January 1582, while yet very young, she had been one of Queen Elizabeth's most favoured attendants. She was then expelled from Court after the usual fall from grace. I cannot believe that she ever did anything she did not choose to do. Who the gentleman was who first dishonoured her, I do not know. I do know that Mr Shakespeare knew her before she came into her own and established the house in St John Street. But where she was and what she was doing when he first met her I have no idea.

She had in her possession seven sumptuous dresses, dresses which Elizabeth herself was said to have given her after wearing them on great occasions. It was one of these dresses, virgin-white, all sugared over with diamonds, which she was wearing the first time I saw her, at the revels in Gray's Inn.

In that seventh chamber of the house of Lucy Negro a shadow prowls back and forth without ceasing. It is the shade of one denied the power to find himself outside these walls. It is the shadow of the late William Shakespeare. There he is who was my friend. A damned soul, madam? He would not have said so, and no more do I. Mr Shakespeare is on the other side of Lucy Negro's seventh door, that's all.

Never elsewhere have I seen such obscene furniture. She keeps two dildoes, crossed, on the wall of her jakes. She is no common doxy, dell, or

bawdy-basket. Some say her mother was Lilith, and that Lilith is the devil. Her cunt is like an oyster with soft teeth.

Lucy Negro called herself a KINCHIN-MORT. These words I cannot find in my father's dictionary. But when I played Pickleherring for the Germans I learned that there a child is called a *kindchen*, and in the Netherlands the name for a brothel is a *mot-huys*. Possibly, though, that MORT is from *amourette*, being French for a passing love affair. Barbarous and beautiful, there was something Babylonian about the woman. She had her own argot. It was the language of a perfect blackness. 'Master Shag-beard, I am your kinchin-mort.'

Call her up now as she appeared to me then, at the Gray's Inn Revels, that year at Christmas. Her pins, her little head, her crown of silver and of lace, her eyes between two shining silver candlesticks, each lifting a trembling flame to worship her, her skin that seems to be *listening* as she stands there on tiptoe, her mouth with that frozen line of irony on her lips, her swaying haunch that speaks of snake-like copulations, her wayward hair, the velvety slope of her breasts – these things are the merest echoes of her presence. Her body is only the perfume of her soul. She laughs and then she is gone. She is melted into air, into thin air.

Poor Shakespeare! Lucy Negro was his punishment. It is a demon's arms that hold him now. Listen, down the maze of the corridors, through the seven airless perfumed rooms, the music of her playing on the virginals. Will the door of that seventh sable chamber ever open again? Will the music of those virginals never end? The sound of the music is like the wash of waves on a far-off shore of sleep. You can scarcely hear it playing. Yet once heard you can hear nothing else. Her fingers play the music of your blood.

They say when she first came to the house in St John Street she called herself Lucy Parker. But always she was known as Lucy Negro. The name came from the colour of her skin. She was a mulatto or quadroon from the West Indies. There was African blood a-coursing through her veins.

Dusky-skinned, with eyes as black and shining as the wings of a raven, her breasts were dun, and her hair was like black wires – it was thick and twisting, curly in the extreme. By no means conventionally beautiful, she was on my oath a woman of rare beauty. Summoned, if she could be said to be summonable, amid candles and mirrors that could not hold her reflection, through flame-shaken gloom, answering to such titles as Black Luce, or (in later years) Old Lucilla, she was in great demand with the young gentlemen of the Inns of Court. For them she wore green gowns, or fragile sheaths of crimson. These were her natural colours. Also the white

of shrouds. What colour she wore for Shakespeare I do not know. I never saw them together. I know that he worshipped her.

At the Gray's Inn Revels, at that masquerade, homage was paid to her. She sat on a throne, and she wore Queen Elizabeth's white gown. Her raven hair was down about her shoulders, her skin gleaming like ebony where she showed her thighs and breasts to her adorers. Lucy Negro came among them with a whip.

It was said that Lucy Negro liked whipping best of all things. She would whip men's buttocks until they were in a frenzy. It is said that men would walk miles with their pricks erect to have her whip them.

Lucy Negro called all pricks WILLS.

'Get out your will,' she would order her servants, 'and let's see what you're made of.'

Or: 'Come here with your will, little man, and let your mother see if you are willing.'

She would wear a will herself, when in the mood. 'Where there's a will, there's a way,' she used to say then. (I wonder why Mr Shakespeare never used that for one of his titles, when he was making up one of those last-minute names which told you he was tired of the whole damned play.) The word WILL occurs 20 times in 28 lines in sonnets 135 and 136, which pun furiously on Lucy Negro's usage, among others.

Lucy Negro was a spirit who sold her body to earn her living. She was a mystery, she was also a common whore. When Rizley came her way, she deserted Mr Shakespeare. She was after the highest game that was available. WS, besotted, forgave them both, though perhaps the forgiveness should not be attributed to the besottedness. To Rizley he wrote:

> That thou hast her it is not all my grief,
> And yet it may be said I lov'd her dearly;
> That she hath thee is of my wailing chief,
> A loss in love that touches me more nearly.
> Loving offenders, thus I will excuse ye:
> Thou dost love her because thou know'st I love her;
> And for my sake even so doth she abuse me,
> Suff'ring my friend for my sake to approve her.
> If I lose thee, my loss is my love's gain,
> And losing her, my friend hath found that loss;
> Both find each other, and I lose both twain,
> And both for my sake lay on me this cross.
>   But here's the joy: my friend and I are one;

Sweet flattery! then she loves but me alone.

I must admit that I do not find this very convincing. It strikes me that Mr Shakespeare was trying to cheer himself up.

The sonnet addressed to Lucy Negro is more truthful. From it, I have sometimes surmised that Shakespeare wanted the three of them in bed together. It would not much surprise me. Lucy Negro's bed was wide. And it is said that when done whipping she liked to have two men pleasure her at the same time, one at the front door, one at the back:

> *Two loves I have of comfort and despair,*
> *Which like two spirits do suggest me still:*
> *The better angel is a man right fair,*
> *The worser spirit a woman colour'd ill.*
> *To win me soon to hell, my female evil*
> *Tempteth my better angel from my side,*
> *And would corrupt my saint to be a devil,*
> *Wooing his purity with her foul pride.*
> *And whether that my angel be turn'd fiend*
> *Suspect I may, yet not directly tell;*
> *But being both from me, both to each friend,*
> *I guess one angel in another's hell:*
>   *Yet this shall I ne'er know, but live in doubt,*
>   *Till my bad angel fire my good one out.*

This, then, was William Shakespeare's true Dark Lady. Lucy Negro, mistress of the enchanted house in St John Street, the Abbess of Clerkenwell, was his 'woman colour'd ill', and his living exemplar of the fact that as he says in sonnet 127, 'In the old age black was not counted fair'. That is the first sonnet which is addressed to the Dark Lady. Mark well that it uses the word BLACK three times in its 14 lines. Not 'dark', sir. BLACK.

Never despise the obvious, my friends. When Shakespeare goes on in these sonnets about the blackness of his mistress, he means just what he says. It should be readily discernible that from the outset it is not merely a matter of the lady having dark hair. It is her total blackness that obsesses and fascinates and torments him. Her hair is black, her eyes are black, her skin is black. No doubt, since he called her his 'female evil', and again characterised her cunt as a 'hell' in the last line of sonnet 129, Mr Shakespeare would have said that Lucy Negro's heart was black as well.

And yet, as I insist, he worshipped her, which is to say that he went on loving her through hate and out the other side. He may still be imprisoned in her seventh room, but the sonnets are not.

Lucy Negro appeared before the Queen's Bench, that year I first came to London, charged with keeping a house of ill repute. Her friends in high places kept her out of jail on this occasion. Later she was not so fortunate. In January 1600, she was sentenced to a spell in the Bridewell, though even then strings were pulled and she was spared the usual carting through the streets. Her name appears on the warrant as 'Morgan or Parker'.

She died in 1610 – of the pox, it was said. She was a queen bee that had buzzed herself to death. It was bruited about that she had the pox as early as 1595, and that she had stung others along the way. It is possible that Mr Shakespeare caught the foul disease from her. That would explain some of the vehemence of his expressions in her regard. It is possible also that Lucy Negro gave him, first, blains, and then the Neapolitan bone-ache, or (as some call it) the malady of France. In short – sigh, Phyllis!

Lucy Negro died a Papist, so I have it on good authority. May her strange soul rest in peace. I thought her, sir, a not dishonest woman. Her house was like no other I was ever inside.

There are several epitaphs, of which I quote one by Davies of Hereford as being typical:

> Such a beginning, such an end. This I'll not applaud.
> For Luce did like a whore begin, but ended like a bawd.

But we can't leave things there, with such hobbling moral comment. Not for one who was in many ways the mistress of her craft. Better to quote Mr Shakespeare's reference to Mrs Overdone in *Measure for Measure* as 'a bawd of eleven years' continuance'. Was he thinking of Lucy Negro when he wrote that? *Measure for Measure* was first performed at Court at the Christmas festivities of 1604, and it was then about 11 years since Lucy Negro first set up her house in St John Street.

What more is there to say of such a woman? Like Cybele, her forehead was crowned with the twin towers of the impossible, those strange second thoughts of all the twice-born in the world. Apuleius, the African from Madaura, had his Lucius the Ass blessed with a vision of her. He called her Queen Isis. Others have called her Ceres and Hecate, Minerva, Diana, Venus, Bellona, Proserpine, Juno, Aphrodite. These are all one. In London, for a spell, she was known as Lucy Negro. She revelled in cynical songs and expressions, and in lascivious attitudes and gestures, and she

came among her followers with a whip, yet she was in her heart what she said she was, a girl-child who had been carried in a sheet on her mother's back, a KINCHIN-MORT. She would furiously demand coitus, yet she gave herself for love because she loved it. Her desire for sexual gratification seemed unlimited, yet there was that in her which lifted her high above her body threshing on the bed, and crowned her head with stars, and made a poet love her and adore her. Like Messalina she was driven to prostitution perhaps in an attempt to find satisfaction and relief with one man after another, yet she became for William Shakespeare his most demanding Muse.

Sometimes I think that Mr Shakespeare lived a life of allegory, and that his work was a commentary upon it. When I think that I think of Lucy Negro. The women in his plays all flow from her. As for the sonnets, they are full of the conflict of the masculine and the feminine, the Apollonian and the Dionysian, and their resolution is the interweaving and fusion of those two great forces. William Shakespeare learned most of Dionysus in the house of Lucy Negro.

'Not many men amuse me by meaning to,' she said once, when I displeased her.

I think that Mr Shakespeare was one of those exceptions. I hope at the end, at least, she knew his worth.

Let Shakespeare's disciple John Weever have the last rhymed word on the subject of Lucy Negro. Among his epigrams there are verses about a woman he calls Byrrha which I am sure are about the mistress of that house in St John Street, Clerkenwell:

> *Is Byrrha brown? Who doth the question ask?*
> *Her face is pure as ebony, jet-black.*
> *It's hard to know her face from her fair mask;*
> *Beauty in her seems beauty still to lack.*
> *Nay, she's snow-white, but for that russet skin,*
> *Which like a veil doth keep her whiteness in.*

Weever was in many respects a weevil, but I always found this moving. He must have followed Mr Shakespeare to the whore-house, and worshipped the Dark Lady from afar.

Chapter Seventy-Eight

Of eggs and Richard Burbage

Anne brought me two more eggs. And she told me her name. It is not Anne exactly. It is Polly!

All this has left me too excited to start writing today's chapter of my *Life of the late Mr Shakespeare*, which should be on the subject of some of the leading actors in our Company, and particularly Mr Richard Burbage. So I'll leave that for a moment. Here is what happened.

Today is the Feast of the Transfiguration, the 6th of August. This is a feast day I have always kept. I love the idea of Christ's shiningness passing from his soul to his body, as he stood on Mount Tabor before St Peter, St James, and St John. The way Luke describes it in his Gospel* it must have been like the atmosphere when suddenly lit up passingly by the sun. As such, a miracle of that kind I can most readily venerate – unlike, for example, Christ's walking on the waves of the sea.

I never tasted fish nor flesh since Jane died. I never drank either wine or any beer. My chief food is oatmeal boiled with water, which some call gruel; and in summer, now and then, a salad of some cool choice herbs which I purchase of Pompey Bum. For dainties, or when I would feast myself, upon a high day such as this, I like to eat the yolk of a hen's egg, if I can. And what bread I eat, I cut out the middle part of the loaf, but of the crust I never taste. Now and then, when my stomach serves me, I eat some suckets – dried sugar-plums. But more commonly I have my mulberries.

Knowing my liking for yolks on such a day as this, you can imagine my delight when I opened my door to a gentle knock and found my whorechild standing there with a basket on her arm and a crisp white linen cloth folded over the basket. I knew at a glance what was under that napkin.

---

* Luke, 9.28–36; also Matthew, 17.1–13, and Mark, 9.2–13.

'Why do you bring me these gifts?' I made bold to ask her.

'Better an egg today than a hen tomorrow,' the sweet girl replied.

This I found extraordinary. I asked her, had she heard of Rabelais? Of course, she had not. Yet it comes in his third book, the self-same saying: *Ad praesens ova, cras pullis sunt meliora*. It is when Bridlegoose is going on about the scribes and scriveners. Perhaps it is one of those proverbs you get in several languages.

Anne looked so innocent, standing there with her little wicker basket. She was wearing a kirtle, grass-green, that came down to her ankles. It was almost impossible to associate this visitor with the naked nymph I had watched at Sapphic work on the body of the Countess. All the same, memories of that other sweetness did float into my mind as she flitted about the room.

I gave her a pickled mulberry. Against my window, the sunlight making a black bonfire of her hair, she leaned and sucked it prettily, and pronounced it good. Her pleasure surprised me, for I do not think she would lie for the sake of politeness. I had supposed the last mulberry was not to her tender taste.

Anne did not stay more than five minutes, but they were the best five minutes I have known for years. The sunlight seemed to follow her about my chamber. She dusted my table with her green sleeve, and fanned her cheeks with the top page of my manuscript. She expressed no interest in it, though it has now achieved the height of a small hill. After she'd gone, I sat and held that top page to my nostrils. It was the last one where I wrote of Lucy Negro. Now it is soaked in the scent of a second KINCHIN-MORT.

When she said she had to go, I made her a bow. 'May I ask,' I murmured, 'to whom I owe the honour of all these eggs?' (I did not want her to know that I knew her name.)

I swear that she blushed! So I'm right, and she can't have been long at the game.

'My name is Anne Flinders,' she said. 'But those who like me call me Polly.'

I stood there, friends, mouth open, in the doorway. I could not move my tongue. She must have thought the old man living up here in the eaves of Pompey Bum's brothel was, after all, an idiot. It was simply too much for me – the thought, all at once, that this exquisite vision of loveliness who has also been so kind to a crazy stranger is known to those who like her by that name which has always been closest to my heart, the name of that girl in the song, *O* (long-lost!) *Polly Dear*.

I kissed her hand, the better to prevent her seeing the tears that had come to my eyes.

She spun in a flurry of green petticoats. Then she was gone.

Those eggs were delicious. I fear I ate each part. This has left me with a torment in my gut, but I do not regret the eating.

It occurs to me that when Anne – when *Polly* first brought eggs to me, why, I ate those first eggs knowing there could be plague in them. Yet that is melodramatic. Of all things brought to eat by other hands perhaps eggs were the safest while the plague still raged in London. There was a shell after all between the meat and any possible contagion. All the same, what if the very chickens were infected? It is, I suppose, not impossible. I think I knew that when I ate them, in some dark antechamber of my mind. Perhaps I longed for death at the young whore's hands? Death as her speckled gift? Death as her bright yolk given to me, a kindness granted to the old crazed man in the attic? Well, had there been death in those first eggs, I would never even have begun my Life of William Shakespeare, let alone got so far along in it as I have now.

The principal actors in our Company, known at that time as the Lord Chamberlain's Servants, were Richard Burbage, William Sly, Thomas Pope, George Bryan, and Will Kempe. Later, Augustine Phillips and Henry Condell, both members of the Lord Admiral's Company, and John Heminges, from the Queen's, joined our band. Some fifteen more players were soon added, the main ones being John Lowin, Joseph Taylor, Alexander Cook, Samuel Gilburne, William Cowley, and your servant. With the exception of Kempe, last seen trying to hop across the Alps to win a bet, all these remained faithful to the Company and died in harness. I tell a lie. Lowin became a publican in his old age, and for all I know is still alive at Brentford. Otherwise, Pickleherring must be the only one of us left.

Reader, I doubt if Mr Shakespeare would have played the leading parts in his own plays even if Richard Burbage had not existed. Shakespeare was not a genius as an actor. Burbage (in my opinion) may have been. Roles such as Romeo and Bassanio and Henry V were made for him to fill. He was a natural lover and soldier, and a hero just to look at, with a very fine rich speaking voice besides, and much grace and charm of movement. There was never an awkward bone in his whole body, and he had that gift which some (very few) actors have, that once he came on stage your eyes never left him.

Though partial to a tot of rum, Richard Burbage never fluffed his lines. He always endeavoured to perform as near the apron as he could, so that his great rolling vocables would reach to the back of the house even when

he whispered. Playing so many girls' parts opposite him, I appreciated that his breath usually smelt pleasantly of aniseed, though I never saw him chew it. So warm he was in the interpretation of his parts, so entirely believable, that he could reduce me to tears on the stage – something no other actor was ever capable of. The audience was similarly affected. One day, when he threw himself into Ophelia's grave, a spectator jumped up on stage and tried to pull him out.

The younger son of anchor-man James Burbage, the founder of our Company, he was about two years older than Mr Shakespeare, but he always looked younger. It was only in the parts of 'potent, grave, and reverend signiors' that our author had the edge – I cannot imagine Richard Burbage playing Prospero, for instance. It was his great personal charm which made plausible in *Richard III* that immediate conquest of the widow of the man he has murdered, a seduction which Burbage used to perform over the very coffin. I have seen other actors attempt this, but none who made it credible.

Madam, do you know why Juliet falls in love with Romeo at first sight, and Rosalind with Orlando? I will tell you. It is because Richard Burbage played Romeo and Orlando first on stage, and he was so good-looking and so full of grace when young.

Sir, do you know why Queen Gertrude says that Hamlet is fat and scant of breath and offers him her napkin during the duel with Laertes? It is because Dick Burbage, when he got older, put on weight, and he found himself often out of breath and mopping the sweat from his brow during this scene, so Mr Shakespeare wrote in those lines for Gertrude to give him a moment to rest during the fight and to provide an excuse and reason for him doing so. This was, I think, a mark of Mr Shakespeare's affection for Burbage, that he wrote this into *Hamlet* just for his sake. It has occurred to me, though, that anyone who does not know the physical shortcoming must find Gertrude's words and actions quite a puzzle.

Othello and Lear were Richard Burbage's other great roles, and he also played Hieronimo in Kyd's *Spanish Tragedy*.

He was a skilled painter in oils, as well as an actor. In 1613 and 1616 he painted the device for the shield of Francis, Earl of Rutland, with Shakespeare writing the motto on the first occasion. He died three years after Mr Shakespeare, and all that was mortal of him lies buried now in the church of St Leonard's, Shoreditch, under a stone that bears a perfect epitaph for an actor:

EXIT BURBAGE.

Talking of eggs, as today I must, I have a story which says much of

Richard Burbage and his appetite for life. I heard him once, at that Oxford inn where our Company were staying when on tour, lean over the bannisters and roar down the stair-well in his best King Lear voice:

'Mrs Davenant! Three of those six eggs you sent up for my breakfast were bad! I've eaten them all, but don't let it happen again!'

As for me, I seem to have written a little song to celebrate Polly's giving me more eggs on this transfigured day. It has nothing to do with the girl or the occasion, that I can see, but the lines came into my head, so I've written them down. Here they are:

> Sing a song of eggshells,
>   Who's to pay the rent?
> What's the use of fairy tales
>   That you never meant?
> What's the use of living?
>   What's the use of jam?
> All you get is what you want —
>   Never who you AM.

But I'm a comedian, not a poet, and the jingle does scant justice to my joy. It even sounds bitter, which might be considered curious and perverse.

Chapter Seventy-Nine

A few more facts and fictions
about William Shakespeare

Listen. I could tell you several more uninteresting things about William Shakespeare, in a line with those one or two uninteresting things which have already crept into this book despite my best efforts. As regards the latter, I mean such things as the fact that the poet was the first son and third child of John Shakespeare, a country trader settled in Stratford, and of Mary his wife. And that he was baptised, for instance, on the feast day of Saints Cletus and Marcellinus, about whom next to nothing is known, and that when he was 18 years old he got with child a woman named Anne or Agnes Hathaway, who was eight years older than himself, and that her relatives saw to it that he married her.

I could tell you, for example, that he had three brothers – Gilbert, Edmund, and Richard – as well as a rather more interesting sister whose name was Joan.

I could tell you also that in 1597 he bought the second largest house in Stratford, and that the death of his father in 1601 brought him possession of the house in Henley Street as well. And that he purchased another 100 acres in Stratford from a family called Combe, and a cottage in Chapel Lane in 1602, and an interest in the tithes of Welcombe and Bishopton as well as Stratford parish.

I could tell you, for example, that he sued in Stratford court for small debts in 1604 (*versus* Philip Rogers, an apothecary) and in 1608 (*versus* a man called Addenbrooke).

I could tell you, for instance, of his 10% share in our Company's profits. Or of how he did his bit (without getting his hands dirty) when we had to dismantle the Theatre at the Christmas of 1598, when our lease ran out,

carrying each brick across the river, rebuilding our playhouse on Bankside as the Globe.

I could tell you of his various London lodgings: of how he lived for a while in a house on the north side of Fleet Street, two doors west of the end of Chancery Lane – thus under the very shadow of Temple Bar; of how subsequently he removed to the seventh house on the west side of Chancery Lane; then of his later lodging in the Liberty of the Clink just round the corner from where I'm writing now; and of his final property transaction – the purchase of the Gatehouse near King's Wardrobe and Puddle Wharf, which he put on mortgage.

When I say that these things are uninteresting I do not mean to deny that there is a certain piquancy, for instance, in thinking of a poet whose name is wedded with lady-smocks and cuckoo-buds living at certain addresses in the din of the heart of London. I mean only that there are things like this in everyone's life, and that they are not what matters in the end, not what makes each one of us unique, although we like to know them.

What I really have to tell you is quite other. It might also strike you as uninteresting, but it is not uninteresting in the way of these dry facts.

What I really have to tell you is not facts at all.

What I really have to tell you consists of fictions.

Reader, our real lives *are* fictions.

Be sure that fiction is the best biography.

Procopius knew this. So did Suetonius. So, for that matter, did the four Evangelists. Nothing better confirms the truth of what they tell us, those four, than the way they slightly contradict each other on matters of fact. They knew that the true story is what cannot be told.

Here, then, as my small contribution to the true story of William Shakespeare are several uninteresting things about him which are not facts. These fictions have at least the interest that you will not have heard them before, and that you will not learn them from any other source if Pickleherring does not put them down now in this chapter.

1. Mr Shakespeare was never at home either in London or in Stratford. He didn't say so. He wouldn't. He was reticent. But you could see he was thinking of something else the way he spoke to his dog. When he spoke to me it was as if he knew I was out of earshot but he didn't blame me. He had also a way of looking at me as if he knew I was somebody else. I didn't like days when he looked at me like that. Not that I wanted him to be kind to me, madam. He had no need to be kind to me. You could say I was kind

to him, but that is an irrelevance. All right – he was a very great poet, but very great natures are not easy to get on with.

2. Truth, now. Mr Shakespeare used to talk a lot about truth. On the first night of *Othello* I remember him saying, 'Truth is a whore, who requires some compensation for being summoned.' It is a wise saying, though personally I have never kidneyed with the creatures. You could not hear him speak and not know what he meant. Clarity like that is not achieved in a day. His whole life was one long summer of creation. His very spit was eloquent, by the end. By the time of *Othello* we had moved from a daylight to a lamplight theatre, which is why I speak of a first night. The lamplight pleased the wits, not so much the groundlings.

3. A day spent with Shakespeare? A day spent with Shakespeare may be in your eyes, madam, something so wonderful to contemplate that you can scarcely understand that I can let many such pass without note or comment. And yet many days we did nothing but rehearse, and then rehearse. And many days we did nothing but sit and watch rats in the river. Those last were the days I felt nearest to him. I cannot recall a word he said about the rats, but I never watched rats so closely when not in his company. With anyone else, I'd have thought I was wasting my time. With Shakespeare, those rats were the meaning of existence.

4. Mr Shakespeare in his youth heard singing masons building roofs of gold. Mr Shakespeare in his middle years drank a drop of happiness, an old brown drop of golden wine. Mr Shakespeare in his last years looked down a well of eternity – the joyous, awful noontide abyss.

5. I never caught William Shakespeare looking at the new moon through glass. He was not fond of the moon, not overmuch. He was fastidious regarding her. But the full moon in the Thames, Mr Shakespeare would smile at that. And the sunsets over the Pool of London, sometimes. Let me get this right, what did Mr Shakespeare say about sunsets? 'I detest sunsets: their composition is careless.' But a moonless night now, that was a different story. Once, about the time when storms destroyed the second Armada, we were looking at the sky above the Curtain, the audience gone home, the stage in darkness, and I made bold to ask him which star he had fixed his eye on, and he answered, 'I am not looking at a star; I am looking past the stars.' His eyes were like icicles, and when I looked into them I saw that it was true – I, Pickleherring, saw beyond the stars, but only in the eyes of William Shakespeare.

6. The day that Mr Shakespeare drank himself blind. He wore a black coat, white gloves, in his hat-band a red rose. His hat itself was grey. It was that sleek copataine, high-crowned, he had been wearing when first I met him. He met John Florio in the park, who was jealous of him. John Florio had cause. They did not speak. Not a word was exchanged between them on this occasion. Mr Shakespeare had a hawk upon his wrist, and he let it fly at the white turtle doves that fluttered about Mr Florio. Blood and white feathers fell about the two men's heads, but they never moved. Mr Shakespeare raised his hat when the slaughter was over.

7. I remember when I played the flute for him at Windsor and he said, 'Don't'. He was right, of course, he had reason. The music made his ear bleed. Though I had something of a reputation, madam, I may say. (All flute-players are mad. In comes music at one ear, out goes wit at the other.) As I was playing I saw Mr Shakespeare's left hand go bloodless. And he never used it well, I think, after that night. Not that it was a blemish. It was an act of criticism.

8. I shall never forget the day he (almost) shook hands with the Earl of Essex. He had been writing *Henry V*, and inventing helmets. Essex was cross. He liked the helmets, certainly. But he said, quote When the sun shines upon them it will give away the disposition of our troops unquote. But Mr Shakespeare was ready for Robert Devereux. He replied, 'If your dispositions are such that they can be interpreted by the enemy I shall take my helmets elsewhere.' The Earl was thunderstruck. It was then that they shook hands, almost. In sight of the whole army. Essex approached from the east. The sun was glinting on his helmet (he had put it on at once). Mr Shakespeare came at him from the north, limping ever so slightly. The plume in my master's hat, green, green as goose turd, tossed in the light summer breeze. Mr Shakespeare never wore a helmet, to my knowledge. Essex marched at a lope. Mr Shakespeare, at a canter. The dogs were scratching themselves in the sun. Towards the end, the Earl, alarmed, saw that the necessary junction of soldier and poet was by no means inevitable. His right hand, outstretched, brushed the shining back of Mr Shakespeare's coat as he sped downhill. Let us recapitulate. Mr Shakespeare is speeding down the hillock towards the south, and indeed towards the Irish rebels. The Earl of Essex, Robert Devereux, is, as it were, unreturnably advanced towards the west, laying his shadow behind him on the evening turf, but nonetheless at some risk. He is already within gunshot of Tyrone's battery on that monticle. The English troops, at a loss, have the sun in their eyes. The Lord Lieutenant and his friend's poet are being unaccountably

careless. Then both men halt, as the bagpipes skirl. They laugh, Mr Shakespeare first, then the Earl joining in, though separated by no less than a furlong of bogland. Tyrone and his cartload of priests are surprised and vexed. I forget what happened next, but it was first-class. Tyrone stamps his foot and all hell's let loose. The Earl of Essex laid men upon the turf, to left and right, until his troops came up, and then sought out Southampton's pet once more. Mr Shakespeare danced among the cannonballs. He spat upon them where they landed, to hear the hot iron hiss. It was against all the proper usages of war.

9. Was Mr Shakespeare mad, madam? The question is ridiculous. He was the least mad man I ever knew. Yet love (if you will pardon me for saying so) is itself a madness, a war, a hell, an incurable disease, and William Shakespeare was in love with Lucy Negro, an impossible object for any man's desire. Let lovers sigh out the rest. I'm sure they will.

Chapter Eighty

In which boys will be girls

Some of those wretched Puritans got it right. They knew, at least, the sex of it, the way the audience's excitement at a performance of *Romeo and Juliet*, say, was something both peculiar and perverse. What was being enacted in our playhouse was the same hot thing that had been enacted centuries before, in the beginning of the theatre, at those exaltations which formed part of the worship of the god Dionysus. Aeschylus calls that god 'the womanly one'. In Euripides, he is 'the womanly stranger'. At times he has also been termed 'man-womanish'. The sexes are fused in him. The arousal he causes in his followers is like nothing else. He is the great enigma at the heart of a mystery.

You get the same idea in alchemy. There the *hierosgamos* or *coniunctio* is the chemical wedding of male and female in one. No alchemist myself, I know what this means.

When I put on my rose-coloured petticoats and my high-heeled shoes with roses, when I wore quilted and beaded under-skirts and long hard bodices stiffened with whalebone and encrusted with embroidery and gold lace, when I pulled up my cart-wheel farthingale to be spanked as the shrew, or bewailed all the perfumes of Arabia as I sleep-walked in Lady Macbeth's nightgown of Judas-colour satin faced with fur, I was both female and male, the flower and the thorn. Sometimes, quite intoxicated by my roles, bewildered and bewitched by all the woman's words I had to say, I think I imagined myself one of those devotees of the goddess Isis, who castrated themselves and changed sex to become her. At such times, no doubt, my performance was particularly good, and in the eyes of the audience I perhaps *became* Cordelia or Desdemona, Cleopatra or Juliet. At other times, though, more thoroughly and more often, I was the perfect

androgyne, male and female in one, changing from boy to girl and back again, to the very great excitement of my audience. That it excited *me*, and how, I have already told you. The fervour and fever in the spectators was mostly to be inferred from their rapt and breathless silence. But once or twice I saw certain poor souls in the shadows quite carried away, jerking off under cover of their cloaks, or pressed up hard against their neighbours. I was never insulted by this. It stood tribute to my art, as to the mystery of our craft.

Consider: in all orgies, at all times in history, cross-dressing has been of the essence. Put a man in a woman's clothes, or a woman in a man's, and you have instantly an invitation to sweet disorder, to sexual riot and confusion, and to a breakdown of all the usual inhibitory canons of behaviour.

I say that the spectacle of boys dressed as women on our stage was *meant* to be erotically exciting. Anyone who tells you otherwise is ignorant or is lying. What's more, Mr Shakespeare's plays, more than any other plays ever written, play about with this sexual confusion to a point where I insist I do not exaggerate by likening their effect to what happened in the worship of the great god Dionysus.

Some of the Puritans knew this, as I said. Here is John Rainoldes (no relation!), writing in 1599 on *Th' Overthrow of Stage-Plays*, after seeing me as Beatrice kissing Benedick at the end of *Much Ado About Nothing*:

'When *Critobulus* kissed the son of *Alcibiades*, a beautiful boy, *Socrates* said he had done amiss and very dangerously: because, as certain spiders, if they do but touch men only with their mouth, they put them to wonderful pain and make them mad: so beautiful boys by kissing do sting and pour secretly in a kind of poison, the poison of incontinency.'

In another passage in the same pamphlet, Rainoldes gets even hotter on the subject:

'Those monsters of nature, which burning in their lust one toward another, men with men work filthiness, are as infamous as *Sodom*: not the doers only, but the sufferers also.'

This Rainoldes must have been a closet sodomite, since that is all the thrust of his argument. No sodomite myself, I say our subversions were more terrible even than he imagined. Making men burn for men was only one aspect of the matter.

Here is Phillip Stubbes, whose *The Anatomy of Abuses* was published in the year that I was born, so he cannot be talking about my performances, yet the general argument is much the same:

'It is written in the 22nd chapter of *Deuteronomy* that what man so ever

weareth woman's apparel is accursed, and what woman weareth man's apparel is accursed also. . . . Our apparel was given us as a sign distinctive to discern betwixt sex and sex, & therefore one to wear the apparel of another sex is to participate with the same, and to adulterate the verity of his own kind. Wherefore these women may not improperly be called *Hermaphroditi*, that is, monsters of both kinds, half women, half men.'

Now, I, old Tiresias Pickleherring, say that there is much truth in Mr Stubbes's wholesome fulminations, and I should know. When I wore a woman's dress and spoke the woman's words written for me by Mr Shakespeare I did indeed PARTICIPATE with a woman's sex, and no doubt (thus initiate) I was guilty of adulterating the verity of my own kind. And yet how sweet, how very sweet it was! And what is my own kind, in any case, since all my long life it has seemed to me that I am Sappho imprisoned in a man's body?

Stubbes does at least do credit to the *general* disorder inspired by our cross-dressing, not just concentrating on the issue of effeminacy to the exclusion of all else. He sees quite clearly that the theatre is a pagan temple (which is why he abhors it), and that the god who is worshipped there is not Jehovah (nor even perhaps a male deity), and that the worshippers leave the place filled with a spirit which moves them to several different expressions of human passion:

'For proof whereof, but mark the flocking and running to Theatres and Curtains, daily and hourly, night and day, time and tide to see plays and interludes, where such wanton gestures, such bawdy speeches, such laughing and fleering, such kissing and bussing, such clipping and culling, such winking and glancing of wanton eyes and the like is used, as is wonderful to behold. Then, these goodly pageants being done, every mate sorts to his mate, every one brings another homeward of their way very friendly, and in their secret conclaves (covertly) they play the Sodomites, or worse.'

Regarding the strange gender of the spirit behind the ecstasy of the playhouse, Stubbes is also on to something real when he associates the practice of cross-dressing with the power of women over men:

'I never read or heard of any people except drunken with Circe's cups, or poisoned with the exorcisms of Medea that famous and renowned sorceress, that ever would wear such kind of attire as is not only stinking before the face of God, and offensive to man, but also painteth out to the whole world the venereous inclination of their corrupt conversation.'

I have just the one more pamphlet in this box. It is the most arresting of them all – the *Histrio-Mastix* of William Prynne, published in London in

1633. Prynne sees that boys dressing as girls not only excites the boys 'to self-pollution (a sin for which Onan was destroyed) and to that unnatural sodomitical sin of uncleaness to which the reprobate Gentiles were given over', it also transforms them into women:

'And must not our own experience bear witness of the unvirility of play-acting? May we not daily see our players metamorphosed into women on the stage, not only by putting on the female robes, but likewise the effeminate gestures, speeches, pace, behaviour, attire, delicacy, passions, manners, arts and wiles of the female sex, yea, of the most petulant, unchaste, insinuating strumpets that either Italy or the world affords?'

This is the finest critique I ever had! That Mr Prynne in his youth had seen me in the part of Cleopatra I have no doubt, especially since elsewhere in his *Histrio-Mastix* he works himself into another lather over such matters as Cleopatra's clothing herself in the habit of Isis during the course of that play, not to speak of her dressing her lover in her own 'tires and mantles' whilst she straps on his sword:

'A man's clothing himself in maid's attire is not only an imitation of effeminate idolatrous priests and pagans who arrayed themselves in woman's apparel when they sacrificed to their idols, and their Venus, and celebrated plays unto them (which as Lyra, Aquinas, and Alensis well observe was one chief reason why this text of Deuteronomy prohibits men's putting on of women's apparel as an abomination to the Lord), but a manifest approbation and revival of this their idolatrous practice. Therefore it must certainly be abominable, and within the very scope and letter of this inviolable Scripture, even in this regard.'

Before I leave the subject, ladies and gentlemen, picture to yourselves for a moment a pretty page boy pulling on a pair of Queen Elizabeth's black silk stockings when his mistress's back is turned. Then think of the boy's prick nestling in a pair of the Queen's warm discarded satin drawers, and being stirred perhaps to tumescence by the touch of their texture and the thought of Her. These images, I submit, excite both men and women. They are indifferent in their sexual excellence. It is the silk excitement makes us hot. It is the mixture of identities and tokens of sex: the Queen, the young boy, the soft and private petals, the sharp upthrusting thorn. It is the silken confusion – that element of the forbidden, the perverse, the opposites kissing as they cross – which so fascinates and engrosses our senses. The dress is female, while groin and fist are male. This is the ultimate and primal image, the mystery enacted in that theatre of the soul which our bodies will avow before our minds. This is the play of all plays, the drama that Mr Shakespeare could not write, but which he wrote over

and over by not writing it. All the secrets of creation can come down to this little scene. It is the secret dream in the darkest chamber. This is what happens in Lucy Negro's seventh room.

Chapter Eighty-One

In which Mr Shakespeare is mocked
by his fellows

William Shakespeare was now so famous and successful that his rivals started mocking him. Such was ever the way of the world. They envied him his fluency and his facility, as well as the great popularity of his work with all manner of people. By this time our upstart crow had produced 8 comedies and 12 tragedies. He had also published two much-reprinted poems that everyone was talking about on account of their high erotic content and mellifluous versification. And besides all this, he had been responsible for adapting and reworking at least a dozen old plays, and was always being asked by the Company to spice up and improve the plays we had in stock.

Given this acclaim, and the spite that comes naturally to certain poets, it is not surprising that some of Mr Shakespeare's contemporaries found fault with him. Ben Jonson, in particular, was very jealous.

There was a deep difference of temperament between the two men. I can best suggest this by remembrance of the few occasions when Mr Shakespeare was persuaded to the Mermaid tavern by his friends (his usual habit, as I have said, being to avoid attendance by sending down a note that he was 'in pain'). Jonson held court in the Mermaid, he was its uncrowned king. His sycophants danced attendance on him there, hanging on his every word, laughing obedience to each laboured joke that fell from his lips, licking his arse as if his shit was nectar. He would sit there sweating in his own carved chair, a mountain of flesh with pock-marked face and albino hair and eyes, wearing a coat like a coachman's, with slits under the arm-pits. He had once been a brick-layer, then he had fought in the wars in Flanders. A mediocre actor, in truth he was at first not much more

successful when he turned playwright. During these difficult years, Jonson quarrelled with an actor of Henslowe's company, a man called Gabriel Spencer, and killed him in a duel in Hogsden Fields. He only escaped hanging by invoking the 'Benefit of Clergy' clause, calling for a Bible and reading in Latin the verses of the 51st psalm. This proof of erudition reduced his punishment, but his thumb was branded with a T for Tyburn.

Down at the Mermaid, he met more than his match in Shakespeare. In their wit-combats, Jonson was like a Spanish great galleon, while our hero was an English man-of-war. Jonson, that is to say, while physically more impressive, and giving every impression of being built higher out of the water in terms of Learning, was but solid and slow in his performance. Shakespeare, our English frigate, lesser in bulk, could out-manoeuvre him in any exchange, being lighter in sailing, and able to turn with all tides, tack about and take advantage of all winds, by the quickness of his wit and invention.

Needless to say, this pleased Mr Jonson no more than the fact that it was only when Mr Shakespeare got our Company to perform his *Every Man in His Humour* with Shakespeare himself in the part of Knowell Senior that he started to get merit as a playwright. The two rival writers passed for the best of friends, and nowadays when people who knew neither of them read Jonson's fulsome eulogy they quickly conclude that this was indeed the case. However, I can tell you that relations between them were always in fact more complicated, on account of Jonson's jealousy. This came out in his losing no opportunity to mock Mr Shakespeare's pretensions to the rank of gentleman. In his satire which appeared the year a coat of arms was accorded to Mr John Shakespeare, Jonson parodies both the 'falcon brandishing a spear' and the device 'Non sans droict', giving to one of his characters, the upstart Sogliardo, similar armorial bearings with the motto, 'Not without mustard'. As for the magnificence of his tribute to Shakespeare in the shape of that ode which Mr Heminges and Mr Condell (in their wisdom) placed as heading to the Folio of 1623, permit old crazy Pickleherring merely to point out that this came only when Jonson's great rival was safely dead and buried, and that then the note of praise seems strained and forced, perhaps out of guilt that he had put the man down when alive.

However, Pickleherring might be wrong to say so. I confess that I never liked either Mr Ben Jonson or his inky plays. Shall I just say that we boiled at different temperatures, before leaving the subject?

In any case, the sharpest mocking of Shakespeare was done not by Jonson but by John Marston in his *Histrio-Mastix or The Player Whipt*. (Yes,

madam, it *is* the same name as that pamphlet of Prynne's which I gave you in the last chapter, but believe me that does *not* mean I am making all this up! If this were fiction, I could change the name, so that there would be no possibility of confusion. But real life is like this, full of meaningless coincidence. Consider the other Reynoldses in my narrative. . . .)

Marston was no albino giant. He had red hair and short legs, and in due course he gave up poetry to become a priest. But in his unregenerate days he had much fun at Mr S's expense with his character called Post Haste.

Post Haste is a playwright in a hurry. He is hasty, he is muddled, and he has to turn out play after play for his company. He is always eager to offer his services to the Truly Great, and glad to give a performance in exchange for a good dinner and a night's sleep in a swansdown bed at any Lordship's house. His repertoire parodies that passage in *Hamlet* where Polonius lists the accomplishments of the itinerant players:

> *The Lascivious Knight and Lady Nature*
> *The Devil and Dives (a comedy)*
> *A Russet Coat and a Knave's Cap (an infernal)*
> *A Proud Heart and a Beggar's Purse (a pastoral)*
> *The Widow's Apron Strings (a nocturnal)*
> *Mother Gurton's Needle (a tragedy)*

What's more, like Mr Shakespeare, Post Haste always has in hand a *new* play, a piece which he is just finishing, something never yet seen but which he intends to stage without delay.

When Post Haste appears on stage his companions bow low. They count on his talents for their cakes and ale. He consents to give the actors a foretaste of his latest work, *The Prodigal Son*, but his voice is so broken by sobs that he can't go on reading. Nothing daunted, he declares that he is equal to improvising a prologue appropriate to every occasion. Post Haste, in fact, has up his sleeve a Universal Prologue and a Universal Epilogue.

Here is the Universal Prologue:

> *Lords, we are here to show you what we are;*
> *Lords, we are here although our clothes be bare.*
> *Instead of flowers in season*
> *Ye shall gather Rime and Reason.*

And this is the Universal Epilogue:

> *The glass is run, our play is done:*
> *Hence: Time doth call; we thank you all.*

However, what Post Haste has in hand for this particular occasion is a play on the subject of Troilus and Cressida, and in case anyone should so far have missed the object of the lampoon when we get to Cressida bestowing her colours on her champion we have Troilus hammering home a pun on Shakespeare's name:

> *When he shakes a furious spear*
> *The foe in shivery fearful sort*
> *May lay him down in death to snort.*

I think this is quite enough to show that Marston certainly had it here in mind to mock both our hero's character and his more perfunctory dramatic procedures. The satire is not without bite, and the feeling of it may even have a touch of affection. Shakespeare's portrait in the person of Post Haste does bear some resemblance to the man I knew.

Talking of which, and since it was at this point in his life's fame that I first met him, let me explain how it happened that Mr Shakespeare was in Cambridge rather than London that day when I jumped off the wall for him in 1596. The Puritans amongst the magistrates of the city of London had just at that time managed to get an order forbidding all plays in the city and its suburbs, on the pretext that large assemblies would create a public danger by increasing the risk of infection with the plague. That there was in that year no plague in London, or anywhere near London, did not deter them. But then in my definition a Puritan is one who objects to bull and bear baiting, not in pity for bull or bear, but in aversion to and envy at the pleasure of the spectators. In a word, a KILL-JOY.

The ban did not last long, yet it was a presage of things to come, when under Cromwell the same spirit triumphed, shutting down every playhouse in the country.

Still, I am grateful to those kill-joys for what they did in the summer of my thirteenth year. Without their mean antics, the Lord Chamberlain's Servants would never have been touring the provinces, their shoes full of gravel and their old blind nag laden down with baskets full of costumes, and I would never have met Post Haste and become a player myself. In

which case, I suppose, it is unlikely that I would now be sitting in the attic of a Southwark brothel, munching pickled mulberries and watching the moon rise over the roofs of the stews. She makes these roofs silver. I wonder how anything can be so white, so perfectly white.

Chapter Eighty-Two

Pickleherring's poem

Last night I dreamt that I was an urchin and Polly was a waif. We were the same age, the two of us, younger than she is now, and we came in together off the street hand-in-hand to present ourselves to Pompey Bum and Lucy Negro.

'Whose house is this?' I asked them.

'It belongs to her,' said Pompey Bum. 'Her name is Madam Mitigation.'

Polly jumped up and down. She was wearing a short white dress, and a ribbon of white velvet in her hair. 'Goody! Goody!' she cried. 'You buy children, don't you?'

They smiled and nodded, nodded and smiled, but Lucy Negro was holding a long whip. 'We do,' she said. 'Jump up on the table and let's have a look at you,' said Pompey Bum.

So Polly and I climbed up on the table in my dream. But I was frightened. 'Why do you buy children?' I enquired.

'For love,' said Lucy Negro.

She was pinching and stroking my calf.

Pompey Bum spread wide his pale pink hands. He looked like a pork butcher. 'That's right,' he said. 'For love. What else?'

Polly pouted. 'Will we have to work?' she asked suspiciously.

'You will work for love, my moppet,' said Lucy Negro.

I didn't like the sound of this, though it seemed not to displease Polly. She gave a twirl where she stood beside me on the table top, showing the adults her bottom. She was not wearing drawers.

'Do you have a lot of love then?' she asked them, giggling.

'My house is made of love,' said Lucy Negro.

She cracked her whip as she said this. I was scared. But Polly jumped up

and down and clapped her hands together. 'Oh, how soon can we have some?' she cried out.

Lucy Negro cracked the whip again, but it was Pompey's fat hand that slapped pretty Polly's impertinent arse. 'Stand still when you're up for sale!' the whoremaster commanded. 'I can't abide a kid that keeps jigging about before the price is settled.'

'They don't love us, Poll,' said I. 'They don't love us at all.'

Some ridiculous antics followed. I can't remember the sequence. At one point, I know, I had to jump through a hoop while Polly stood on her head in the corner and Pompey Bum inspected her. At last the owners of the brothel professed themselves satisfied. It was to me that Lucy Negro turned, and she took me by the hand. 'You see, little pickerel,' said she, 'we *do* love you, and you will find out how much just as soon as the contract is signed.'

'To whom should we make payment?' said Pompey Bum. He was tossing a bag of money from hand to hand.

I very much wanted to piss. And I wanted to leave. But Polly was dancing about again on the table. 'Mr Bum and Miss Negro,' she cried, 'we belong to the river.'

'We can't pay the river,' Lucy Negro said. 'The brat must mean Mr Shakespeare.'

Pompey Bum, though, seemed delighted that the two of us should belong to the River Thames. 'River children! River children!' he chanted. 'They are children of the river! Down you come!'

When we came down off the table he wanted to know if we had come upstream or downstream. I said nothing. I just wanted to piss. Then he asked us if we had seen a boat with a white female figurehead and a captain by the name of William Shakespeare. A man without a memory, he said.

Polly put on a serious face. It didn't suit her. 'Yes, sir,' she said. 'I think I met the gentleman.'

'Liar!' I cried. 'You're just saying that to please them.'

But Polly insisted. 'He was at the lock above Alveston,' she went on. 'It was the day that Pickleherring went to the fair. Captain Shakespeare put a kiss in my hand and he asked me if I would stay with him until dark. I said I would. He smelt like trees in a forest. He said, "Tell me a story." So I told him about the swan that was cut open on Thomasina's birthday and they found a mirror inside it. It was a little mirror, with an ivory handle and a silver back. When you looked in it, you saw yourself clearer than you are. He didn't like that story.'

'That's our friend,' said Pompey Bum. 'Did he mention me?'

Polly shook her head. 'He didn't say much about himself,' she explained.

'But he liked me. He made me take all my clothes off and we played a wee game. All about me being a wolf and he was the chickens. I wished that Captain Shakespeare was my father.'

Pompey Bum and Lucy Negro were falling about. They seemed delighted by this story. As for me, I just wanted to have a good piss and the dream to end. You know how it is in some dreams – that you start to wake up in them. I was reaching that stage, being conscious that I wanted it to end. Meanwhile, Pompey Bum was asking Polly what the game was called, and Polly replied that the game was called PILLICOCK HILL.

I had had enough. 'Don't believe it, sir and madam!' I cried out. 'She's wanted to be deflowered for simply ages. Terrible she is. You can have no idea what her brothers have had to put up with. Anyway, you can't have me without her, so make up your minds.'

'Take them,' said Pompey Bum to Lucy Negro. 'What else is there to do when two lives come to join yours?'

'It's an odd story,' Lucy Negro said.

'You can say that for a week,' said Pompey Bum. 'You will still take them.'

But Lucy Negro was shaking her lovely head. 'I do not believe the girl's story,' she announced. 'William Shakespeare would never use a word like PILLICOCK.'

That's where you're wrong, lady, thought I to myself in the dream, for he uses that word in *King Lear*. But I was not going to tell her. Instead, I woke up and had a good piss in my chamber-pot. As I pissed I reflected that it is Lear's *'Twas this flesh begot / Those pelican daughters* which prompts Edgar (outcast, and posing as the idiot Poor Tom) to chant: *Pillicock sat on Pillicock Hill.** PILLICOCK means the male generative organs, with *pilli* as the testicles and *cock* the penis. As for PILLICOCK HILL it is the Mount of Venus + the *pudendum muliebre* itself. So Pillicock sitting on Pillicock Hill describes the deed of darkness by which Lear's flesh begot his daughters. No doubt it meant the same in my foolish dream.

When I was finished pissing I heard Polly at work in the room below, but I did not want to look. Don't ask me why, sir. I just didn't feel like it.

That word PILLICOCK comes somewhere in one of John Florio's word-books, by the by, which is a source from which Mr Shakespeare drew many choice vocables. It comes also in my mentor Urquhart's translation of Rabelais, but that of course was after Shakespeare's time.

Marston has Post Haste have a word-hoard: *Plenty of Old England's mother*

* *King Lear*, Act III, Scene 4, lines 74–5.

319

words. So he did, and only a fraction of it from Florio. Florio, for that matter, might have garnered PILLICOCK from Shakespeare, learning the word from him during the course of a game at tennis on Rizley's second-best court for all I know. It is not (I just looked) in my father's kidskin dictionary.

Since in my last chapter I disparaged Mr Ben Jonson's famous verses about Mr Shakespeare in the First Folio, it is only fair that now I should give you my own verses about Mr Shakespeare which I contributed to the Second Folio. These appeared there amongst the preliminary matter in 1632, but with no name attached at my request. As you will see, the verse turns on the degree to which Shakespeare is to be found rather in his works than in Droeshout's copper-plate engraving for the title-page. Here is my poem:

Upon the Effigies of my worthy
Friend, the Author Master William
Shakespeare, and his Works

Spectator, this life's shadow is. To see
The truer image and a livelier he
Turn reader. But observe his comic vein,
Laugh, and proceed next to a tragic strain,
Then weep. So when thou find'st two contraries,
Two different passions from thy rapt soul rise,
Say (who alone effect such wonders could)
Rare Shakespeare *to the life thou dost behold.*

Chapter Eighty-Three

*In which Mr Shakespeare plays
a game at tennis*

William Shakespeare and John Florio enjoyed a game at tennis. They played in a walled and roofed court belonging to the Earl of Southampton. This court was 110 feet long by 38 feet and eight inches wide, though the floor measured but 96 feet long by 31 feet and eight inches wide, the difference being the width of a roofed corridor, the 'penthouse' which runs along the two end walls and one of the side walls of all such arenas.

Across the middle of the court a tasselled rope is stretched, and I will tell you that the first object of the game is to strike the ball over this with a bat called a racquet. The rope is five feet high at the ends, and three feet six inches high in the middle, and divides the floor into two equal parts, the 'service' side and the 'hazard' side.

Sometimes I stood in the 'dedans' to watch them play. The dedans is an opening in the end wall on the service side, under the penthouse, where provision is made for spectators, who are protected by a net.

The game is very fierce. It goes like this.

The players decide who shall serve by spinning a racquet on its head. Mr Shakespeare would spin and Mr Florio would call 'rough' or 'smooth', the 'rough' side of the head of the racquet showing the knots of some of the lower strings. The winner takes the service side, service being an advantage.

The server may serve from any part of the court, and in any way that he thinks best to serve. (Mr Shakespeare would spin the ball high with his fingers and then hit it hard with his racquet as it came down.) The ball must then fly over the rope, and strike the side penthouse, and fall into the service-court. The opponent (or 'striker-out') tries to return the ball over

the rope before it has touched the ground a second time. He may volley it if he can, or he may half-volley it. For a stroke to be 'good' it must be made before the second bound of the ball, and the ball must go over the rope (even if it brushes it), and the ball must not strike the wall above the play-line, nor touch the roof or rafters. The first point to be attained is thus to be sure of getting the ball over the rope, and the next to do so in such a way as to defeat your opponent's attempt to make a 'good' stroke in return.

It often happens that a player, either intentionally or from inability, does not take or touch a ball returned to him over the rope. In this event, a 'chase' is made, the goodness or the badness of which depends upon the spot on the floor which the ball touches next after its first bound. The nearer this spot is to the end wall the better the chase. Strokes into the galleries and doors count as chases. The making (or as they call it, the 'laying down') of a chase does not immediately affect the score: it has to be won first, *i.e.* the other player tries to make a better chase; if he fails, the original maker wins. The winner of the chase scores a point. A point is scored by that player whose opponent fails to make a good return stroke, or who strikes the ball into a winning opening, or wins a chase, or to whom two faults are served in succession. A player loses a stroke who strikes the ball twice, or allows it to touch himself or his clothes.

The game is marked, 15, 30, 40 (or advantage), equality of numbers, and then victory. The players wear felt shoes for play on the smooth tiled pavement, with caps held on by a band which goes under the chin. The balls are small and hard, being made of whiteleather and stuffed with dog's hair and other such stubble.* The racquets are woven from strings such as might otherwise be found on a six-stringed lyre.

Mr Florio was an excellent player at tennis, with a subtle understanding of all the game's finer points. Even if you had never seen him in action on Rizley's court, you might deduce as much from his *Second Fruits* (1591), where the value of chases is discussed at length.

Mr Shakespeare was an altogether wilder sort of performer. He struck the ball well and he was agile in his volleying and his bandying, but when it came to the chases you could tell his mind was somewhere else. This did not bother me as his spectator. In fact, what I liked best was the stream of invective which would flow from his lips when he was *losing*. I never heard anything to match it, not even among the tinkers and mountebanks busy at Bartholomew Fair.

One morning when the game went all Florio's way, I took paper and

---

* Cf. 'The barber's man hath been seen with him; and the old ornament of his cheek hath already stuffed tennis-balls.' *Much Ado About Nothing*, Act III, Scene 2, lines 45–7.

jotted down some of the choice names which my master called his opponent as each point was lost. Here is that riot of insults:

You drone!	You slug!	You patch!	You punk!
You clog!	You bubble!	You sprat!	You sot!
Dog-ape!	Odd worm!	Garbage!	Fishmonger!
Unpaved eunuch!	Jack-sauce!	Miscreant!	Mouse!
Spongey officer!	Fire-drake!	Mongrel!	Chewet!
Libbard's head!	Rash wanton!	Detested kite!	Lack-love!
You mere gypsy!	You gibbet!	You foul blot!	You thing!
Notable lubber!	Coistrel!	Gross lout!	Camel!
Such a snipe!	Botchy core!	Sir knave!	Cuckold!
Minion!	You drone!	Malt-horse!	Shrike!
Coxcomb!	Boggler!	Carbonado!	Toad!
Mechanic slave!	Serpent's egg!	Dullard!	Popinjay!
Capering fool!	Foolish cur!	Silly dwarf!	Hulk!
Whoreson zed!	Rebel's whore!	Sly divel!	You chaos!
You ronyon!	You polecat!	You baggage!	You bead!
You saucy friar!	You prodigal!	You Lucifer!	Thou cat!

There were other choice phrases of abuse also, more in the nature of complete sentences, which Mr Shakespeare uttered when he had his breath back. Amongst these I noted:

'You very superficial, ignorant, unweighing fellow!'
'You wimpled, whining, purblind, wayward boy!'
'You logger-headed and unpolish'd groom!'
'Red-tailed bumble-bee! Foul indigested lump!'
'You are the son and heir of a mongrel bitch!'
'You dainty dominic! You stretch-mouthed rascal!'
'You minimus, of hind'ring knotgrass made!'
'Mad mustachio purple-hued maltworm!'
'Thou little better thing than earth!'
'Foolish compounded clay-man!'
'A dog-fox not proved worth a blackberry!'
'King-Urinal! Monsieur Mock-water! Thou finch egg!'
'Thou idle immaterial skein of sleeve silk!'
'Thou green sarsanet flap for a sore eye!'
'Thou bright defiler of Hymen's purest bed!'
'You bawling, blasphemous, incharitable dog!'

'Thou disease of a friend!'
'Thou thing of no bowels!'

And so on, and so forth. Mr Shakespeare was a master of this craft or sullen art. He could go on for minutes on end, insulting Mr Florio without ever repeating himself once.

I remember one game where Mr Shakespeare kept on serving what they call double faults. Of course, he blamed his opponent for this small deficiency. John Florio, he said, was a KNAVE. Then, standing at the tasselled rope, racquet in hand, which he waved above his head to punctuate each verbal thrust, he gave it as his opinion that John Florio was not just a KNAVE, but a foul-mouthed and caluminous KNAVE, and not just a foul-mouthed and caluminous KNAVE, but a wrangling KNAVE, a poor, decayed, ingenious, foolish, rascally KNAVE, a KNAVE that smelt of sweat, a shrewd KNAVE and unhappy, a sly and constant KNAVE, a lousy KNAVE, a bacon-fed KNAVE, a counterfeit cowardly KNAVE, a crafty KNAVE, a subtle KNAVE, the lying'st KNAVE in Christendom, a beastly KNAVE, a stubborn ancient KNAVE, a muddy KNAVE, a whoreson beetle-headed, flap-ear'd KNAVE, a base notorious KNAVE, a KNAVE very voluble, a pestilent complete KNAVE, a KNAVE fit only to be beat into a twiggen-bottle, an arrant, malmsy-nose KNAVE, a KNAVE most untoward, a muddy KNAVE, a ruddy KNAVE, a base, proud, shallow, beggarly, three-suited, hundred-pound, filthy worsted-stocking KNAVE. In short, a *villain*.

And not just a villain, of course, but a bloody, bawdy villain, a remorseless, treacherous, lecherous, kindless villain. A honeysuckle villain. A villain fit to lie unburied. Even a chaffy lord not worth the name of villain.

Mr Shakespeare had a very good line in expletives, also. Here are just a few which I recall from the tennis court – William Shakespeare's tennis court oaths:

Cupid have mercy!
What rubbish and what offal!
O, vengeance, vengeance!
Pish for thee!
Figo for thy friendship!
Plague of your policy!
Froth and scum!
Divinity of hell!
Pow-waw!
My breath and blood!

O woeful day!
Pluto and hell!
Chops!
By Chrish, la!
Bedlam, have done!
Good worts!
By cock and pie!
O blood, blood, blood!
Fut!
O curse of marriage!

Fire and brimstone!
Goats and monkeys!
A pox of wrinkles!
Tilly-vally!
Disgrace and blows!
Let all the dukes and all the
                        devils roar!
Foh! Fie!
For the love of Juno!

Hell gnaw his bones!
Puttock! Puppies!
Chaff and bran!
God's lid!
O piteous spectacle!
A bugbear take you! O
         plague and madness!
Leprosy o'ertake!
O viper vile!

And so on. But his favourites, in the expletive art, were *'A pox on this gout! or a gout on this pox!'* (which line he gave to Falstaff), and (if he noticed me, note-taking in the dedans) *'A plague o' these pickle-herring!'*

As this will indicate, some of these terms of abuse were borrowed from his own plays, but there were as many or more which he had not used in his work at the time when he uttered them extempore.

All of which makes me think that William Shakespeare employed his games at tennis to put some critical part of his mind to sleep in action, and to see what words and phrases would bubble up from the depths if he lost his temper as a result. Not that he ever did lose his temper; not exactly. He would let himself go just far enough to have access to his great store of original invective. Then he would turn his fury into words. Then he would stop playing tennis. Often I thought he was playing some other game all the time.

Chapter Eighty-Four

What Shakespeare got
from Florio
+ a word about George Peele

I am apt to believe that Mr Shakespeare's skill in the French and Italian tongues exceeded his knowledge in the Roman. For we find him not only beholding to Cinthio, Giraldi, and Bandello for his plots, but also able to write such a scene as that in *Henry V* where the princess Katharine and her governante converse in their native language quite believably. More cogent, though, to my memories of the playwright's performance on the tennis court is the very great number of Italian proverbs scattered up and down in his writings. Where did these come from if not from John Florio?

Southampton's tutor had been born in London, the son of an Italian refugee of Jewish ancestry. He was educated under the direction of the scholar Vergerio at Tubingen. He travelled through Italy and returned to England in the middle 1570s. Here he made a living from private lessons, taught at Oxford, and was authorised to wear the gown of Magdalen College. Patronised by Walsingham, he was recommended to Lord Burghley, who appointed him as tutor to his ward. This would have been at the start of the Nineties, about the time when Shakespeare was beginning that monumental work more durable than bronze or stone, the immortal sonnets, which as we have seen began as advice to the pupil Rizley.

So we have this interesting little triangle if not trinity – rich patron, learnèd teacher, eager poet. I think it was Rizley's wish to see some of the furnishings of Italian romance transported to England, and Shakespeare's wish both to please him and to have a certain edge over his rival playwrights by substituting for their classical scenes the much more colourful Italy of the Renaissance. As for the pedagogue, he was happy

enough no doubt to have found both a powerful nobleman and a poet of genius to act as propagandists for the culture he personified.

Florio's library was magnificent. It contained more than 300 volumes. It was this precious collection, to which Shakespeare soon had access, which provided the plot source of nearly every one of the early plays. Here he found the *Novelle* of Cinthio, and Luigi da Porto, and Boccaccio, and Bandello. Here he found the works of Machiavelli, and Ariosto, and Ser Giovanni, and Florio Fiorentino, and Petrarch, and Aretino, and Dante. Many of these texts were not yet translated into English, but with Florio to guide him to the treasures in the magic cavern the man from Stratford was soon rubbing lamps and releasing genii for himself. Everything he found got thoroughly turned into English in the process of his imagination, but Florio should be acknowledged as the one who gave him access to the cave.

All Mr Shakespeare ever needed to set his mind a-racing was a few words, the merest outline of a plot. Often, hearing of some such, I saw him stop his ears, covering them suddenly with his hands, rather than listen to the actual conclusion of the story. He always preferred to hear half a promising tale, and then let his own wild fancy do the rest. In this way several of his plays had their beginnings.

John Florio was a curious gentleman. The feature of him which I remember best was his little wax-like hands. When he had completed a game at tennis the smell that his body exhaled was of sweet earth-flesh, the odour of mushrooms. He had long bristling moustaches which he would twist between his fingers and thumbs as he talked to you. As his several books show, he was a man of incontestable erudition and culture, even if he did like torturing rats.

To give you some idea of Mr Shakespeare's debt to Mr Florio, I think I will quote first from the latter's *First Fruits*:

'We need not speak so much of love; all books are full of love, with so many authors, that it were labour lost to speak of love.'

That saying, of course, gave Mr Shakespeare the title of one of his first plays, *Love's Labour's Lost*.

Among the 300 proverbs which Florio boasted of having introduced into England from Italy, Shakespeare uses (to my count) more than 30, and there are a few of them which the poet quotes more than ten times. It is interesting and revealing, your author suggests, to see the manner in which Shakespeare incorporates Florio's 'golden sentences' in his dialogue or fits them into his verse:

'All that glistereth is not gold . . .' (Florio, *First Fruits*, page 32)	*All that glisters is not gold* *Golden tombs do dust enfold . . .* (Shakespeare, *The Merchant of Venice*, Act II, Scene 5)
'More water flows by the mill than the miller knows . . .' (*First Fruits*, page 34)	*More water glideth by the mill than wots* *the miller of* (*Titus Andronicus*, Act II, Scene 1)
'When the cat is abroad the mice play . . .' (*First Fruits*, page 33)	*Playing the mouse in absence of the* *cat . . .* (*Henry V*, Act I, Scene 2)
'He that maketh not, marreth not . . .' (*First Fruits*, page 26)	*What make you? Nothing? What mar you* *then?* (*As You Like It*, Act I, Scene 1)
'An ill weed groweth apace . . .' (*First Fruits*, page 31)	*Small herbs have grace; great weeds do* *grow apace* (*Richard III*, Act II, Scene 4)
'Fast bind, fast find . . .' (*Second Fruits*, page 15)	*Fast bind, fast find,* *A proverb never stale in thrifty mind* (*The Merchant of Venice*, Act II, Scene 5)
'Give losers leave to speak . . .' (*Second Fruits*, page 69)	*But I can give the loser leave to chide,* *And well such losers may have leave to* *speak* (*Henry VI*, Part II, Act III, Scene 1)
'The end maketh all men equal . . .' (*First Fruits*, page 31)	*One touch of nature makes the whole* *world kin . . .* (*Troilus and Cressida*, Act III, Scene 3)
'Necessity hath no law . . .' (*First Fruits*, page 32)	*Nature must obey necessity . . .* (*Julius Caesar*, Act IV, Scene 3)
'That is quickly done, that is done well . . .' (*First Fruits*, page 27)	*If it were done when 'tis done, then 'twere* *well it were done quickly . . .* (*Macbeth*, Act I, Scene 7)

In each and every case, of course, Shakespeare has improved on Florio. For instance, how much more fleeting his water-by-the-mill because it *glideth*, a word which has both the movement of the river and the sunlight on it, and so is more ephemeral than the Italian lexicographer's *flows*. For instance, how much more immediate the poet's *one touch of nature makes the whole world kin*, where TOUCH and KIN bring home the mere abstraction of the original.

You may say, madam, that proverbs are much the same in any language, but surely you will concede that there are so many striking verbal similarities between Florio and Shakespeare as to make it likely that here we are not just up against coincidence. Besides, in *Love's Labour's Lost* (whose very title is borrowed, as I have shown, from the Italian-English manual), Shakespeare goes so far as to quote Florio *in the Italian original*, when he makes Holofernes say:

'Ah! good old Mantuan. I may speak of thee as the traveller doth of Venice: *Venetia, Venetia, Chi non te vede, non te pretia.*'

Florio had written: '*Venetia qui non ti vedi non ti pretia; ma chi ti vede ben gli costa!*' You will find this also in his *First Fruits*, published in London in the summer of '78.

These two volumes of English and Italian dialogues, Florio's *First Fruits* and his *Second Fruits* published some 13 years later, seem to me to have provided Mr Shakespeare with a most unusual source of material. That the influence extended both ways might be surmised from the fact that while the subject of Love was omitted from the *First Fruits*, in the *Second Fruits* Mr Florio devotes no less than 60 pages to the tender passion, quoting Ovid constantly. I smell my master's hand in this, not least in Florio's conclusion that Love is as indispensable to mankind as eating or telling lies.

Incidentally, in the course of the *Second Fruits* John Florio not only gives us his opinion of the state of the English stage, but sets this in the context of a tennis game exactly like the ones he played with William Shakespeare. This is how the game is led up to:

'Let us make a match at tennis.
Agreed, this cool morning calls for it,
And afterwards we will dine together;
Then after dinner we will go see a play.
The plays they play in England are not right comedies;
Yet they do nothing else but play every day.
Yea, but they are neither right comedies, nor right tragedies.
How would you name them then?

Representations of histories without any decorum.'

I suggest that Mr Shakespeare's eye certainly passed over these dialogues, which are spoken prose set out with some of the appearance of verse. Whether he thought that Florio was having a hit at *King John* and his *Henry VI* trilogy with that remark about 'representations of histories without any decorum', I could not tell you. The criticism bears some truth within it. Though it might be just revenge for a lost game at tennis.

Florio's major work came out in 1603 – his Englishing of the *Essais* of Montaigne. There can be no doubt that Mr Shakespeare read this carefully. He makes use of Montaigne's essays on cannibals and on cruelty in passages of *The Tempest*, and I think there are traces of the Frenchman to be found in *King Lear* also, and the last revision of *Hamlet*. Montaigne's thoughts on Death were much to Shakespeare's taste in his later life. I have his copy of the *Essays* in Florio's translation, with his signature in it, which is followed by the words MORS INCERTA in his neatest hand.

John Florio's star rose highest after his years with Southampton, when he was appointed to be one of the tutors of the greatly gifted but ill-fated Prince Henry. When that boy died young, this gentleman's fortunes waned. He died of the plague at Fulham in 1625, having spent his last years in vain bickerings with his daughter Aurelia and his son-in-law, Dr Mollins. His wife Rose Spicer had been a sister of the poet Samuel Daniel, of whom I once heard Mr Shakespeare remark that he could never trust a poet whose name rhymed with itself.

This was, for him, an uncommonly harsh criticism. He was nearly always generous in his appraisal of other writers – saying nothing if he could not say something good. Even of Henry Chettle, that fat fool who was responsible for publishing Greene's upstart crow libel, he managed to find lines to like. Not that Diaphenia like the daffadowndilly (heigh-ho) nonsense, but *Aeliana's Ditty*.

The late Mr Shakespeare's usual practice, if you happened to mention a poet's name, was to remember at least one good line that the man had written. For that matter, if he heard good told of anyone, he would rub his hands together instinctively.

Most poets die poor, and consequently obscurely, and a hard matter it is to trace them to their graves. Not so, of course, with William Shakespeare. But it *was* so in the case of a now obscure writer whose work (if you will forgive the pun) certainly much appealed to WS. I mean George Peele.

Poor Peele. He died young, and of the pox, and after his death for some reason he passed swiftly into legend as the very emblem of the witty poet,

the so-called *Merry Conceited Jests of George Peele*, published in 1605, consisting for the most part of jokes and stories fathered on him. The author of *Polyhymnia* deserved a better fate. I often heard Mr Shakespeare refer with affection to him, and more than once I heard him quote the song that concludes that long poem, the lyric that begins *His golden locks time hath to silver turned.*

His favourite amongst Peele's poems, though, was not that, nor the famous *Bethsabe's Song* which begins *Hot sun, cool fire, tempered with sweet air,/ Black shade, fair nurse, shadow my white hair*, although for sure I know that he loved the latter. Mr Shakespeare esteemed his friend George Peele most highly on account of nine lines in his *The Old Wife's Tale*, a song sung by a voice that speaks from a well. That song goes like this:

> *Fair maiden, white and red,*
> *Comb me smooth, and stroke my head;*
> *And thou shalt have some cockle bread.*
> *Gently dip, but not too deep,*
> *For fear thou make the golden beard to weep.*
> *Fair maid, white and red,*
> *Comb me smooth, and stroke my head;*
> *And every hair a sheave shall be,*
> *And every sheave a golden tree.*

It was the fourth line in particular that Mr Shakespeare loved. *Gently dip, but not too deep.* I often heard him murmur it to himself, apropos as it seemed to me of nothing.

George Peele was only 38 when he died. Some called him 'the English Ovid'. The product of London streets and gutters, brought up in the shadow of an asylum for the poor, he is said to have been frivolous, shiftless, sensual, drunken, dissipated, and depraved. His physical person went like this: squint-eyed, short of leg, swart of complexion, his voice high-pitched like a woman's. I never met him, as he perished the self-same year that I first came to London. But I revere his memory for the reason that Mr Shakespeare did, for the way his spirit triumphed over every adversity to write that song that comes out of the well. His last act in this world, so Mr Shakespeare told me, had been to write a letter to Lord Burghley, begging for some assistance as he lay dying. Burghley, it goes without saying, did not bother to reply.

Chapter Eighty-Five

Deaths, etc.

But George Peele was not Mr Shakespeare's favourite poet amongst his contemporaries. That high honour went to Edmund Spenser.

It was Spenser's way with words that Shakespeare loved. He told me once that he thought our language began with him. Notice he did not say just his own language, or the language of modern poets in general. Shakespeare seemed to credit Spenser with tapping into a vein of English which everyone could speak. He praised his older contempoary's ear, the perfection of the music of his verse. But it was Spenser's *tongue* that he loved. I remember two lines in especial that Mr Shakespeare delighted to repeat, and about which he would always murmur, 'That is the very tongue of truth.' The first is the refrain from *Prothalamion*:

Sweet Thames, run softly, till I end my song.

The other, odder, rougher, comes (he assured me) somewhere in *The Faerie Queene*, though I confess I have never myself had the patience to find it:

Let Grill be Grill, and have his hoggish mind.

I think Mr Shakespeare revelled in these two extremes, for he would sometimes recite the lines as if they belonged together, which of course they do not, neither in provenance nor in spirit. As to the rest, I remember him remarking idly that the entrance of Belphoebe in *The Faerie Queene* was like Aphrodite being born from the sea, and on another occasion I heard him laugh and tell someone who was objecting to the rape and carnage in *Titus Adronicus* that far from being put in to please the groundlings he had intended it as a parody of Spenser. But I admit I do not know what he meant by this latter remark.

Anyhow, what I am trying to make clear is that Shakespeare revered Spenser more for his manner than his matter. In this, as in much else, my friend's opinion stood in direct contradiction to that of Ben Jonson, who

liked to bellow in his cups that Spenser 'writ no language'. Shakespeare, on the contrary, would have praised Spenser for being what Spenser called Chaucer – a *well of English, undefiled.*

The century died with Spenser. He had been driven out of Ireland, where he did the Queen's work, by peasants who set fire to his house in the night. The poet's baby son was killed in the conflagration, and the final cantos of *The Faerie Queene* were also destroyed. Arrived back at Court on Christmas Eve, he received £8 for his service, then took lodgings with his wife and remaining three children in King Street, where he died in poverty.

When he heard of the death of Edmund Spenser, Mr Shakespeare shut his eyes. Then he laid down his pipe as gently upon the fender as if it had been spun from the unravellings of a spider's web.

'Let us go to Lucy Negro's house,' said he.

This was ever his way. The shadow of Thanatos, dark-robed lord of the dead, always drove him to the worship of Eros, god of that frenzy and confusion which some call love. Love and Death were like twin sisters in the poet's mind. The kiss of one would lead him to seek oblivion in the arms of the other.

So we went down to Lucy Negro's and fucked out the night.

The Earl of Essex paid for Spenser's funeral. His coffin was carried from King Street to Westminster Abbey by eight of his fellow poets – Thomas Campion, George Chapman, Samuel Daniel, Michael Drayton, Hugh Holland, Ben Jonson, John Marston, and William Shakespeare. Spenser was buried beside Chaucer in the Abbey, the poets consigning his body to the earth. As the coffin went into the grave each poet with bowed head dropped on it a scroll with an elegy and quill attached thereto. Some of the poets kept copies of their elegies, but Shakespeare did not. When I asked him why, he shrugged and said only, 'I wrote it for Edmund Spenser, not for posterity.'

This was the first of three deaths that left their mark on Mr Shakespeare, as on all of us alive then. The second came two years later when the man who had paid for Spenser's funeral ascended the scaffold at the Tower. Essex had been found guilty of treason after his abortive attempt to raise the citizens of London against the Queen's counsellors. Southampton, his right-hand man, was fortunate, as I have said, to be reprieved from execution, though he remained in prison for what was left of Queen Elizabeth's reign. Mr Shakespeare himself, although the least conspiratorial of men, and by then at some convenient distance from Southampton, hardly found favour at Court because the ill-planned coup had begun with the conspirators commanding our Company to a performance of *Richard II*, where Essex loudly applauded the deposition scene.

I always considered the Earl of Essex insane. But then I was only a youth in those long-ago days, and perhaps the poor fellow was merely vainglorious and headstrong. His manners were never those of a successful courtier. Witness the famous occasion when the Queen boxed his ears and he drew his sword in anger at her behaviour.

People say that when he heard the sentence of death passed upon him, he looked as calm and contented as if invited to dance with the Queen. There is a story that Elizabeth had given her favourite a ring at the height of her love for him, promising that whatever might befall in the years to come she would grant him any wish or pardon him any offence at the sight of this jewel. Essex is supposed to have sent the ring from the Tower by the Countess of Nottingham, who was to present it to the Queen as a token of his repentance, but the Countess preferred to keep the ring for herself. Those who can credit this story say that both Essex and Elizabeth were victims of the Countess, with the Earl believing up to the last moment that the sight of the ring would save him, and the Queen only affixing her seal to her former lover's death warrant when she took his apparent failure to send her the ring as evidence of his pride. Pickleherring has an open mind on this romantic subject. But I will tell you in a minute of something that might confirm that the story is true.

Elizabeth did make one concession, even without the ring. The sentence of hanging and quartering went too far, she decided. Essex should be beheaded, *tout court*, and his body could be buried in the Tower chapel, instead of being distributed to the four corners of London for public show.

Her lover was no doubt grateful for this favour. On the appointed day, he mounted the scaffold clad in a long robe of embossed velvet, over a suit of black satin with a short white collar, and with a black felt hat on his head. When asked to pray for the Queen, he said: 'May God give her an understanding heart,' and then repeated the fourth psalm. The executioner was clumsy. The first blow struck the Earl of Essex aslant. He knelt there, half-dead, his bleeding head on the block, while the executioner turned away his face to redouble the blows.

The third death came again after an interval of two years. Just as the second death had been the death of the man who had paid for the funeral of the first to die, so the third death was the death of the woman who had commanded the execution of the second to die. It is said that Queen Elizabeth complained more than once to her confidantes that she had never known a moment's happiness since the death of Essex. In the spring of 1603 she left her palace for the last time to visit the bedside of the dying Countess of Nottingham. There she learned that this lady was wearing her conscience

on her finger. It was Robert Devereux's ring – the one the Queen had given him. The Countess confessed that he had confided it to her to take to the Queen, but that she had kept it. It is said that Elizabeth dealt the dying woman such a blow that her demise was hastened.

Nor did the Queen recover from the shock of this interview. She returned to her palace at Richmond, where she could neither eat nor sleep yet refused to go to bed, crying out that under the heavy state canopy she had been visited by strange and terrible apparitions. Three days and three nights the Queen sat upright in a chair, too frightened to be put to bed, sucking her thumb like a child. She died on the 24th of March, 1603, without speaking a word.

Mr Shakespeare once observed to me that all those of us who lived during the last century would always remember exactly where we were and what we were doing when the news came to us that Queen Elizabeth was dead. For all her age and infirmity, we never counted on the death of Gloriana. For my part, when the news came I was shaving my legs in the tiring-room at the Globe and trying to learn my part of Cressida for the first performance of *Troilus and C.* When I asked Mr Shakespeare where *he* was he said that he had been in Stratford, sitting in the window of a house near to the church which overlooks the charnel. He was reworking the cemetery scene in *Hamlet*, he said, and finding some inspiration in the view, when his daughter Judith brought him a pippin from his orchard and the message from London that the Queen was dead.

He might have been mocking my sense of the appropriate, of course. But he had a nose for death, and I should not be surprised if his tale was true.

I wonder if it is simply because he is dead that the life of William Shakespeare seems so much neater and more complete than my own life, so much more shapely and formal and sensible. Does not death confer a *sense* on any life? Perhaps I write this book in part because I have had to learn that. Good friend, perhaps you read it because you like to have assurance of a life making more sense than your own. This new cult of biography, this great passion for Lives – what if it is based upon nothing more profound or noble than our separate several feeling that life is such a mess?

O my little heart! Misprision in the highest degree! A plague o' these pickle-herring! All this stuff about Lives, deaths etc. is just a way of avoiding the question that really consumes my heart and my mind this minute, namely:

Where is my dear Polly, my own Anne?

Chapter Eighty-Six

'Mrs Lines and Mr Barkworth'

Between the second death and the third death, William Shakespeare published his obscure and enigmatical poem of *The Phoenix and the Turtle*.

First, though, the matter of Polly. She is gone, my little egg-girl. I have not seen her now for some three days. Pompey Bum smiles when I ask him about her absence. He is so vague and dismissive on the subject that his manner implies she might never have existed. 'What moppet?' he says. 'We never have moppets in here.' He would like me to think that my mind is going. If he could get me carted off to Bedlam then my boxes would be his, and this book as well.

He appeared suddenly on the stairs yesterday as I was carrying out the slops. He was wearing something on his head that looked like a drowned water-rat. He called it a PERUKE, and claimed it as the very latest fashion.

'I'm all behind!' he complained, when I asked him about my love's whereabouts.

Pompey Bum is forever saying this, and patting the seat of his vast breeches whenever he says it. No doubt some pun is involved, and I am supposed to be bemused as he changes the subject. He means, my great whoremaster of a landlord, not just that he has many tasks to do but that he wears much horse-hair stuffing in his breeches. He always has a face like a man at cack.

'Polly who?' he said, when I persisted with my queries.

'Flinders,' I said. 'But I heard you call her Anne.'

'Not me,' said Pompey Bum, grinning. 'And we never have no Annes.'

Then he was off down the stairs, like a big monkey in trousers, holding the rat in place on his greasy skull, and chanting just to mock me a rhyme that children sing: *'Little Polly Flinders / Sat among the cinders / Warming her pretty*

little toes! / Her mother came and caught her / And whipped her naughty daughter / For spoiling her nice new clothes!'

This left me feeling hot and sick and hopeless. The blackguard had succeeded in turning my flesh-and-blood darling into something ghostly and unsubstantial by this suggestion that I had dreamed her up from a character in a nursery rhyme.

Or perhaps it is the girl herself who has mocked me – by claiming 'Polly Flinders' as her name? This further thought (which came later), that she was herself the author of the fiction, was hardly comforting. Whatever, she was gone, and she is still gone.

All night I kept hearing sweet imagined noises from the room below. But each time I fell out of bed in a sweat and removed my Ovid, only darkness met my eye when I applied it to the peep-hole. Darkness and silence. There was no one there.

The Phoenix and the Turtle first appeared in 1601 in an octavo volume called *Love's Martyr*, commemorating the marriage of Sir John Salusbury to Ursula Stanley, illegitimate daughter of the fourth Earl of Derby. The longest thing in the book is a terrible set of verses by one Robert Chester, allegedly translated 'out of the venerable Italian Torquato Caeliano'. So far as I know, Torquato Caeliano never existed, and Robert Chester was certainly no poet. Here is a sample of his versification:

> *Where two hearts are united all in one,*
> *Love like a King, a Lord, a Sovereign,*
> *Enjoys the throne of bliss to sit upon,*
> *Each sad heart craving aid, by Cupid slain:*
> *Lovers be merry, Love being dignified,*
> *Wish what you will, it shall not be denied.*
> *Finis quoth R. Chester.*

Finis, indeed. When I asked Mr Shakespeare who R. Chester was he told me he was Salusbury's secretary. Salusbury himself was a Papist Welshman, knighted by Elizabeth as a reward for his loyalty during the Essex rebellion. He had married the bastard Ursula some 15 years before, and in fact she had given him 11 sons and daughters, which might make WS's praise of *married chastity* seem a bit odd. Still, no doubt the phoenix and turtle-dove imagery of Chester's original rigmarole was appropriate at the time of the marriage, since Mr Shakespeare explained to me that Salusbury was then the sole remaining male in a family seeking to win back its good name and perpetuate it in a love-match – John Salusbury's elder

brother having been executed for complicity in the Babington Plot. Salusbury was a pugnacious character, a wine-bibber, a friend of poets, and he may well have reminded Mr Shakespeare of his own father in that year when Jack Shakespeare turned Papist and died. For whatever reason, he liked Salusbury well enough to let him use his own poem on the phoenix and the turtle theme in an appendix to the Chester drivel. Other poet-friends of Salusbury's also contributed to the volume: George Chapman, John Marston, and Ben Jonson. But it is William Shakespeare's poem that stands out.

The Phoenix and the Turtle is certainly a strange and difficult poem. To unassisted readers, it would appear to be a lament on the death of a poet, and of his poetic mistress. But the poem is so quaint, and so charming in diction, tone, and allusions, as in its perfect metre and harmony, that I for one would be sad to have its meaning ever explained. I consider this piece a good example of the rule that there is a poetry for poets proper, as well as a poetry for the world of readers. This poem, if published for the first time, and without a known author's name, would find no general reception. Only the poets would save it.

The Phoenix and the Turtle is William Shakespeare's darkest allegory of love. It celebrates a marriage in tones more appropriate to a funeral. It talks of love in terms of perfection, and of perfection in terms of a love that is transcendental and sublime without ever ceasing to be physical. Its distillation of the nature of self-hood in love (*Either was the other's mine*) reminds me of such things as John Donne's *The Ecstasy*, which I know that Mr Shakespeare read in manuscript when it was circulating in the Inns of Court. Donne's obscurities are mere smoke, though, compared with the blazing bonfire of Shakespeare's thought here. The poem is such a pure, such a concentrated mystery that we ought just to point out the simple things that can be said about it, before submitting our minds to the power of its music. All but six of its 67 lines are in truncated trochaic tetrameters; the other six employ the final syllable of the trochaic line. The only action takes place in the sixth stanza, where the two birds flee away together. All the rest of the poem is preparation for this action and comment upon it. The birds are a female phoenix and a male turtle dove. Here is the poem:

> Let the bird of loudest lay,
> On the sole Arabian tree,
> Herald sad and trumpet be,
> To whose sound chaste wings obey.

But thou shrieking harbinger,
Foul precurrer of the fiend,
Augur of the fever's end,
To this troop come thou not near.

From this session interdict
Every fowl of tyrant wing,
Save the eagle, feath'red king;
Keep the obsequy so strict.

Let the priest in surplice white,
That defunctive music can,
Be the death-divining swan,
Lest the requiem lack his right.

And thou treble-dated crow,
That thy sable gender mak'st,
With the breath thou giv'st and tak'st,
'Mongst our mourners shalt thou go.

Here the anthem doth commence:
Love and Constancy is dead;
Phoenix and the turtle fled
In a mutual flame from hence.

So they lov'd as love in twain
Had the essence but in one;
Two distincts, division none:
Number there in love was slain.

Hearts remote, yet not asunder;
Distance, and no space was seen
Twixt this turtle and his queen:
But in them it were a wonder.

So between them love did shine
That the turtle saw his right
Flaming in the phoenix' sight:
Either was the other's mine.

Property was thus appall'd,
That the self was not the same;
Single nature's double name
Neither two nor one was call'd.

Reason, in itself confounded,
Saw division grow together,
To themselves, yet either neither,
Simple were so well compounded

That it cried, 'How true a twain
Seemeth this concordant one!
Love hath reason, Reason none,
If what parts can so remain.'

Whereupon it made this threne
To the phoenix and the dove,
Co-supremes and stars of love,
As chorus to their tragic scene.

THRENOS
Beauty, Truth, and Rarity,
Grace in all simplicity,
Here enclos'd, in cinders lie.

Death is now the phoenix nest,
And the turtle's loyal breast
To eternity doth rest,

Leaving no posterity:
'Twas not their infirmity,
It was married chastity.

Truth may seem, but cannot be;
Beauty brag, but 'tis not she;
Truth and Beauty buried be.

To this urn let those repair
That are either true or fair;
For these dead birds sigh a prayer.

This is my favourite of all William Shakespeare's poems outside of his plays. I do not understand it, but I know what it means. I have copied it out now in my own handwriting because that is something I always like to do. If you copy out *The Phoenix and the Turtle* in your own handwriting you discover that you know what it means, even though you do not understand it. I recommend the exercise to every reader.

Spiritual ecstasy is the only key to work of this kind. To the reader

without that key it can only be so many strange words set in a noble rhythm for no apparent cause.

Poetry moves in many ways. It may glorify and make spiritual some action of man, or it may give to thoughts such life as thoughts can have, an intenser and stranger life than man knows, with forms that are not human and a speech unintelligible to normal human moods. This poem gives to a flock of thoughts about the passing of truth and beauty the mystery and vitality of birds, who come from a far country, to fill the mind with their crying.

Yet, human nature being what it is, basic and obstinate questions remain. *Who was the phoenix? And who the turtle?* And if we knew, would we know or understand the poem any better?

I have heard men say that *The Phoenix and the Turtle* refers to the love of Elizabeth and Essex, but I cannot for the life of me see how. It seems even less likely that it refers to WS and Rizley, and I do not see myself in the part of either bird. For what it is worth a number of Sir John Salusbury's own acrostic lyrics, included in *Love's Martyr*, make it clear that he was at least as much in love with his wife's sister Dorothy Halsall as he was with his wife. It is just possible that Dorothy Halsall is the phoenix and John Salusbury the turtle celebrated by all the poets in the book, including Shakespeare. Such a secret and forbidden love would at least explain the obscurity which cloaks all the poems, as well as the fact that all the poets seem to know who they are talking about. Dorothy may have been one of those women in whom the divine is sometimes felt to be incarnate. Never forget that it is Beatrice, not Virgil, who guides Dante through Paradise.

Yet, for all that, I fear that I must close the mystery up only by creating another. For once, not long after these baffling and immortal verses first appeared, at a point where I found myself confronted by the torment of their memorability, aware that for the rest of my life now I would be unable to get them out of my heart and my head, I asked Mr Shakespeare, point-blank, one thunder-rumbling London afternoon, to identify his creatures.

'Who is the phoenix?' I asked him. 'And who is the turtle dove?'

'Mrs Lines and Mr Barkworth,' said Mr Shakespeare.

But I never could get him to say another word on the subject, and he might have been joking.

Chapter Eighty-Seven

Shakespeare in Scotland
& other witchcrafts

D^o you know the real names of the three witches in *Macbeth*?
Agnes Thomson, Violet Leys, and Janet Wishart – that's who.

You will find their names in that book by King James called *News from Scotland*. In it he describes the atrocious life of the notable sorcerer, Dr Fian, whose trial he followed, and whose interrogation he conducted. The King was present at many other trials of the sort. Witchcraft was his passion – I mean, the elimination of it. In 1596 he set up a commission including the provost of Aberdeen to judge witches and sorcerers. In the course of that year, 23 women and one man were found guilty of sorcery, and put to death. James himself was present at the trial of Agnes Thomson and other witches who boasted of having raised a storm while the King of Scots was on a voyage. She was sent to sea with a whole concourse of sister-witches, each one riding in a riddle or sieve. They took hands and danced singing all in one voice while the master of their coven, Giles Duncan, played upon a Jew's trump. At the trial this scene was re-enacted to the King's satisfaction. Agnes Thomson confessed that 'she took a black toad and did hang the same up by the heels three days and gathered the venom as it dropped and fell from it in an oyster shell'. She also took a cat and christened it which caused such a tempest that the vessel perished 'wherein was sundry jewels and rich gifts which should have been presented to the now Queen of Scotland'. The ship in which James sailed would have met the same fate if the King's 'faith had not prevailed above their intentions'. All this you can find for yourselves, good readers, in that silly *News from Scotland*.

I call it silly since I think James was. What Mr Shakespeare thought of

him I do not know. I do know that he wrote *Macbeth* in part to please him. So he worked in bits and pieces borrowed from the King's writings on the theme of witches and witchcraft – from James's *Daemonology* as well as *News from Scotland*. He wrote it very swiftly, while our Company was in Scotland. We went there after the Essex affair, when we were in disfavour with Queen Elizabeth on account of that performance of *Richard II* commissioned by the plotters in trust that it would stir up feeling against her. We were not punished, but we made ourselves scarce.

We played before King James in Edinburgh. After, we went by royal orders to Dunfermline, where we played before his Queen in the palace of Linlithgow. At Aberdeen, we were received in pomp by the provost William Cullen. We stayed there for most of the month of October, performing in the town hall to great audiences. The Scots are very good to strolling players. In Aberdeen we dined at the town's expense. At Linlithgow twelve of us players slept in feather beds.

Sir William Davenant, the poet's godson, claims to have in his possession a letter to Mr Shakespeare signed by the King of Scots, and highly complimentary. I have not seen this letter, but I do not disbelieve in it. King James enjoyed the theatre, and he liked his Shakespeare. That, at least, is one of the things Ben Jonson got right in his Folio eulogy.

Macbeth is soaked in WS's experience of Scotland. Banquo's first question 'How far is't called to Forres?' sounds rather more Scotch than English to my ear. QUELL for murder, SKIRR for search, LATCH instead of catch, GRUEL for broth, SLAB for sticky, CRIBBED for enclosed, all these are northern words which Shakespeare uses only in *Macbeth*. The receptiveness of his ear was quite remarkable. I was in lodgings with him at Inverness, for example, and our hostess remarked approvingly of the porridge which she had boiled for us that it was *thick and slab* – the phrase went straight into the Scottish play, used of the contents of the witches' cauldron.

At Inverness, the close proximity into which we were thrown enabled me for the first and last time to observe Mr Shakespeare at work from the inception to the completion of a play. With Holinshed's *Chronicles* open at his elbow, and the Scottish King's two books of witchcraft not far away across the table, he sat down to write on a rainy October morning. He wrote fast and he did little crossing out. The first two Acts of *Macbeth* came in a single marvellous day and night. Words poured from Shakespeare's pen in a torrent like one of those I watched tumbling down the mountainside. He created all those early scenes at the gallop, and the power and the urgency of their writing shows (in my opinion) both in the intensity of the verse and the way those scenes always play themselves fast

in the theatre. The rest came more slowly, with pauses for reflection, but without apparent trouble. Sometimes he muttered phrases to himself, once or twice I heard him chanting them quite loudly. For example, *'And pity, like a naked new-born babe,/Striding the blast, or heaven's cherubin, horsed/Upon the sightless couriers of the air.'* I remember that particularly because it made the hairs stand up on the back of my neck when I first heard it, and I'm sure it would do so still if I was able to get to a modern playhouse and there was a performance that did not cut it out. Such things are omitted in these enlightened days. How, they would say, can a baby stride a blast? It is a prime example of what is now regarded as Shakespeare's barbarity.

I regard it as a prime example of his genius, friends.

Mr Shakespeare's writing method was straightforward. Each page was divided into columns. On the left-hand side he would put the name of the speaker, on the right-hand side he would put the exits and the entrances. The poetry was written in the middle. He would write 50 lines on one side, 50 lines on the other. Sometimes, in full flood, he would forget to write the name of the speaker, and just make a squiggle in the margin, for the initial letter of the character's name; then he would go back and spell out the identity later. Similarly, with the exits and the entrances. Each page got dropped to the floor as soon as he had written it. At the end of that long first night in Inverness, as the sun came up, I woke from fitful slumbers and saw Mr Shakespeare still crouched at his table, his eyes red and staring, his hand scuttling back and forth across the page like a crab trapped in a bucket, the sweat running down his face, and the floor of the room covered with sheets inscribed with his rustic gothic handwriting, all straight-flowing letters. It is something I'll never forget. It was like waking and finding yourself in the cavern of a demi-urge, or in some place where a man takes dictation from angels.

Mr Shakespeare stared sightlessly at me. Then he blinked. 'What's for breakfast?' he demanded. 'I'm starving! Be a good lad and fetch me some pippins, will you? Or a taste of dry biscuit. Or a slice of salted pork. Anything but Mrs MacDiarmid's porridge!'

Did a discarnate spirit guide my master's pen in Scotland? He said he was in the grip of Hecate when he wrote that play, but he said it with a grin and a shrug, and at such times I could never tell if he was serious. Later, though, I remember him remarking that the Witch Sycorax had him in her power when he wrote much of his last play of *The Tempest*.

It is possible that he always wrote his first drafts very fast, and that these first drafts (with some notable exceptions, such as *Hamlet*) were not much changed before it came to performance. I know that *The Merry Wives of*

Windsor was written, rehearsed, and performed in the space of a fortnight, at Queen Elizabeth's express command, Her Majesty having declared her wish to see a play done at Court which would show 'Sir John Falstaff in love'. *Twelfth Night* was such another, hurriedly prepared for a royal command performance at Whitehall on the twelfth night of January, 1601, at which the Duke Virginio Orsino, newly arrived in London from Italy, was gloriously entertained.

Perhaps what I saw for myself in Scotland was William Shakespeare's usual practice. In the *Dream* he speaks of the poet's *fine frenzy*. Against this, the character called Poet in *Timon of Athens* is made to say

> *Our poesy is as a gum which oozes*
> *From whence 'tis nourisht.**

Frenzy or gum, as Mr Heminges and Mr Condell report in introducing the works in the Folio, there were never many blots in William Shakespeare's foul papers.

And that night in Inverness I thought the page would catch fire from the fury of his quill.

Unlike mine, in this. There is still no sign of that sad adorable enchanted child who told me her name was Polly. I would be heart-broken were it not that I have had no heart to break after poor Jane. Even as it is, I can barely lift my pen, it seems so heavy, and as for the ink it smells like juice of wormwood.

Reader, I know I ought to cut out every reference to this whore-child in my book. She is not relevant to my Life of Shakespeare. All that she did was fetch me a few eggs, then make my fancy dance with her girlish ways. Sir, I resolve to effect this act of exorcism as soon as it comes to the time for revision.

Madam, Jane my wife is a different case. She has had her part to play from the time of my Acknowledgements. Without her, I would not be where I am. I said that then, and I say it now again. The difference is that the first time I said it, you did not know where I was, whereas now you know I'm an old mad man who lives at the top of a brothel.

I suppose things started to go wrong when Jane started walking behind me in the street, imitating my walk. My wife would copy every single movement that I made. If I ran, she ran; if I dawdled, she dawdled; if I stopped, she stopped, so that I could never stop her. When I tried to talk to her about it, she laughed and denied that she was doing it. I was going mad

* Act I, Scene 1, lines 23–4.

with all my play-acting, she said; I was imagining things. She had better things to do, she said, than copy me. Yet it was not long before her mimicking of me extended to my gestures. It was cruel. People would stop to watch us in the streets, and they would laugh at the pantomime. I did not laugh. I tried not looking round at her. But I knew when she was there. I knew all right.

Then, one day, Jane fell down, and I fell down. I can't explain it. First I felt a sudden stab of pain in my leg, then I fell down. My wife had fallen down first. But her fall was deliberate. She had mimicked me so exactly, with such perfection, that it was as if she had *become* me, so that I fell down in the street as an echo or an answer to her fall. I considered this, at the time, a form of witchcraft. In fact, I read somewhere of witches who do no less. They follow their victims, they copy their victims' every movement, then by their falling down they make their victims fall and break their necks.

I did not break my neck. It was Jane who broke hers, though not in the street and not when copying me. She took a lover. Then she took another. One night I watched her at it with her lover. Another night I watched while the second man had her. I never said what I had seen her doing. I never repeated the words I heard her say – not deliberately. Did Jane know I had watched her? Did my actions or reactions betray to her my knowledge? I don't know. That is something I will never know, not in this life. All I can say is that my very living once depended utterly on my close observation of women, and my imitation of them, and it is possible that I repeated in bed with Jane some word or trick of one of her lovers, or more likely of her own, and thus betrayed to my dear wife the fact that I had watched her do it with other men. It is possible, as I say, but it is not likely. It is not impossible, but it is, I think, unlikely.

In the morning I found her hanging there from the rafters. She was wearing her shift as if it was a shroud. Over it she wore her black top-coat that always smelt of pepper. She was strangled in her own hair as well as the rope. Hair and rope were all twisted together where she had twined and plaited them. I had to cut her hair to cut her down. With all the while that peppery scent in my nostrils.

It was then I suppose that I determined to write my Life of William Shakespeare, though the relation between the two things is something I cannot explain. It took me, of course, many years to get this book started. First there were the years of collecting all the matter for it. Then came the years of clearing my head for the writing. And now I have the writing to keep me going.

But I owe my Life of Shakespeare to the death of my wife Jane. Don't ask me why or how, for I could not tell you. But that the one followed the other as the day the night is something I know in my bones, and can never forget.

Mulberries are grateful, and they are cooling, and astringent. I have a jar of pickled mulberries beside me as I write. I do not write quickly. I suck on a mulberry and think, and I chew and I scribble. I have a pot of good mulberry jam also, though the top is furred over, all that is left of the several Jane made for me from the fruit I once stole from Mr Shakespeare's mulberry tree. I spread it on my crusts that I get from the pie-shop in the basement.

Chapter Eighty-Eight

About Comfort Ballantine

It was not long after the coronation of King James that Mr Shakespeare carried the canopy in the royal procession,* and then elected to change his London lodging. He took rooms in the house of a Huguenot wigmaker, Christopher Mountjoy, who lived with his wife and daughter in a handsome twin-gabled building at the corner of Silver Street and Monkswell Street. Here the first thing he wrote was *Measure for Measure*, a new kind of philosophical comedy which (like *Macbeth* in a different mode) was designed to appeal to the King's tastes and interests. The Duke in *Measure for Measure* has more than enough of James in his character. I admit that I found the part of Isabella difficult – her heart's aspiration to divine love being perhaps beyond my range. After a few unfortunate perform-ances, the role was taken over by a new boy who had caught my master's eye, John Spencer, then up and coming, in due course to be my principal rival and enemy, especially in his incarnation abroad where he took that humorous alias of Hans Stockfish just to spite me. I remember his Isabella: a holy dog-faced dwarf in a cart-wheel farthingale. But Stockfish can be kept for another day.

Mr Shakespeare found himself now in a fashionable part of town. Mountjoy, his landlord, made not only wigs but those pearl-sewn and jewelled head-dresses then much in favour with the ladies of the Court. One of the Huguenot's clients was Queen Anne herself. By moving to this

---

* See sonnet 125. The procession went from the Tower through the City, passing under 7 triumphal arches. At every halt a speech or song by Thomas Dekker greeted the King and Queen, to their eventual less than delight. The great canopy over their heads was carried by 8 senior members of our Company. I can't remember which, but certainly Burbage and Heminges took part, as well as Mr S. They all wore red and black livery, with scarlet cloaks, and walked bare-headed.

well-to-do quarter, north of the river and away from the stews of Southwark, Shakespeare was showing how far he had risen in the world.

Not that everyone in the Mountjoy household considered him respectable. The Mountjoys kept a cook called Comfort Ballantine, a formidable woman, originally from the north country, who in addition to providing for the Mountjoys' stomachs also took a keen interest in the welfare of their souls. For Comfort Ballantine was a Puritan. While not so extreme in her views as some of her brothers and sisters in that tendency, she still rated players as masters of vice and playwrights as teachers of wantonness. When the critical cook heard that William Shakespeare was taking two rooms in the house she gave it as her opinion to the Mountjoys that this was decidedly 'poor policy'. POOR POLICY was one of Comfort Ballantine's favourite phrases. She was forever telling Mrs Mountjoy that she thought it would be Poor Policy to do this and such. Taking in as lodger a player/playwright with as facile and likeable a reputation as William Shakespeare's was perhaps the Poorest Policy she had ever heard of.

It is a measure of Mr Shakespeare's charm that he won Comfort over. She very nearly quit when he first came to Silver Street. But before long she was tidying his papers whenever he left the house. This tidying she called REDDING UP.

'What are you doing, Mrs Ballantine?' I heard our hero ask her, the first time it happened, him fearing no doubt that she was about to consign his blossoms of sin to the flames of her kitchen stove.

'I am redding up for you, Mr Shakespeare,' the cook replied, beaming.

And from that day forth, so he told me, he never had a moment's fear but that when he returned from his daily stroll down Wood Street and through Cheapside to get a wherry across to the Globe, and back again, he would find all his scattered papers neatly assembled on his table by the window at the Mountjoys. Not that Comfort Ballantine read them. She could not read.

Consequently, of course, the papers were often in the wrong order. But William Shakespeare knew better than to complain because of that.

It was not the theatre that Comfort Ballantine changed her mind about, only Mr Shakespeare. 'Players live by making fools laugh at sin and wickedness,' she said to me once. I did not argue with her. Who am I to disagree?

As for Mr Shakespeare's success in winning the respect of this worthy woman, that was just the lively face of something I find at the heart of his art. William Shakespeare was the least of an egotist that it is possible to be. He was nothing in himself; but he was all that others were, or that they

could become. He not only had in himself the germs of every faculty and every feeling, but he could follow them by anticipation, intuitively, into all their conceivable ramifications, through every change of fortune, or conflict of passion, or turn of thought. He had a mind reflecting ages past and ages present – all the people that have ever lived are there. He had only to think of anything in order to become that thing, with all the circumstances belonging to it. Thus he was capable even of being Comfort Ballantine, who considered all rhymers plain rogues. He treated her with dignity, accordingly, and the cook adored him for it in return.

Comfort Ballantine was a great frequenter of the public sermons of those times, of course, which sermons were called 'prophecyings'. Because she could not read it was her practice to commit the substance of all that she heard at a prophecying to memory, so that she might regurgitate it later, and dwell upon its sapience in her mind. For the help of her memory she had invented and framed a girdle of leather, long and large, which went twice about her waist when she went to the conventicle. This girdle she had divided into several parts, allotting each book in the Bible, in its order, to one of these divisions. Then, for the chapters, she had affixed points or thongs of leather to the several divisions, and made knots by fives and tens thereupon to distinguish the chapters of each book. And by other points she had divided the chapters into their particular contents and verses. This girdle she used, because she could not use pen and ink, to take notes of all the sermons which she heard; and she made such good use of it that when she came home to the Mountjoys from the conventicle just by fingering her girdle she could repeat the sermon through its several heads, and quote the various texts mentioned in it, to her own great comfort, and to the benefit of Mr Shakespeare.

This girdle of Comfort Ballantine's was kept by William Shakespeare, after the cook's decease, and he would often merrily call it his Girdle of Verity.

Chapter Eighty-Nine

*In which Pickleherring plays Cleopatra
at the house in St John Street*

I have often regretted my failure in the part of Isabella. My heart could do
with a measure of divine love. The dignity of Portia, the energy of
Beatrice, the radiant high spirits of Rosalind, the sweetness of Viola – I was
shaped by the female parts I had to play, and I am missing some hunger for
heaven in my make up. Had I been able to make a success of Isabella's
character I would have less of that wretched Petrarchan worship of the
unattainable female in my soul. It is not really worship. It is lust.

But Isabella, I found, has impossible things to say. I mean, things that
your humble servant finds impossible. Of course, madam, you are right –
no one in real life ever spoke like any of William Shakespeare's characters.
His language hovers on the threshold of a dream. Yet I say that he
possessed an implicit wisdom deeper even than consciousness. *There is
another comfort than this world.* ... Had I been able to say such things with
conviction doubtless I would have been a better player and a better man. I
would certainly have been one less obsessed with the divinity of breasts like
ivory globes circled with blue, or for that matter with hell heard in the
shriek of a night-wandering weasel.

But without more ado about nothing, permit me to tell you that Mr John
Fletcher mutilated that song *Take, O take those lips away** when he dropped
the echo of 'Bring again' and 'Seal'd in vain', thus achieving the
remarkable feat of turning a nightingale's song into a sparrow's. I never
had much time for Mr Fletcher, and not just because he called me
mediocre. The man was an opportunist. The blossoms of his imagination

---

* *Measure for Measure*, Act IV, Scene 1, lines 1–8. Fletcher's plagiarism occurs in his play *The Bloody
Brother*

draw no sustenance from the soil, but are cut and slightly withered flowers stuck into sand. He had a cunning guess at feelings, and betrayed them. Nothing shows this better than that terrible thing he did to the song sung by the boy servant to the foresaken Mariana.

To this period of Mr Shakespeare's sojourn at the Mountjoys, with his soul and his papers under the watchful eye of the cook Comfort Ballantine, belong some of his greatest writings. I mean: *Othello*, *King Lear*, and *Antony and Cleopatra*. There are odd links between them, not always noticed. You may not know, for instance, that on the 27th page of the first volume of Holinshed's *Chronicles* (which was always at Shakespeare's elbow when he was composing) there is a rough woodcut of a fellow with a villainous look and underneath it no story but a title in capital letters

IAGO

and that opposite this woodcut, on the facing page, there is a picture of Cordelia, named as daughter of King Lear. These images sank deep in our poet's imagination, coming up in separate plays, yet beginning together. The sound of the name Iago must have seemed especially evil to Mr Shakespeare, since later in *Cymbeline* he rang the changes on it, and adopted for his new villain, whose character was almost as atrocious as the cunning Venetian's, the name of Iachimo. As for the name Othello, it came (so he told me) from Moghrib: *Hawth Allah*. We performed the play for the first time on November 1st, 1604, in the presence of King James, Anne of Denmark and her brother Prince Frederik of Wurtemberg. It became a very popular and profitable piece. Within months Burbage reported that someone in his parish of St Leonard in Shoreditch had christened their newly-born daughter with the name of Desdemona, hitherto unknown in England. I was much flattered. Mr Shakespeare, however, quickly brought me back down to earth by telling me of another man who had called his pet rat Desdemona in honour of my performance.

Beyond these trivialities, I would like to observe that it seems to me that two things were happening in Mr Shakespeare's work about this time. First, with the accession to the throne of King James, he found a better patron than the Earl of Southampton, not in the sense that James gave him £1000 gifts or anything of that sort but in the sense that some of Shakespeare's earlier work had been written to divert or enflame the fancy of Southampton, ten years his junior, and that this rather led the poet into idylls. What I am trying to say is that the aristocratic futility of Southampton bred a certain kind of gold fire in WS's works which were written if not to please him then at least with that possible pleasure

sometimes in mind. When James became the chief member of WS's audience then new elements came in – some good, some not so good, but all of them more serious. Perhaps it is just that Shakespeare grew more serious himself, though I hesitate to offer such a banality. The middle age of Mr S was all clouded over, certainly, and his days were not more happy than Hamlet's who is perhaps more like Shakespeare himself, in his common everyday life, than any other of his characters. Yet having said that, I want to withdraw it on the instant. William Shakespeare is never to be identified by pinning him down as 'like' or 'unlike' any single one of his characters. He was like and unlike them all. He was Iago as well as he was Cordelia. Those crude remembered woodcuts were mirrors of his soul. In short, it was only by representing others that Shakespeare became himself. He could go out of himself, and express the soul of Cleopatra. But in his own person, he appeared to be always waiting for the prompter's cue. In expressing the thoughts of others, he seemed inspired. In expressing his own thoughts, he was a mechanic. Witness even how from the beginning of his career he found himself in others – for it was only in adapting plays which had been written by other men that he first discovered his own powers. And then even when he was gradually drawn on to write original plays of his own, he nearly always derived his subjects for those plays from histories and their substance from collections of prose tales written by others.

The second thing I want to say generally about Mr Shakespeare at this point in his life is that it seems to me that with this graver tone he also turned not so much his back on fame and favour, but *aside* from fame and favour. From now on he was after more difficult and even more fleeting game. I will not say that it was better game, since I am no moralist. But it is surely not irrelevant that from this time forth he began to spend more time in Stratford than he spent in London. Perhaps you are right, sir, and he simply preferred having Anne Shakespeare redding up his papers. But I think there might have been more to the matter than that.

Cleopatra as I have said was the height of my performance as a woman. I confess that I was freakish, and that my piping voice was a long time a-breaking. (And now I am old I squeak again like a boy.) Wigged, singed, perfume-sprayed, with smooth-shaven armpits and gilded eyelids, I was the fleshpot of Egypt. It was out of deference to my being no longer in the first flush of youth that Mr Shakespeare makes Cleopatra 36 years old at the opening of the play, with 20 years having passed since she subdued Caesar, and it being now 10 years that Antony has been 'caught in her strong toil of

grace'. In fact I was 24 at the time of our first performance. I have never forgotten the last rehearsal Mr Shakespeare made me do for it.

I had realised from the start, of course, just who I was playing. *Age cannot wither her, nor custom stale / Her infinite variety: other women cloy / The appetites they feed: but she makes hungry / Where most she satisfies.** Who else could this be but Lucy Negro? It is as if the Dark Lady of the sonnets stepped forth on the public stage. Note some of the other things that are said about Cleopatra – particularly her habit of hopping to fetch her breath short for men's arousal. This is Lucy Negro to the life. *Vilest things* are said to *become themselves in her*, and the holy priests to *bless her when she is riggish*. All this sounds like the tone of the sonnets to me, and the last phrase reminds me especially of a story Mr Shakespeare told me of how Lucy liked to go to confession and excite her confessor with details of her sins of lasciviousness. Since RIGGISH, besides, is the very word that my master always used of the Abbess of Clerkenwell ('Lucy was unslakedly riggish with me last night,' and so on) I had no doubt from the first moment I began to learn my lines who it was that he was wanting me to portray.

So what we have here is a very queer kettle of fish. For Lucy was Shakespeare's Muse, but so now was I. I was Lucy interpreted, Lucy played, Lucy made quick and amenable, the living Lucy perfected by his art and *said* by me. She had been turned into words and I was their incarnation. It is indeed a complex and a sinister process. Mr Shakespeare was using me to tame and to interpret his vision of the female sex. It is in this sense, best of all, that I was the master-mistress of his passion, and that I had *one thing* which was to his purpose *nothing*. He gave Lucy Negro the royal dignity of the Queen of Egypt, and then had me, a bastard boy from the fens, turn the queen back into riggish quotidian life. Never forget why Cleopatra kills herself: because she cannot bear the prospect of being paraded in parody in Caesar's triumph——

> *I shall see*
> *Some squeaking Cleopatra boy my greatness*
> *I' the posture of a whore.*

But Lucy *was* a whore, and I *was* a boy. I played Cleopatra as myself playing Lucy Negro for the pleasure of the man she had given the pox. And for our final dress rehearsal, Mr Shakespeare had me go with him to the house in St John Street, where poet and Muse dressed me in one of Lucy's

---

* *Antony and Cleopatra*, Act II, Scene 2, lines 235–8.

best Queen Elizabeth gowns and I was commanded to act out my part under their glittering critical eyes. My performance seemed to satisfy them. That is, she sat on his lap to watch me, and kept wriggling her haunches, and I was dismissed from their presence long before it came to asp-time.

Consider, all you who are either true or fair, could play go further?

What the Abbess of Clerkenwell made of my impersonation of her I cannot tell you. I do know that Mr Shakespeare added two words to *Antony and Cleopatra* on our return to the Globe. They come where the lady Charmian follows her mistress in death, her last words as she applies an asp to her own breast: *Ah, soldier!* That simple phrase marks the height of Shakespeare's genius. Dante would never have thought of it, nor Homer neither.

My dear Polly is back! Last night I looked through the hole, without hope, and there was my love!

Polly was lying on her back, below me, with her candles burning. She was naked save for a pair of black silk stockings. Her sweet face was most curiously made up, as though beginning with the eyes she had not had time to finish, for the rims of her eyes were dark, the rims only, and not the lids, no, not the lids at all. This effect is achieved, and achieved exclusively, by applying mascara under the lids alone. This I know well.

My heart leapt to my lips when I beheld her. They framed her name, although I did not speak.

For her part, Polly looked up at me, and she was smiling. Then she waved her hand to me, a circle in the gloom. It was a regal wave. Like Queen Elizabeth. My poor waif, my child of shame, my bride of darkness, daughter of the night, and yet for me *the fairest of erth kinne* – she knew I watched her, and she smiled at me; she knew I saw her, and she waved to me.

> *On yonder hill there stands a creature.*
> *My lemmon she shal be.*

O Polly dear.

Naked, on her back, and in her white bed, Polly saluted me gaily and gravely. My heart bowed down.

Chapter Ninety

Tom o' Bedlam's Song

Where Polly has been I don't know, but she brought me back a present. It is a curious thing – an Aeolian harp. I never saw anything like it before.

Aeolus in Roman mythology was the god of the winds. This wind-harp is a box on which strings are stretched. You do not play it, but you let it play. Polly showed me how. You hang the harp in the window, or stand it up on the windowsill. The breeze passing freely over the taut gut strings produces a haunting, long-drawn chord, rising and falling. This music is for all the world like the cry of some coy young maid half-yielding to her lover.

Hark! The wind kindles the strings again. This simplest lute placed length-wise in the casement is now my constant companion. It is as if Dame Nature told her secrets on the strings of the human heart.

Life is other than what one writes. When I thanked Polly for her gift, and made bold to kiss her hand in token of my gratitude, she spun three times round like a sweet little dervish, and then asked would I like to know what it is about me that touches her. Remembering that the night before last I am certain she knew that I spied on her naked in her bed, I hesitated. But the dear child took my hesitation for compliance, and so whispered her approbation in my ear. It is – in the way I think and speak, in my whole manner, apparently (and this is one of the compliments which has moved me most in my whole life) – my *simplicity*.

A harp, though a world in itself, is but a narrow world in comparison with the world of a human heart. And tonight the music of my wind-harp is not all I hear. It is raining. The rain drips and gathers in the eaves. The sound of the rain in the eaves is like Jane's laughing.

I have a note in this box about Cordelia Annesley. Her story is soon told.

She was the daughter of Sir Brian Annesley, a Kentish landowner who had been a Gentleman Pensioner to Queen Elizabeth. In the autumn of 1603 this poor fellow's two older daughters tried to have their father certified insane so as to get their hands on his estate. Their names were Lady Sandys and Lady Wildgoose. Cordelia, his youngest daughter, protested against this proposal in a letter to Secretary of State Cecil. She urged, as an alternative, that a guardian should be appointed for her father. On Sir Brian's death the Wildgooses contested his will, but they failed in their attempt to stop Cordelia inheriting what was rightly hers. This woman became in 1608 the second wife of Mr W. H. – Sir William Hervey, widower of the dowager Countess of Southampton, Rizley's mother. I think Cordelia Annesley's story gave Mr Shakespeare some of his plot for *King Lear*.

I was the first Cordelia, of course. (John Spencer Stockfish was well-cast as Goneril.) My part contains only 100 lines – 40 in the first Act, 60 in the last. But my influence is felt throughout the play, and I believe beyond it. Mr Shakespeare played the part of Kent in the early performances – a role which much suited him, and also allowed him to be frequently in the wings directing what we did.

Notice the sound of the words NOTHING and PATIENCE in this play. *King Lear* rings with them, just as *Othello* is a kind of fugue on the word HONESTY. I never hear any of these words spoken but I think of Mr Shakespeare.

Reader, have you ever remarked that Cordelia and the Fool are never on the stage at the same time? This cunning of Mr Shakespeare's was quite deliberate. It permitted me to play both parts in the play. He had me cut out for a fool as well as a truth-teller. So that when Lear says *And my poor Fool is hang'd* he means not only his one honest daughter who truly loved him.

Let me tell you something strange. Just as I sometimes think that William Shakespeare dreamt me up that afternoon in Cambridge, creating me as I jumped down off the wall, so it has also occurred to me that in making me double the parts of Cordelia and the Fool he taught me the voice in which I have written this book you are reading. Did Mr Shakespeare know that I would one day write his Life? Of course not. But he must have heard in me the possibility.

In this my 90th box I have kept a poem of Mr S's that you will not know. It is a ballad sung by Edgar in *King Lear*. We used it to cover the noise of scene-shifting between the third and fourth scenes of Act II. For some reason it does not appear in the play as printed in the Folio. I suppose WS never wrote it down into his fair copy. He produced this song on the spot

when we realised we needed it, saying it followed on naturally from Edgar's declaring *Poor Turlygod! Poor Tom!/That's something yet: Edgar I nothing am*, and his lines about becoming a Bedlam beggar. When Burbage said it was several verses too long for the time it took to change our scene from the wood to Kent in the stocks before Gloucester's castle, Mr Shakespeare scowled, then grinned, then scrunched up the offending stanzas and kicked them into the pit.

Here is the poem. It has no title, but I call it *Tom o' Bedlam's Song*:

> *From the hag and hungry goblin*
> *That into rags would rend ye*
> *All the spirits that stand by the naked man*
> *In the Book of Moons defend ye!*
> *That of your five sound senses*
> *You never be forsaken*
> *Nor wander from yourselves with Tom*
> *Abroad to beg your bacon.*
> > *While I do sing 'Any food, any feeding,*
> > *Feeding, drink, or clothing'*
> > *Come dame or maid, be not afraid,*
> > *Poor Tom will injure nothing.*
>
> *Of thirty bare years have I*
> *Twice twenty been enragèd,*
> *And of forty been three times fifteen*
> *In durance soundly cagèd*
> *On the lordly lofts of Bedlam*
> *With stubble soft and dainty,*
> *Brave bracelets strong, sweet whips ding-dong,*
> *With wholesome hunger plenty.*
> > *And now I sing, etc.*
>
> *With a thought I took for Maudlin*
> *And a cruse of cockle pottage*
> *With a thing thus tall, sky bless you all,*
> *I befell into this dotage.*
> *I slept not since the Conquest,*
> *Till then I never wakèd*
> *Till the roguish boy of love where I lay*
> *Me found and stripped me naked.*
> > *And now I sing, etc.*

358

When I short have shorn my souce face
And swigged my horny barrel
In an oaken inn I pound my skin
As a suit of gilt apparel.
The moon's my constant mistress
And the lonely owl my marrow,
The flaming drake and the night-crow make
Me music to my sorrow.
       While I do sing, etc.

The palsy plagues my pulses
When I prig your pigs or pullen,
Your culvers take, or matchless make
Your chanticleer, or sullen.
When I want provant, with Humphrey
I sup, and when benighted
I repose in Paul's with waking souls
Yet never am affrighted.
       But I do sing, etc.

I know more than Apollo,
For oft when he lies sleeping
I see the stars at bloody wars
And the wounded welkin weeping;
The moon embrace her shepherd
And the queen of Love her warrior,
While the first doth horn the star of the morn
And the next the heavenly Farrier.
       While I do sing, etc.

The Gipsy Snap and Pedro
Are none of Tom's comradoes;
The punk I scorn and the cutpurse sworn
And the roaring-boys' bravadoes.
The meek, the white, the gentle,
Me handle, touch, and spare not,
But those that cross Tom Rhinoceros
Do what the panther dare not.
       Although I sing, etc.

With an host of furious fancies
Whereof I am commander,

With a burning spear, and a horse of air
To the wilderness I wander.
By a knight of ghosts and shadows
I summoned am to tourney,
Ten leagues beyond the wild world's end –
Methinks it is no journey.
      Yet will I sing 'Any food, any feeding,
      Feeding, drink, or clothing'
      Come dame or maid, be not afraid,
      Poor Tom will injure nothing.

Reader, does this song trouble your memory? Does it make you feel that you have heard it somewhere before? Mr Shakespeare used to say that poetry is original not because it is new but because it is both new and old, something you seem to remember the first time you hear it. Poetry is original because it deals in origins. Something in poor Tom o' Bedlam's song reminds me of Adam. Something in poor Tom o' Bedlam's song reminds me of us all.

It is easy to clothe imaginary beings with our own thoughts and feelings. But to send ourselves out of ourselves, to *think* ourselves into the thoughts and feelings of beings in circumstances wholly and strangely different from our own, and yet make those beings remind us of us all – *hoc labor, hoc opus!* Who has achieved it? Only Shakespeare.

Chapter Ninety-One

In which William Shakespeare
returns to Stratford

Here are Anne Shakespeare and her daughter Judith, sewing. They sit on low stools by the window that looks out into the garden of New Place. Anne has a green shield across her eyes, for the evening sun is bright and the work particular. The sunlight glints on the gold medal between Judith's breasts.

Here is a neighbour come calling – Mrs Judith Sadler, perhaps, wife of the baker Hamnet Sadler, Mrs Shakespeare's lifelong friend. She rallies Mrs Shakespeare on her industry, remarking teasingly that all the wool spun by Penelope 'did but fill Ithaca full of moths'. They talk over various items of gossip: who's dead, who's dying, Anne's beloved granddaughter Elizabeth chasing a golden butterfly, the fruit of the mulberry tree which is too soft to stand touching just now, the price of needles. Meanwhile, the evening makes a glory of all Stratford. There was a shower just before my chapter began, but now it has stopped the rabbits are emerging from their burrows. Tradesmen are singing in their shops. Boys play at bowls on the slippery ground, one of them tumbling past his own throw.

How do I know these things? I admit I do not. I have transposed them from a charming scene you will find in *Coriolanus*. That scene is not in Plutarch. It is pure Stratford.

Mr Shakespeare's mind was at all times possessed with images and recollections of English rural life – but there is more to it than that. I have yet to learn that his fancy could not luxuriate in country images even amid the fogs of Southwark and the Blackfriars, but from about the time of his daughter Susanna's wedding he had no need to feed on memories, for after that happy event he spent more and more time in the town of his birth,

where his heart always lay. The masque in *The Tempest* was used originally in honour of Susanna's wedding, by the by. She was always her father's favourite. Having known her, I can inform you that she flits in and out of all his later works – she is Mariana in *Pericles*, and Perdita in *The Winter's Tale*, and Miranda in *The Tempest*. A woman with a pale, ugly, clever face, she resembled neither of her parents save in her wit.

Mr Shakespeare never thought of taking a great house or a high place in London – he rather kept retired, in modest lodgings, and saved money. He was always a good man of business. By 1589, when he was only 25, he was a minor shareholder in the Blackfriars Theatre, and of course he was afterwards a leading shareholder in the Globe. As a writer of plays for both these houses, he realised great gains, and from his 33rd year on he was investing his profits in property in his native town. It was typical of him to return to Stratford, though none of us knew he was doing it until it was done. There was no dramatic exit. Rather, he transformed his residence by degrees. Certainly by the time we did *Coriolanus* he would have been able to observe at first hand a scene such as his wife and daughter sewing, any day of the week. Such domesticities became much to his liking in his later years. The plays become full of forgiving wives and daughters, critical and original women who yet pardon their men. What part his daughter Judith played in this I could not tell you. She never seemed to me to have forgiven her father for his long years of absence, but then indeed she never seemed much interested in William Shakespeare at all. (She once told me she would prefer to talk of Sir Francis Drake!) She was an altogether enigmatical woman. The poet's widow had her mysteries too, but her silences were of a different order, and I always sensed that she had welcomed her husband's return, and made much of it, and him, and the two of them together. Yet there can be little doubt, I think, that the prime mover in the drama of the playwright's later years in Stratford was his daughter Susanna, by then married to Dr John Hall. We shall notice in due course that she was the principal beneficiary of his will. Her epitaph deserves repeating in this connection:

> *Witty above her sex, but that's not all,*
> *Wise to salvation was good Mistress Hall.*
> *Something of Shakespeare was in that, but this*
> *Wholly of him with whom she's now in bliss.*

In other words, Susanna was a good Christian as well as a good

Shakespearean. I like to think of her as the last of her father's heroines, and as open-eyed and original as any of the others.

I like also to think of the late Mr Shakespeare spending the latter part of his life as all men of good sense will wish theirs to be – in ease, retirement, and the conversation of his friends. Of course it was not exactly like that, but while we are in the mood for idylls let us picture to ourselves, madam, the poet seated one warm evening at that same window where we just spied Judith and Anne. His hand moves on his tablet. He is engaged, no doubt, in the composition of his latest play. Again and again he is distracted, breaking off to watch his daughter Susanna and her little child Elizabeth as they run here and there among the borders of summer flowers. It crosses his mind, maybe, idly to wonder as the sunbeams seek to pierce the shadows of the rose trees and a distant drowsy humming makes soft music in his ears which thing it is he likes the better – that freshly fashioned Ariel song of his:

> *Where the bee sucks, there suck I:*
> *In a cowslip's bell I lie . . .*

or – the real sound of the bees, and the reality of the child and her mother there among the flowers?

New Place was a very fine house, the embodiment and emblem of Mr Shakespeare's success in the world. He had built it up over the years, entrusting the supervision of these improvements to his cousin Thomas Greene. I measured it once: it was 30 yards long, and 30 feet high. The main facade with its wide bay windows, columned doorway and three ornamented gables stood imposingly on Chapel Street. Walking up to it, you couldn't help thinking it was quite a palace for a butcher's son who had once wielded the sledded pole-axe and spat on his palm himself. The house contained ten rooms and cellars, apart from the large central hall. A staircase of carved oak led to the upper floor. I will tell you soon enough what I found and did there.

In this grand house, with its orchards and gardens, surrounded by his family, William Shakespeare now wrote three new plays in a final style: *The Winter's Tale*, and *Cymbeline*, and *The Tempest*. From each is derived an impression of moral serenity. Even *Cymbeline*, which the author calls a tragedy, ends in reconciliation. I always thought myself, when young, that Posthumus in that play gets forgiven too quick and easy. But Mr S would have it no other way. And now that I am old I complain no longer.

Living mostly in Stratford, eating according to the recipes in Mrs Shakespeare's cook-book, Mr Shakespeare cultivated in his latter days a

considerable belly. Anne Shakespeare had a huge manuscript book of recipes. It was the only book I ever saw her keeping company with. Cooking and sewing were her life, I think. Her room at New Place after her husband died was adorned with needlework of various kinds, cut works, spinning, bone-lace, and many pretty devices, with which the cushions, chairs, and stools were strewed and covered.

Mr Shakespeare's corpulence never quite rivalled that of his own Falstaff, but it might have done had he lived long enough. He could well afford to eat, and to eat well. By the time of his retirement to Stratford, he was oozing with gold. You can see from the bust that Dutchman did for his memorial in Trinity Church just how fat the Bard got. He had in addition three false teeth. His first false tooth was made of iron. His second false tooth was made of silver. His third false tooth was made of gold.

The return to Stratford was a confirmation of the roots of Shakespeare's art. It took a poet's imagination to realise the debt owed by humanity to the rude mechanicals of Warwickshire. Had the drama not been deeply rooted in the native soil, it could not have borne such excellent fruit. It was to the village festival and the goat song in honour of Dionysus that Shakespeare returned.

In his native place, I noticed that people tended to favour a short pronunciation of the first syllable of our hero's name: *Shax* rather than *Shakes*. This makes me think it possible that the name derives after all from the Anglo-Saxon personal name, SEAXBERHT.

Idylls over, good friends, I think at the end that Mr WS was bored with people, bored with real life, bored with drama; that he was bored, in fact, with everything except poetry and poetical dreams. In these last years at Stratford I see him as half-enchanted by visions of beauty and loveliness, and half-bored to death.

He also had barns full of grain, at a time when there was a general shortage. But we'll speak no more of that. Sufficient to say that Mr John Shakespeare was not the only one in the family with a Midas touch of the usurer about him. William Shakespeare drew Shylock out of his own long pocket.

But what is the point of dwelling upon such things? They contribute nothing to our gratitude, and gratitude is all that we should feel. If you have to be negative, better to try to conceive of a world without Shakespeare. It is only by holding our breath that we begin to understand how necessary breathing is. And the best way of bringing before our minds the true magnitude of our debt to Shakespeare is to imagine for a moment or two

that he never existed. His faults then pale into mere significance. He was a necessary man.

Even so, reader, I confess it – that the closer I get to Shakespeare, the more I recoil from him. That villain had all my life. He had my youth in my playing. He had the rest in that the rest followed on from my playing – I mean what Jane did, and what Polly is. And now he has my age which I have spent in writing about him. I have given him my life to write his Life.

That man deceived me. I used to have a trusting nature. No more the spaniel now, sir; my innocent old eyes worship him no longer. I have my Aeolian harp, if I want music.

I had a wife once. I failed her. That's the way of the world.

My mother, though, she is a different story. Her name was Lalage. Her hair was the colour of blazing treacle and her eyes were reticent. Women can see through you when they want, but mothers don't do it. I loved this mother, this Lalage. I had a song about her:

> *Weeny weedy weeky said Caesar,*
> *Weeny weedy weeky said he.*
> *Weeny weedy weeky said that old Roman geezer*
> *In the year 44 BC.*
>
> *I love Rome, I love Gaul,*
> *I love politics, but best of all*
> *I love Lalage.*

More about her? More about Lalage? Very well, sir. She had a rocking-horse. She sat me on the rocking-horse and she rocked it to and fro, to and fro, the rain falling, the window open, the fire burning, and all the time she sang. Such long, long music. It was the song of La Belle Dame sans Merci. But it came out to the words of O Polly Dear.

You shut me up, sir?

Madam, you are right. In truth the only thing I remember about my mother was the way she used to shave her legs. All the way up. And every day.

And *this* happy song which she sang to me:

> *I'm not Hairy Mary, I'm your Ma!*
> *I'm not Hairy Mary, I'm your Ma!*
> *I'm not Hairy Mary,*
> *I'm your father's fairy!*

I hope that makes you smile. That would be something.

Today I have practised smiling in new ways. Listening to the breeze on the strings of the harp that Polly gave me, I have practised a smile for death. Listening to the rats in the wainscot, I have practised a smile for ugliness. Listening to nothing in particular, I have practised above all a smile for the next time I see Polly. I shall have also a special smile for the beggar I refuse a penny to. And another smile for the spaces between the stars.

The only trouble is: I have no mirror.

Steady now, Pickleherring. But consider this, old pickpocket. Leonardo *made* a smile. First he cut up the mouth and looked at the muscles, and maybe he pulled them this way and that to see how they moved. Then he sat this lady down and taught her to pull her mouth up at the edges. The lady was irrelevant, but the smile is immortal and much discussed and it means nothing at all but Smile. It is the record of the muscles of the mouth.

To such experiment I lay my hand. I have a lot to learn in the way of smiling. But I shall become the master of the rictus. And I will not go out of the door of this room of mine again until I am borne hence in a last black box on the shoulders of six men.

Talking of Leonardo, it occurs to me to say in all modesty that if ever I had been good for anything besides play-acting it would have been as a painter. I can fancy a thing so strongly, and have so clear an idea of it. But I've a turnip that bleeds for a heart, so there's an end of that. Without an old gossip like me there would be no remembrance. And if you find fault with Pickleherring for saying this, then I can only agree; yet I'd say that it is my faults that give my work vivacity, and perhaps also vitality, and (I trust) a palpable sincerity.

Here is a question for you: *Did Shakespeare write Bacon?* I knew a man once on Primrose Hill who affected to believe that it was possible. (I knew another who said that the Bard kept a shed full of monkeys, and that these monkeys wrote *Hamlet* for him. I have forgotten why they did not succeed in writing the other plays. But that man ended up in the Bridewell.) Anyway, if Shakespeare did write Bacon then it must have been in his Stratford days, I reckon. He would not have been so philosophical in Southwark, nor dared to deceive so much at the house of the Mountjoys under the kindly eye of Comfort Ballantine. A third picture for your inward eye, dear reader: Shakespeare in his retirement from the stage, under his mulberry tree, dashing off *Novum Organum* in the gathering gloom.

I have also heard it said from time to time that the divine William is not dead. Such pious belief would have it that he went to Iceland. There the poet was trapped suddenly in an iceberg. Mr Shakespeare will remain in that Iceland iceberg for a thousand years. He awaits a virgin who will weep warm tears for him, or a winter of exceptional mildness.

Chapter Ninety-Two

Bottoms

Have you ever noticed how poets borrow not just from each other but from themselves? Upstart crows are thieves no less than magpies. But sometimes it's their own shed plumage that they steal.

In this my 92nd box I have a note concerning an interesting item of self-borrowing I once discovered in the works of Mr Shakespeare. BORROWING is perhaps not quite the word for it. Nor is REMEMBERING, though we'd better not forget that Memory was the mother of all the Muses. Anyway, can I please point out that there is something small in *Titus Andronicus* which might have 'suggested' something big in *A Midsummer Night's Dream*? I mean that the very name of Bottom and the line

It shall be called Bottom's dream, because it hath no bottom

came to Shakespeare because of the line in *Titus*:

Is not my sorrow deep, having no bottom?

Reader, it is obvious that here we are over the border of biography. I can neither prove nor can you disprove my case. Shakespeare wrote *Titus Andronicus*, or much of it. Shakespeare wrote the whole of the *Dream*, there is no reason to doubt. That is all that a biographer can say. The rest is poetry.

The common reader or playgoer is misled by the fact that such plays as *Titus Andronicus* and *A Midsummer Night's Dream* have apparently nothing in common. But to the poet's mind such differences are irrelevant. What the two works have in common is *him*.

Sir, poets frequently, if not always, borrow from other poets. Pickleherring is here to remind you, madam, to what extent they do, and must, borrow from themselves.

My wife Jane had a particularly handsome bottom. It was her finest

feature. I saw a man in Covent Garden once take off his hat to it as she passed by.

On the other hand, the late Mr Shakespeare's bottom was nothing to write home about. But then I must confess it did not interest me. In fact it was one of those things about him which I think I found boring. There were some few such, as I have admitted.

A thing you may not know is that he once slipped when about to throne himself upon a piss-pot, and marked himself severely on the arse. (Madam, I do apologise for the inclusion of such base matter, but then without it my anatomy of Shakespeare would be incomplete.) The great man thus had this anal stigmata, as it were, in the form of a crucifixion on his bottom.

So are our heroes somewhat less than gods, though they may carry emblems of divinity in the most unlikely places on their persons.

Chapter Ninety-Three

Some sayings of William Shakespeare

I have given Polly my father's kidskin dictionary. This present seemed to please her. She gave me in return for it, fishing beneath her bodice, a locket she once received as a prize at her convent. I expressed tender delight at a gift warmed by her contact and for so long worn by her intimately, *i.e.* between her breasts.

What have these things to do with my Life of William Shakespeare? Reader, I will tell you. They have everything to do with it, and so does Jane. I confess that I have only learned this in the writing. When I began, for instance, it was my intention that my late wife would have only a walking-on part in this book. It is, after all, supposed to be not my life, but the Life of William Shakespeare. Yet even at the start I think I knew that the biographer is part of the story in any biography. Otherwise why should I have felt the need to tell you that I am the bastard son of a priest's bastard? But beyond that, even, there is the natural need to confess where one stands (or falls) in love.

It is by suffering in love, erotic suffering, that we all grow. The Greeks knew this. Their novelists were interested in stories of EROTIKA PATHEMATA, and so was Mr S, and so am I. The engrossing experience of love, that is the thing. It is the theme of Parthenius (Virgil's Greek teacher). Later, among the Latin authors, it is the great theme of Petronius in the *Satyricon*. It is the theme, above all, of that great *Metamorphoses* of Apuleius – I mean the *Asinus Aureus* or *Golden Ass*. These are the works I love, the love-works against which I would match my Life of Shakespeare. But this book is intended also as a kind of *Secret History*, like that of Procopius.

Talking of love, Anne Shakespeare is of course the living statue of Hermione in *The Winter's Tale*. There was never a more beautiful or

touching embodiment on the stage of re-awakened love, in my opinion. (I am vulgar and bold, mind you; a sentimentalist, sir.) In Greene's *Pandosto*, whose plot Mr Shakespeare follows up to this point, Queen Hermione dies of grief and King Leontes promptly falls in love with his newly found daughter Perdita, thus making his suicide inevitable. By resurrecting Hermione and giving Perdita the husband of her choice, Shakespeare makes possible Leontes' repentance and his wife's pardon. To this end our dramatist was obliged to invent a means by which Hermione *could* forgive her husband, and take up life with him again, after some sign that he has shed his former jealousy and that he loves her – some sort of moral rejuvenation put on stage. The problem must have been a difficult one. The Bard's solution is nowise short of brilliant.

Leontes must be compelled to recognise in his wife other qualities than charm and beauty. She is now 16 years older than when he last saw her, and bears the marks of all that she has been through. Shakespeare hits on the idea of the kissed statue. If you ever want proof of his genius, this is it. Before revealing that Hermione is still alive she must be exhibited to the King as a marble statue placed on a monument – a statue of her not as she was 16 years ago, but as she would be now had she lived on.

Leontes gazes a long time at the statue. Then overcome by emotion he cries out. No matter how mad he seem, he must kiss her lips.

Then, as we all know, the statue trembles. And Hermione steps down from her pedestal, and herself embraces Leontes.

It is a moment of pure magic. I should know, for I played it.

How so? Why did I not play Perdita? Not, I assure you, because John Spencer Stockfish was considered my superior for any part. It is just that by this time I was in fact too old for the roles of young girls. Consequently I was a natural for the part of Hermione. I believe, in any case, that Mr Shakespeare wrote that character with me in mind, wanting me to represent on stage his own wife Anne. He wished me to embody the way he was declaring he could still love her, and she love him, after their own little interval of 16 years or more. And doubtless it appealed to his sense of irony, too, to have the once master-mistress of his passion now enacting the part of the forgiving and pacific wife. After our first performance of the *Tale*, permit me to mention, Mr Shakespeare and I played again at cards for kisses. This time there was this difference from the time when I had been his Rosalind. This time I did not let my master win.

The late Mr Shakespeare used to say that woman's point of view is not necessarily foreign to man's.

The late Mr Shakespeare used to say that words cool more than water, or are perhaps less likely not to.

The late Mr Shakespeare used to say that the void, the good void, the aching void of the good, which was his source and port and target, the wordless bourne of his every fugue, however sudden and eccentric, was the last place anyone would think of looking for him, the well-known long sweet home, the room where music plays itself.

Mr Shakespeare said that he was not here, being there, and having no whereness anyhow.

Mr Shakespeare said that music made his ears bleed.

Mr Shakespeare (as he lay dying) said that he really ought to try not to die, and that the light was badly painted on the wall.

Also, Shakespeare said his body was his grave;

That when it rained he fell;

That his scabby heart was unquiet if full of truth;

That his head was beginning to stink of innocence;

That he had St Catherine's uncouth wheel printed in the roof of his mouth;

And that he was over and above the dark, one of her dateless brood all right, but still serving his apprenticeship down here.

All these things were said by William Shakespeare as he lay dying. I do not know what they mean. I am only a comedian.

Chapter Ninety-Four

A word about John Spencer Stockfish

The Tempest, the late Mr Shakespeare's last play, seems to me as perfect in its kind as almost anything we have of his. One may observe that the classical unities are kept here with an exactness uncommon to the liberties of his writing. It is a play about magic, and that magic has in it something very solemn and very poetical. I would draw your attention in particular to the character of Caliban. It is certainly one of the finest and most uncommon grotesques that ever was seen, but what is then remarkable is that it is to this uncouth wild figure that Shakespeare gives the most delicate poetry in the play – I mean the speech beginning *Be not afeard; the isle is full of noises.* . . . Only a writer at the very top of his powers could have dared to do this. It seems to me that Shakespeare not only found out a new character in his Caliban, but also devised and adopted a new manner of language for that character.

The name Caliban is a phonetic anagram of CANNIBAL. Mr Shakespeare pointed that out to me himself, one day when showers had ruined our rehearsal. As for the name Ariel, he took that from his friend Thomas Heywood's rhymed catechism of the occult, the *Hierarchy of Blessed Angels*. In that work Ariel is named as the spirit who commands the elements and governs tempests. As for Setebos, the god adored by Caliban, that name was printed first in Thevet's *Cosmographie*, but I think it more likely that WS got it from a popular source, probably Eden's *History of Travayle* (1577). He only ever needed a few bits and scraps like this to set his mind in motion. And of course once he got going the whole play became profoundly autobiographical. In Prospero we look on Mr Shakespeare's likeness. The magician breaking his wand and retiring to Naples is the poet breaking his pen and retiring to Stratford.

We had a great metal bowl with a cannon ball in it. This was our thunder for *The Tempest* (and *King Lear*). Ben Jonson makes fun of our effects in the prologue to his *Bartholomew Fair*, offering ironic excuses for not having sought applause by staging monsters (an allusion to Caliban), and for hesitating to unleash nature, 'like those that beget Tales, Tempests'. Mr Jonson missed the point, as usual. It was not the stage properties that made *The Tempest* so moving and so memorable. It was the words.

Too old for Miranda, I took the part of Ariel. But there was more to this casting than the matter of my age. I think that Shakespeare wrote the part of Ariel *for* me, since Ariel is a spirit, something beyond man or woman. I had served my master well, and I had gone for him through the female and the male. In Ariel he recognised and rewarded my service in the sexual journey, the ways in which I had enacted on the stage the secret dreams and dramas of his heart. He set me forth now as a creature neither male nor female, and beyond either condition. Then, at the play's end, he set me free, even as he freed himself in the person of Prospero. No doubt it was his recognition that he had ruined my life, even as he had also made me.

If I could, would I fly backwards from the garden and up onto the wall, and unsing *Polly Dear*, and never know him?

I would not.

I am happy enough to be Ariel.

Call me a little epitome of the leavings of Dame Nature's workshop, a compound of all sorts and sexes, a wheyfaced hermaphrodite. I shall not care to quarrel with those callings. I am what I am, and William Shakespeare made me.

Note Ariel's last words to Prospero, my words to Mr Shakespeare in that part:

Was't well done?

That is the only question I care to ask. His answer to it, spoken aside, still more than contents me:

Bravely, my diligence. Thou shalt be free.

I always took that for my approbation. My master's approval of my career in his service. Not that I am free, not yet, not quite. Nor shall be till I have finished with this my book.

John Spencer Stockfish played the part of Miranda. John Spencer Stockfish had several qualities in common with Susanna Shakespeare, so shall we say that this part suited him down to the ground?

John Spencer Stockfish was my Caliban, madam.

John Spencer Stockfish was a shit, sir, yes.

Chapter Ninety-Five

*Pickleherring's list
of things despaired of*

I once heard Dr Donne preaching in St Paul's. He spoke of 'that glorious creature, that first creature, the Light.' The remembrance that the Light was the first created thing has stayed with me since. I always recall it when I get up early and witness the dawn, as today.

This morning I met Pompey Bum on the stairs. The sun not long risen, that greased cruel potbelly whoremaster was already drunk. He sat at the turning of the bannisters, his mouth agape and drivelling. He was reading a book, with his bottle beside him. His eyes went to and fro. He read from left to right, lips moving, silently, then bent to kiss the page where he had read it. He wept and trembled. Then he burst out with a lamentable cry, saying, *'What shall I do to be saved?'*

When I asked him what he meant, he wept the more. Then he told me that he was for certain informed that this our city of London will be burned with fire from heaven, in which fearful overthrow we shall all miserably come to ruin.

I comforted my landlord as I could, and advised him to take more water with it.

Then I came in here to attend to my Aeolian harp. But the day is close and windless, and the strings will not speak.

The end of my book is in sight, yet there are a number of things which I meant to include in it but which now there will be no room for. Fatigue and my lack of competence may be blamed. All these are matters recorded on notes which I have accumulated in my boxes, but which now it is too late to work into the fabric of my book. Here is a list of things despaired of, things

that belong in my Life of William Shakespeare but which now I must leave for others to write about:

Abraham men	alarums	aprons mountant
artichokes	asphodel	aspic
aunts	bankrout beggars	barber-surgeons
Basimecu	bat-fowling	bed-pressers
bed-swervers	Belgia	bogs
bona-robas	bonfires	bottom-grass
breaking wind	brewers	bubukles
bullets	cabbage	cabinets
caddis-garters	cannibals	cataplasm
catastrophe (tickling of)	caudle-cups	chop-logic
christom children	clergy in WS's works	cock-fighting
comfits	cony-catchers	copyright
cries of London	cross-gartering	Cutpurse Moll
dropsy	Dudley Digges	duelling
dulcimers	eclipses	eglantine
elephants	elixirs	endives
eringo	excursions	faggots
fairies	falcons	fern-seed
fewmets	fleas	fools (at Court)
fools (on stage)	football	fustian
galliards	ghosts	giants
glanders (in horses)	glow-worms	grace (at meals)
hair-pins	handkerchiefs	hautboys
heart-burn	hedgehogs	hemlock
hobby-horses	howlets	humours (the 4)
impresas	Ireland	jennets
Jones, Inigo	jordans	Kendal green
knot gardens	ladysmocks	lethargy
mackerel	maggot-pie	mandragora
marchpane	medlars	mermaids
microcosm	motley	mumchance
Neapolitan bone-ache	novum quinque	nutmeg
oats	onions	oranges
osprey	ouches	palsy
pantofles	partelets	passing-bells
passy-measures	peasecod	pissing-conduits
plainsong	poking-sticks	politics

poor-laws
prickets
projection (alchemical)
ragged robin
Ratsey the highwayman
rogero (dance)
silkworms
snapdragon
sorcerers (Lapland)
strawberries
table manners
tooth-brushes
tuckets
Vice (in moralities)
whirligigs

porcupine
pricksong
pumpions
raisins
rebatoes
salamanders
slops
snipe
spoons
sublimation (in alchemy)
tadpoles
trash (of hounds)
valerian
walnuts
wild-goose-chasing

potatoes
progresses (royal)
quotidian fever
rascal (deer)
Rhenish
shoemakers
slugs
soap (cost of)
still music
sweating sickness
tinkers
troll-my-dames
Venus' glove
wasters
wormwood

Chapter Ninety-Six

Shakespeare's Will*
(with notes by Pickleherring)

In the name of god Amen I William Shakespeare of Stratford upon Avon in the countie of Warr gent in perfect health & memorie god be praysed doe make & Ordayne this my last will & testament in manner & forme following. That is to saye ffirst I Comend my Soule into the handes of god my Creator, hoping & assuredlie beleeving through thonelie merittes of Jesus Christe my Saviour to be made partaker of lyfe everlasting, And my bodye to the Earth whereof yt is made.

Item I Gyve & bequeath unto my ~~sonne-in-L~~† daughter Judyth One Hundred & ffyftie poundes of lawfull English money to be paied unto her in manner & forme following; That ys to saye, One Hundred Poundes *in discharge of her marriage porcion* within one yeare after my deceas, with consideration after the Rate of twoe shillinges in the pound for soe long tyme as the same shalbe unpaied unto her after my deceas, & the ffytie poundes Residewe thereof upon her Surrendring *of*, or gyving of such sufficient securitie as the overseers of this my will shall like of to Surrender or graunte, All her estate & Right that shall discend or come unto her after my deceas or *that shee* nowe hath of in or to one Copiehold tenemente with thappurtenaunces lyeing & being in Stratford upon Avon aforesaied in the saied countie of Warr, being parcell or holden of the mannour of Rowington, unto my daughter Susanna Hall & her heires for ever.

---

* WS prepared the first draft of his will in January 1616. A month later, his daughter Judith was married to Thomas Quiney, the ne'er-do-well son of one of his old schoolfellows. A month after that, his new son-in-law was charged before the Church Court at Stratford with getting another local woman pregnant, and sentenced to do public penance in a white sheet. This disgrace may have hastened Mr Shakespeare's end. The signed will is dated 25 March 1616, the day before Quiney's disgrace. Within a month, the poet was dead.

† All passages thus have been deleted from the first draft.

Item I Gyve & bequeath unto my saied daughter Judith One Hundred & ffytie Poundes more if shee or Anie issue of her bodie be Lyvinge att thend of three Yeares next ensueing the daie of the date of this my will, during which tyme my executours to paie her consideracion from my deceas according to the Rate aforesaied. And if she dye within the said terme without issue of her bodye then my will ys & I doe gyve & bequeath One Hundred Poundes thereof to my Neece Elizabeth Hall & the ffiftie Poundes to be sett fourth by my executours during the lief of my Sister Johane Harte & the use & profitt thereof Cominge shalbe payed to my saied Sister Jone, & after her deceas the saied l^h shall Remaine Amongst the children of my saied Sister Equallie to be devided Amongst them. But if my saied daughter Judith by lyving att thend of the saied three Yeares or anie yssue of her bodye, then my will ys & soe I devise & bequeath the saied Hundred & ffytie poundes to be sett out *by my executours and overseers** for the best benefitt of her & her issue & *the stock* not *to be* paied unto her soe long as she shalbe marryed & covert Baron by-my-executours & overseers, but my will ys that she shall have the consideracion yearelie paied unto her during her lief & after her deceas the saied stock & consideracion to bee paied to her children if she have Anie & if not to her executours or assignes she lyving the saied terms after my deceas. Provided that yf such husbond as she shall att thend of the saied three Yeares be marryed unto or attaine after doe sufficientlie Assure unto her & thissue of her bodie landes Awnswereable to the porcion by this my will gyven unto her & to be adjudged soe by my executours & overseers then my will ys that the said cl^li shalbe paied to such husbond as shall make such assurance to his own use.^†

Item I gyve & bequeath unto my saied sister Jone xx^li & all my wearing Apparrell to be paied & delivered within one yeare after my deceas, And I doe will & devise unto her *the house* with thappurtenaunces in Stratford wherein she dwelleth for her natural lief under the yearelie Rent of xij^d.

Item I gyve and bequeath Unto her three sonns Welliam Harte *[blank]* Hart & Michaell Harte ffyve poundes A peece to be payed within one Yeare after my deceas. to be sett out for her within one Yeare after my deceas by my executours with thadvise & direccions of my overseers for her best proffit thereof to be paied unto her.

Item I gyve & bequeath unto her *the saied Elizabeth Hall* All my Plate (*except my brod silver & gilt bole*) that I now have att the date of this my will.

Item I gyve & bequeath unto the Poore of Stratford aforesaied tenn poundes, to mr Thomas Combe my Sword, to Thomas Russell Esquier

---

* All phrases in italics are additions.
† All this reflects WS's anxiety about Quiney, and his wish to protect Judith's inheritance.

ffyve poundes, & to ffrauncis Collins of the Borough of Warr in the countie of Warr gent thirteene poundes Sixe shillinges & Eight pence to be paied within one Yeare after my deceas.

Item I gyve & bequeath to ~~mr Richard Tyler~~ thelder *Hamlett Sadler* xxvjˢ viij^d to buy him A Ringe, *to William Raynoldes* gent xxvjˢ viij^d to buy him A Ringe*, to my godson William Walker xxˢ in gold, to Anthonye Nashe gent xxvjˢ viij^d, & to Mr John Nashe xxvjˢ *viij^d in gold, & to my ffellowes John Hemynge Richard Burbage & Henry Cundell xxvjˢ viij^d A peece to buy them Ringes.*

Item I Gyve Will bequeath & Devise unto my daughter Susanna Hall *for better enabling of her to performe this my will & towardes the performans thereof* All that Capitall Messuage or tenemente with thappurtenaunces *in Stratford aforesaied* Called the newe place wherein I nowe dwell & twoe messuages or tenementes with thappurtenaunces scituat lyeing & being in Henley streete within the borough of Stratford aforesaied, And all my barnes stables Orchardes gardens landes tenementes & hereditamentes whatsoever scituat lyeing & being or to be had Receyved and perceyved or taken within the townes Hamlettes villages ffieldes & groundes of Stratford upon Avon Oldstratford Bushopton & Welcombe or in anie of them in the saied countie of Warr, And alsoe All that messuage or tenemente with thappurtenaunces wherein one John Robinson dwelleth, scituat lyeing & being in the blackfriers in London nere the Wardrobe, & all other my landes tenementes and hereditamentes whatsoever; To Have & to hold All & singuler the saied Susanna Hall for & during the terme of her naturall lief, & after her Deceas to the first sonne of her bodie lawfullie yssueing & to the heires Males of the bodie of the saied first Sonne lawfullie yssueing, & for defalt of such issue to the second Sonne of her bodie lawfullie issueing and ~~so~~ to the heires Males of the bodie of the saied Second Sonne lawfullie yssuieing, & for defalt of such heires to the third Sonne of the bodie of the saied Susanna Lawfullie yssueing and of the heires Males of the bodie of the saied third sonne lawfullie yssueing, And for defalt of such issue the same soe to be & remaine to the ffourth sonne ffyth sixte & Seaventh sonnes of her bodie lawfullie issueing one after Another & to the heires Males of the bodies of the said fourth fifth Sixte & Seaventh sonnes lawfullie yssueing, in such manner as yt ys before Lymitted to be & Remaine to the first second and third Sonns of her bodie & to their heires Males;[†] And for defalt of

---

* I believe this should have read *Robert* Reynolds, and that the passage belongs with the one referring to Shakespeare's other 'fellows' following. I bought a ring at my own expense, and wear it in his memory.

† WS was baffled in his desire to leave New Place and the bulk of his fortune to male descendants. Susanna had no son.

such issue the said premisses to be & Remaine to my sayed Neece Hall & to the heires males of her bodie Lawfullie yssueing, and for defalt of issue to my daughter Judith & the heires Males of her bodie lawfullie yssueing,[*] And for defalt of such issue to the Right heires of me the saied William Shackspere for ever.

Item I gyve unto my wife my second best bed with the furniture.[†]

Item I gyve & bequeath to my saied daughter Judith my broad silver gilt bole.

All the rest of my goodes chattels Leases plate Jewels & householde stuffe whatsoever, after my dettes and Legasies paied & my funerall expences discharged, I gyve devise & bequeath to my Sonne in Lawe John Hall gent & my daughter Susanna his wief whom I ordaine & make executours of this my Last will and testament. And I doe intreat & Appoint *the saied* Thomas Russell Esquier & ffrauncis Collins gent to be overseers hereof. And doe Revoke All former wills & publishe this to be my last will and testament. In witness whereof I have hereunto put my ~~Seale~~ *hand* the daie & Yeare first above Written.

By me William Shakespeare.

---

[*] Judith's sons died young and without progeny. The first, christened Shakespeare, lived only a few months.

[†] Why did Mr S leave his wife only his 2nd best bed, and that as an afterthought? I have heard it remarked that no slight or insult was intended and that while the main part of his estate was bequeathed to Susanna, he would have taken it for granted that Anne would continue to live with her daughter at New Place. While there may be something in this, I still say that to claim that it meant nothing to use the term SECOND BEST BED in connection with your wife is to deny all Mr S's power and virtue with regard to words. He knew what he meant. And he meant what he said. And the rest of his will (particularly as regards his daughters) is very carefully worded. I think he did not leave Anne Shakespeare that second best bed lightly, even if it was only thought of at the last moment. Did he leave it to her darkly then, remembering Lucy Negro? Mrs Shakespeare smiled when I asked her about the bequest, a most singular smile, but she would say nothing.

Chapter Ninety-Seven

Fire

It had been my intention to write in this chapter of how Mr Shakespeare was dogged by fire in the last years of his life. It was as if the element followed him around, sir. There was first the outbreak of fire that destroyed our Globe theatre, and was responsible for the destruction of many of Shakespeare's manuscripts in the process. Then there was the great fire at Stratford in the summer of 1613, when 54 dwellings and numerous barns and stables stacked with hay, wood, and fodder fell a prey to the flames. I have notes on both these conflagrations in this first of my four remaining boxes.

But all such fire past has been overtaken now by another fire, a very present fire, an immediate conflagration. This broke out last night here in London, and already threatens to engulf the city.

Pompey Bum declares his prophecy has come true. He says it is the wrath of God, to kill us. He has all his whores running up stairs and down in a high state of excitement, I can tell you. He roars it is the end of the world, and the poor girls scream. I saw two of them on their knees, and not giving head. There's no sign of Polly in the general confusion that prevails here.

The fire seems at present confined to the north side of the river. It seems to have broken out somewhere close to the Tower, some say in Pudding Lane, but others in Fish Street. The worst of it is that the wind is high, and that this wind veers about with unaccountable caprice, blowing now east, now north, so that the flames roar before it like the devouring tongue of some marauding dragon. The weather has been hot and dry for weeks now, and the very air seems ready to ignite. The old houses catch the fire and they burn like tinder-boxes. In the middle of the night, last night, I was

woken by the *sound* of the conflagration. The sky was full of forks and spears of flame. How Shakespeare would have liked it! I was reminded as I stood there in my nightcap of the days when he peddled his squibs in Warwick market.

But this morning through the triangle of my window I can see nothing that could give any man or woman pleasure, save perhaps a Guy Fawkes. What I behold is a very dismal spectacle indeed – the whole City in dreadful towering flames right down to the waterfront. All the houses and other buildings from the Three Cranes down to Cheapside, all Thames Street, and right on down to the Bridge itself are being steadily consumed in this flagrant and mortifying fire.

Unknown friends, shall I tell you the strangest thing of all? It occurs to me that what I write comes true! It had been my intention to write of Shakespeare and fire, and here is London straight caught fire in the night before I wrote it! So it seems to me that what I have in mind to write may already be the truth, but I make it true by my writing of it. And this has been my task right from the beginning: to make truth come true. Mr Shakespeare did no less in his plays and his poems. Much of what he put on the stage proved strangely prophetic. *Macbeth* says much about Cromwell, and *King Lear* prefigures poor King Charles I – the king hunted, like an animal, through his own land. The late Civil Wars are everywhere foreshadowed in Shakespeare's imaginings.

But these are fancies compared with the fact of the fire. With the wind like this, and the weather like this, what can save us? The whole of London north of the Thames is already a raging inferno.

Wormwood is the name of the star that spells destruction in the Book of Revelation,* and there I set it down (with only Hamlet in mind, and Juliet's nurse remembering the day of the earthquake) at the end of my list of things despaired of. Can a word set the world on fire? If I write of a thing, must it follow?

I have now to write of the death of William Shakespeare. I think my own death won't be far behind.

* *The Revelation of St John the Divine*, Chapter 8, verse 11.

Chapter Ninety-Eight

The day Shakespeare died
(with his last words, etc.)

Shakespeare, Drayton, and Ben Jonson had a merry meeting, and it seems drank too hard, for Shakespeare died of a fever there contracted.

Who killed Cock Shakespeare?

I, said Ben Jonson, with slow-acting poison. . . .

Well, ladies and gentlemen, what if his great rival did murder him? It is a possibility I have considered. Some slow-acting poison (fly-agaric, say, or colocynth) could have been slipped into Shakespeare's cup by the bricklayer's hand at that merry meeting. (Slow acting would suit Mr Jonson right down to the ground.) Of course we shall never know now if this is what happened. But I wouldn't put such a stroke past the author of *Sejanus*. The fellow was when all is said and done a proven assassin. In fact old upright Alleyn always called him so. Bricklayer and assassin, I mean, rather than poet and playwright. With reference to Jonson's early trade as a builder's labourer, and then to his killing that actor Gabriel Spencer with a long foil. And Alleyn, note, was a sober man, and a pious, a man in the habit of writing JESUS at the top of each page of his account books at the playhouse.

But perhaps William Shakespeare died of a broken heart? That Quiney business must have got him down. I mean the discovery that his son-in-law had knocked up another woman while engaged to marry Judith. It might not break your heart, but it would make you dispirited and sick. And then you might drink too much, not long after the wedding, and with the funeral of your sister's husband* to remind you of your own mortality, face to face

---

* William Hart the hatter was buried 8 days before WS.

with despair that your daughter was now married to a scoundrel, and if you had no brains or guts for drinking it could make you sick to death.

The poet's health had not been of the best for some time. He could not eat but little meat; his stomach was not good. He had this lump I noticed, by his left eyelid. It came up after he pricked his eyeball on the thorn of a sick rose. This might have been the true cause of his death. It is just the sort of accident that people do die of. After all, as he had me say as Rosalind, men have died from time to time, and worms have eaten them, *but not for love.*

For love or not, the death of William Shakespeare took place in another cruel and rainy April, on another St George's Day, 23rd April 1616. So if the poet was really born on that day, I think we should applaud him for his neatness. Unfortunately the only other notable I can think of who performed this feat of dying on his own birthday was the late and unlamented Oliver Cromwell. The coincidence is worth remark. It provides your humble servant with an opportunity to say that Cromwell and Shakespeare had nothing else in common.

Forgive me, reader, but I suppose we have to consider the vulgar matter of Mr S's last words. What were they? Some say that he said, 'I have had enough.' Others again report that he called out 'More light!' – at which the casement window was opened for him, only for those in attendance at his death-bed to realise that their beloved Will was speaking of spiritual illumination. Then there are those who claim that the poet's last words were those of his own Hamlet: 'The rest is silence.' This last, in my opinion, is less than likely. WS was not much in the habit of quoting his own works, and I feel sure that a man of such fluency would have found new words for what was after all a unique occasion. On the other hand, there are those who assert that the Bard's eloquence deserted him at the end, and that with his final breath what he really said was a laconic, 'Now what?'

One strange report has it that as Shakespeare lay dying he kept shouting 'Reynolds! Reynolds!' all through the night. I cannot say I would care to believe this either. But others more credibly claim that his final earthly utterance was a whispered, 'Lord, help my poor soul!' This, I think, is my favourite from amongst his reputed Last Words. Though, at the other extreme, there is something to commend Mrs Shakespeare's claim that on returning from his 'merry meeting' her husband declared: 'I've had 18 straight brandy-wines. I think that's the record!' (Those who credit this would also say that WS thus died of 'an insult to the brain'.) After this boast, Mrs Shakespeare said, she cradled her husband's head in her arms, and he said, 'I love you, but I am alone.' Too touching, perhaps, to be true.

Then again, some lovers of taciturnity claim that at the end William Shakespeare said nothing at all, but just smiled.

I say I hope the man laughed.

Anyway, it is not true that he called out for two meat pies as he lay dying.

Reader, he died a Papist. Nor should this surprise you. It was the faith of his mother and his father, and who could deny that you find in the plays what I would call a catholicity of images? That is to say, it is a catholic view of things which WS most readily employs and inhabits in his works, a habit of thinking through images, and while there are no strong personal expressions of belief there, and indeed there is as I have said a cast of mind at work in them which is neither Protestant nor Papist, it should not surprise us that at the end the poet chose to return to his own beginnings.

Mary Arden was always an adherent of the old faith, though she made no fuss about it, and drew no attention to herself by recusancy. As for John Shakespeare, I have heard that he once prepared and signed a Papist last will and testament of the spiritual kind – but I never saw a copy of this, I admit. Such documents were brought into England in the last century by Jesuit missionaries. They consisted of a simple declaration of orthodox faith, in 14 articles, following the model composed by St Charles Borromeo, the Cardinal Archbishop of Milan.

The testator would declare, principally, as follows:

I am myself an unworthy member of the holy Catholic religion;

I crave the sacrament of extreme unction;

I ask the Blessed Virgin Mary to be my chief executrix;

I accept my death however it befalls me, bequeathing my soul to be entombed in the sweet and amorous coffin of the side of Jesus Christ;

I beg that this present writing of protestation be buried with me;

And I beseech all those who love me to succour me after my death by celebrating Mass.

I never heard it claimed that William Shakespeare signed such a document himself, nor do I suppose for a minute that one now lies buried with him in Holy Trinity Church. As I say, I simply heard it claimed that his father John Shakespeare had signed one. And that the old sinner's notorious failure to attend at Anglican celebrations of the Eucharist may not always have been for fear of having writs for debt served on him.

As regards WS: I do not claim that the mystery of his religious thought can ever be sounded. Angels can fly because they take themselves so lightly. I ask the reader only to notice that the language which he gives to his ecclesiastics, from the haughty Bishop of Carlisle to the humble Franciscan

friars, Laurence, Patrick, and their brothers, shows that the Roman doctrine, its liturgy and dogmas, were familiar to him, indicating that his youthful days had been passed among those who remained faithful to the ancient church. *Measure for Measure* is the key play here. It seems to me the work of a lapsed Catholic who is intimating that one day he may return to the church against his will. But perhaps I go too far in saying this. My point is just to remark that it was common knowledge in Stratford that the late Mr Shakespeare died a Papist, and that in this he was not so much converted as reconciled to the religion of his ancestors.

Unknown friends, let us put our religious cards on the table. My name is Robert Reynolds, called Pickleherring. I am by birth a Papist, by life abused, by copulation disappointed. Does this surprise you, sir? (I knew it would not surprise you, madam, bless you.) I think I have made no secret of my own birthright, right from the start. My being a Papist myself is why I have denigrated all fellow Papists throughout this black book. We deserve to be denigrated, reader, for Jesus Christ's sake. And when for example I said that about Nicholas Breakspear being the only Englishman who had *sunk so low* as to be made Pope, why, I was speaking of his noblest and proudest title, and the most true – that the Pope is the servant of the servants of God. Think about it, will you, when you have a moment?

For this comedian, your humble servant, I do not think my view of God is small. And when my own end comes I hope to pray with all the means that God has let me have. I pray on my feet, sir. A man may pray on his feet, on his knees, on his back, on his head, with his mouth, and with his bones (if they should come to hand, madam). There is no rule on how to talk to God.

Your humble servant – this useful civility and self-definition came first into England with Queen Mary, daughter of Henry IV of France, wife of King Charles I. The usual salutation before that time was 'God keep you!' or 'God be with you!' and, among the vulgar, 'How dost thou?' accompanied by a hearty thump across the shoulders.

Reader, I am your humble servant, but I still prefer old ways, so God be with you!

When William Shakespeare was dead his body was disembowelled and then embalmed for display. All that was mortal of him lay in state at New Place for two days and nights in a simple oak coffin of the English sort, that tapers from the middle like a fiddle.

I have my Aeolian harp hung up in the window. It plays fierce music with the wind of the great fire. The smoke of that fire lies over the city like a fog. There is darkness at noon. Many have already perished, consumed in

the flames, or crushed by the falling buildings. The river is crowded with boats where others flee away. Even the people who live on London Bridge are fleeing away. The houses there are old and as dry as any tinder. If the wind should switch round to the north, then the flames will be blown across the Bridge and we are all done for. The fire will cross the river and that will be that.

I can feel the heat of the flames as I sit here and write by my window of the death of William Shakespeare.

Chapter Ninety-Nine

About the funeral of William Shakespeare
& certain events thereafter

At this book's beginning I told you how I first met Mr Shakespeare. Here's how he said goodbye to me, and I to him.

Picture the scene for yourselves, my dears. To the tolling of the surly, sullen bell of the Guild Chapel (it sounds cracked and dust-tongued) the poet's body is being borne from New Place to be buried in Holy Trinity Church by the rain-swollen River Avon. Six men, all in black, are carrying the bier on their broad shoulders. It is heavy, for William Shakespeare at the end was a substantial man. The six tread carefully between the April puddles. The big oak coffin gleams on its bed of black velvet and worsted and stretched canvas.

The poet's family walk along behind – Mrs Anne Shakespeare, tall and thin and proud; his eldest daughter, whey-faced Susanna, with her husband, the physician Dr Hall, and their little daughter Elizabeth, aged eight; rosy-cheeked, buxom Judith, with her recently acquired husband Thomas Quiney, whose step is complicated by alcohol; the poet's sister Mrs Hart, greasy Joan, in widow's weeds, who trod this way just a week ago to bury her husband, with her three sons aged respectively eight, eleven, and sixteen walking beside her; and, finally, red-haired Thomas Greene, lawyer, Town Clerk of Stratford, the poet's cousin.

Inside, behind the closed curtains, New Place is hung with black drapes from top to bottom. Out here, in the bright April weather, the cracked bell tolls on. And now it is joined by another iron tongue in mourning, the great bell of Holy Trinity itself, a deeper and more doleful note, as if gravely to welcome home the body of William Shakespeare to the green churchyard where his father and his mother and his own son Hamlet lie buried.

All eyes are on Anne Shakespeare. She is dressed in widow's black from head to foot. Her kirtle is fashioned of camlet, her gown of pure silk. She wears a black beaver hat with a sable silk band. She carries in her black-gloved hands a garland of spring flowers and sweet herbs, the only spot of colour about her person, from which two long black ribbons trail down to the ground. This garland she will cast in the grave with her husband. Her face is white beneath a veil of double cobweb lawn, her eyes bright with tears. Despite her age, there is something still youthful about her. She appears like a queen, like a nymph, by her gait, by her grace. Watching her walk you might well remember that hot day long ago when Will Shakespeare was caught by her wiles in Henley Street. Watching Anne Hathaway still at work in Anne Shakespeare as she follows her poet to his grave by the green flowing river you can be sure that this woman has been to him what Helena promises her lover she will be in *All's Well That Ends Well*:

> *A mother, and a mistress, and a friend,*
> *A phoenix, captain, and an enemy,*
> *A guide, a goddess, and a sovereign,*
> *A counsellor, a traitress, and a dear.*[*]

But it was as the mourners passed through the lych-gate that my friend and master signalled his farewell to me. The bier had been set down a moment on the greensward to await the emergence from the church of the vicar, the Reverend John Rogers, and now as it was lifted again aloft Mr Shakespeare's coffin-lid shone and blazed forth in a sudden great bedazzlement of sun. It was like a wave of his hand as he went to his grave inside the church. They buried him close under the north wall, not far away from the altar.

After William Shakespeare's funeral, there was a feast. This went on for three days and three nights, in which length of time as in other respects it far surpassed the common country custom. It was as if all Stratford was unwilling to believe that its greatest son was dead. It was as if the force of life itself wanted to hold on to him.

Among notable Stratford residents in attendance at the funeral and the wake, your author counted as follows: Francis Collins, Thomas Combe, Thomas Lucas, George Quiney, William Replingham, John Robinson, Thomas Russell, Hamlet and Judith Sadler, Julius Shaw, Richard Sturley, Richard Tyler, the Reverend Richard Watts (curate to John Rogers),

[*] Act I, Scene 1, lines 173–6.

Robert Whatcott, and Mr Shakespeare's little godson William Walker. Most of the gentlemen had their wives with them, and in several cases their whole families, but I do not know the names of every single one.

From London came Comfort Ballantine, John Black, Cuthbert and Richard Burbage, Henry Condell, Thomas Dewe, Leonard Digges, Richard and Jacqueline Field, John Heminges, John Jackson, William Johnson (landlord of the Mermaid Tavern), John Lowin, Robert Pallant, John Rice (the best of my rivals in women's parts when a boy, but who gave up the stage to become a cleric), Richard Robinson, William Rowley, Thomas Sackville, James Sands, John Shank, Richard Sharpe, Martin Slaughter, Elliard Swanston (the only actor I know who took the Parliament side in our late Civil Wars), Nicholas Tooley, and Jacky Wilson. Again, many of these brought their families with them, so well was William Shakespeare loved and mourned.

I have inspected the roll of accounts of the expenses of that great funeral feast. Provision was made of 13 barrels of beer, 27 barrels of ale, and a runlet of red wine of 15 gallons. Meat, too, was provided in proportion to this liquor. The country round about Stratford-upon-Avon must have been swept clean of geese, chickens, capons, and such small gear, all which, with 500 eggs, 30 gallons of milk and 8 of cream, 12 pigs, 13 calves, and seven neats, slain and roasted on spits and devoured, contributed to the fearful festivity.

Mrs Anne Shakespeare presided over the feast. There were fiddlers (which thing, I think, her puritanical son-in-law John Hall much abhorred). She sat straight-backed and bright-eyed in a tall black chair at the head of the table, eating little and drinking less, but seeing to it that her guests were well provided for. She wore a black silk calimanco gown, with a head-dress of black tiffany upon her thick black hair that was streaked with silver at the temples. Susanna sat on her right hand, wearing a black camlet kirtle and a gown of fine black silk also. Judith sat on her left hand, again all in black, with that medal between her breasts which she kept showing me when there was no need for me to see it.

The three women looked like three versions of the one face.

At the height of the wake, as the fiddlers sawed at their instruments till the horse-hair frayed, I stole away silently from the feasting and the drinking. I had a singular need that just had to be satisfied. I went like a man in a dream, but I knew where I was going. Unobserved by any, or so I believe, I crept from the hall of New Place, and ventured where my longing was directing me – up the broad oak staircase to the room that held the second-best bed and other secrets.

Many speak of Robin Hood who never shot with his bow. I suppose I was determined that Pickleherring should do otherwise, although my will in the matter was fleshly. I had this thirst which could only be slaked the one way. If I wanted to rationalise it, I could say that I had my own way of mourning Mr Shakespeare, and of asserting and celebrating what all his works are an assertion and celebration of – the force that through the green fuse drives the flower. I had a hard on. Funerals have this mandrake effect on me, madam. I do apologise, but my root was up. Remember, I was William Shakespeare's joculator.

That's a good word, that JOCULATOR. It means more than just a jester, or a minstrel, or jongleur. It means a fool who knows the wisdom of foolishness. You get this wisdom in Shakespeare which you do not get in Dante or in Homer. That's why there is nothing in either of those great poets that gets under your skin like Feste's song at the end of *Twelfth Night*:

> *When that I was and a little tiny boy,*
> *With hey, ho, the wind and the rain;*
> *A foolish thing was but a toy,*
> *For the rain it raineth every day.*

Never forget that SILLY once meant BLESSED. Nor that the first Christians were proud to be miscalled Chrestians, meaning *simpletons*. Nor that transvestite boys with phalluses erect led the Greek sacred processions of the Dionysian Oschophoria.

I stripped off all my clothes with the bedroom door shut close behind me. Putting on Anne Shakespeare's things was ever so lovely. She had presses full of the most adorable gowns. Her wardrobe was packed with petticoats and bodices, all scented sweetly of her perfume, with ruffs and cuffs and farthingales and things. I plucked out a stomacher of incarnadine satin, smooth as snow or swansdown, that you had to lace up with two broad silver laces. Standing before her pierglass, I laced this stomacher so tight that it hurt me, quite deliciously. Then I could wait no more, but plunged my engorged and rampant member in a deep cool pool of her petticoats. When I found the drawer that held the lady's most intimate articles of apparel, her shifts and her camisas, her silken drawers and her black and her white silk stockings, soft to my touch as cobweb, I could scarcely contain myself. I hung a pair of her drawers on my pintle while I explored. Among the items of her toilet I found powder-puffs and paints and paint-sticks, false curls and curling irons, lacquers and lip-salves and feathers for applying henna. Mrs Shakespeare had a box of Cordovan

gloves, embroidered sheaths that were shaped to the clench of her fingers. I found to my delight that they fitted me. She possessed diamond and cornelian rings, and garnet brooches, and plaits of pearls, and necklaces of sapphires. It was plain that she favoured certain colours – scarlet and black – both for her choicest gowns and her flimsiest undergarments. That she sometimes adopted worsted hose of different hues – sometimes blue, sometimes grass-green – was a small enough matter for me to regret. (Not so much for the colours, but for that one absence of silk.)

I pulled on a pair of Anne Shakespeare's silk stockings, black as night, just like the ones she had worn to the funeral. I selected a sweet pair of garters, rosy rosettes, and smoothed and adjusted the stockings, consulting the pierglass. Lines of my parts as Juliet and as Cleopatra and as Lady Macbeth came coursing through my head and I spoke them softly aloud, my lips kissing my own image in the mirror, so that soon the glass was clouded with my breath. I selected black silken drawers from the tangle of worn garments in her linen basket. I sniffed at the gusset before I put them on. Anne Shakespeare's drawers smelled deliciously of comfrey fritters: her essence.

I was posed and poised at play there, black silk dress and petticoats up, casting sidelong glances at my image in the pierglass, calling the one there *Sir* or *Madam*, depending upon what was permitted to be shown, flirting with my unruly will, having it hide between my silk-clad legs and then prick out, making it throb and dance to the flick of the gloves, I was at work there, merrily, merrily, in the last throes of the hottest and sweetest ecstasy of self-caressing I ever knew in my life, when the door was suddenly flung open and the mistress of the house burst into her own bedroom and upon me.

Mrs Shakespeare screamed three screams, each one richer and shriller and more blood-curdling than any scream I ever heard screamed before, as she took in the scene that met her wide blue eyes. Then she seized a birch broom from the corridor, and drove me from the house all garbed as I was in her garments. I ran around the mulberry, scattering seed.

Reader, I have no regrets. It was worth the expense of spirit in a waste of shame. Besides, I have reason to believe that Mrs Shakespeare came to forgive me my trespass. At least, she never again referred to the matter, when I went back to New Place more than once to ask her various questions for my planned Life of William Shakespeare. She merely took care to see that I was never allowed to go upstairs alone to enjoy her private treasury of enchantments.

I confess that I would dearly love to have performed the same necessary

office dressed in Susanna's clothes and then in Judith's too. Susanna used spectacles, and she carried a silver whistle for her little dog, suspended at her girdle. She kept a throstle in a twiggen cage. It would have been both interesting and delightful to inhabit her woollen gown and blow the silver whistle for the dog and see what dog and bird made of their master-mistress. Mr Shakespeare's younger daughter was an even greater temptation, since her mysteries were more provocative. That medal bewitched me. And her wardrobe contained at least one fine gown of musk-coloured taffeta that made me almost swoon whenever I saw her wearing it. It had lots of petticoats and smelt peppery to the nostrils as she swished past. When she rode out to hounds at Stratford I saw her decked in a bastard scarlet safeguard coat and hood, Polonia style, laced with red and blue and yellow trimmings, which mightily appealed to my poor senses. I heard her giggle and say once, Judith, that none of her dresses was made by female hands. I suppose the word for this is boasting. She was a boastful creature. I could wear myself to a frazzle just thinking of her boots.

In this penultimate box, though, I do have a pair of Susanna Shakespeare's gloves, filched long ago from Hall's Croft when no one was looking. Sometimes I slip these on and I play Rosalind. Beside them, my other secret treasure is a pair of Mr Shakespeare's sister's Zebelah stockings. (Zebelah is Isabella colour, a shade of tan.) These inhesions of greasy Joan have been my comfort on many a long night. I have also Lucy Negro's handkerchief. Don't ask me how I got it. Once it smelt of white heliotrope. I never washed it. It is quite stiff now with seed and tears, quite yellow. But it is years since I managed either sperm or tears.

The great fire rages on. North of the river it is all on fire. Last night I watched the burning of St Paul's. The stones flew up into the air like grenados, the melting lead ran down the streets in a stream, and the very pavements burned red as the floor of hell. All the sky seemed on fire, like the top of a burning oven.

This morning I can see from my window the way the flames leap after a prodigious manner from house to house and street to street, at great distances one from the other. The clouds of smoke are dismal – they must stretch from here to the Essex coast. All the Inner Temple is assuredly destroyed, all Fleet Stret, the Old Bailey, Ludgate Hill, Warwick Lane, Newgate, Paul's Chain, Whitehall, Exchange, Bishopsgate, Aldersgate, out to Moorefields, the Cornhill, and Watling Street, all, all reduced to ashes.

Oh miserable and calamitous spectacle! The world has not seen the like of it since its foundation, nor will this terrible fire be outdone till the universal conflagration.

Pompey Bum has gone, and all the whores. This building is deserted now, apart from Pickleherring. Pompey Bum belaboured me to leave. He roared that it is only a matter of time before the flames destroy the whole of London, and his last word to me was that packs of rats on fire have been seen running from north to south across London Bridge.

I have no more Life of William Shakespeare left to write – and only one word more about his death. I will sit here and wait for the fire to come. If the conflagration takes my book, that is the will of God. It will not take Pickleherring. Wait and see.

I pray only for Polly to be delivered from the flames, wherever she is. Polly, Polly, you whom everything identifies with dayspring and whom, for that very reason, I shall not see again – O Polly dear, I'm glad you are not here.

Chapter One Hundred

In which Pickleherring lays down his pen
after telling of the curse
on Shakespeare's grave

The last poem written by William Shakespeare is inscribed upon his gravestone. It looks like this:

> GOOD FREND FOR ÍESVS SAKE FORBEARE,
> TO DIGG ᵺE DVST ENCLOASED ᕼEARE:
> BLESTE BE ᵞ MAN ᵞ SPARES ᵺES STONES,
> AND CVRST BE HE ᵞ MOVES MY BONES.

That is from a rubbing of the stone which I made myself. Here is the verse written out in a modern spelling and punctuation, just for your ease of reading:

> Good friend, for Jesu's sake forbear,
> To dig the dust enclosèd here!
> Blessed be the man that spares these stones,
> And cursed be he that moves my bones.

Who is the GOOD FRIEND thus addressed? I think it is the sexton, both now and to come. The sextons of Trinity Church have been known to dig up old graves to make room for the newly deceased. The bones they uncover are then thrown upon others in the charnel-house, which stands adjoining the north wall, no more than a dozen strides from Shakespeare's

grave. As I have told you, the poet had a horror of that charnel-house. But there is more to it than that.

William Shakespeare lies full seventeen foot deep in Trinity Church, deep enough to secure him, and he placed that curse upon his grave to make sure not just that he was not taken out of it but that no one else got into it. He liked in his later years to sleep alone. He did not want his grave raped, nor broken up to entertain some second guest. So he placed that curse there to make sure, I think, that he was not disturbed by *anyone* in his final slumbers. If for ANYONE you read Anne Shakespeare or Susanna Hall then I shall not deny you. For when Anne died seven years after her husband I heard that she left instruction that she was to be buried in Shakespeare's grave, and that so did Susanna when she died in 1649, but no sexton could be found who was willing to lift that nameless flagstone and incur the poet's curse.

Reader, I have heard it said that William Shakespeare did not write this verse himself, and that it is doggerel. I tell you he did write it, and that it is not. The test of any poem is this: *Does it work?* I say these four lines work very well indeed. They have done what the poet intended them to do, and they will go on doing it. No one will ever knave William Shakespeare out of his last bed. No one will ever dig up William Shakespeare while that curse is on his grave. His dust will lie there undisturbed till the day of judgement.

Besides which, just ask yourselves, ladies and gentlemen, would any of WS's relatives or friends have chosen or dared to have written a rhymed inscription of such an unusual kind to place on his grave? The idea that Shakespeare did not write it is absurd. And that four-beat measure, far from being doggerel, is in fact his favourite metre outside the iambic pentameter which comes so naturally to the speaking voice of a man or a woman in good health.

In any case, listen closely to the words. These phrases have his ring right to the echo. GOOD FRIEND as a direct form of address, occurs at key points in his works – for example, Miranda thus addresses Ferdinand in *The Tempest*, and Hamlet says it to Horatio just arrived from Wittenberg. JESU for Jesus is the poet's preferred formulation – he invokes the holy name like that all over the plays. As to FORBEAR – that is a favoured verb, and often as an imprecation forbidding *touching*, as in the second *King Henry VI*: *Lay not thy hands on me; forbear, I say*. Then there is the fact that when Mr Shakespeare thought of death it was often to link the word ENCLOSED with the word DUST (or some similar word meaning mortal remains), as for example in *Henry V*, Act IV, Scene 8, line 129, where you will find *The dead with charity enclosed in clay*. One of the final plays, *Cymbeline*, employs that BLEST BE formula half

a dozen times. While CURST BE comes in *The Tempest*, as well as in the first *Henry VI*, *Richard III*, *Titus Andronicus*, and *Pericles*. CURSED and BONES come together in *The Rape of Lucrece*, line 209.

In short, that poem is Shakespeare's in phrase and pulse as surely as if he had written it in his own blood on parchment made from his own skin.

The grave, I think, was William Shakespeare's best bed. Have you ever noticed how much sweet, dreamless, and untroubled sleep is longed-for throughout his life's work? Sleep was for him God's greatest benison. May he sleep now in blessings! May he rest in peace and his faults lie gently on him!

And so, good reader, pray for me, your Pickleherring. I have done what I promised I would do. I have told you all that I know about the late Mr Shakespeare. And now that it is done, now that I have finished, this whole book I dedicate to my friend's memory in the same words that he used to dedicate his *Lucrece* to the Earl of Southampton: 'What I have done is yours; what I have to do is yours: being part in all I have, devoted yours.' Unknown friends, this has been a lover's book.

What I have to do . . . What I have to do is make my exit. I just looked down this minute through my peep-hole. The room where Polly was is now all flames. The wind in the night must have blown from the north, and the fire come. But that may not be necessary. I am telling you something new about hell-fire.

Bear with me. My old brain is troubled. Brightness falls from the air. Pickleherring's mad again! I can see nothing. I can hear nothing. I can taste nothing. I do not know what comfrey fritters smell like.

Sir, did you expect me to lie down in my Juliet dress and wait for Romeo to come in a cloak of fire? Madam, would you have me robe and crown myself as Cleopatra and clasp the flames to suck on my wrinkled dugs? Shall my last act be to encounter darkness as a bride, and hug it in my arms?

I tell you, none of these is Pickleherring's exit. Nor have I caught an everlasting cold. Nor is old Pickerel, who was once your little Pickle, in the way to study a long silence.

In the beginning, when I was a boy, the late Mr Shakespeare made me jump down from the red brick wall to meet him. In the middle, the late Mr Shakespeare made me a woman before I was ever a man. But at the end, friends, at the end the late Mr Shakespeare kindly made me Ariel. This is Pickleherring's great secret. I am a spirit. I can fly away!

I will take my harp in my hand and rise above the city where it burns. I

will go not just to the harp's defunctive music but my own. I will fly high above the flames, O Polly dear.

I think that is enough about what I have to do. I think that I have done enough already. I think that is enough about the late Mr Shakespeare.

An

ever

writer

to a never reader

F A R E W E L L

Postscript

This book contains quotations from (and variations on) the lives and works of: John Aubrey, W. H. Auden, William Barnes, John Berryman, William Blake, William Bliss, Jorge Luis Borges, André Breton, Robert Burton, John Bunyan, Sir Edmund Chambers, the Comtesse de Chambrun, Samuel Taylor Coleridge, Daniel Defoe, John Donne, John Dryden, T. S. Eliot, Ralph Waldo Emerson, John Florio, Edgar I. Fripp, Robert Graves, Lady Charlotte Guest, Ivor Gurney, John Orchard Halliwell-Phillips, Thomas Hardy, Frank Harris, G. B. Harrison, William Hazlitt, Warren Hope, Henry James, Samuel Johnson, James Joyce, John Keats, Malcolm Lowry, Edmond Malone, Christopher Marlowe, John Marston, John Masefield, Marianne Moore, Thomas Nashe, Lady Anne Newdigate-Newdegate, Robert Nye, Eric Partridge, Georges Perec, Robert Pinget, Edgar Allan Poe, John Cowper Powys, Marcel Proust, François Rabelais, Sir Walter Ralegh, James Reeves, Edwin Arlington Robinson, Nicholas Rowe, S. Schoenbaum, William Shakespeare, Dame Edith Sitwell, Caroline Spurgeon, Laurence Sterne, Lytton Strachey, Arthur Symons, Dylan Thomas, Anthony à Wood, Charles Williams, John Dover Wilson, and Ludwig Wittgenstein.

A PENGUIN READERS GUIDE TO

THE LATE MR.
SHAKESPEARE

Robert Nye

An Introduction to

The Late Mr. Shakespeare

I am writing this book to tell you all I know about the late Mr.
Shakespeare. I knew him well, which is also to say that I knew him
well enough to know that I know nothing. There's little to know, but
there is much to tell.

In a little triangular room above a London brothel, retired actor
Robert Reynolds, a.k.a. Pickleherring, begins the book he has
waited the whole of his life to write. The book is an account of the
life and work of Pickleherring's mentor and friend, the man who
persuaded him to be an actor, the late Mr. William Shakespeare.

Pickleherring knows and freely admits to his readers that he has
taken on an impossible task. Shakespeare was an enigma even to
the actors who shared the stage with him and spoke his lines.
Pickleherring himself, as a young boy playing women's parts, was
one such actor, the first to fill the roles of such great female
characters as Juliet and Lady Macbeth, eventually playing Ariel to
Shakespeare's Prospero. Yet despite his intimate friendship with the
Bard and his overwhelming admiration for him, Pickleherring
cannot say who Shakespeare truly was. There were times, he
comments, when Shakespeare seemed like nothing at all, having
immersed himself so fully into his varied characters that he escaped
having any identity of his own. Pickleherring provides all the
concrete facts about Shakespeare on a single page of his manuscript,
demonstrating that such evidence reveals nothing about the man
and doesn't begin to explain how he wrote his remarkable plays.
The subsequent pages of Pickleherring's book contain much less
concrete data, instead reveling in legend, conjecture, and the
pleasure that comes from a good story.

According to Pickleherring, the tales surrounding Shakespeare bring those who are curious closer to the man than mere facts ever could. Shakespeare, after all, was a poet who imagined exotic worlds and invented remarkable beings. Pickleherring tells us, in candid passages, that Shakespeare even invented Pickleherring. For what would Pickleherring have been, if the Bard had not summoned him to live the life of an actor and speak the greatest lines ever composed in the English language? Now, years later, it is Pickleherring's turn to invent Shakespeare, relying on memory and embellishment. Combining tall tales, bawdy jokes, outrageous lists (of Shakespeare's childhood illnesses and their cures, of his favorite curses, of the four dozen variant spellings of his name), English folk yarns, and personal observations, Pickleherring forms a composite portrait of Shakespeare more guessed at than clearly understood, more imagined than verified, yet fitting the facts known of the playwright's life and work.

Pickleherring's stories provide very probable explanations of the identity of the "Dark Lady" present throughout the sonnets, and of Shakespeare's model for the character of John Falstaff. They also provide less probable conjectures as to Shakespeare's parentage, such as one story where Shakespeare's mother is forbidden from saying "yes" to the lecherous clergyman of Stratford-upon-Avon, and the even more preposterous yarn of John Shakespeare's fathering his famous son during a prolonged improper encounter with Queen Elizabeth (as boasted by John Shakespeare). Pickleherring speculates about his mentor's lost years between his leaving Stratford and his arrival in London, when he worked as either a lawyer, a fireworks salesman, or a sailor with Sir Francis Drake.

The tales reveal the adventurous, squalid, and extraordinary years at the close of Elizabeth's reign, an era alive with dynamic poets and playwrights, ravaged by fire and plague, triumphant in warfare. For Shakespeare it is a time of pageants and patrons, of fame and unparalleled creativity. For Pickleherring, his years as a player in Shakespeare's company are the most remarkable in his life.

In telling how he came to play Shakespeare's heroines and speak their lines, Pickleherring delivers another set of eyebrow-raising stories. Arriving in London at the age of thirteen, he became a significant performer of women's roles, meeting the great actors and playwrights of his day and touring England in Shakespeare's plays. He soon came to understand a secret about the dramatic arts. The theater, according to Pickleherring, is more than a place of entertainment; it is a temple of Dionysus, where boys in women's clothing were just one of the several sexually liberating customs which Shakespeare recognized and put to good use. The theater is a realm of transformations, beyond everyday conventions and banalities. It is the country where peasants' sons become kings, where mortals become spirits, and where actors as well as audiences drop their collective proscribed behaviors to participate in mystery and passion.

In recounting the life of Shakespeare, Pickleherring discovers that a biographer, even a fictional one, inevitably reveals himself in writing about his subject. Pickleherring accepts this, confessing that he is writing his book to gain a fragment of eternity for himself as well as his subject. Language, he reveals, is capable of such things: Just as speaking Shakespeare's lines changed him as a young man, Pickleherring discovers the world around him changing as he puts words down on the pages of his manuscript, reality following what he writes.

In *The Late Mr. Shakespeare*, Robert Nye not only revisits Shakespeare's life and the world of Elizabethan drama; he also explores the nature of biography, the suspect nature of truth, and the power words have to transform life and bring people closer to immortality.

A Conversation with Robert Nye

Writing a novel about Shakespeare is almost like writing a novel about Jesus; the main character is basically unknowable in the academic sense, yet a lot of people have very strong opinions about who this person was and what his life must have been like. Did it ever seem to you that, in writing about Shakespeare, you were heading for trouble? That is, that you were bound to run up against purists and scholars who see Shakespeare as a figure too grand and too complex to be portrayed in a work of fiction?

Well, I always head for trouble if I can. It's where the treasure lies. Though I must say that scholars have been kind about my book, on the whole, and even done me the honor of supposing that I'm one of them myself, which I am not. Seriously, I don't think that anyone is too complex or too grand for fiction. The more complex, the more mysterious, the better. Poetry and the novel might even be called the right places for what is unknowable in the academic sense. They admit all those notions of truth as consisting sometimes of contradictions and ambiguities which are anathema to theologians. The novel in particular is a house for everything that's human, and part of Pickleherring's joy in Shakespeare is that Shakespeare is as human as we come.

Would you say The Late Mr. Shakespeare *is more a book about Shakespeare or a book about Pickleherring?*

I'd say that's for each reader to decide for himself or herself. For me, Pickleherring began as not much more than the figure in the corner of the picture—the one that architects include in order to give perspective to their drawing. He was just a device, a way of getting at the material. When I started, you see, I didn't know anything about him, but then quite quickly this little man began to tell me unexpected things about himself as well as about

Shakespeare, and to dance about in the foreground. He's an actor of course, and all actors like to be center-stage, don't they? Some readers have told me that they loved Pickleherring, that they found him lovable, and I like that. But William Shakespeare is the hero of the book, of course. Pickleherring's hero, and my own.

Where did Pickleherring come from? Was there a real boy-actor in the Lord Chamberlain's Servants, Shakespeare's troupe, upon whom Pickleherring was based?

There really was an actor called Robert Reynolds who flourished in Shakespeare's day, but he seems to have worked mostly with Queen Anne's Men, not Shakespeare's company, and there's no evidence to say that he was ever a boy actor playing female parts. On the other hand, there's no evidence that says he wasn't. Anyway, this historical Reynolds went off abroad, possibly for religious reasons, after Shakespeare died, and he toured Germany until about 1640, using the comic name "Pickleherring" as an alias. He really did that. But what happened to him later, or whether he ever lived on boiled eggs in an attic above a whorehouse at the time of the Great Fire of London, nobody knows. He told me that he did, and I believed him. I plucked his name out of a playbill because I liked the name Robert Reynolds and I liked the name Pickleherring even more. Only after I'd been listening to his voice in my head for about half the book did I realize that my own name was there inside his, with my surname spelt backwards. About the same time I consulted the Oxford English Dictionary and I learned that the word "pickleherring" (meaning a clown or a buffoon or merry-andrew) first came into English from the German in 1620. It appears then as the name of a humorous character in some little plays, a sort of seventeenth-century vaudeville. And what this character delivers is a series of "pickelheringspiels" or "songspiels." I took this etymology as confirmation that I was on the right track in what I was writing. I liked it that here I had a sort of archetypal

verbal clown, a storytelling droll, and that probably the historical Robert Reynolds had been in his German guise the original for this pickleherring work in English. The historical Reynolds really did have a wife called Jane, by the way. But only her name has come down to us. I made up the rest.

How many of Pickleherring's opinions and speculations on Shakespeare are yours? Does the author of The Late Mr. Shakespeare *intersect at any point with the narrator of the book?*

Well, that's a hard one. I wrote another novel called *Mrs. Shakespeare: The Complete Works,* five years before this one, and in that earlier book there is for a start quite a different speculation concerning the identity of the Dark Lady of the sonnets—one that is there under Pickleherring's nose, incidentally, but he never sees it, namely that Shakespeare's wife was also his mistress, and that *she* was the Dark Lady, even though in that book she doesn't know it herself, never having taken the trouble to read her husband's works. I suppose you might say I share a number of Pickleherring's opinions regarding Shakespeare as a poet, but not so many of his opinions of Shakespeare as a man. I doubt if Shakespeare was tall, for instance. I just think Pickleherring thought Shakespeare was tall, because Pickleherring was only a boy when he first met Shakespeare and at that age most impressive men give you an impression of tallness. As for Pickleherring's tall stories about Shakespeare, of course I don't have to believe them, though some of them are what Robert Graves used to call "philosophically true"— meaning true to the essential spirit of the man, if not actually true.

Similar to the play Rosencrantz and Guildenstern Are Dead, *in which Tom Stoppard borrows characters and situations from* Hamlet *and creates a very different play, you openly borrow from English folktales, Welsh legends, and ghost stories to create something that is very unlike a typical Shakespeare biography. Examples include the eerie*

tale of Martin Jimp, the tailor, and young Shakespeare stirring the cauldron of Inspiration and Science, taken from the Mabinogion. *By borrowing from these diverse sources, are you tying Shakespeare into the weave of English literary history? Are you simply having Pickleherring recount stories that he likes?*

Both. Not just English folklore and literary history either—the Taliesin story is Welsh. I think there's this sense in which Shakespeare is the *genius loci*, what the ancients used to call the spirit of the place. The whole of the matter of Britain flows through him, and of course he's at the heart of the English language, with more citations from his works in the thirteen volumes of the *Oxford English Dictionary* and its various supplements than from any other writer in the language. I wanted Pickleherring to celebrate Shakespeare as the spirit of England, the one who retells the old tales lest Englishmen forget them. But at the same time Pickleherring is just telling us stories that he likes, as you say. But then Pickleherring in my story was created by Shakespeare, he is Shakespeare's creature, so what Pickleherring likes tells us something about Shakespeare, or so I hope.

You are also clearly familiar with antique English rhymes and folk songs. How did you discover "O Polly Dear"? (Or is it one of your works?)

I'm particularly glad you asked that question. "O Polly Dear" is in fact an original poem of my own. I wrote it in December 1996, though four lines of it first came to me as long ago as 1968—I had to wait for the rest. The poem came before the novel, anyway, and was in a sense the seed of it. Working out where the poem might come from, and who would sing it, and what it was about, became my way of thinking about Shakespeare without thinking about Shakespeare. So the novel was written to accommodate the poem, to give it a home, to match it. But if it sounds like an old

anonymous English folk song, so much the better. I wanted that poem to run through the novel like a tune you keep forgetting and remembering. As for the actual music given for the supposed song, in chapter 22, that was written a bit later by my stepdaughter Sharon Nye, because she liked the words. As it happens, a lot of my fiction has begun this way—either with a poem, or with some poetic obsession that I work out later in prose. There are usually years of brooding on or avoiding the subject, then a burst of concentration and swift writing. *The Late Mr. Shakespeare* took five months to write—a long while for me. That earlier novel I mentioned, *Mrs. Shakespeare*, was written in eleven days—and nights—but I got the bones of it ten years before.

Presumably, parts of the book are true, while other parts sprang from your imagination. Is the depiction of John Shakespeare accurate? Did you hammer out any details to make the readers believe that he was the basis for Falstaff? How much of Lucy Negro and her brothel is historically accurate? Do readers who care about these sorts of things miss the point of your chapter on country history?

If you will allow, I'd put it slightly differently: What is most true in *The Late Mr. Shakespeare* is precisely what springs from the imagination. The rest is just biography, or fact, or dross of one sort or another. You have to have a certain amount of dross to prove the gold. Was John Shakespeare really the basis for Falstaff? I don't know. Maybe his son didn't know either. I think the father drank too much and that is why he fell from public office in Stratford, but I couldn't prove it in a court of law. My evidence would include Hamlet's diatribe on the perils of drunkenness. Inadmissible hearsay! Was John Shakespeare a Roman Catholic? Well, that Roman Catholic will is historically true—the document was found hidden in the thatch of his house years after his death. The stuff about his cronies having the same names as two of Falstaff's, Bardolph and Fluellen, that's documented also. And there was

absolutely a Lucy Morgan nicknamed Lucy Negro and she did run a brothel in St. John Street, believe me, but whether Shakespeare ever went there, and what he did if he did—who knows? In my novel what goes on in that brothel owes something to an opium dream of Edgar Allan Poe's, while the themes of the seven rooms follow certain of my other books. I've written about Faust and Merlin and Joan of Arc and Gilles de Rais, so those rooms are like rooms in my head, you might say. Still, black people were not that common in Elizabethan London, but Lucy Negro was black and sometimes I think that Shakespeare's harping on about the lady's blackness in the sonnets has to do with her skin as well as her hair. But of course I don't know and nobody knows or is ever going to know and a good thing too. That's one of the beauties of what Pickleherring calls country history. You can believe different things on different days. They may all be true. Or none. But never dismiss the truth of the imagination. Aristotle once said that a poem or a story can give you the essential *general* truth about something more effectively than any particular historical record can.

You've written several other books combining the lives of real people (Lord Byron, Sir Walter Raleigh) with fiction. How do you know when to create fictional events, and when to stop and stick to a version of events closer to the accepted truth?

Instinct, I suppose. But I'm nearly always skeptical or suspicious when it comes to the "accepted" truth. One of the things I like about Pickleherring is that he takes nothing for granted. That's a decent habit in a narrator.

Many of Pickleherring's stories are sexual, and some are openly pornographic (such as when Pickleherring spies on Polly and "The Countess" pleasuring herself with an enormous dildo). Yet none of the stories are out of place, since Pickleherring more than once points out the erotic nature of the theater, how it is a kind of temple to carnality.

Do you think Shakespeare represents this more, or in a more clever way, than any other playwright?

I do, though some of those old Greeks run him close, Euripides for instance in the *Bacchae,* where you get an even more explicit enactment of the idea that it might be some erotic nerve that connects us to the divine. As for pornography, that dildo comes straight out of *The Winter's Tale* where a servant says that Autolycus has songs to sell about dildoes. I think myself (Pickleherring doesn't say this, does he?) that Shakespeare saw poetry as another form of lovemaking. Shakespeare knew Lust by day, with raw unsleeping eye, as Laura Riding says in one of her poems. It's all through the plays, all over the sonnets, and *Venus and Adonis* and *The Rape of Lucrece* made his reputation early as an erotic writer. I remember they were the first poems that turned me on, when I was still a schoolboy, back in grammar school. There's a serious point to this. Shakespeare is without question the most sexy poet in English, in world literature perhaps. Sex runs through his language like wildfire. That's one of the things that make him superior to Homer, and to Dante even.

You acknowledge in the Postscript that The Late Mr. Shakespeare *borrows from the lives and works of many modern writers. The line "He said that sometimes he felt as if his works had been written by someone else of the same name" is from Borges, who himself used Shakespeare in his fictional writings. Other writers you name at the end include André Breton, Georges Perec, T. S. Eliot, and Ludwig Wittgenstein, to name a few. How did you bring these writers into the book, and why?*

Did Borges say that as well? I think it was first said by the poet James Reeves in 1934. He published this essay called "The Romantic Habit in English Poets" in which he argued that the point of the old joke about Shakespeare's plays having been written

by another man of the same name is that the man of the other name is the biographical Shakespeare. That's to say that the life of a poet is his poetry; his biography is just his history in time. I got a lot from that, as from the linguistic and psychological commentaries in the original-spelling edition of the *Sonnets* done by Martin Seymour-Smith in 1963. Reeves is acknowledged in the Postscript. Seymour-Smith isn't, his influence was too pervasive, but there's a reference to him on page 271. As for the others you mention particularly . . . André Breton comes in because of his novel *Nadja*, a book I love, one of the necessary books about Woman and her mysteries as the key to truth, completely poetic. Eliot because of what he said about Fletcher, and about poets borrowing from themselves. Wittgenstein because he was the one who asked if people are really murdered in tragedies or not—which I put straight into Pickleherring's Shakespeare Test. In my first novel, *Doubtfire*, I called Wittgenstein a humorist. Because he wasn't aware how humorless he was he could be amusing, as when he observed that death is not lived through. Perec is an altogether different kettle of fish. I like him. You'll have noticed maybe that *The Late Mr. Shakespeare* is partly dedicated to his memory. He was so funny and inventive, a poet of fictions, and the structure of my novel owes a trick or two to his *La Vie mode d'emploi*. But none of this is important, not in the final analysis. I'd say it's a bit like the matter of the Homeric parallels in *Ulysses*—someone asked Joyce to explain their significance and he said, "That was just a way of marching my troops over the bridge."

One of the modern writers listed in the postscript is . . . Robert Nye. Does Shakespeare or Pickleherring quote from any of your other books?

That's my little joke. Of course there are more words in this novel by Robert Nye than by anyone else. But yes, Pickleherring does quote from a version of the Mabinogion's Taliesin story that I once did for children. And the tale of Anne Hathaway's scandal

problems in the dung outside John Shakespeare's shop comes from a sort of all-purpose universal folktale called *The Same Old Story* which I wrote in the Sixties. The Lord Fox story was in there too— I seem to have been telling versions of that all my life, but then it's a very old story, an English variation on the Bluebeard legend, and I'd be surprised if Shakespeare didn't hear it somewhere in his early days, especially since he has Benedick allude to it in *Much Ado About Nothing*. What else? Oh yes, Pickleherring picks up towards the end on the beginning of my first novel, *Doubtfire*. So I come full circle, if you will forgive that pomposity. *The Late Mr. Shakespeare* will be my last novel, you see. I didn't know this when I started it. But when I read the final sentence I saw what it said, and that I meant it: *An ever writer to a never reader FAREWELL.*

Beyond that—as to *why* I worked in all those writers, ancient as well as modern by the way—I suppose I thought it might be entertaining and instructive to have a miscellany of Shakespeare criticism in the form of a novel, with just about all the key things that anyone has said about him over four centuries being said by someone who knew him (or says he knew him) in his lifetime. Also, as regards the stories about Shakespeare, I wanted him to become as it were the complete poet-hero, a kind of epitome of all the poets. A small example that springs to mind is how when Shakespeare dies Pickleherring repeats various reported last words, and one of these is that Shakespeare tells his wife he's just drunk eighteen straight brandy-wines. Now nothing is known of Shakespeare's last words, but there is a story (first collected by a Stratford clergyman within fifty years of the poet's death) that he died as the result of a drinking bout, a merry meeting with his fellow poets Jonson and Drayton. And in our century Dylan Thomas died rather famously of drink in New York and his last words were "I've had eighteen straight whiskies—I think that's the record!" So I applied Dylan Thomas's words to William Shakespeare. At the same time, in that chapter, I have Pickleherring say that Shakespeare's last words were "More light!" (which were

Goethe's last words), and then "What next?" (which was what my friend William Saroyan said when he rang up Reuters to tell them he was dying), and the "Reynolds! Reynolds!" and "Lord help my poor soul!" (which were Edgar Allan Poe's last words as he lay dying in drunken delirium in the hospital at Baltimore). I wanted Shakespeare's death to be the death of all poets, as it were. I wanted Shakespeare to have become by this point a giant who absorbed all others, like the Gargantua of Rabelais and Joyce's Humphrey Chimpden Earwicker. Lots of fun at Will-y—um's wake!

Pickleherring says that no biographer can write a life of another person without revealing himself as well. Is this your hint or warning to your readership that you are revealing yourself in this book as well? Or, also following Pickleherring's lead, are we to assume that the work sometimes comes from outside the writer and says little about him?

Ah, well, it may be interesting that I make Pickleherring contradict himself. When he says that no one can write a biography without revealing himself as well I'm having him make a general remark about biography—that it can't really be as objective as it pretends to be—and a particular criticism of biography of Shakespeare, where the actual amount of biographical material is so sparse that it invites speculation or invention. Writing a biography of Shakespeare must be like looking at a shadowy portrait in some dim-lit gallery. You think you see a face, then you realize that the face you see is your own face reflected in the glass. But then we have Pickleherring's second remark—that the work sometimes seems to come from outside the writer, and says something about more than the writer. That's nearer my own position, actually. It reminds me of the argument that Proust put up against the critic Saint-Beuve, who wanted to interpret works of literature as though they were autobiographical. Not so, said Proust, because the man who creates the work is not the man with the good manners and the vices. In other words, in Shakespeare's case, that "man of the

same name" again. So while writers may seem like good candidates for biography—and we have this whole modern cult of biography which I have Pickleherring condemn—in fact writers are the worst candidates for biography. Because their works are acts of imagination, not gestures of self-expression.

I'd like just to say as well that the reason why *The Last Mr. Shakespeare* seems to me to fall into Pickleherring's second category is precisely because it isn't a biography. It's only a novel. Only a novel, as Jane Austen* would say. Only a novel.

*What Jane Austen says comes in her *Northanger Abbey* (chapter 5): *'And what are you reading, Miss—?' 'Oh! it is only a novel!' replies the young lady; while she lays down her book with affected indifference, or momentary shame. — 'It is only Cecilia, or Camilla, or Belinda;' or, in short, only some work in which the most thorough knowledge of human nature, the happiest delineation of its varieties, the liveliest effusions of wit and humour are conveyed to the world in the best chosen language.*

QUESTIONS FOR DISCUSSION

1. At one point, Pickleherring says that he is Shakespeare's creation, like one of the plays; at another point, he says that Shakespeare dreamed him. Why does he think that he owes his existence to Shakespeare's imagination?

2. Pickleherring frequently addresses the audience of the book, calling them "Sir" and "Madam." In what other ways is the book theatrical—in what ways is it less like a text to be read and more like a presentation to be watched?

3. What, according to Pickleherring, is the difference between country history and town history? Why does he prefer country history? Why is "The Man in the Moon" the patron saint of

country history? Why does Pickleherring put the explanation of country history in his book on the life of Shakespeare?

4. Pickleherring claims that Shakespeare's plays must be performed with boys in the female roles. This is, he points out, how Shakespeare wrote them. What are some scenes in Shakespeare's plays in which a boy in the female role is essential? What, according to Pickleherring, happens to the plays when women play these parts?

5. Pickleherring mentions other famous English poets and playwrights—among them Christopher Marlowe, John Milton, and Ben Jonson. Pickleherring rates Shakespeare as a greater artist and more complex person than any of them. How, according to Pickleherring, was Shakespeare different, and how were his works more innovative and original? Do you agree with Pickleherring?

6. In addition to great poets, Pickleherring's stories also mention other famous Elizabethans such as Sir Francis Drake, King James of Scotland, Sir Francis Bacon, and Queen Elizabeth herself. How does Shakespeare measure up as a kind of Everyman of the era?

7. Of all the Shakespearean heroines that Pickleherring portrayed (especially Rosalind, Cleopatra, Cordelia, and Lady Macbeth), what is the role with which he most closely identifies himself? Ariel is not exactly a female part, yet Pickleherring identifies very strongly with that role. What is different about Ariel? How is Ariel a kind of culmination of all of Pickleherring's female roles?

8. Why do you think Nye includes chapters about Anne or "Polly," the prostitute who lives below Pickleherring? Pickleherring compares writing a biography to voyeurism, and he frequently spies on Polly. How else do the events in Pickleherring's relationship with the girl reflect events in his book on Shakespeare?

9. Pickleherring writes his book to grasp Shakespeare, to reach some understanding of a man who was always an enigma to him. Does he succeed? If so, what has he come to understand about the man in the end? If not, what keeps Pickleherring from viewing the book as an exercise in futility?

10. Pickleherring's manuscript opens with the line "A never writer to an ever reader." At the end, the formula is reversed; the manuscript closes with "An ever writer to a never reader." What do these lines mean? Do they reflect a change that Pickleherring has undergone during the writing of his manuscript? Do they reflect his opinion of literary immortality?

For authoritative and informative editions of Shakespeare's works, look for the **Pelican Shakespeare series** available from Penguin. For more information on Shakespeare's times look for Penguin Classics editions of the works of John Donne, Ben Jonson, Christopher Marlowe, Thomas Nashe, and other Elizabethan and Jacobean writers, and visit www.penguinclassics.com.

For information about other Penguin Readers Guides, please call the Penguin Marketing Department at (800) 778-6425, E-mail at reading@penguinputnam.com, or write to us at:

Penguin Marketing Department CC
Readers Guides
375 Hudson Street
New York, NY 10014-3657

Please allow 4–6 weeks for delivery.
To access Penguin Readers Guides on-line, visit Club PPI on our Web site at: http://www.penguinputnam.com.

FOR THE BEST IN PAPERBACKS, LOOK FOR THE Ⓟ

In every corner of the world, on every subject under the sun, Penguin represents quality and variety—the very best in publishing today.

For complete information about books available from Penguin—including Puffins, Penguin Classics, and Arkana—and how to order them, write to us at the appropriate address below. Please note that for copyright reasons the selection of books varies from country to country.

In the United Kingdom: Please write to *Dept. EP, Penguin Books Ltd, Bath Road, Harmondsworth, West Drayton, Middlesex UB7 0DA.*

In the United States: Please write to *Penguin Putnam Inc., P.O. Box 12289 Dept. B, Newark, New Jersey 07101-5289* or call 1-800-788-6262.

In Canada: Please write to *Penguin Books Canada Ltd, 10 Alcorn Avenue, Suite 300, Toronto, Ontario M4V 3B2.*

In Australia: Please write to *Penguin Books Australia Ltd, P.O. Box 257, Ringwood, Victoria 3134.*

In New Zealand: Please write to *Penguin Books (NZ) Ltd, Private Bag 102902, North Shore Mail Centre, Auckland 10.*

In India: Please write to *Penguin Books India Pvt Ltd, 11 Panchsheel Shopping Centre, Panchsheel Park, New Delhi 110 017.*

In the Netherlands: Please write to *Penguin Books Netherlands bv, Postbus 3507, NL-1001 AH Amsterdam.*

In Germany: Please write to *Penguin Books Deutschland GmbH, Metzlerstrasse 26, 60594 Frankfurt am Main.*

In Spain: Please write to *Penguin Books S. A., Bravo Murillo 19, 1° B, 28015 Madrid.*

In Italy: Please write to *Penguin Italia s.r.l., Via Benedetto Croce 2, 20094 Corsico, Milano.*

In France: Please write to *Penguin France, Le Carré Wilson, 62 rue Benjamin Baillaud, 31500 Toulouse.*

In Japan: Please write to *Penguin Books Japan Ltd, Kaneko Building, 2-3-25 Koraku, Bunkyo-Ku, Tokyo 112.*

In South Africa: Please write to *Penguin Books South Africa (Pty) Ltd, Private Bag X14, Parkview, 2122 Johannesburg.*